TO FLAIL AGAINST INFINITY

D1523461

J.P. Valentine

To anyone and everyone who's offered their feedback.

1

The day I died started off as boring as the day before it.

My holopad beeped angrily that Foreman expected my brother and me five minutes ago, but I ignored it. I could wait for Brady at the locker room, or I could wait for him here. I liked it here better.

I breathed deeply into my belly as my eyes drifted over the viewing deck window, my mind at rest as I contemplated the vastness of the nothing that awaited just beyond a few inches of reinforced glass.

Every day I came up here, taking Brady's *excessive* morning routine as an opportunity to gaze off into space and clear my head in my own, mortal simulacrum of actual meditation. None of the sects bothered to teach lowly vac-welders fuck all about cultivation, but I'd seen the way they breathed, and gods knew they meditated a lot.

I just did it because it felt nice. It kept me calm. It stopped me from thinking too deeply about just how many punctures I'd sealed up in this tin can we called a home. Hey, just 'cause I wasn't meditating to manipulate qi or sense the way of the world or whatever spiritual bullshit didn't mean it wasn't *useful*. You should try it some time.

"Keep that up and I'll have to report you for VIP."

1

"Maybe someday that joke'll be funny, Brady. Looks like it's not today." I turned away from the windows to face my older brother. Growing up, people always thought we were twins. We shared the same sickly-pale skin, over-pronounced cheekbones, and soft jawline. Hell, we even smiled the same lopsided grin when we thought we knew something somebody else didn't.

These days, we differentiated ourselves with our hair. He kept his head shaved, as if anybody wanted to see *more* of his uv-starved skin, while I maintained as much of my brown locks as would fit inside a vac helmet. It wasn't much.

"Maybe I'm serious," Brady said. "You spend too much time up here. People will start to think you're losing it."

"I'm not a cultivator. How am I gonna get VIP?"

"Knowing you?" Brady snorted. "You'll discover a whole new type of crazy, all your own."

I rolled my eyes. "C'mon, we're late. Foreman'll be pissed." I stepped past him, putting an end to the conversation even as my gaze lingered on the poster next to the door.

"Know the Signs of VIP," it read, just above a series of images in that hyper-generic corporate art style we all know and hate. The posters were everywhere, everywhere enough that I'd long memorized every inch of them, including the bit depicting a cartoon man staring forlornly into space.

Obsessive thoughts about space was symptom number one of void-induced psychosis, a disease, I repeat, that I very much *did not have*. It was just common enough for people to worry about it, but not quite common enough for them to actually do anything about it.

Other warning signs included pallidification of the skin, depression, extreme and insatiable appetite, and, finally, homicidal rampage. Basically, every once in a while, a cultivator in deep space goes batshit from the lack of qi in the environment. They start running around draining the qi from everything and everyone they can get their hands on, until either someone puts them down, or all the foreign qi kills them. A bronze core cultivator can chew through about a dozen mortals before that happens. Keep that in mind.

Our station—officially RF-31, but we all called it roofie—floated far enough from literally anything that we had these VIP prevention posters all over, not that VIP ever manifests on tiny refueling stations *with no cultivators*. Still, our ambient qi levels sat low enough that Allcorp regulation mandated we keep the posters up, so up they stayed. Brady liked to wonder how a bunch of mortals were ever supposed to stop a void psycho, but whenever he asked, the higher-ups just regurgitated some line about catching it early.

Our roofie sat on the proverbial crossroads of two midsized long-haul shipping routes. Most freighters didn't need the re-up, but every once in a while they had to burn some fuel to escape pirates or reroute around a void beast. When that happened, they'd stop here to replace what they'd spent.

We didn't get many visitors. Other than our quarterly resupply, someone'd stop by every other week or so, but nobody stayed long. The cultivators especially hated it out here. VIP aside, the low ambient qi made their lives harder. We liked it that way. Our little family got to steer clear of the arrogant bastards.

Roofie kept on a small full-time crew to keep the lights on, about half of which were vac-welders like my brother and me. Our job was to patch up the various holes in the hull caused by random bits of space debris—a common hazard on these trade routes. Between us, management, agri-production, and maintenance, RF-31 employed and housed a grand total of seventeen people. Remember that number.

"Hey, I didn't know we had visitors." Brady's voice pulled me from my thoughts as we passed the window to dock four. Sure enough, the gangway led to a small skiff.

I squinted through the glass as we walked to try and get a glimpse of its name, but the angle was wrong. All I got was pristine matte white paint and a single, off-center orange stripe. "Can't be many of them on a ship that small," I reasoned. "And gotta have one hell of a reactor to make it out here in that thing."

"We could ask," Brady offered.

"We're *already* late," I countered. "If they're still here once Foreman's done with us, maybe we can find 'em. Otherwise…" I shrugged.

"Where the hell have you two been?" Foreman's voice greeted us on cue the moment we stepped through the door into the locker room.

"Brady spent all morning getting his hair *just right*," I muttered.

"Cool it, Cal," Foreman snapped at me. "You're both late."

"Yeah, Cal," Brady said, gently ribbing me with his elbow, "cool it."

The six-foot-four hunk of meat before us glowered. Foreman—his real name was Josh. Jacob? Jackson? I don't fucking know; everybody called him Foreman—shoved our vac suits at us. "Suit up. There was a pirate skirmish a few weeks away, and I want us whole as we can get before any of that debris gets here."

"Sir, yes, sir," I said with a slight grin and a sloppy salute.

"And steer clear of our guest. He catches you saluting like that, you might not like the outcome."

Brady blinked. "We have a cultivator on station?"

"Yup," Foreman answered. "I'd tell you two not to piss him off, but we all know *that's* beyond you, so instead, you're gonna spend the entirety of his visit outside." He once again shoved the vac suits in our direction. "Understood?"

"Understood," I muttered, taking my suit and beginning the long process of putting it on. There was a reason nobody liked cultivators. They tended to find disrespect wherever they looked, and boy, they did *not* take it well. Thankfully, odds were our mystery cultivator was off sipping spill-off qi from the station's reactor rather than watching us mortals refuel his ship. Brady and I would probably still be out working when he left.

My ears popped as my suit pressurized, the locker room going silent until the shitty comms crackled in my ear.

"You hear me okay?"

"Yes, Brady, I can hear you," I spoke into my mic. "You ready?"

"Let's do this."

We grabbed our weld kits and waddled over to the airlock—yes, *waddled*. Three years we'd been doing this job, and neither one of us had gotten remotely better at walking in a pressurized vac suit, but I digress.

My hud flickered to life on the glass face of my suit as the airlock hissed open. Another step, and we'd left the station's artificial gravity.

Most people hate spacewalks. It's one thing to perceive the vastness of space on a screen or through a window, but out there, when it's all around you, it fucks people up. Some folks start screaming the moment they step outside, and they don't stop until they feel gravity again. Most just get used to it over time.

I loved it. There was something peaceful about all that nothingness, like it put everything into perspective. I think you have to truly grasp the concept of nothing before you even begin to comprehend the idea of *something*. I tried explaining that to my brother once, and he asked who on roofie was mixing narcotics.

Skipping past the more boring aspects of it, our job mostly involved crawling around the outside of the station until we got to where our huds told us to go, patching up whatever hole or damage we found, then doing it all again. It was boring, arduous, repetitive work that only paid a decent wage because we did it in a place nobody wanted to be—bumfuck nowhere.

We were about two hours into our shift, and my lower back was killing me when the lights went out.

It happened all at once. I like to imagine there was this great big *perklunk* as every system on roofie went down at the same time, but obviously *I* didn't hear anything— vacuum of space and all that. Brady and I were perched up on the wall overlooking dock three when it happened.

"What's that? What's going on?"

"Caliban to roofie, Caliban to roofie, do you read me?" I spoke into the mic, but no response came. I exhaled. "Comms are dead."

"Shit," Brady cursed. "They would've told us if they were planning a reactor reboot today, right?"

I scowled. "I didn't see anything on the docket, but it could've been a last-minute addition. We *were* late this morning."

"We should go in. Maybe something's wrong."

"If they wanted us in, they would've called us in. Come on, we're almost done with this one."

"I don't know, Cal," said Brady. "They wouldn't just leave us out here like this, would they?"

"They would if we, I don't know, had *work to do*. Now, come on, help me finish this." I held down the piece of sheet metal as Brady tacked it on, reinforcing the dented hull enough that it *probably* wouldn't puncture if something else hit it. I'd just pulled back to admire our work when the panic returned to Brady's voice.

"Cal, you should look at this."

"Look at what?"

"Your fucking hud. You know, the thing they pay you to look at?"

With a sigh I tapped the button on my wrist that marked the current job as done and glanced up at my hud to read the next one. None appeared. "It's gone."

"You're damn right it's fucking gone," Brady cursed yet again. "We need to go back. Something's wrong."

"Alright, alright," I breathed, fighting back my own mounting sense of trepidation. "Lead the way."

We took turns trying the comms again as we crawled hand over hand across the patchy hull. With every failed attempt my anxiety grew. As long as we'd been on roofie, maintenance had never taken the reactor down for more than a few minutes. By the time we reached the airlock, it'd been twenty.

Luckily for us, some engineer three centuries ago had the bright idea that airlocks should stay tied to the back-up batteries just in case a pair of vac-welders got caught outside during a reactor failure. While they weren't *quite* as important as, well, *clean air*, Brady and I certainly appreciated it. Well, *I* appreciated it. I think Brady was busy thinking about other things.

Namely the corpse on the staging room floor.

If I were one of those *biased* narrators, this would be the part where I claim I heroically rushed to Foreman's side to take his pulse and call for help. I would absolutely *not* stand perfectly still for three heartbeats then vomit in my suit.

"Foreman!" Brady tore his helmet off and heroically rushed to Foreman's side to take his pulse. "We need help down here!" he shouted. "Somebody!"

7

His voice echoed pitifully through the empty staging room. No-one came.

"Cal, help me with him!" Brady yelled at me, already shoving Foreman on his back and getting on top of him. "He's not breathing!"

Adrenaline finally kicking in and banishing the nausea, I wiped my mouth as best I could and darted to my brother's side as he started chest compressions. A hideous crack rang out as Brady broke one of Foreman's ribs. I tapped my foot to the rhythm, clapping Brady on the back to help him keep time. That's when I saw it.

"His eyes, Brady," I managed at little more than a whisper. "Look at his eyes."

"Shit." Brady deflated as he saw what I saw, stopping CPR the moment he realized its futility. "He has all the signs."

"I—" I stuttered, "I didn't notice—I didn't think—pallid and clammy skin are classic signs, but Foreman's *always* had pallid and clammy skin."

"The eyes confirm it," Brady said, his own gaze fixed on the milky white orbs that had once shined deep azure.

The posters listed three telltale symptoms of lethal qi depletion. Sickly and sweaty skin we could excuse, but I only knew of one thing that could drain the color from a person's eyes so quickly and so completely as Foreman's.

"We need to find the others!" Brady shot to his feet, not even bothering to strip out of his suit before he moved for the door.

"Are you kidding?" I shouted at him, already reaching for my sick-filled helmet. "We need to get the fuck out of here. If that cultivator's gone VIP, there's nothing we can do to stop him. Our best bet is to get back outside and hope he doesn't notice us."

"I'm not gonna hide while some void psycho kills my friends."

"*Our* friends," I corrected him. "And if they're smart, they're hiding too. Now, come on, we need to—" Before I could even finish, Brady had darted out of the room, leaving me, Foreman, and a vac suit full of vomit.

I chased him.

Before anyone starts calling me a coward for wanting to hide outside instead of trying to help people, it's important to understand that *I was right*. The most good any of us could've hoped to do was warn someone to hide before the void psycho found them, but what with all those enhanced senses cultivators have, the mere act of warning someone meant practically shouting our location to the high heavens.

As it turned out, we didn't need to shout or warn anybody at all. The mere sound of our feet against the metal walkway was enough.

He appeared out of nowhere, seeming to pop out of thin air as he stepped in front of Brady faster than my eyes could register the motion. Brady slammed into him, the entire body mass of my six-foot-one older brother failing to budge the cultivator an inch. Some dozen yards behind, I skidded to a halt.

The void psycho leered down at my brother with eyes as black as the abyss. Sweat dripped down his brow. One of the muscles on his face twitched uncontrollably, forcing his mouth in and out of a one-sided smile with no discernible rhythm. He wrapped a shaky hand around my brother's throat and licked his lips.

If this were a lighthearted, fun, adventure story, this would be the part where Brady broke free and escaped down the hall, all the while shouting some line like, "he's got the signs, Cal! He's got the signs!" Then we would've outwitted the insane cultivator, saved someone's life, and in the process won the approval of some powerful benefactor who'd whisk us away from this mundane existence to begin our true journey down the path of cultivation.

This isn't that story.

My brother's corpse hit the deck with a wet thump.

The cultivator shivered, his entire body quaking as he drank of Brady's qi. For a moment, for a brief, horrible, precious moment, there was only me and him.

I didn't see red. My heart didn't race with undying fury. My soul didn't wail with helpless sorrow. Somehow, in the maelstrom of fear and adrenaline and grief and hopelessness, my mind found itself at the eye of the storm, and a sense of calm overtook me.

I had two options. I could pray to whichever god would listen that Brady's had been the last foreign qi the VIP could handle, or I could go down swinging. With all the rational forethought of a man staring down his brother's murderer, I made my choice.

The cultivator didn't even look at me as I charged him. He didn't break from his stupor as I lunged over Brady's lifeless body. He didn't so much as flinch when my fist struck his jaw. I may as well have punched the outer hull.

Later on, I would learn that the most forceful punch of my mortal life was strong enough to break three bones in my forefingers, and one in my hand itself. At the moment, I just knew it hurt like hell.

The cultivator laughed.

It started low, a soft, quick, rhythmic exhalation as I first recoiled and clutched my injured hand. It built from there, rising in pitch and volume until his cackles echoed hauntingly down the metal hallway. He clutched his belly and doubled over, apparently finding my attempt at fighting back too funny to remain standing.

I ran.

The thick boots of my vac suit clanged against the walkway as I sprinted for my life, mind racing in desperate panic. *He's dead. He's dead. They're all dead. No. Stop. That doesn't matter right now. I need to do something or I'll be dead.*

I ran and I ran and I ran, taking corners at random, leaping over the pale corpses of my crew-mates as I found them. I didn't bother to check for a pulse. I didn't dare look back.

I knew it was futile. I knew there was nowhere I could hide where the cultivator wouldn't find me, nowhere I could run faster than he could follow. All I had was a paltry few moments of head start while he cackled. If he'd already made his way through the reactor core and the other crewman without dying to qi poisoning, nothing would stop him from taking me too. Nothing, unless...

"Scan for life signs on the ship in dock four!" I shouted the command at my holopad, taking a sharp left at the next available turn before its response even appeared. The display popped into view above my left wrist—no life signs, no lockdown.

I plotted the route in my mind, opening doors and making turns on instinct over anything else. Fear and adrenaline spurred me onward, my heart pounding in my chest as I kept imagining the void psycho popping out of nowhere directly in front of me, just like he did Brady. Brady...

I shook the thought from my mind. *Survival first, grief second*, I told myself.

The first glimmer of real hope sparked when I rounded the bend onto the gangway. The door to the cultivator's skiff hung open, its interior the only space free of the dull back-up lighting. I chanced a grin—the ship's reactor was online!

I booked it down the gangway, feeling the narrow passage shake as my feet impacted against it. I was so close. So close. I just had to—

The doors slammed shut in front of me. I collided with

them, my face pressing up against the small glass porthole. My panting breath fogged it up as I gazed through it, watching with desperate eyes as my only chance drifted away.

Unoccupied, unpiloted, seemingly of its own volition, the skiff abandoned me to die.

"No," I breathed, pounding my fist against the door. I felt the hope drain from my body as the skiff distanced itself, as more and more hard vacuum separated me and it.

"And then there was one."

I jumped as the singsong voice breathed down my neck, spinning in place to find the cultivator standing directly behind me. I panicked. I scrambled back, feet scraping against the floor as I pushed myself as far away as I could manage. My back pressed up to the gangway door, to the vacuum beyond.

The cultivator tilted his head. The spasms on his face had grown more frequent, more intense. He wrapped a hand around my throat.

There can be no words to adequately describe how it feels to have your qi torn from you, to have your life force so completely rent from your body that your every spiritual and biological function shuts down at once. There was pain, but no working nerves to register it. There was sorrow, but no working tear ducts with which to cry. There was torment, but no air with which to scream.

"Yes, yes!"

The man's hand twitched and released me. I slumped to the floor.

He turned and began to limp away, the spasms spreading and intensifying throughout his body as his muscles seized with foreign qi. He made it four awkward, jerking steps before he turned on his heel, opened his mouth as if to speak or to shout, and promptly exploded.

Blood and viscera rained down on me. Bone fragments

pierced my vac suit and the flesh beneath it in a dozen places, but I didn't care.

I was dead.

My only regret, in that moment, was that I wasn't lucid enough to truly enjoy the gruesomeness of the psycho's death.

But already I'd breathed my last. Already the color faded from my eyes. In those final seconds, as the neurons in my brain fired their desperate final thoughts, something miraculous happened.

I understood.

For all the time I'd spent gazing out at the stars, for all the contemplation I'd done, all the spacewalks I'd taken, it took all this to truly understand it. It took existing on a dead station in the middle of nowhere without a living soul around. It took the realization of how truly meaningless my life had been. It took experiencing true emptiness, *lethal* emptiness.

The void was infinite, and the void was nothing, and yet in its infinity, the void rendered all else nothing in comparison.

I was nothing. Roofie was nothing. The cultivator had been nothing. The scale of our existence touched so little that any distinction between us and the infinite nothing broke apart.

For all my life I've felt the call of the void, but it was there, alone, bleeding from a dozen small punctures and a shattered hand, my brain shutting down from qi deprivation, that I called back.

And the void answered.

Energy flooded through me, energy I didn't recognize yet knew like a close friend. I seized as my brain fired back up. I coughed great, horrible, full-body coughs as the air returned to my lungs and found them full of blood.

I made it eight seconds before the pain crashed into me,

a tidal wave that rippled up from my very soul only to wash against my various injuries like an acid bath. I lasted three breaths more before it proved too much for my overwhelmed mind, and at long last, consciousness escaped me.

According to my holopad, I was mentally, physically, and spiritually dead for four minutes and twenty-three seconds. I can't say for sure whether or not I woke up the same person. All I know is that *I* woke up, and, including the cultivator, seventeen men and women aboard RF-31 didn't.

And I hadn't the slightest idea why.

2

"Caliban? Caliban, can you hear me?"

The words drifted through my mind even as consciousness eluded me, the first trickle in the oncoming storm of sensory information to break through the blackness around me. It sounded distant and tinny as if it echoed from down the hall, yet a distinctly feminine character survived the trip to my ears.

"Caliban, you need to move."

I groaned and rolled my head to the side and muttered the only response my addled brain could think of in the moment. "It's Cal."

The feminine voice let out a patient sigh. "Alright, Cal, listen to me. I know you're in a lot of pain, but you need to —"

"Pain?" I mumbled. "What pain are you—" It hit me all at once. "Oh. There it is." My head throbbed like an army had marched across it. My right hand sent stabbing jolts up my arm, a curious reaction considering it hadn't been my hand that'd been stabbed.

It'd been the rest of me.

All across my torso and legs, small spots of red burned with their own rumbling infernos. Blood trickled down my leg, my side, my chest, its warmth and wetness sticking my clothes to the wounds. A hole in my left lung hissed air with every pained breath. A puncture in my abdomen wafted a foul stench into the hallway, indicating intestinal damage. Neither of these individually life-threatening injuries gave me much pause.

The three-inch shard of bone sticking through my upper chest did. The fact I hadn't kicked it *quite* yet meant it must've missed my heart, but if the pain was any judge, it'd certainly hit *something*. What felt like the rhythmic crashing of waves upon a beach slammed against the bone shard, each sending ripples of agony down my entire body. That single wound on its own almost drove me back into unconscious delirium, but the voice had other ideas.

"Cal, you need to move. Cal? Caliban! Stay with me. Cal, can you hear me? Open your eyes if you can hear me."

I gritted my teeth and blinked my eyes open. Well, eye. Despite my best effort, my left eye opted to remain shut.

A horror scene greeted me. An even layer of blood splatter coated the floor and walls in a circle around where the cultivator had once stood. Bones and bits of tissue lay scattered about the floor and walls.

My holopad blared with a dozen alarms, but I ignored them all. I already knew I was fucked up. It was the loud and unceasing whistling sound that grabbed my attention, a sound I'd come across all too many times in my line of work: depressurization.

My eye darted left to the source of the noise, where I found a hole roughly the width of a rib in one of the viewing ports. The bone had pierced the window clean through.

One of the problems with living in deep space is that you can't crack open the windows whenever you want a bit of fresh air. In fact, 'keep the windows closed' was a very important lesson that I was already in the process of learning the hard way.

"Cal," the feminine voice returned. It sounded middle-aged, soft, and comforting, a weird set of characteristics with which to be shouted at from a distance. "Cal, you need to get out of there. The gangway is losing pressure. Can you move?"

I grunted.

"I'm going to take that as a yes."

I certainly hadn't intended it as a yes, but who was I to argue with the mysterious disembodied voice that called to me in my dying moments?

"Okay, Cal, I need you to follow my voice. Can you do that? I can't help you if you can't get to me."

I tried lifting my head first, making it a full inch off the ground before a twitch in my spine sent the back of my scalp slamming into the metal grating. The pain barely registered as it added itself to the pile. My injured right arm lifted easily enough, though the act of lowering it again sent fresh and unpleasant sensations rocketing up my shattered hand. My left arm refused to budge below a gash in my bicep.

Standing was right out, but I did manage to drag my heels up half the way to my ass, even if my knees fell to the side rather than actually raising up. As I pushed my ankles away, the second miracle of the day occurred.

My body shifted backwards. I'd only made a few pathetic inches of progress in the direction of the closed end of the gangway, but I would take pathetic. I could work with pathetic. I couldn't work with dead.

Now I just needed to figure out a way to turn around so I could—

"Yes! Cal, that's perfect. Keep that up!"

What? But I'd moved the wrong way. If I kept going I'd just end up at the door that'd shut in my face before… I let the thought die before unwanted memories could derail my focus. I coughed. Blood dripped down my chin.

In more of a twitchy flop than anything that could really be called a glance, I tilted my head back to look for the dead end that had sealed my fate.

It wasn't there.

The door at the end of the gangway stood open, the dingy, depressurizing hallway coming to an abrupt end as a well-lit, pristine airlock took its place.

There was a ship here. Someone had come to save me!

"Don't stop!" the voice called from aboard the vessel.

I obeyed, too wrapped up in the idea of rescue to bother wondering who could've come to my aid. We weren't due another fuel shipment for three weeks, and not once in my years on roofie had we gotten two visitors in one day. I also didn't waste time asking why whoever it was refused to leave their ship.

I couldn't exactly joke about making the mortally wounded man come to you when I couldn't breathe deeply enough to get out more than one word. Well, I guess I *could have*, but the timing would've been all wrong.

So back I inched, pitifully, painfully, desperately. Hair tore from my scalp as it caught in the grating. New pain rose up to join old as I tugged on muscles that had previously known rest. All the way the voice cheered me on, telling me how good of a job I was doing even as I bled out. I kept my breathing shallow, terrified of the coughing fit I'd trigger if I inhaled too much. The increasing thinness of the air exacerbated things, constantly reminding me of the need for haste.

Not that I needed much reminding.

The sliding door slammed shut behind me the moment my feet cleared it. Fresh air filled the bright airlock, forcing my lungs to start sputtering up blood as they clamored to fill themselves. I didn't stick around long enough to start coughing. The last I remembered was a prick at the base of my neck and the words, "You did it, Cal," before the blessed darkness reclaimed me.

* * *

I awoke in a fog.

My thoughts slurred as my eyes drifted open, panic and pain driven away thanks to whatever drugs were being pumped through me. I glanced down to find myself lying on a bed, the blankets stripped away to leave me upon just the fitted sheet. My vac suit and the jumpsuit I'd been wearing under it were gone, leaving my bare skin exposed to the open air.

What little bare skin that wasn't covered in bandages, that was. About as much of me was hidden beneath strips of white cloth as was actually exposed, though whoever'd bandaged me hadn't bothered to cover my uninjured... *private* portions.

Saliva pooled in the back of my mouth, but as I tried to swallow it, the tube down my throat got in the way. Oh. I had a tube down my throat. As I glanced to the side, the clear tubing seemed to be coming from a four-wheeled cart that also contained various medical supplies, equipment, and the bags of whatever high-quality narcotics ran through my IV.

Before I could get much of a look around the unfamiliar room, the voice came back. "You're awake. Good. I need your help with something."

The voice spoke in the same nurturing tones as before, yet this time it sounded as if the speaker was right next to me. However I angled my eyes, I couldn't find her.

"Don't try to talk. You have a tube down your throat."

Yeah. I'd noticed that.

"I've fixed you up as well as I can, but this last injury is more... complex. A qi-infused bone fragment has punctured your blood meridian. Right now it's holding

19

the hole shut, but if I take it out while you're unconscious, all that qi in your system is going to rupture it. The problem is, you can't integrate the qi with your meridian blocked up. Here's what I need you to do. You're going to reign in that qi you absorbed and keep it out of your blood meridian as best you can while I remove the bone fragment. Then, I'll apply a patch to the meridian that'll hold long enough for you to integrate the qi. Understand?"

I shook my head no as vigorously as I could manage.

"Okay, that's okay," the voice reassured me. "How long have you been cultivating?"

I blinked in surprise. I'd been cultivating?

The voice let out a breath. "It's okay. It's okay. Can you at least sense the qi you took in?"

I nodded.

"Is it hostile?"

I raised an eyebrow.

"Is it all one type of qi?"

I nodded. Whatever energy had flooded me after I'd been drained was definitely uniform.

"Is it bucking wildly or just trying to run through your injured meridian?"

I raised an eyebrow again, unsure how to answer an either-or question with a nod.

"Blink once for the first option, twice for the second," the voice offered.

I blinked twice. The energy felt familiar, not foreign, and much as it sent waves of anguish through my body, it did so in a rhythmic manner as it crashed against the bone in my chest.

"Okay, good. That's good," the voice reassured me. "I don't know where you managed to find that much qi all the way out here, but it's good you did. Okay, I want you to shut your eyes and focus inward. Give me a nod when you're ready."

I obeyed, the calm and soothing voice helping to keep the fear at bay.

"Good, good.   Normally I'd give you a breathing technique for this, but the ventilator will do that for you. You just focus on keeping that qi away from your meridian. I'll know when you've done it."

I didn't bother nodding my assent. That she'd tactfully neglected to mention what a ruptured meridian meant implied she didn't want me thinking about the consequences of fucking this up. Still, my instincts urged me to trust this woman. It probably had something to do with the genuine sense of *care* in her voice, along with the fact she seemed to have done a damn good job of patching up the rest of me.

I reached for the swelling mass of energy within me. It reacted in exactly the wrong way, gushing with renewed vigor against the blockage. I struggled to constrain it, my will grasping like fingers through vapor. I realized then and there that that's what it *was*, vapor broadening in volume as pressure drove it to fill as much space as possible. If I wanted it to stop, I only had one option.

I had to condense it.

Rather than pushing away from the blockage, I *stretched* my will across my entire body, encircling the gaseous energy in a bubble of sorts.   At least, that's how *I* envisioned it. The bubble had other ideas, specifically, one other idea: popping.

I tried and I tried and I tried to completely wall in the qi, each time holding it in for just a few moments longer before my control inevitably wavered. Still I pushed, the tubes, the IV, the entire outside world fading away as the energy claimed the forefront of my mind.

It was like trying to catch an air bubble rising to the surface of a pool, except the bubble was as big as I was and *very* determined. Luckily, it wasn't the only determined one. Imminent death makes for a hell of a motivator.

I don't know how long it took. Some combination of my meditative focus and all of the drugs blurred the minutes into hours as attempt by attempt, I reigned the qi in. The first time a droplet formed on my imaginary walls, my excitement shattered my focus. After countless tries and unknowable hours, I managed to form a small pool of liquid qi at my center while the gaseous stuff continued to condense.

That's when she yanked the bone out.

The sudden shock and pain of the reopened wound blew a hole clean through my tight focus. The liquid qi stayed put, but what remained of the vapor spilled out into the hole. Fighting through the pain, I redoubled my efforts, capturing as much as the spilled qi as I could and continuing my condensation. I dared not stop. Already a dangerous amount of energy had slipped my grasp. The more I could condense, the less havoc it'd wreak before my meridian had a chance to heal.

A complex web of foreign qi pressed itself upon the chest wound, sealing the spiritual hole for the time being. Still I condensed, unwilling to cede an inch of the progress for which I'd fought so valiantly.

Nanometer by nanometer my imaginary bubble pulled in, forcing more and more of the vapor to condense as the pressure within built. The process grew both easier and more difficult as it went, easier as I reduced the total surface area I had to maintain, yet more difficult as the pressure grew. Rather than broad, consistent control, now I needed only sheer force of will.

Compared to my crawl off the gangway, it was a piece of cake.

A jolt ran through me as the last bit of vapor disappeared, leaving only a calmly-rippling pool that filled the lower quarter of my center. Carefully, I withdrew my will.

The qi stayed in place.

Elation filled me at my success just long enough to break my meditative state and return my senses to the world around me. A bandage pressed down against my sutured chest. The tube chafed against my dry throat. The disembodied voice was mid-sentence.

"—an't believe you managed to condense it! I just needed you to hold it back. This is… this is good. Great, even. It'll make the next step easier."

If I could've, I'd have let out a groan. Why was there always a next step?

"Don't worry." No hand touched my own, but I felt a comforting presence in the room with me as the voice spoke. "The worst part's over. The blockage is out and the patch is in place. You just need to cycle qi through your blood meridian. The patch will take what it needs to fix the hole and direct the rest where it needs to go. If the meridian wasn't open before, the good news is, it's about to be. Try to keep your focus on that."

I blinked. The meridian certainly *hadn't* been open before—I think I would've known if I'd secretly been a cultivator all this time. I didn't know much about meridians, you know, not secretly being a cultivator all this time, but I knew they were passages for qi that corresponded with particular body parts, and I knew opening all twelve of them was the first stage of cultivation.

What I didn't know at the time, was that opening a meridian was a famously unpleasant process. Curiously enough, the comforting voice neglected to share that information.

"Take your time," she urged me. "I'll be right here with you."

Ignoring the fact that I *knew* I was in an empty room, I obeyed the instructions. She'd gotten me this far, after all. Under the forcedly rhythmic breathing of the ventilator, I fell back into a meditative trance, and the pool of qi returned to the forefront of my mind's eye. With every beat of my heart it thrummed with power, a ripple spreading from its center out to its edges and back again. As my will touched it, it stirred in answer.

I directed a trickle up away from the pool and into my blood meridian where its entrance sat just beside my heart. It swept in slowly and weakly, a scarce few drops entering the passage at a time.

Agony erupted throughout me as qi ran through my blood meridian for the very first time. The body's longest meridian ran a full loop through every limb before returning back to the heart, spreading the anguish of this first traversal across every inch of my body. Less qi came out the other end than went in, some going to reinforce the meridian as a whole while the rest joined the patch across my spiritual wound.

I forced more qi into the meridian.

The pain intensified as more of the liquid energy surged through my blood meridian, opening it up and clearing out two decades of toxins. It wasn't long before I managed a continuous stream, yet bolstering and thickening that stream took yet more effort.

Bit by bit I purged my blood of impurities, opening and stretching my meridian while I fed the stranger's patch the qi it needed. I lost myself in the rhythm of it, sweeping up new qi into the channel even as old qi came out, until, at last, the pain abruptly ended.

The qi still flowed, looping around and around, but no more impurities impeded it, no more patch drank it up. My blood meridian, my longest meridian, my *punctured* meridian, was whole and clean and, most shocking of all, *open.*

And I still had qi to spare.

I'm not going to pretend my next decision was particularly informed, well-thought out, or even good. It was more the product of me being elated at my success, brimming with qi, and hopped up on drugs I'd never even heard of than anything resembling rational thought. Put simply, I got overexcited.

I tugged once more at my reserves of qi and sent a trickle towards the next closest meridian: my heart.

It splashed against it like spit against the ground.

A single, sharp stab of pain echoed from my heart as it skipped a few beats, but its pounding did return. I tried again, launching more qi at the barrier this time. Again I failed.

My third attempt finally forced through.

It also stopped my heart.

Ignoring pain that didn't hold a candle to my earlier crawl, I pushed through, forcing the cramped and polluted channel to widen and clear itself to fit the growing deluge of qi. Toxins secreted from my stilled heart into my blood, where the open and clean meridian whisked them away, or would have, had my heart been beating.

But I'd been through this once before, or at least something like it. If I could cleanse one meridian, I could cleanse two. I just had to finish up before the hypoxia caused permanent brain damage. Simple.

My extremities numbed. My thoughts slowed. A low ache spread throughout my entire body.

And then it didn't. Just like before, the pain stopped all at once. The qi flow solidified.

My heart beat once more.

Learning at least a little bit from my mistake, I opted to leave my brain meridian alone. With my newly cleansed heart and blood, my limited anatomical knowledge led me to what *I* thought was the obvious next step: my kidneys.

I began the process anew, embracing the pain as my qi battered through the various toxins that blocked the meridian. I was ready for it this time, ready to steel my will against it, and confident in the knowledge that I had what it took to accomplish my goal.

By the time my third meridian of the day came open, my pool of qi had depleted to little more than a puddle. I had enough to cycle through my new channels, enough to minutely reinforce my heart and blood and kidneys, but a dubious quantity to go for a fourth. Instead, I allowed the qi to still, and returned my focus to the world at large.

The world at large stank.

All the toxins I'd purged had excreted through my skin and various orifices I'd prefer not to list, soaking my bed and bandages with foul-smelling grime. The disembodied voice of my benefactor greeted my return to awareness.

"You did well," she cooed in my ear. "You did so well. So, so well. But it's time for rest now. I know you have questions, and I'll be here to answer them when you wake. Don't worry. I'll be right here."

The gentle comfort in her voice paired beautifully with the mental, physical, and spiritual exhaustion that filled my body to send my mind right to the brink of sleep. The fun new meds she pushed through my IV knocked it over.

My final thoughts weren't of my accomplishments, nor of my survival, nor even, I'm ashamed to admit, of my brother. No. As peaceful slumber drew in, I thought of the cultivator. I thought of the way I'd broken my hand against his jaw, of the speed and power with which he'd moved. I thought of how helpless I'd been before him.

And I thought of *never* being helpless again.

3

I dreamt of a soft bed and a cool pillow and a woman with a warm smile and silver streaks running through a golden braid. She sat at my bedside, watching over me and stroking my hair as I slumbered. I never questioned why she did this, never doubted this stranger's intentions. It felt nice. It felt safe.

Behind her, darkness lurked. Dread and despair loomed in the shadows, ready to inflict harsh reality upon the pleasant dream.

"Shhh," the woman calmed me. "You poor thing. Rest now. I'll keep them at bay until you're ready."

The words seemed to echo through my head.

"Until you're ready."

"Until you're ready."

My eyes snapped open.

The room had changed. Gone were the sterile white walls and the barren twin bed. I lay in a suite built for a king, or at least what I assumed kings liked. Navy-blue silk sheets caressed my skin beneath a remarkably soft blanket and a silver-embroidered quilt. The dark blue and silver palette extended to the walls and trimmings respectively, bestowing a somber, royal aesthetic to the decor.

For all the copious use of silver, the cabin itself was remarkably minimalistic. No portraits hung upon the walls, no decorations nor knickknacks nor real signs of character filled the space. If anyone had ever lived here, they'd either packed up well or been a particularly boring person. The only furnishings were the massive four-poster bed, a bare desk with a single, wheeled office chair, a few rows of empty shelving on the walls, and the medical cart, which still beeped along at my side.

That's when I noticed the tube was gone. Only the IV continued to tether me to those damn machines.

I inhaled deeply, eager to savor the sensation of once more breathing under my own volition, until the cool air passed through my throat and I realized my mistake.

Wow was I parched.

My eyes darted around until I found a pewter tray with a pitcher and cup sitting atop the medical cart. I didn't bother with the cup.

Screw post-workout water. I'm done with ice water on a hot day. Three AM water can go fuck itself. Those first gulps awake after extubation were the gods damned elixir of life. Say what you want for saline drips, but nothing deals with a dry throat like a good old fashioned sip.

Once I'd had my fill, I set the half-empty pitcher back on its tray and took stock.

The bandages were gone. In their place was a pale green garment that could charitably be called robes and more-accurately called a nightgown. Peering beneath it, I found no scars where any of the various punctures had been, save for a curved line just next to my heart. Only the bone that had pierced my blood meridian had left its mark.

I glanced at the back of my left wrist to summon my holopad, which readily displayed all the vital signs it broadcast to the machinery on the cart. Apparently they were pumping me with saline, a nutrient mix, and some drug I'd never heard of. That latter bore a little note that read, *to counteract the sedatives.*

A part of me wanted to do that thing holo characters do where they dramatically rip out their IVs and go wandering around. That always seemed stupid to me. I'm no doctor, how should I know how important the IV is or how to safely remove it?

So I did the much more sensible thing and started talking to the empty room. "Hello? Is anyone there?"

"Good morning. How are you feeling?"

I jumped as the familiar voice emanated from the empty air right next to me. "I'm... um... okay, I guess. Where are you?"

"I'm right here," the voice replied, her tone soft if a bit patronizing. "I know it doesn't seem like it, but I am."

"Um..." I managed, the height of eloquence. "And where is here? It can't be a ship, not with all these unsecured objects."

"You're in a midsized pocket dimension. It's where we keep living quarters, amenities, and cargo away from all the jostling of space travel."

"So we *are* on a ship. Kind of." I scowled. "Who's 'we'? Is someone else here?"

"I'm sorry." The invisible woman's voice fell. "It's just me, now. You don't have to worry about him anymore."

Something in the back of my mind burned at the mention of this 'him,' but I pushed past it. "Why can't I see you?"

"You can," she explained. "I'm all around you."

"Wait," I breathed as the realization sunk in. I raised a hand to my forehead in shock. "You're *the ship*." I blinked. "I'm on a fucking soulship."

"Language!"

"Sorry." Something in her tone brought me to apologize

without thinking. I *never* apologized for the way I talked, especially when I found certain words warranted.

In this case, they *were* warranted.

For an inanimate object to grow a soul, it has to experience a critical mass of life as well as the entire breadth of purpose for which it was designed. For a sword, that's easy: cut things, maybe parry a few blows, maybe impress some cute girls. For a ship? Those massive juggernauts with six-figure crews take *centuries* to gather enough experience for a soul. A skiff like this with a crew of no more than two at any given time would've taken millennia. Multiple millennia.

If your ship told you it was probably a couple *thousand* years old, you'd swear too.

"How did I get here? How did you find me?" I paused for a moment before building up the courage to add, "Why did you help me?"

Sorrow and regret colored her voice. "You came to me in your hour of need, and I abandoned you. I feared for my life, so I left you to your fate. Only when the threat was... gone, dared I return to find you by some miracle alive. Restoring you to health as best I could but scratches the surface of the debt I owe."

My heart quickened. "You couldn't have stopped him."

"No, but I could've given myself. My core alone holds more qi than most of your crew put together. How many died so that I could live? How many innocent souls were lost to save the one who delivered such destruction to them?"

"He was insane! There was nothing you—"

"Thank you, Cal, for your forgiveness, but absolution isn't yours to grant. It's mine to find. I fear I'll carry this shame for the rest of my life, but in the meantime, I swear by the stars, the galaxies, and the threads that bind them, I'll aid you in whichever way I can."

There was a weight to the words, a solemnity that carried past the voice itself and deep into my core. I knew, in that moment, more than I'd ever known anything, that I could trust this woman.

I swallowed and blinked away the gathering moisture in my eyes. "Thank you," I managed.

The conversation lulled for a few breaths as I collected my thoughts. I couldn't even *think* about what'd happened back on roofie. Every time the thoughts bubbled up in my mind, they seemed to blur and distance themselves. I think the ship might've had something to do with it.

Mentally referring to her as 'the ship,' brought me to my next question. "What do I call you?"

"My official designation is LC-81535, but my former partner called me—"

"Lucy," I murmured. Apparently cultivators and mortals used the same naming conventions.

"Indeed. I quite liked it."

"Lucy it is then," I said, a smile stretching across my face. "You really did a bang-up job on my injuries." I tensed and stretched my once-shattered hand. "No residual pain, no stiffness, only the one scar." I glanced down at my holopad. "It says here I was dead for a few minutes?"

"That's not the strange part. The strange part is that you both died and came back to life *before I found you*. As far away from any gravity well as I've ever been, you managed to find enough ambient qi to not only restart your heart, but open three meridians."

That last bit came with a hint of disapproval that for some reason hurt far more than it should've. "Was I not supposed to? I thought that's what cultivators did."

"That's what cultivators do in a safe and stable environment under experienced supervision. You did it sedated, intubated, and with a hole in your chest. The

31

damage to your blood meridian may've forced your hand, but it was foolish to continue as you did. It's a marvel you didn't hurt yourself."

I blinked. "I didn't? Well that's good, at least. I'm new to this whole *cultivation* thing."

Lucy let out a patient sigh. "How much do you know?"

"Um... I know it's all about taking in qi from the environment and circulating it through meridians. I know once you've opened all twelve you start forming a core. Cultivators judge each other based on how big their core is?"

"How dense," Lucy corrected.

"Sure. How much energy is in there, anyway. There are..." I tallied them up in my head. "Twenty-two core levels, categorized into five stages. I think advancing from stage to stage is supposed to be significantly harder? I don't know. The strongest cultivator I ever saw had a titanium core, so still in the metal stage. I know they meditate a lot, and they breathe a certain way, and they care way more about respect and their little hierarchy than any sane person should." I paused for a moment as I tried and failed to remember anything else before I asked, "How'd I do?"

"You sound like a mortal," Lucy answered.

"I should hope so. I *am* a mor—shit."

"Language."

"Sorry," I exhaled, the words soft on my tongue. "I'm a cultivator now."

"Barely," Lucy said. "Three open meridians does not a cultivator make, and this far away from any gravity wells, you'll have a hard time finding enough qi to open a fourth, let alone the full twelve."

"But I found some before. Maybe I could find it again."

"Perhaps, but I don't consider recreating your prior circumstances a viable option." She paused for a moment, allowing the silence to hang in the air. "How did you do it?"

"I don't know. I was drained. I was dying—or dead, I guess, and I had a thought about the infinite void of space, how my emptiness and its emptiness were the same and its vastness rendered my existence nothing in comparison. So… not the most *poetic* of dying thoughts."

"An epiphany, then," Lucy muttered. "Epiphanies bear great power as we forge a connection to one of the threads that binds the universe. You mentioned meditation. One of the reasons cultivators meditate is in contemplation of life's great mysteries in the hopes of bringing about such an epiphany. You must have touched upon something truly great to survive as you did."

"So that explains it, then? I realized something and got a bunch of qi as a reward?"

"Not quite. It explains how you went from a clueless mortal to someone who could sense and manipulate qi enough to take it in, condense it, and open three meridians, but it doesn't explain where it came from, nor its… unique properties."

I scowled. "What properties."

"It doesn't exist."

"Excuse me?"

Lucy let out a breath. "Well, obviously it *exists*. It saved your life. It opened your meridians. But no matter how I look at it, it just isn't there. When your holopad gave me access to your vitals, I could deduce its presence. I could see how the bone in your chest shook with each impact. I could feel how the pressure in your core fell to zero as you condensed it. I could watch your meridians clear themselves of impurities. I could see the ways it acted upon the world—"

"But you couldn't see *it*," I finished. "What does that mean?"

"I don't know. You seem to have stumbled upon something I've never heard of. I'm sure someone somewhere knows something of what you've done. It's possible it took having the epiphany you did while being utterly drained of your natural qi to even sense the energy you found. I doubt many—if any—have accomplished such a thing, but the cosmos is vast."

I nodded along. "I can't be the first, right?"

Lucy didn't answer.

In case you were wondering, uncertain silence is an even *more* disconcerting answer coming from a thousand-year-old spaceship. I bit the inside of my cheek, gaze flitting around wildly as my instinct to avoid eye contact clashed with Lucy's lack of eyes. "What happens now?"

"If you're feeling up to it, I think your first step should be to see if you can find this qi of yours again."

"Okay. How do I do that?"

"First you leave," Lucy replied. "Whatever you found, I doubt it was hiding in a pocket dimension. You'll have to come out to the upper deck."

"Yeah, just let me…" I reached down to remove my IV, but already the needle was gone from my vein, a small bandage in its place. "The fuck?"

"Language," Lucy chided, sounding more bored than irate.

"Sorry. How did you—"

"How did I remove your IV? A bit of qi manipulation. How did I do it without you noticing? A bit of *very gentle* qi manipulation," Lucy bragged.

"Impressive," I said, with no idea whether or not that was impressive. I pulled the blankets off me to reveal my gorgeous green cotton nightgown. "That's how you treated me?"

"That's how I do most things. Like you humans, ships don't come with mechanisms for moving things around inside us."

Opting not to make the 'inside you' joke to someone who chided me for swearing, I swung my legs around and pushed myself out of bed. I almost collapsed then and there, not from weakness or anything, but surprise at what awaited my bare feet. "Holy shit. You have hardwood floors. Actual, real, hardwood floors."

"Language."

"Sorry." I recollected myself. Why had I believed pocket dimensions and a living soul but not a wooden floor? Shaking my head, I moved for the room's only exit. The metal door slid open for me as I approached, reacting quickly and suddenly enough that I didn't even have to break my stride.

At least until I stepped through it and realized my dilemma. "Um... which way?"

"Left." Lucy's voice made me jump as it sprang from the empty space in front of me rather than the empty space in the bedroom I'd grown accustomed to. This whole disembodied voice thing was gonna take some acclimation time.

The hallways kept the wood flooring, but forewent the blue and silver for a soft eggshell white with distressed-wood crossbeams. It made for a jarringly rustic aesthetic, as if I'd stepped from a spaceship into a medieval reenactment.

Lucy directed me past a number of unmarked doors and even a long window into what looked like a garden before we arrived at a matte white set of metal sliding doors, their hue just different enough from that of the walls to be unsettling. Like the bedroom, the doors opened automatically to admit me into what I could only assume was the ship proper.

As I'd have expected from a skiff, space was tight. Matte white panels coated the floor, ceiling, and inner wall of the four-foot-wide hallway. The first four feet of the outer wall housed a curved-top enclosed space for storage and cabling, above which only a single panel of glass separated me from the vacuum of space.

I gaped. Lucy had a fucking *hallway* with a window as big as the entire viewing deck on roofie.

Misreading the sudden pause in my step, Lucy raised her voice in concern. "Are you alright?"

"I'm fine, I just…" I trailed off, eyes glazing over as I gazed out into space. It beckoned to me, whispered promises of infinite mystery and untold adventure, of hope and possibility in limitless supply. I found music in the dark between the stars, a tune at once that urged I listen, a song I dreamt one day to sing.

Of course, I couldn't explain any of this to Lucy.

"Cal?" Lucy pulled me from my reverie.

"Yes, yes, sorry, just… contemplating." She'd said cultivators did that, right?

She led me down the almost painfully white hallway until it curved back around at the skiff's rear.

Glancing down, I saw how the windowed outer hall seemed to traverse both sides of the skiff, leaving various small rooms and the entrance to the pocket dimension—or 'lower deck'—in the middle. We didn't head that way. Instead, Lucy led me through a door at the very back of the ship.

The ten-by-ten room inside had padded flooring, a drain, various painted qi formations that I didn't even come close to recognizing, and a nuclear reactor.

As it turns out, the only difference between the fusion core a high-level cultivator will eventually develop and the fusion core that powers a ship or a station like roofie is whether or not it's inside a living human. As it turns out, sustained nuclear reactions, qi-based or chemical or otherwise, are a lot easier to set up *outside* the spiritual space of the human soul.

The two *did* work a bit differently in practice. There were all manner of corners to cut in the manufacturing process that led to most ship reactors burning a bit dirty, and of course, since ships didn't gain energy from eating like us fleshy meatbags, most of the qi output went towards keeping the lights on and the thrusters working.

When the void psycho had drained roofie's core, he hadn't actually *drained* it, but rather pulled enough qi that the station's other demands overwhelmed it and caused it to fail. It wouldn't have taken much. A sentient ship could, in theory, advance its core enough to generate excess for personal use and empowerment, but Lucy didn't know any that had, at least not into the next core level.

The reactor sat within a metal pillar at the room's center. Only a small glass window revealed the core itself. It looked like a ball of metal that glowed bright yellow, not quite as bright as a star, but bright enough it made me squint to look at it.

"This is the core room," Lucy explained. "Cultivators spend their time here, cycling and absorbing any qi that inefficiencies in the reactor give off. It's not much, but it's better than nothing. It should go without saying you only take the spill-off. Draining the reactor itself will kill it." The following 'and me' went unsaid.

"Right," I said, scratching the back of my head. "So I just…"

"Take a seat," Lucy instructed. "Anywhere works."

I obeyed, plopping down right where I stood into a cross-legged pose.

"Good. Now straighten your spine. Shoulders back. Eyes level." She went on for some time, making smaller and smaller corrections to my basic posture before at last saying, "Cultivation takes time. You may or may not perceive it, but odds are you'll be sitting in this same position for hours. If your posture's not right, you'll hurt yourself."

I nodded, which apparently moved my neck and back enough to warrant a whole new set of posture corrections before she was finally satisfied. From there she guided me through a breathing exercise, which turned out to be less about breathing into your belly through the nose and out through the mouth or whatever, and more about keeping the correct rhythm.

Humans are actually pretty shit at keeping time. Our heartbeat, our pulse, the rhythm that drives our entire biology, keeps changing. The next time you hear a crowd clap along to live music, listen for how out of time they get.

All this to say, it took about an hour before I managed to breathe right. Lucy told me it'd get easier with practice, but I think cultivators just stop realizing they're fucking it up when instructors stop looking over their shoulders.

"Okay," Lucy said once I'd learned how to breathe. "Next I want you to visualize your core."

I gave a slight nod. This part was easy; I'd done it already when I'd opened my meridians. I just had to—

"In, out, in, out," Lucy started counting as my breathing once again fell out of time.

Okay, maybe the ventilator had helped a bit. I tried again, focusing on my breathing until I could trust my subconscious enough to take over. I focused inward, searching for that pool of mysterious energy that'd saved my life. I found little more than a puddle. Apparently recovering from all those shrapnel wounds had cost a bit of qi.

"Good, good," Lucy said, somehow aware that I'd successfully visualized my core.

I'd have wondered if I needed to revoke her access to my holopad's bio-data, but *that* train of thought would've earned me another hour of breathing lessons. I kept focused.

"Next, I want you to circulate your qi. Split it evenly between your three open meridians, even if that means they aren't flowing at full capacity. We're not trying to reinforce your meridians, just increase awareness."

I wordlessly obeyed, splitting the liquid qi into thirds and sending a stream through each meridian. I made it four seconds before inhaling for just a *little* too long.

"You're doing well," Lucy reassured me. "You're doing very well. Now, again. In, and out."

She counted me back into time and I delved once more into my core. This time, I lasted nine seconds.

We progressed from there, repeating the frustrating start-and-stop as I progressively managed to maintain my breathing for longer and longer. At something like attempt number eighteen, gods know how many hours in, I finally reached the next step.

"Okay," Lucy spoke the word carefully as if afraid of upsetting my focus. "Now in the same way you're visualizing your qi, I want you to expand your focus outward. Start slow, maybe just an inch away from your skin. Don't think about the air or the floor or the ship. Think about qi. There's energy all around you. How does it feel?"

It felt loud, loud and weak like a sick child crying for attention. It grated against me, foreign and wrong and asserting its existence as if for some reason I should care. It was strange. I'd expected it to be scarce. I'd expected it to be thin, so little that I could barely perceive it, but the opposite was true.

I perceived it so much it hurt. Okay, maybe not quite *hurt*. It was more like a fly buzzing in my ear, small and annoying and useless but impossible to ignore. So little couldn't possibly overwhelm my senses, but it could certainly distract them.

It went away the moment I opened my mouth to relay all this to Lucy.

"That's… not how I would describe it," she said once I'd finished my explanation. "I'd call it… warm, full of life, eager and energetic. Yes, the qi here is weak, we *are* in deep space, but you're the first I've heard liken it to a crying toddler."

"What does that mean?"

"It means we all perceive qi in our own way?" Lucy offered. "I've known a lot of cultivators, child, but I haven't studied the art. I'm a ship, not a teacher."

I took no offense at her calling me child. After however many millennia she'd lived, the difference between twelve and twenty-two didn't *really* matter. "Back to it, then?"

"Back to it," Lucy agreed, counting off once more.

I was thankful when she didn't let me try and take in any of the hyperactive qi. I found it almost repulsive. Imagine that—a vac-welder from bumfuck nowhere turning his nose up at qi on his second day cultivating. I could already feel myself becoming the entitled asshole most cultivators were. I guess when you spend all day looking inward, it's easy to think the world revolves around you.

Instead, we worked on expanding my external perception beyond the first few inches. Lucy told me that the wider a cultivator's sphere of influence, the more qi they could take in. How *much* of the qi within your radius you managed to gather was an entirely separate axis of improvement we hadn't reached quite yet. For the time being, she just wanted me to touch the boundaries of the core room.

I made unsteady progress. Sometimes my reach would leap a foot or more in a single go, others I'd manage barely an inch before losing focus or hitting some block, but on we pressed.

At one point Lucy pulled me from my meditation to reveal a ham sandwich and a glass of lemonade had magically appeared at my side. I gaped at that, barely holding back profanity as I realized that a thousand-year-old soulship had *made me a sandwich.*

I still wasn't quite over the whole *soulship* thing.

I devoured the delicious lunch with all the reverence and grace of a twenty-two-year-old vac-welder, thanked Lucy profusely, and went back to the grindstone.

When my senses reached the reactor core, that buzzing in my ear turned to a scream. My focus fell apart as I gasped and clutched at my ears, a headache building behind my temples. I fell back against the padded floor.

"Cal! Are you okay? What's wrong, child?"

"It's loud," I managed through gritted teeth. "It's so *loud.*"

"Shh, shh, it's okay. You're okay," she cooed.

Patronizing as her words were, they *worked.* My heart stopped pounding, the ringing faded from my ears, and the headache drained away. I sat back up. "Okay," I echoed. "I'm okay."

"Do you want to stop?" Lucy offered. "Perhaps it would be best to wait until we can find an instructor who knows what loud qi means."

"No." I straightened my posture, getting back into position to try again. "Again."

She didn't question me.

I tried to prepare myself for the onslaught of overstimulation, but the mere act of bracing set my breathing off and forced me to start over. The second time I sensed Lucy's core, I was ready for it. I knew going in that the obnoxious demands of the weak ambient qi would explode into an onslaught of noise.

It still took me by surprise. It still shattered my focus in under a second.

"Again," I grumbled through my headache, jumping right into it before Lucy could talk me down.

The essence of cultivation, I discovered, seemed to be learning new skills through brute-force repetition. I had no idea if I was acclimating myself to the brightness of the core the *correct* way, only that if I tried it enough times, I'd get there eventually.

It took a few hours before I could reliably maintain my focus and breathing with the fusion core screaming at me, an hour more before I could keep expanding my senses past it. I'm hesitant to say I got *used to* the core's presence, but I at least made decent progress towards learning how to ignore it.

I'd dismissed two of my holopad's bedtime reminders before my qi sense finally touched the boundaries of the room—directly to my left as I wasn't sitting *quite* center. I suppressed my elation, eager to push on as much as I could before my concentration inevitably lapsed. *Just a few more inches*, I told myself. *Just a few more inches and I can—*

The core went silent. The buzzing in my ear faded away. The floor beneath me, the air around me, Lucy's calming presence all vanished as the leftmost point of my perception passed the outer hull to touch hard vacuum.

It was right there. It had always been there. It was cold and comfortable and quiet and dark. It demanded nothing. It didn't impose its existence upon me; it asked not for attention or influence. It simply was.

From barely grazing the edge of space, I went from a man squinting at the sun to one standing upon a flimsy raft in an endless ocean. No more could the core perturb me, for noise could find no footing in the face of so much silence. In its vastness, I was nothing, yet how could it be vast without something by which to measure it? As it defined me, so too did I define it.

I reached for it, longing to once more sip from these

eternal waters that had deigned to spare my life. It heeded my call, rushing in to join with its kindred spirit. I drank it in, eager and joyous and rejuvenated in the bounty of the infinite sea.

Until the waves came crashing down.

4

I should've panicked. I should've withdrawn my senses, broken my focus, altered my breathing.

Instead, as the riptide of qi bore my consciousness away, I rode along with it. It felt right, like the time had finally come to commune with the great nothing to which I'd always felt some connection.

But nothing communed with *me*. No great sage bestowed their wisdom, no horrible monster lurked in the darkness, no god ruled over the void, nor, as it happened, did the void rule anything else.

It simply was.

Vast and empty and unknowing and unwanting, the void accepted all that came, made way for the insistence of existence, and swept in as the existence departed. It sat still, unstirred by the tides and currents of needless motion.

The first thing I realized as my consciousness drifted, was that the qi had only come to sweep me away because I'd called for it. So eager I'd been to drink of this vast reserve of energy, I'd underestimated my influence upon it. Such was its way. Emptiness didn't assert itself the way existence did. It simply came to whichever space offered itself.

But I'd known my whole life about the vastness of space. For decades I'd pondered the nature of nothing. That wasn't new.

The qi was.

How could there be qi where there was nothing? From whence could come this colder energy that seemed to so flood the corners of dark infinity? And how was there so fucking much of it?

A single sip had saturated my soul, setting my meridians alight and my center overflowing. Was I so weak that but a taste of real power overwhelmed me, or was the void so brimming as to make such power plentiful? I settled on both, with the caveat that perhaps all cultivators shared my weakness. How could a man be anything *but* weak in the face of such might? How could a god?

I found beauty in that. To the void, all were equal, for no finite gap in power could bridge the way to infinity. To the void, all were neutral, for morality could only exist where there were decisions to be made. To the void, nothing mattered.

Nothing mattered.

Nothing mattered.

So I drifted. I had no cause to return when cause itself no longer *was*. I had no tasks to complete when any action I took could change nothing in the scope of reality. I had no dreams to chase when even my wildest fantasy meant naught to the sea in which I swam.

I can't say how much time passed. I can't say if time passed at all. What was a second, a minute, a lifetime to cold uncaring infinity? Here, there could be no joy, no sorrow, no love, no hate. There could be no life, no death, no knowledge shared or secrets kept. There could be no fond memories, no soul shattering trauma.

I ached. I ached, but I knew not why. My spiritual self,

the only part of me that could embark on this voyage, seemed whole. The wound to my meridian had long closed, and while the surplus qi ran rampant throughout me, its was the realm of cool comfort, of welcoming darkness and sweet relief. Pain belonged to the living.

I found the source hidden away atop my still-closed brain meridian, a wildly complex weaving designed to be unnoticeable. Compared to the void, it shone like a beacon. With a dull thought, I swiped away life's annoying insistence, my own minute share of the infinite sea more than enough to wash it away.

I remembered.

I watched in my mind's eye as the cultivator twitched, as he moaned with euphoria, as my brother's corpse landed at his feet. I felt again the desperate race of my heart as I'd fled, the crushing hopelessness as Lucy's doors had slammed in my face, the maniacal laughter that had echoed through the halls behind me.

I didn't care. It didn't matter. Nothing mattered. Horrific as those events may have seemed, they'd barely caused a ripple in the infinite sea. All it would take was time, minuscule, pointless *time*, before those ripples calmed and the waters stilled again.

But I was still here. I yet drew breath, yet maintained life's unique capacity to effect change, as much as finite life could alter the infinite.

Perhaps that explained it. Perhaps that displayed why cultivators drove themselves towards immortality, dedicated their lives to the hopeless chase of infinity. On the scale of forever, no man, no woman, no star, no black hole could hope to leave a mark upon these endless waters.

But they could make a splash. Their ripples could spread to the furthest corners, reverberate across time and space for unmeasurable eons before they too finally faded. If there was beauty in the eternal, could there not too be beauty in the fleeting?

By the curse of opportunity, did I now bear the burden of greatness? In the aftermath of RF-31, of the void psycho, of *Brady*, did I now owe it to them to make as big of a splash as I could? Whether or not I saw value in pointlessly defying eternity, I was roofie's last scion, the only one who could spread their ripples across the uncaring dark. Is that what they'd have wanted? Did their wants even matter? I thought nothing mattered.

It had mattered to them.

Was I so much greater, so much more enlightened to believe I knew better than they? I may have been the first to sense its qi, but all had glimpsed the void—by its nature it was everywhere. My failure to find meaning in it didn't negate their successes.

Those successes deserved to live on, to make an impact, to reverberate through the heavens for all to hear. Perhaps that's what it was to live, to seek out and glorify every bit of meaning to be found. Ancient wisdom said that to cultivate was to defy the heavens. I wasn't sure I agreed.

To cultivate was to flail against infinity, to stoke the flames of discontent at one's own smallness, to glimpse eternity, recognize the hopelessness of it all, and *fight back anyway*.

If not meaning, I found at least beauty in that thought. Maybe that could be enough.

I followed that beauty, that dream, that hope, back through the endless dark. It led me to a raft, a tiny blip forcing itself upon the emptiness, an island of blinding light and deafening cacophony and boundless love. It led me home.

The world came back all at once, the padded floor beneath me, the roaring fusion core ahead, the walls on all sides. Lucy's presence warmly welcomed my return, her silent comfort some solace against the maelstrom to come.

The memories struck like a blade through the gut. Foreman, Brady, the cultivator, images and emotions ravaged my spirit with neither Lucy's enchantment nor the void's numbness to shield me. I collapsed onto my side. I quivered and quaked and curled into a ball beneath the weight of it all.

And I wept.

5

Lucy let me cry.

She didn't interrupt to ask if I was alright, she didn't try to stop me or convince me it would all be okay or to look on the bright side or any other meaningless bullshit. She stayed present, her perception lingering in the core room ready to listen or remind me I wasn't alone, but she made no attempt to halt the outpouring emotions.

A blanket found its way around my shoulders. A tray with a couple of cups, a pitcher of water, and a bottle of bourbon materialized on the floor next to me. A thermos of chicken soup shortly followed.

I partook in all three, nourishing and hydrating and intoxicating myself in turn. I found the latter's numbness more acceptable than that of the infinite sea, more human in the way it left my emotions ragged and raw rather than entirely detached. From whiskey I knew I'd eventually sober up. If I waded back into those eternal waters, gods knew if I'd ever return.

Sleep took me before my eyes could fully dry, thrusting me cruelly into an endless race down twisting hallways with demented laughter echoing behind me and a twitching cultivator around every corner.

I awoke to a dull headache and faint nausea, symptoms that I knew Lucy could probably treat yet felt appropriate. I rubbed the grogginess from my eyes and forced myself to my feet, leaving the blanket draped over my shoulders as I picked up the tray with the half-empty bottle and used dishes. I shuffled over to the door before muttering my first words since my return from the infinite sea.

"Where're the showers?"

"In your quarters."

"What? All of them?" The joke came half-hearted and poorly timed, the best I could manage given the circumstances.

Lucy laughed anyway. "Just yours."

"And where do I...?" I trailed off and gently shook the tray in my hands.

"I'll take care of those," Lucy said as two strands of gray and golden qi whisked the dirty dishes away. "You go take that shower, and then we can see about the full tour. You remember the way back?"

"Yeah, thanks."

I truly, deeply, meant it, but at the moment I lacked the mental capacity to fully express my gratitude. Instead I shuffled off, retracing my previous steps back into Lucy's pocket dimension and my luxurious bedroom. Sure enough, opposite the entrance were two more doors, one that led to a walk-in closet, and another that opened to a private bathroom, complete with sink, shower, and a massive open tub that I couldn't comprehend filling.

Pocket dimensions really broke down the basic rules of voidcraft design, huh?

I let my nightgown fall to the tile floor and embarked upon the umpteenth revelation of the past few days.

Seriously, this shower changed my fucking life. A sensor in the wall must've measured my skin temperature or something, because the moment I tapped the touchpad, a mid-sized creek's worth of perfectly-heated water rushed from the head above.

People who talk about water pressure are full of shit. How fast the water comes out of the pipe is only ever relevant if there isn't *enough* of it, and let me tell you, speed makes a poor substitute for quantity. Or is that a pour substitute?

Either way, the shower didn't blast me with water or attempt to pressure-wash my skin off. It simply let fall under Lucy's artificial gravity the bounty it had to offer, a waterfall of such warmth and mass that it relaxed muscles I didn't even know I had. Did all cultivators shower like this? 'Cause honestly, if so, fuck immortality, I was in it for the showers.

Feeling refreshed down to my very soul, I emerged from my new favorite room, toweled off, and strode back into the bedroom to face my next conundrum: clothes. I assumed Lucy had disposed of the vac suit and underclothes I'd been wearing when I came aboard, especially since she'd have had to cut them off me to get to my injuries.

I made a beeline for the closet. Given how thoroughly she'd cleared out the rest of the cabin, I could think of no reason beyond my own use that the clothes should've remained. An embarrassing amount of digging around in drawers and trying things on later, I left wearing a T-shirt that bore the logo of some qi supplement brand I didn't recognize and a pair of what I've decided to call 'cultivator pants.'

The dark brown synthetic-cotton bottoms hung just loosely enough to allow the full range of motion as they tapered down in a slight cone towards the feet. They felt like just a *bit* too much fabric to comfortably fit under a vac suit, but if I needed to kick somebody in the head, I'd have that option. The loose elastic bands around the ankles would even keep them from bunching up or getting caught in any hatches or doorways.

To my eyes they looked a touch too much like sweat pants or pajama bottoms, but the strength of the fabric and the complete lack of any other style in the closet confirmed that this was just how cultivators dressed. The void psycho had been wearing something similar when... you know.

I shook the thought from my head as I stepped back into the hallway. I didn't even have to open my mouth before Lucy greeted me.

"Feeling better?"

"A lot, thank you," I replied. "Seriously, thanks. I haven't exactly been the best houseguest, and you've been absolutely amazing to me."

"It takes a million little goods to pay off one great evil," Lucy said, an uncomfortable darkness to her voice. "But enough of that. Can I get you some breakfast? Tea? Or would you prefer to start the tour right away?"

"The tour," I answered. "Then I'll know where to get my own breakfast. I can't have you doing *all* the work around here."

My ears thought they picked up something akin to a patronizing laugh, as if my words had been those of a naively cute child rather than a guest offering to help out, but the noise just as easily could've been the air-scrubbers kicking in. Either way, Lucy didn't give me much chance to analyze the noise, whisking me away on a tour of the lower deck.

I had absolutely no frame of reference by which to judge the size of her soulspace, so I just decided to be deeply impressed by everything she showed me. What I had originally thought to be a two-man skiff actually housed a crew of five, climbing to eight if the three king-sized beds slept two.

None of the cabins matched mine for size or luxury. The two larger rooms each contained their own closets and washrooms and workspaces, while the two smaller quarters only housed twin beds and had to share a bathroom.

Though it had been deeply cleaned, the smaller room in which I'd first awoken still reeked of the impurities I'd expunged when I'd opened my meridians. I gagged as I stepped inside before thanking Lucy then and there for not treating me in the captain's quarters. The core room had a drain in the floor for a reason.

Beyond the surplus of bedrooms, the lower deck contained a fully-equipped gym, a sparring ring complete with blunted wooden weapons, and a fucking *swimming pool*. Lucy could've easily housed fifty people and carried enough cargo to make a fortune in inter-station shipping with all the space she'd devoted to amenities for her crew of five. Fucking cultivators.

Past the exercise wing, I found the garden. Three rows of mint and basil and other basic cooking herbs filled one side, but six rows of fertile soil sat unsown, as apparently neither Lucy nor her former partner had the necessary training to cultivate the rare and valuable plants for which the space was designed. That made three of us. I made a mental note to either learn some herbalism or recruit someone who already practiced the craft before the absolute insanity of the thought struck me.

I'd known Lucy for all of two days and already I wanted to recruit new crew members.

The water and biomass recycling systems sat understandably close to the garden. I nodded along as Lucy explained how all of it worked, pretending I understood half of what she was saying. I was a welder, not an engineer. Point me to a hull puncture, and I'll patch that son of a bitch right up, but life-support systems? They may as well have been black magic.

Having had my fair share of black magic over the past couple of days, we moved past the deep freezers with enough food to last twenty years and into the most important room on the whole ship: the kitchen.

Fire qi direct from the fusion core powered the stovetop and oven, next to which sat a holopad-integrated terminal for requesting ingredients. I simply had to wirelessly sync up to view inventory and press a few buttons to summon a freshly-thawed ingredient warmed to my desired temperature and peeled, chopped, or sliced however I needed.

A set of knives and cutting boards sat ready should I want to prepare the food myself, and I'd have to combine and cook it all manually either way, but the sheer convenience of it all astounded me.

A twenty-foot bar separated the kitchen from what appeared to be a combined dining room and lounge. A wooden table long enough to host dinner guests sat closest to the bar, beyond which rested a plush red couch and two armchairs overlooking the room's most absurd feature.

A fucking fire crackled in the hearth.

"The logs are carbon cellulose composites," Lucy explained at my aghast expression. "It takes a fair bit of energy to reform them from their component parts after they're burnt up, but I have the qi to spare."

I decided she could show me the holotheater and upper deck another time. I was gonna sit by the fucking fire for a bit.

Moments later found me leaning forward in the soft armchair as I stared into the flames, a mug of earl gray in my hand. The sheer opulence of it staggered me. Back home on Veruma, mom used to put on a fire every night, but that'd been a prebuilt holo with heat and sound effects.

The real thing had a smell to it, a cozy smokiness that

my body found relaxing even if my brain knew it was technically poisonous. The air around it moved in subtly different ways, pulling in and up rather than blowing out into the room. That was it. Those were the only differences. And here Lucy was, spending absurd amounts of energy to manufacture her own sustainable firewood. I repeat myself: Fucking *cultivators*.

"Cal," Lucy broke me from my musings, "it's time we talked about what's next."

"I'm a cultivator now, right? I guess I should do... cultivator things?"

She sighed.

"Okay, okay, seriously," I said. "I want to learn more. I want to finish opening my meridians; I want to form a core; I want to *cultivate*. I want to be strong enough that the next time someone comes for me and mine, I can do more than run and hide, and I want to find out where all this qi is coming from. Why does the qi in your core feel so wrong to me, and why am I the only one who can pull from the vast supply of qi out in space?"

"So you did find it again," Lucy breathed.

Right. I hadn't told her. I'd been so caught up in my whole nihilistic crisis and overwhelming grief I'd forgotten to mention the gods damned ocean of qi out there. "I did. I found a *lot* of it. It's different from your qi, quieter and stiller and dark in nature."

"That might explain why you thought my qi was too loud," Lucy said. "The qi you'd found, the first qi you'd sensed, is silent. If it's incompatible with normal qi, that could be why you only discovered it once all the regular qi had been drained from your system."

I snorted. "Of *course* I stumble down the only cultivation method that requires you to *die* before you even begin."

"The weft and warp are never simple," Lucy calmly

restated the ancient phrase about the threads of fate. "You'll be forging your own path for some time, possibly your entire life."

"Which leaves one question. What's the next step?"

"You need guidance," Lucy said with no uncertainty. "I can guide you through the absolute basics, but the complexities of human cultivation are beyond me. My tutelage will just as likely leave you dead or permanently spiritually stunted as help you."

I nodded along.

"You'll have to join a sect," she continued. "The Dueling Stars system is your only option if you don't want to wait through a two-year-journey, but it's a *good* option. The sects there are weak enough that their outer stations might accept new recruits even if they can't sense your qi, and their affiliation with Eternity's Maw means there'll always be opportunities for advancement."

I blinked. Even vac-welders from bumfuck nowhere knew of Eternity's Maw. Built around a massive black hole, they were the strongest sect in viable distance. That meant to find anyone stronger, you'd have to either be a powerful enough cultivator to walk the threads or somehow survive a two-hundred-year trip sub FTL. All this to say, Eternity's Maw was the biggest fish in a *very* big pond.

Lucy wanted me to join one of their subsidiaries, and from the sound of it, not one of the stronger ones. It made sense. We all had to start somewhere, and a three-week trip certainly seemed preferable to a multi-year one.

"Okay," I finally said. "Dueling Stars it is. I assume we have enough fuel to make the trip?"

"We do," Lucy acknowledged. "We only came to RF-31 to avoid going out of our way to visit that backwater."

I cringed internally at the thought of my first sect being a backwater, but coming from roofie, anything under a year away fit the definition to a T. "Alright." I stood. "We're good to go, then?"

"Cal," Lucy stopped me, hesitation in her voice, "we're still docked. All you had on you when you came aboard was a torn-up vac suit and your holopad. You should go back and get—"

"No," I cut her off. My heartbeat sped. "We should go."

Lucy's tone dripped with patience. "Cal, we won't be coming back. You had a life here. You had family. I really feel it would be best if you brought something with you to —"

"To remember them by?" I exploded at her. "Is that what this is about? You don't think I have those people imprinted on my fucking soul? How dare you. How fucking dare you. I could run to the gods damned edge of the galaxy and I'd still see Brady's face whenever I close my eyes, still watch him rush out to help people when he could've hidden, still hear the sound he made when his corpse hit the floor. You don't get to tell me what is and isn't best for me, and you *cannot* make me set foot on that station."

For the first time, Lucy didn't chastise me for my profanity. She didn't sigh, she didn't raise her voice, she simply spoke in a soft whisper. "I've lost people too, Cal."

"Yeah, well, at least I brought you a few chunks of his bones to remember him by."

The room went silent. The crackle of the fire washed through the still air. My heart pounded. Adrenaline rushed through me. I breathed in sharp and shallow breaths until I forcibly slowed them. I swallowed. "I'm sorry. That... that was cruel."

"It's alright." Her voice sounded tired, not sad, not angry, just tired. "You're grieving. It's natural." She let out a long, drawn-out breath. "Is there anything I can say to change your mind?"

I shut my eyes for a moment—a moment was all it took —and the memories came flooding back. I shook my head as I realized it wasn't anger that had driven my outburst.

"I can't go back there."

"Okay." Just like that, she let it go. "I'll set course for The Dueling Stars. You're welcome to come up to the upper deck to watch us depart, or stay down here and enjoy the fire or other amenities. And Cal, remember, if you ever want to talk, I'm here."

"Thanks," I murmured, my eyes fixed on the empty tea mug in my hand.

I can't quite explain what Lucy's presence felt like, and thus find it difficult to relate how I knew she'd departed. Even with the warmth of the fire, the room seemed to grow slightly colder, somewhat less comfortable and welcoming than it had been before. It was the only indication I received that she'd diverted her attention elsewhere.

I sat back down and took a long, deep breath. The pocket dimension felt none of the telltale jerks of undocking, but I knew the procedure well enough to imagine them. I didn't bother returning to the upper deck to watch roofie fade in the distance. Instead, I gazed into the fire.

The past could go fuck itself. There, staring into the flames, into this crackling, warm, cozy symbol of unimaginable opulence I found, for a few precious minutes, a glimpse of the future.

The Dueling Stars, Eternity's Maw, the great and terrible world of cultivation awaited me. For the first time in my life, I stood at a precipice of countless mysteries and untold opportunity. For the first time in my life, I had a way forward. For the first time in my life, the path ahead of me was mine to build and mine to tread.

I just had to start walking.

6

I have a theory. You see, I think cultivators are so obsessed with their ceremonies and their honorable combat and their *constant* drama because none of them have jobs. You can only meditate so long before the boredom sets in, and with the mortals doing all the actual work, the cultivators have nothing better to do than argue over petty bullshit and hit each other with sticks.

My first trip with Lucy reinforced this theory.

Prior to this, the only interstellar travel I'd done had been the four-year trek out to roofie from my home system. Brady and I had hitched a ride on a long-haul freighter, which meant working through the journey. We probably spent as much time crawling around outside as actually aboard the ship. If RF-31 hadn't offered us shorter hours, we'd have kept on for another two years to make it to the Riala system.

Lucy didn't need any vac-welding—her qi barrier deflected any debris before it could get to the hull. She handled maintenance, cleaning, and food production entirely on her own, the latter of which I took some issue with.

It wasn't that I thought I could do better—gods knew

Lucy was a better chef than I'd ever be. It just drove me crazy to wander about aimlessly while someone else worked. All my life I'd had to pull my weight, and I'd be damned if I stopped now.

Problem was, Lucy had an annoying tendency to step in and take over the moment I tried to cook something for myself. Start to make an omelet? Lucy's ground the pepper before I've even cracked the second egg. Grab the ingredients for a sandwich? Lucy's already slicing the tomato and toasting the bread. Hell, I couldn't pour a bowl of cereal without a strand of qi adding the milk.

That's how I discovered her weakness.

Day four into our three-week trip, I managed to finish two entire pancakes before Lucy swooped in to cook the rest. Turned out she'd been fixing a leak somewhere in the garden's sprinkler system, which meant one thing and one thing only to my competitive nature.

Her perception could only be in one place at a time.

I tested my hypothesis on laundry day, waiting until she'd begun folding to sneak into the kitchen and make a sandwich. By the time her defeated presence made it back to the galley, I'd already taken my first bite.

From there it turned into a game. Once every other day or so, I'd dream up some way to distract her so I could cook behind her back, bonus points if I managed to do all the dishes before she noticed.

She responded with heightened vigilance at mealtimes, but that didn't stop me. Whether or not I'd just eaten lunch, if Lucy went off to do some chore elsewhere on the ship, you'd better be sure I was cooking *something*. Usually the results of my efforts wound up in the fridge for later, but reheated pasta was a small price to pay for that little *huff* she made whenever she caught me doing things for myself.

To be clear, I wasn't *entirely* unproductive. I spent long

hours meditating in the core room, forcing myself to grow accustomed to the deafening qi. I couldn't spend my whole life floating through deep space, and I wouldn't make much of a cultivator if I got a migraine from *being around qi*. I knew whatever barren rock I ended up on would be a thousand times worse than Lucy's core, so I had to get as comfortable around it as I could get.

I kept my senses constrained to the ship, refusing to touch the vast reservoir of calm qi outside. Once already I'd nearly lost myself to it, so Lucy and I agreed I should leave it alone until we got to The Dueling Stars. Presumably *somebody* there would know how to fetch a wandering spirit.

I *did* try taking in some of the reactor's spill-off qi like normal cultivators did, but my body rejected it. With a bit of concerted willpower, I could pull some of the obnoxiously bright energy towards me, but it refused to enter my core.

On the bright side, even though I couldn't cultivate any new qi, my previous foray into the infinite sea had left me absolutely brimming with the stuff. The act of condensing it took on a whole new level of difficulty without a ventilator doing my breathing for me, but I managed it after a few days.

It's remarkable the things you can accomplish when you don't have anything better to do.

From there I experimented. Cycling qi through my different open meridians had different effects on my body, effects I grew to realize differed from what I might've expected.

Cycling through my heart meridian, for example, slowed my heart rate, evening it out to solid, powerful thumps. Lucy told me most cultivators experienced the opposite, their pulses quickening as they cycled. Similarly, while it still improved my circulation, cycling through my blood meridian cooled me down rather than warming me up. I found it pleasant. I hated being too hot.

My kidney meridian—which also governed the liver, I discovered—had no immediately discernible effect. Most people can't actually tell how well their kidneys or liver are doing unless the answer is 'catastrophically poorly,' so I just assumed my qi cooled them and made them run more effectively, if more slowly.

I practiced all sorts of different variations. I cycled one after the other. I cycled them all at once. I experimented with giving them each fresh qi, looping them so the qi out of one meridian went straight into the next, flickering them on and off like light switches, anything I could think of, really. Lucy didn't bother trying to instruct me one way or the other, claiming circulation techniques weren't relevant until I had all twelve meridians open. I practiced anyway.

The only trick I didn't master was cycling qi without entering a meditative trance first. It was the one thing Lucy kept pushing me to work on, presumably because anything you can only do in a meditative trance isn't actually that *useful*. I made a *bit* of progress towards keeping my cycling going after breaking meditation, but nothing inspiring. Hey, we can't *all* be instant masters.

Imagine that, an instant master. *Just add water.*

Lucy outright forbade me from opening any more meridians, citing the inherent danger in doing so unsupervised. I told her I'd already opened three. She told me any more would raise suspicion in a new recruit. I told her she wasn't my real mom.

One more wouldn't hurt, right?

It hurt like hell.

I settled on my lung meridian, hoping it would help with my breathing and assuming its proximity to my heart and blood meant something. The qi channel itself was shaped like, well, lungs, looping out to one side before swinging back to the other. Its entrance and exit both rested at the base of my throat.

I started by cycling my open meridians on the logic that my blood and kidneys would help purge the toxins I was about to force out. The slight spiritual numbness that came from circulating my particular qi had nothing to do with it, because I absolutely wasn't afraid of repeating the painful opening process. Nope. No fear of pain here.

The first time I slammed a wave of qi into my clogged lung meridian my focus shattered like a wine glass hit by a cannon—not a cannon ball, a *cannon*. I fell backwards and gasped for air, but none came.

Panic mounted. My heart raced. The harder I pulled, the more my diaphragm refused to budge. This was it. This was the danger. I hadn't listened, and now I was gonna suffocate because I'd thought I could fuck around with my lungs unsupervised.

Second by second, the air slowly came. It was a torturous process, my lungs expanding ever so slightly more with each failed breath. By the time the blue tone had faded from my face, I'd switched from asphyxiating to hyperventilating.

And it didn't stop.

With just a trickle of qi running through my mostly-closed meridian, my breath ran away from me, energized and out of control. Trouble was, unlike my heart stopping when I opened its meridian, regulated, rhythmic breath was central to cultivation.

It came down to a race. Either I'd manage to recenter my focus while hyperventilating, or my lungs, diaphragm, meridian, or all three would give out, you know, *exactly* the perfect scenario for seeking inner peace.

Laying on my back with my knees in the air, I slammed my heel into the padded floor, establishing a tempo triple that of my normal breathing. If I was going to hyperventilate, at least I could hyperventilate *in time*. Triple proved too slow.

A fog swept through my brain. The room spun. My throat grew parched then inflamed as I sucked back more and more air. Still I tapped my foot, four, five, six times as fast as normal breath. I forced my eyelids shut.

My center reappeared in my mind's eye in flickers, blurry and unstable as my focus wavered. I fixated on it, clinging desperately to my one and only hope. I grabbed the liquid qi with all the restraint of a starving man before a four-hour meal, snatching it up and throwing it against my lung meridian.

I coughed. Breath left me again, a momentary relief from my hyperventilation until, as before, it came back, and the cycle began again.

I don't actually remember exactly how many pushes it took to finally clear out my lung meridian, but I'll never forget the relief that washed over me as I finally inhaled at a pace of my own choosing. I'll also never forget Lucy's tone as I exited my stupor.

"Go wash up," she'd simply said, disapproval clashing with concern in her voice. "I'll take care of the mess here."

I slunk away as she got to work cleaning the grime I'd expunged from the reactor room floor.

I took the longest shower of my life that day, first scrubbing the foul-smelling gunk that'd coated my skin, then simply standing there and letting the water wash over me. I thought about a lot of things, from how close I'd just come to death to what exactly had driven me to take such a risk. I refused to believe boredom and impatience had been enough, but the harder I looked, the less I liked what I found.

By the time I finally shut the water off and emerged from the shower, two conclusions had solidified themselves in my mind. The first was never to let my desire for progress cloud my better judgment.

The second was to *always* listen to Lucy, even if she wasn't my real mom.

* * *

In the days following that particular adventure, Lucy made more of a concerted effort to keep me busy. My days started with an hour on the treadmill followed by another hour of weight training, rotating muscle groups as Lucy instructed. Apparently I was just copying the exercise routine one of her other passengers had used, but I supposed if it was good enough for them it was good enough for me.

After the gym, I'd eat breakfast and meditate through the morning, practicing cycling and all that other stuff I already told you about. Lucy would eventually pull me back to the lower deck for lunch, and then it was off to the sparring ring.

I'd never been a fighter. Sure, I worked with my hands so my body had *some* strength to it, but vac-welding was more of an endurance exercise than an agility one.

Lucy's inexperience in the field didn't help. She had an entire library of holos she'd recorded of her various passengers' practice sessions, but even slowed to ten percent speed I could only hold my own against a handful of those. I tried emulating the forms as best I could, but mimicry could only go so far.

The best I could really say for my martial progress was that I grew comfortable holding a sword. It was better than nothing.

After what could only loosely be called combat training, I'd shower and retire to the lounge for a cup of tea. I'd spend the hours before dinner reading fiction on my holopad or pestering Lucy with questions about her past. She proved adept at avoiding straight answers, distracting me instead with tales of great battles or legendary cultivators she'd met. The stories would persist through dinner, after which I'd recline in the theater to watch a holo or two before bed.

It was simultaneously the busiest and least busy I'd ever been. I spent all day every day doing *something*, but almost none of it could've been considered actual work. Exercising, cultivating, reading, even sparring all felt like practice at worst and leisure at best.

I had hours and hours of free time, yet all of it somehow ended up filled by one activity or another. I started to think all those bored cultivators with nothing better to do than duel each other or start drama were just lazy, but I supposed there were only so many books to read and holos to watch.

On the twenty-first day since our departure from roofie, my post-dinner routine went slightly differently. Rather than immediately whisking the dirty dishes away, Lucy simply left them on the counter and returned with a glass of port. I raised it to my nose. It smelled like raisins. I took a sip. It tasted like alcoholic raisins.

"Early tomorrow morning, we'll land on Fyrion, an inhospitable dwarf planet which hosts the smallest and weakest outpost of the Dragon's Right Eye sect. Once there, you'll beseech the local elders for a chance to join their sect. Before that happens, there are a few things we need to work out."

"Like what I'm going to tell them," I said.

"Precisely. An unaffiliated initiate with four open meridians is going to raise questions, especially one with so little training and such peculiar qi. You should know the answers to those questions before you set foot on Fyrion."

I raised an eyebrow. "What's wrong with the truth?"

"Do you want to be a cultivator or a science experiment?" Lucy asked bluntly. "You should tell them as little as possible. Cultivators are famously secretive, an unfortunate byproduct of their competitive nature. Openly sharing information like that will get you exploited or killed. Avoid outright lying—anyone with an open sense meridian will sniff you out immediately—but don't be afraid to stretch the truth."

"Um… okay. So what *can* I tell them?"

"Lean on me," Lucy said. "One of the perks of being around a few thousand years is your juniors assume you have some ineffable reason for everything you do. You were a vac-welder on a long-haul freighter until a soulship found you and gave you some basic training. That's all they need to know."

I sipped my port and nodded. "I like it. Short, sweet, and mysterious enough to explain anything weird I do while still maintaining plausible deniability. Anyone asks, I can just tell them that even *I* don't know why you picked me."

"Exactly. It explains your origin, your behavior, and your open meridians."

"And what do I say when they ask why they can't sense my qi?"

"The magic words."

"The magic words?"

"Repeat after me," Lucy said. "It's a part of my Way."

"It's a part of my way."

"Great. Now say it again with a bit more reverence to the word 'Way.'"

"It's a part of my Way?" I tried.

"Better. You still sound like a confused vac-welder."

"That'd be because I *am* a confused vac-welder."

Lucy sighed. "Every cultivator has a Way, the path they follow on their journey to grasp one of the threads that bind the universe. A cultivator's Way encompasses all the techniques they learn, the way they fight, the truths they contemplate, *everything*. It's an intensely personal thing, and pressing someone on the details of their Way is an insult at best and a challenge to a duel at worst."

"So they'll think I'm hiding my qi on purpose? Won't they ask why?"

"That's the beauty of it; asking any more questions would be disrespectful, and cultivators *loathe* disrespect. That's why they're the magic words. Whenever a cultivator asks a question you don't want to answer, it's a part of your Way. Got it?"

"It's a part of my Way," I repeated. "What else should I know?"

"Salute everyone higher ranked than you. When a higher-up is in the room, don't speak unless you're spoken to. Err towards being overly polite." Lucy sighed. "I don't know all the protocols myself, and I *really* don't know which are basic human behavior and which are unique to cultivators. Your background as a simple vac-welder will earn you some leeway, but don't abuse it."

She went on to coach me on the proper form and posture for a salute, the common greetings and different levels of respect each carried, and a hundred other little things I'd forget the moment I was in front of an actual human being. The longer the onslaught of instruction dragged, the less excited I grew for the inevitable sneers I'd get when I messed something up. A part of me didn't believe it. Cultivators couldn't have a stick *that* far up their collective ass, could they?

As the etiquette discussion wound down, Lucy moved on to sharing what little she knew of The Dueling Stars. It wasn't much.

A binary pair of red dwarfs sat at the center, one for each of the two sects that governed the system. Unoriginally named Dragon's Right Eye and Dragon's Left Eye, the rival sects were identical in all but name, which was apparently enough of a difference to fuel a generation-spanning hatred for each other.

Each sect had three outposts scattered between the various barren planets, as well as a large station around their respective star. All the core members lived on the starbases, seeing as their proximity to the stars meant they had access to the most qi. I'd be starting as far from the red dwarfs as it got.

The majority of the mortal population lived on Ilirian, the system's sole habitable world and the source of most of its food. Lucy wasn't sure which sect controlled it, but I sincerely doubted they shared.

That was it. That was all the background information I'd get on the people to which I was about to entrust my entire future. It was better than nothing.

As I finished my port and finally rose from the dining table to adjourn to my quarters, Lucy left me with one more lesson.

"The one thing you need to know," she said, "more than how to salute, more than the magic words, more than *anything*, is that every cultivator thinks it's gonna be them. Once you realize that, everything they do starts to make sense."

"What are you talking about?"

"You think it, don't you? You think you'll be one of the incredibly few to reach the peak, to touch the threads, to attain immortality. That's good. You *need* to think that. But you should know that every single cultivator thinks it's not gonna be you, it's gonna be *them*. Some are boastful about it—they're annoying but generally harmless. It's the ones that pretend to be humble you need to worry about. Those are the ones that want something."

"So I should just trust no-one? That doesn't seem like it'll get me far."

"Trust the ones that are open about it," Lucy said.

"Better yet, find the few idealists who think you can all make it, the ones who believe in rising tides. It's a pit of vipers you're about to enter, and you'll need friends who can show you the way through it." She exhaled. "I wish I could help you more, but you won't understand until you experience it for yourself. Only the flame can temper the sword."

"Tides, vipers, and flames." I counted on my fingers. "Really pushing the metaphors, huh?"

Lucy let out a long-suffering sigh.

"I'm kidding, I'm kidding," I laughed. "Thanks for the advice. I needed it. *All* of it, metaphors included."

"Goodnight, Cal," Lucy called an end to the evening. "I'll see you in the morning."

"Goodnight," I bid her in turn as I left the galley and made my way to bed.

All jokes aside, I did deeply appreciate her words, even if they felt overblown. A den of vipers? Seriously? I knew cultivators were all over-the-top batshit insane; I knew they were competitive; I knew they obsessed over decorum and protocol and hierarchy, but they were still *people*.

How bad could they be?

7

"Soulship LC-81535 requesting permission to land."

"LC-81535, I don't see you on our docking schedule for toda—wait. Did you say *soulship?*"

"I did."

"Holy fuck. Let me just—"

"Language!"

"Oh, yes. Sorry ma'am. You're clear for dock sixteen. Welcome to Fyrion. Somebody fetch Elder Berkowitz! We've got a—"

I couldn't hold back my laughter as the poor dock worker reacted to Lucy almost exactly as I had, with the added bonus of shouting at someone before his mic cut off.

Lucy sighed. "Don't ever do that where they can hear you."

"What? Laugh?"

"Not unless somebody's purposefully made a joke. Laughing at a cultivator is a surefire way to wind up in a duel—a duel you'll *lose* because you can barely hold a sword."

"No duels. Got it," I said, trying and failing to wipe the grin from my face.

I watched our approach from Lucy's bridge, or what

71

might've been the bridge a thousand years ago. No longer needing human controls, Lucy had converted the room at the bow into a viewing deck. Leather chairs with full impact harnesses lined the back wall of the mostly empty space. From the floor a large table could emerge for meetings and meals with guests unwelcome in her soulspace, but we didn't anticipate its use.

Fyrion was two things—small and gray. A complex web of dark lines coated its surface, formations carved into the planet itself to direct its qi towards its only settlement. Such enchantments weren't even close to fully efficient, but they'd still make the outpost far and away the best place to cultivate. Given the planet's lack of atmosphere, it was also the *only* place to cultivate.

The settlement, confusingly also called Fyrion, had the population of a mid-sized freighter: about a hundred thousand, of which five thousand cultivated. The mortals did all the actual work of keeping the city running, from commerce to hospitality to maintenance to mining the planet's rich silver deposits, a lucrative business that the Dragon's Right Eye taxed heavily in exchange for their governance and protection from raiders and void beasts.

Fyrion-the-city sat at the center of the web of trenches, a mass of glass and metal with all the aesthetic design of a prison. The docks were far and away the tallest part of the structure at some eight stories tall. I supposed with an entire planet at their disposal, building *up* wasn't strictly necessary.

I strapped in as we neared dock sixteen, tugging the harness over my dull red T-shirt and brown leather jacket. I'd found the latter garment hanging in my closet, part of a collection that came in every color the cultivator pants did. For such an important day, I wore a matching set, first impressions and all. None of the clothes quite fit me, of course, but already in my time with Lucy I'd bulked up a little. She assured me by the end of the year I'd fill them out quite nicely.

We attached to the docking arm with a remarkably slight jerk, an unsurprising testament to Lucy's experience as a pilot. As the gangway telescoped out to meet us, I unclipped my harness and made for the airlock. My suitcase awaited me there, packed with the various belongings Lucy had given me.

I saluted and I fought to slow my racing heart as the airlock hissed open to reveal three people in pale gray cultivator pants and matching military-style button downs, each bearing the sect's insignia and a sigil displaying their rank. Apparently such hierarchies varied from sect to sect, so I didn't have the faintest clue whom I was dealing with.

On the left stood a severe-looking man with short, gray-flecked black hair. On the right, a middle-aged brunette woman sized me up. In the center, a woman who looked like she had great great grandchildren hunched over a black wooden cane. She didn't even look at me, casting her gaze upward and speaking to the open air.

"Welcome, venerable ancient. I am Elder Berkowitz, Matriarch of Fyrion. With me are Elders Lopez and Smith. We hope you'll find what you're looking for on our humble home."

I almost burst out laughing then and there at a woman *that* old calling Lucy ancient, but I managed to stifle it. It seemed the people who ran the place had come to greet Lucy personally, and the last thing I wanted to do was piss them off.

"I hope so too," Lucy replied, cutting right through the formalities to answer the elder's not-so-subtle question. "I have a student for you, a promising young cultivator I found in deep space. He's opened four meridians almost entirely on his own, and shows the ambition it takes to defy the heavens."

That last bit was her polite way of referring to my foolhardy push to open my meridians in less than ideal conditions. Whether or not the elders picked up on that meaning remained a mystery.

The man, Elder Smith, scowled. "All potential cadets are welcome to undertake our entrance exa—" He cut off as Elder Berkowitz elbowed him in the ribs.

"Of course, honorable ancient. The Dragon's Right Eye is happy to accept such a..." She looked me up and down. "...*unique* pupil. May I ask what he was doing in deep space?"

I opened my mouth to answer before remembering I was supposed to keep silent in the presence of the elders.

"He worked as a vac-welder," Lucy answered. "Remarkable, isn't it, that he managed to make the strides he has under such circumstances? I'm sure under your fine tutelage, he'll continue to thrive. I ask no favoritism, simply that he receive the same opportunities as your other students. I've taken an interest in his progress, but it must remain *his* progress, understood?"

"Absolutely, wise ancient," Elder Berkowitz replied. "We shall make the utmost strides to look past his... mortal upbringing and consider him one of our own."

That didn't bode well. Not once has anyone uttered the words 'mortal upbringing' with good intentions. Those words were for discriminating and for pretending you weren't discriminating, the latter of which seemed to be Elder Berkowitz's case.

"As well you should," Lucy said. "I entrust him into your care."

"Good," the old woman barked. "Elder Lopez here will get him situated while we discuss details and answer any questions you may have."

"With me, cadet!" the middle-aged woman ordered before turning on her heel and striding away.

I broke my salute and scurried after her. The end of the gangway opened up into a cavernous dock complex abuzz with activity as workers went about the daily business of loading and unloading various bits of cargo.

I didn't worry too much about what Lucy and the other elders were talking about; I already knew the gist of it. They'd flatter and appease her in the hopes of winning her favor while she gathered as much relevant intel about the sect as she could. In the end she'd refuel, vacate the dock, and enter low orbit, where she'd be a comm link away. Ten times out of ten I'd have preferred to stay with Lucy over whatever lodgings the sect offered me, but their sect, their rules.

Word of the soulship had apparently spread like wildfire through the mortal population, as countless eyes tracked Elder Lopez and me from the moment we stepped into view. Luckily enough, the elder set such a quick pace that I didn't find much opportunity to gape at the attention.

She led me up a set of metal stairs to a platform for a transport tube, from which promptly emerged a single sleek, gunmetal gray pod. Inside sat two opposing rows of pristine leather seating, complete with a wooden table and porcelain tea set.

"Greetings, Elder Lopez. Where are you headed today?"

I wondered if the artificial voice synced with her holopad, or if this was her personal transport pod. Knowing the excess of cultivators, I leaned towards the latter.

"Student Housing D," she said, sitting in the rear-facing row. I sat opposite.

"Very well," the tin-can voice replied. "Destination: Student Housing D. ETA: eighteen minutes."

The door shut behind us and the pod took off, accelerating gently yet consistently for some time. Elder Lopez wasted no time.

"Give me your hand."

I blinked in confusion before obediently resting my right hand, palm up, on the table between us. She grabbed it.

"I'll have to appraise your cultivation. Let me in if you can."

Before I could nod my assent a spear of foreign qi shot through me. Instinctively my own qi rose up to fight off the invasion, washing against the vibrant energy like a tidal wave of cool darkness. I stabilized my breathing and fought to pull my defenses back, but already the elder's qi had pierced them.

The probe darted around, poking and prodding at the walls of my center and the entrances to all twelve meridians. It ran right through my four open ones, sending jolts of heat and discomfort through my body. I grimaced and bore through it, maintaining my focus and holding back my qi as best I could until at last she retreated.

"Your control is awful. It's a wonder you've survived opening the meridians you did."

I lowered my head. "So I've been told."

"Whatever foolishness possessed you to start with your vital organs has no place here on Fyrion," she continued.

"Yes, elder. I have a lot to learn."

"You have too much to learn," she snapped. "But you've found yourself a powerful benefactor, so you'll be taught." She swiped around on her holopad for a bit before returning her attention to me. "Can you cycle?"

"I can, but only with my full attention."

"That's a no, then." She tapped on her holopad again. "I'm enrolling you in meditation one, cycling one, and combat one. You'll be in class with our pre-recruits, children of sect members who aren't yet old enough to fully join. If you have as much potential as your benefactor claims, I'm sure you'll catch up to those your age within the year. If not, I'm sure she'll understand your failure."

I silently nodded, taking note of the entirely unsubtle threat. Advance out of the kiddie class or get out. I could do that.

"You'll take morning workouts and meals with the others in your housing block. Try not to make any mortal enemies of your neighbors. We determine sect ranking based on scheduled and unscheduled duels, and more than one grudge match has ended fatally. Given their role in evaluating cadets, fighting is mandatory. If you reject an official challenge, you *will* be removed."

I gulped. Now I couldn't just avoid fighting, I had to avoid getting challenged in the first place. They really weren't going to make this whole 'no duels' thing easy.

"I'm understood then," the elder said as she noted the look on my face. "Now," she said, sitting back dangerously casually, "tell me how you're masking your qi."

I blinked in surprise.

"It's obviously a technique of some sort. I could feel its resistance, but I couldn't feel *it*. You're like a corpse. What have you done? Is this something the soulship taught you?"

"It's-um... a part of my Way?" I tried.

She huffed, the annoyance in her voice undermining the words she spoke. "Close to the chest. Smarter than you look. Perhaps we can make something of you yet. You should know that the sect will pay handsomely for knowledge of any technique outside our database."

I kept silent.

"Think on it," she told me, her tone carrying the subtext that I'd be an idiot to miss such an opportunity. "You may find it in your best interests to stay in your elders' good graces."

I decided I didn't like this woman.

The pod came to a gentle halt as we reached our destination, and the door swung up to reveal a luxurious lobby. Uniformed cultivators milled about, reading and chatting and drinking tea as they lounged on the various couches and armchairs. A number of hanging potted plants and an entire green-wall brought life to the space, a gorgeous yet undoubtedly expensive-to-maintain way to decorate.

Two dozen sets of eyes burned a hole in my back as we crossed the lobby. I could *feel* the cultivators sizing me up, judging my hair, my clothes, the look on my face, the size of my suitcase, the way I walked. To them, I wasn't a peer. I wasn't a potential friend. I wasn't a human.

I was a threat.

A circular desk sat at the chamber's center, behind which sat a mortal man with a startled look on his face. He jumped to attention at our approach.

"Elder Lopez, ma'am," he greeted us. "The dorm you requested is ready."

"I should hope so. I gave you ten whole minutes."

Ten minutes didn't seem like a lot of time, but I didn't question her.

"Number three-oh-one," the man said. "He'll be the only one on the third floor." The man gave me an apologetic look, one I didn't quite understand. An entire floor to myself? Yes fucking please.

"That will do. Take him to his room. I have more important matters to attend to."

"Yes ma'am," the receptionist said, still not breaking his salute.

"Go with him," the elder ordered me. "You'll have the day to situate yourself, but tomorrow you're to arrive at class on time, understood?"

"Understood."

She glared at me.

"Understood, ma'am," I corrected myself.

"Good," she grumbled. "You're dismissed."

I saluted once more as she turned on her heel and departed, leaving me in the care of the mortal receptionist.

"Right this way," he said, leading me towards a grand arcing staircase. "Can I take your bag?"

"No, no, I got it," I said with a smile. "I'm Cal, by the way."

"Oh, I'm-uh… I'm Arthur," the man replied, visibly taken aback.

"So tell me, Arthur, how'd I get so lucky as to get an entire floor of my own?"

He laughed as if I'd said something funny. "Our lower floors are all taken, unfortunately. You could move down if you found someone willing to share a room with you. That's what most third-floor cadets wind up doing."

"And I would do that because…?"

Arthur faltered. "For the qi. You *are* a cultivator, yes?" He exhaled. "Housing D is already the furthest from the formation's center. Climbing away from the planet's surface only makes it worse. You'll find yourself at a disadvantage compared to your peers, spiritually and socially. Your sect mates will see accepting such a poor placing as a sign of weakness."

"Oh. That makes sense. Sorry. I'm a bit new to all of this."

"I picked up on that," Arthur said. We passed the second floor and continued on to the third, where we stopped at the very first door. "Three-oh-one. Welcome home." He swiped his holopad. "Access codes for your room and for the building. Bathrooms are down the hall; cafeteria is on the first floor. If you'll forward me your measurements, I'll arrange for some uniforms to be brought up."

A request for sizing data popped up on my holopad, and

I tapped accept.

"Perfect," Arthur chimed. "I think that's it then. I'll let you get settled in. If you have any questions, I'll be downstairs."

I bid him thanks and stepped into my new home. The door slid shut behind me.

Room 301's full bed, simple wardrobe, and lack of en suite bathroom made for a definite downgrade from Lucy's luxurious captain's quarters, but having it all to myself automatically made it better than my cabin on roofie or the freighter before it. At least I had a window, a long horizontal thing that stretched across the entire back wall. Even standing in the doorway I could see the stars. Somehow, they were the most comforting sight I'd found on Fyrion.

I plopped my suitcase down onto the bed and went through the motions of unpacking, which mostly consisted of tossing clothes into drawers and stashing the bottle of whiskey I'd stolen from Lucy's storage between two pairs of pants. Hey, I had to make friends *somehow*, right?

That done, I sat cross legged on the carpeted floor and set to meditating. I still had about two thousand questions I needed to ask about how this place worked, but my first priority had to be acclimating myself to the local qi. I didn't know how long it would take, and I couldn't very well show up to my first classes getting a headache every time I tried to cultivate. I mean, I *could've*, but it wouldn't have been a very good look.

I evened out my breathing, visualized my center, and sent qi running through my four open meridians, reveling in the sense of cool, quiet comfort the process generated. I cycled for a few minutes before I stretched my perception beyond the boundary of my skin, experiencing the spiritual environment of Fyrion for the first time.

It felt like standing on the sun.

Heat and light and *noise* blasted me from all directions as it emanated from the planet below and saturated the very air. There was less of it than in Lucy's fusion core, but it spilled out and forced itself upon me rather than keeping mostly to itself. If Lucy's cultivation room was a sauna, my dorm on Fyrion was a pot of boiling water.

My focus shattered. I returned to reality with a pounding headache and blood dripping from my nose. I groaned. This was going to take a while.

I stopped for all of two minutes to grab a tissue for my bleeding nose and a few gulps of water before resuming once more. Still it burned, still it blinded, still it screamed, and still I tried.

In adherence to my earlier promise, I won't bore you with the details of my continued attempts to acclimate myself to all the qi. Just rest assured it was a long and painful process that I very much did not finish.

It took four and a half hours before I could consistently maintain my focus under the barrage of qi, and however horrifically unpleasant I still found its presence, that would have to do for the time being. I pushed myself to my feet and stripped out of my sweat-soaked clothes, rubbing my temples to combat my aching head as I did.

I found a towel folded in my wardrobe, so I wrapped it around my waist to protect my precious modesty. I may have had the entire floor to myself, but that didn't mean there wouldn't be staff members wandering the hallway between here and the shower. The last thing I wanted to do was blind some poor maintenance worker with my pasty ass.

So it was that drenched in sweat, with a line of dried blood down my upper lip, fighting off a brutal migraine, and wearing nothing but a towel, I left my room to find an absolute ox of a man with an untamed mop of blond hair and a cultivator's uniform grinning down at me.

"Newcomer!"

My aching head throbbed as he practically shouted the word.

"I, Xavier Honchel, future champion of the Dragon's Right Eye, hereby challenge you to a duel!"

I sighed. Gods damnit.

8

I blinked. I looked back at the still-open door to my room behind me. I looked down at my sweaty, towel-clad self. I looked up at the cultivator who'd challenged me to a duel on my first day.

"How long have you been waiting here?"

"Two hours!" he proclaimed with both too much pride and too much volume.

My brow furrowed. "And you didn't... I don't know, knock?"

"I did. You didn't answer."

I rubbed at my temples. "Right. Sorry. I was cultivating."

"All the way up here? No wonder your core is so weak! I can hardly sense it."

"No, no, you can't sense it at all. It's not..." I trailed off as I realized the futility in trying to explain my peculiar qi. "Look, can this wait? I was just about to take a shower."

Xavier squinted at me. "You'd rather shower *before* you fight? Wouldn't you just have to shower again after?"

"Good point." I sighed. "Alright. Let me just put some clothes on and we can get this over with."

"Of course! I shall await your return!"

I slipped back into my room, wondering if all cultivators were this extra or if Xavier was a special case. By the time I'd re-donned the clothes I'd arrived in, I concluded both could be true.

Xavier didn't shut up a single time as he led me down the steps and across the lobby to a well-decorated hallway. He swore up and down that he was the most motivated person here, that the thin qi on Fyrion wouldn't stop him from rising the ranks, and that his position at the absolute bottom of the sect rankings didn't truly reflect his talent or his grit.

Over the course of the five minute walk, he used the phrase 'future champion of the Dragon's Right Eye' a grand total of eight times—more than once per minute. I counted. I might've asked what it meant had I been able to get a word in edgewise, but my head still hurt and my cultivation session had left me far too exhausted to compete with his seemingly boundless love for his own voice.

Ego notwithstanding, there was a certain sincerity to the man I couldn't help but appreciate. Xavier said what he thought and he wore his feelings on his sleeve, two traits I'd come to appreciate all the more since entering the world of cultivation. I remembered Lucy's words about all cultivators thinking they were special. She'd said I could trust the ones who were open about it.

I don't know how much more open anyone could possibly be.

His boastful rambling and my analysis of his character were almost enough to make me forget he'd already declared his intent to beat the shit out of me. Almost.

The hallway spat us out into a cavernous gymnasium. Every type of exercise equipment I could imagine and a few dozen I couldn't lined the outer walls. An elliptical running track that must've been over a mile long separated the weights and treadmills and other machines I'd never learn the names of from the room's dominant feature.

A dozen elevated sparring rings ran in two rows down the room's center. Each came with their own rack of wooden practice weapons, padded floor, and no walls or railings. Around the ones currently in use, a pale blue dome surrounded the combatants, keeping them and any wayward projectiles from escaping the ring. I imagined with a bunch of cultivators throwing qi attacks at each other, such precautions were necessary.

Fascinating as I found the sheer scope of the gymnasium or complexity of the automated qi barriers, *my* favorite attribute was the ceiling. Instead of the normal bare metal or plaster, a single, gargantuan pane of glass kept the atmosphere in. I stopped in my tracks just to gape at it, the engineering in making such a thing a marvel in and of itself. The fact it made for the best view of space I'd ever seen didn't hurt.

"This way, newcomer," Xavier pulled me from my state of awe back into my gallows-walk to the nearest open arena.

A mortal woman with her holopad out greeted us. "Back again, Xavier?"

"Of course! Nothing shall stop me from proving my might!"

"Alrighty then. Registered duel between Xavier Honchel and…" she trailed off and looked at me.

"Caliban Rex," I introduced myself. "Nice to meet you."

"Likewise," she muttered, not bothering to give me her name as she entered mine into her holopad. She looked to Xavier. "I assume you're the challenger?"

He nodded.

She turned back to me. "That means you get to choose the weapons."

"Oh—um… no weapons, please." If I was going to get

my ass kicked, I preferred if the guy doing the kicking didn't have a fucking sword.

Xavier clapped me on the back. "A traditionalist! Man after my own heart! Why allow a few paltry pieces of wood to get between two cultivators in the throes of combat?"

I groaned.

"You two are good to go. Best of luck." The woman didn't wait for us to mount the steps of the arena before she walked away, screaming something about a cultivator misusing a piece of exercise equipment. It was only as I watched her go that I noticed the crowd gathering around us.

I wasn't sure if registered duels were always spectacles, if they'd come to evaluate the newcomer, if they just wanted to see bottom-ranked Xavier flounder, or some combination of the three, but something like thirty cultivators in sect-member gray watched us with expectant eyes.

With a sigh, I climbed the steps to the arena.

The ring stretched forty feet across, plenty of space for us both to move about, but absolutely minuscule for the speeds I knew cultivators could travel. I supposed Fyrion had to have larger sparring arenas somewhere else. For us underlings in housing D, forty feet was plenty.

The padded floor had just enough give to it to add a slight spring to my step, but not enough that a fall wouldn't hurt. It visibly bent under Xavier's weight.

Whispers of 'where's his qi?' and 'how weak *is* he?' spread through the crowd around us, questions I'd have to get used to hearing sooner or later. They didn't matter. All these people were about to watch Xavier absolutely thrash me, so whether or not they could sense my qi, the answer to their second question was going to be '*very* weak.'

I sized up my opponent. He was bigger, more

experienced, and probably a higher-level cultivator than I. I almost certainly had more qi, but I hadn't even managed to cycle while standing up, let alone while *fighting*. At least I knew I could take a punch. A lifetime spent saying things I maintain were absolutely *hilarious* had earned me that much.

A gong rang out.

I darted in, eager to at least land a hit. Xavier let me come.

I learned, in that moment, how he'd landed at the absolute bottom of the sect rankings as Xavier went on to block my punch with his face.

I got him in the jaw. His head jerked to the side from the force of the punch, but only by an inch. Immediately it spun back, his eyes focused on me. He smiled wide and let out a bright, boisterous laugh.

I blinked and the arena was gone. The gym was gone. Fyrion was gone.

I stood in a narrow metal hallway under the pale glow of the emergency lights.

Xavier's eyes turned black. Sweat dripped down his brow. His upper lip twitched arrhythmically. His laughter echoed through roofie's dark hallways.

I froze. My heart pounded against my chest. My breath came quick and shaky and shallow. My eyes shot wide open. "No," I muttered, the terror clear in my quivering voice. "No, no, not again."

My throat tightened. My stomach dropped. I stared into his void-darkened eyes, refusing to look away, refusing to look down. I already knew what I'd find if I looked at the floor beneath his feet.

I wanted to run. I wanted to hide. I wanted to cry for mercy, for rescue, for a quicker death. I didn't. I couldn't. I stood, petrified, as he came for me.

The punch knocked me flat on my back.

I curled into a ball, protecting my stomach and face from further assault. The cold metal of roofie's flooring pressed against my exposed skin. Tears streaked down my cheeks as I trembled there, waiting for the void psycho to finish me off. "No. No. No. No," I whispered the word to myself like a mantra, as if my desperate denial would stop the walls closing in on me.

A dozen voices murmured taunts and jeers in the distance, but they didn't matter. They weren't *here*.

Xavier knelt over me. "Newcomer! Newcomer, are you alright? I didn't punch you too hard, did I? Of course I did. My might has overwhelmed you! I'm so sorry, newcomer."

"It wasn't you, you idiot," an unfamiliar female voice rose up from the fray. "He's having a panic attack. My father still gets them after the void horde."

That shut the onlookers up. It was like magic.

A gentle hand touched my shoulder. "Newbie, can you hear me?" the woman asked. "Newbie, it's alright. You're safe. You need to stop cycling. Cycling makes it worse."

Cycling? But I wasn't—wait. Cycling! That was a great idea. I pulled and the qi came readily. It rushed through me, spreading cool calm through my blood, slowing my heart, deepening my breathing.

My eyes flicked open and upward, past the worried faces of the two cultivators kneeling over me to the glass ceiling above and the stars beyond. The infinite dark sang comfort in my ear, serenaded me with the petty smallness of my fears and pains.

Reality eased back into place. The whites returned to Xavier's eyes. The metal hall gave way to the padded floor of the arena.

I exhaled, qi still racing through me as I perceived the world around me. It was the first time I'd cycled without meditating, but the achievement felt hollow given the circumstances.

"I'm alright," I panted. "I'm okay."

I sat up, ignoring the silently gaping crowd to get my first look at the girl who'd come to my defense. She had long, perfectly straight light brown hair and a pair of black-rimmed glasses. What kind of cultivator needed *glasses*? To top it off, even beyond the concern in her eyes, she had a look to her like she knew something you didn't, a kind of quiet sense of superiority that at once left me feeling stupid and insulted.

Xavier offered me a hand. I took it, and he pulled me to my feet. "A valiant effort, newcomer! The first of many defeats on the road to endless victory!"

"Um, thanks," I managed, unsure if I liked or hated that he was talking about the fight as if that was all that'd happened.

"Come on," the girl said, a hand on my back, "let's get away from the peep show."

"They're just here to revel in my triumph!"

"No, Xavier," I muttered. "They really aren't."

The crowd parted for us as we climbed down from the sparring ring and through the gymnasium. My cycling slipped as we walked, and the weight of everything that'd happened struck me like a piece of space debris.

Was there a prize for worst possible first impression? Fuck, I hoped so. I had a strong candidacy.

As we left the gym behind and entered the wide hallway, I broke the uncomfortable silence. "Thanks for the help back there. I... that's never happened before."

"It'll happen again," the girl said. "Every time you cycle you put yourself at risk. Higher blood pressure, heart rate, body temp, none of it's good for panic attacks. Your options are stop cultivating or find a way to work through whatever's wrong."

I opted not to mention that my qi had the opposite

effects. "I'll... work on that. Thanks." I held out my hand. "I'm Cal, by the way."

She shook it once, a prim, deliberate motion. "Charlotte. Charlotte Velereau."

She said her last name as if I should've recognized it. After the way mention of her father had silenced the crowd, I put two and two together. "I take it your father's someone important?"

"Important?" Xavier burst. "He's a hero! He saved the entire sect!"

"There was a void horde a few cycles ago." Charlotte sighed. "I don't like bringing him up, but sometimes it's warranted. None of those idiots have seen real combat, so none of them know what it costs." She looked up at me. "They'll all think you're weak because they don't know what you've been through."

I raised an eyebrow at her. "And you do?"

"Gods no. For all I know, you just have a crippling fear of cultivators."

I gulped at that, but she seemed not to notice.

"The point," she continued, "is that you're not necessarily weak, you're just facing greater challenges than they are. That's good. Meditation and practice and epiphany are all well and good, but overcoming adversity is just as important if you want to progress. The road to immortality is paved with conflict."

"Welp," I exhaled, "it's looking like I've got adversity in spades."

"The good news is, now you've lost to this buffoon, nobody'll challenge you any time soon. Nothing to gain and everything to lose fighting the bottom rank."

"Thank gods for that," I said, relief clear in my voice. "I've had enough dueling for a while."

"Enough dueling for one day!" Xavier countered. "The real advantage of sitting at the bottom is having so much further to climb."

"No, no, I think I'm good where I am, thanks."

Charlotte snorted. "If that's your mindset, you can go ahead and leave now. Ambition isn't optional."

"I didn't say I wasn't ambitious. I said I'm happy with my rank."

"You shouldn't be," she argued. "It might seem like a lot now, but the qi in D-block is *very* thin, especially all the way up on the third floor. Once you start trying to develop a core, you're going to start living for those two hours per week you get in a focus room."

"What's a focus room?"

Charlotte looked side-eyed at Xavier. "Where did they find this guy?"

"Deep space," I answered. "Assume I know nothing."

"You opened your qi sense in *deep space*? That's incredible. *I* can hardly sense fusion core spill-off. No wonder D-block feels like enough qi to you."

Now *that* was interesting. I'd found Lucy's core spill-off overwhelming. If other cultivators thought it barely perceptible, what did that say about me?

Charlotte exhaled. "Anyway, the formations on the planet direct its qi towards the outpost. Formations in the *outpost* direct its qi to the seventy-seven focus rooms. Each sect member gets two hours per week to cultivate in one of the focus rooms. You can earn more time, but only by being *useful*. In those two hours, you'll get more qi than the rest of the week combined."

"Huh." I blinked. "Can I trade away my hours?"

"Only if you need a *really* big favor," Charlotte explained. "Like I said, once you start building your core, you'll need every scrap of qi you can scrounge up. The focus rooms are essential—use them for breakthroughs if you can. Outside of that, if you want more qi, you'll need to earn a better housing placement. It takes top four thousand to make it to C-block, and to make top four thousand, you'll have to *duel*."

Xavier clapped me on the back yet again. He seemed to have a thing for that. "Imagine it! Endless opportunities to challenge yourself, endless progress to be made. It's beautiful."

"I think you and I have different definitions of the word 'beautiful,'" I told him. My gaze slid back to Charlotte. "So how does the daughter of the sect's savior wind up in housing D?"

She glared at me. "I don't see you offering up *your* life story."

"Fair point."

Our conversation faded as we reached the lobby. Various bored cultivators eyed us as we made for the stairs, doubtlessly coming to all sorts of conclusions about me based on everything from my current company to the particular tempo of my stride or some other bullshit. I'd been here less than a day and I was already tired of it.

I stopped at the base of the steps. "I think I can make it from here, unless you were planning on showering with me."

Charlotte's nose turned up at the comment, but Xavier let out a laugh. At least somebody appreciated my comedic mediocrity.

"Thank you for the duel, my friend." Xavier slapped me on the back. I wasn't sure exactly how many times it was appropriate to slap someone on the back in a ten-minute period, but I was pretty damn certain Xavier had passed it. "Best of luck on your struggle to the top!"

With that he walked away, leaving Charlotte and I both squinting at his confident stride.

"He's... a lot," I said.

Charlotte nodded.

"Very self-assured for someone at the bottom of the

rankings."

"At least he has *you* below him, now," Charlotte said.

I chuckled. "Glad I could be of use." I smiled at her. "Thanks again for the assist. And for the info. It's really a big help."

She smirked. "I'm sure you'll find a way to pay me back."

I cursed to myself as she walked away. Of *course* she expected me to repay her. Fucking cultivators. Maybe I could give her one of my focus room hours. It wasn't like *I* had any use for them.

I reflected on the day's events as I made my way up the stairs and to the third-floor showers. I thought of Elder Lopez's disdain and veiled threat, of Xavier's challenge and the crowd's judgmental eyes, of Charlotte's help at an unnamed price.

The system was rigged.

It'd taken a fucking soulship just to get me in the door, and all the sect had offered was the worst room they had, three children's classes, and a literal punch in the face. How was anyone without generational wealth or powerful friends ever supposed to succeed? How could one climb the ranks if everyone above them had access to more resources?

I had a long road ahead of me—meridians to open, techniques to master, combat to learn, and *maybe* a bit of unresolved trauma to work through, but at least I seemed to have taken strides towards making friends, egotistical and/or manipulative as they may've been.

Better yet, for all the hurdles in front of me, I had one inalienable advantage they couldn't even comprehend.

They could set the rules. They could mark the cards. They could stack the deck. But in the end, none of that would matter.

I wasn't even playing the same game.

9

There are only two things you need to know about meditation class. The first is that it consisted almost entirely of thirty ten-year-olds and one twenty-two-year-old trying to meditate while a pair of instructors wandered the room randomly hitting them with sticks. The second is that I was absolutely godawful at it.

I understood the necessity. A cultivator couldn't afford to lose his focus for any reason, *especially* in the middle of a fight, but that didn't change the fact that the normal human reaction to getting smacked with a cane is a sharp intake of breath.

I hissed and rubbed at the back of my head, the repeated smackings compounding into an ache that echoed back and forth across my skull. The rhythm of my breathing shattered, I glanced up at my most recent antagonist.

Senior Cadet Stevens glared down at me. I averted my eyes, opting to avoid drawing any more of the cadet's ire. I watched as Senior Cadet Park rapped one of the children on the arm, her strikes upon them far gentler and less frequent than those upon me. I didn't complain. I let out a breath and returned to my meditation.

Truthfully, their attention didn't bother me. Whether

they hit me harder to punish the upstart mortal, to put the newbie in his place, or simply because they thought the adult could take more of a beating didn't really matter. Training was training, and I needed all that I could get.

That thought felt foreign to me at first. Beyond how deeply it contradicted the classically cultivator obsession with disrespect, it seemed like it contradicted *me*. I mean, hell, they'd been hitting me with a cane for two hours and I hadn't made a single wisecrack. It was like someone had secretly replaced my brain with that of a mature adult.

Come to think of it, ever since I'd touched the void I hadn't been big on holding grudges. Sure, I was traumatized and I was sad and I was detached, but even when I'd snapped at Lucy I hadn't really been *angry*. I didn't blame Xavier for challenging me. I didn't blame Lucy for abandoning me. For fuck's sake, I didn't even really blame the void psycho for what he'd done. It wasn't *his* fault deep space had driven him homicidally insane.

Okay, I know that last bit makes *me* sound a bit insane, but something about comprehending infinity makes being angry at people feel like a waste of time.

And hey, if the instructors were hitting me more, that meant they were hitting the kids *less*. I'd happily take a couple of extra thwacks if it meant fewer ten-year-olds got hit. Seriously, I think part of why everyone on Fyrion was so fucked up might've had to do with getting repeatedly smacked as a kid. I had sympathy for the kiddos, even if a bit of tough training was nothing compared to what Brady's and my—

Thwack.

"Fuck," I swore and rubbed at my sore temple before realizing I'd just cursed in a room full of kids. I could practically hear Lucy chiding me. "Sorry," I muttered and returned to my meditation.

I fought off the urge to cycle. They technically *wanted* us cycling, but I'd figured out by then their qi sharpened the pain of the blows. Mine numbed it. If I'd been willing to risk it, I could've drifted off into the infinite sea and not even literal torture would've broken my meditation. I couldn't let that happen. Shortcuts wouldn't prepare me for the pain of opening my next meridians, nor that of actual combat.

By the time their three hours were up, Park and Stevens had left a myriad of welts on my head and a crisscross of bruises down my back. Not once had I managed to maintain my meditation through their abuse, but by the end I *did* successfully suppress the sharp intake of breath. I counted that as progress.

A few of the young'uns followed the seniors out of the classroom, but most stayed behind with me. We had a half hour before cycling class, and whoever was in charge of such things had had the kindness to keep the introductory classes in the same room. I pressed off against the padded floor and stood up to stretch, casting my gaze across the class as I realized my mistake.

Each and every one of the remaining kids pulled a lunchbox from among their belongings.

"Note to self," I muttered. "Pack a lunch."

My holopad beeped to confirm it'd recorded the note. "Oh, shit, delete that," I ordered it. I didn't need the thing reminding me at some odd hour. I looked up from the holographic screen to find every child in the room looking up at me.

"Sorry, pretend you didn't hear that."

None of them looked away.

"Um, hi," I tried. "I'm Cal."

"Mister Cal?" one of the kids in the back asked. "What's a fuck?"

I froze. "Uh... you should ask your parents that. Tell them you heard it from Senior Cadet Stevens." Okay maybe I wasn't as immune to grudges as I thought. Remember when I said my sense of humor had a tendency to get me in trouble?

Three of the kiddos snickered amongst themselves, but didn't explain it to the others. Whether they knew the meaning of the word or just that it was bad escaped me, but I had no intention of pursuing the matter. That sounded like an entirely unfunny kind of trouble I *really* didn't want.

Another kid spoke up, one of the younger boys near the front. "Where's your lunch, Mister Cal?"

"It's just Cal," I told him, masterfully evading the question. I tapped the symbol on my sect uniform. "I'm the same rank as you." *Technically*, as pre-cadets, none of the kids even had ranks, but I was at the same cultivation stage as they were and I considered those basically the same thing. I still didn't know what all of the insignias actually *meant*, but I figured the hollow circle on my uniform meant I hadn't formed a core yet.

"Did your mom forget to pack you one?" the boy asked, laser-focused on my lack of lunch for some reason.

"Don't be stupid!" the girl next to him elbowed him. "Grown-ups make their own lunches."

I sat back down and smiled at the boy. "My mom is *very* far away." That reminded me, I owed Lucy an update on everything that'd happened. Wait. Why had that reminded me of Lucy?

"Oh," the kid said. He rifled through his lunchbox and pulled out a peanut butter sandwich, half of which he grabbed and held out towards me. "You can have half of mine. My mom forgets my lunch sometimes too."

"No, no, I can't take this," I said, fighting off my urge to give in to the overwhelming cuteness of it all. What kind of person would I be if I took some kid's lunch? "That's yours."

Just as the boy started to pull his proffered sandwich back, my body betrayed me in the most primal of ways.

My stomach growled.

The boy shot to his feet, plodded right up to me, deposited the half-sandwich on my knee, and returned to his seat. I looked down at it and up at him, tactfully ignoring the spot of peanut butter he'd smudged on my uniform, and picked up the food. "What's your name?"

"I'm Vihaan."

"Well, thank you, Vihaan. It's very kind of you." I gave the morsel a try.

The sandwich was painfully bland and it stuck to the roof of my mouth something awful, but my empty stomach and cuteness-overloaded heart didn't care. I scarfed it down in three bites.

What followed could only be described as a donation drive as kid after kid walked up to offer some portion of their lunch. It wasn't until half of them had stopped by that I realized I'd accumulated a surplus of carrots, celery, and nutri-shake, and an absolute dearth of sweets. Were these kids just pawning off the parts of their lunch they didn't want to eat?

I devoured it all anyway, thanking each of them for their generous gift as I assembled a full lunch from a pile of kid-sized portions. By the end, I wasn't entirely sure who had taken advantage of whom, but that uncertainty seemed par for the course on planet cultivator.

Ahead of schedule, a pale woman with dreadlocks stepped into the classroom, her uniform marking her as part of the sect. Cries of 'Miss Chrissy!' greeted her.

She looked right at me. "Caliban Rex?"

I jumped to attention, saluting my superior just a few moments too late. She let me slide.

"At ease. I'm Senior Cadet Chrystalia, but you can call me Chrissy. Elder Lopez says you'll be joining my class?"

"Yep," I said, already appreciating her laid-back attitude. "I'm very new to all this, so they've got me down here with the kiddos." I grinned back at them. "I'm already making friends though."

"That's something, at least," Chrissy replied. "Other than friends, I'm not sure what I can offer you."

I raised an eyebrow. "Why do you say that?"

"Right now we're working on exercises for the bone, skin, and stomach meridians, none of which you've opened. Soon the class'll shift gears to preparing to open our kidney meridians, which you already *have* opened."

I blinked at her use of the first person plural to describe the class as if she were learning along with them. I wondered if that was a personal quirk of hers, or if Chrissy did it as a way to connect with the kids. "Okay, um... do any of the exercises apply to the other meridians?"

"The focus ones do, but your meditation training will help with that more than anything I can teach you. I'd give you some exercises for the meridians you *do* have, but I'm not authorized to teach those. We don't open our blood or heart until cycling two, and lungs aren't until cycling three."

"Hmm," I wondered aloud. "Any tips for opening those three you mentioned, then? Those are the easiest, right?"

"That's why we start with them," Chrissy confirmed, "but easier doesn't mean easy." She nodded towards the kids happily eating their lunches. "I have a few minutes before I have to start with them. Let me guide you through our pre-meridian exercises."

As I learned over the following minutes, pre-meridian exercises entailed sensing your core, condensing your qi, and practicing moving it around a little bit—basically everything you could do without any open meridians. By the time I'd mastered and remastered the extremely basic exercises, Chrissy's calm and rhythmic voice was already guiding the kiddos through some cycling technique.

I followed as best I could, simulating the starts and stops and twisting qi patterns with my differing set of meridians. I had no idea if it was any use, but I dutifully cataloged how each technique affected my body. Of course, none of it matched what Chrissy described, but I was cycling different qi through different meridians, so… duh.

I came away from the experience feeling calm and refreshed—if a bit bored. My relaxed posture clashed with the energized children, but I figured everyone looked calm compared to a bunch of kids who'd been cooped up inside for six hours. I lingered as they practically trampled over each other in their rush to combat class. "So how'd I do?"

Chrissy shrugged. "As well as you could do, given the circumstances. Usually once a child can sense their qi we go straight for the bone meridian, and you're well past that. I'd start saving up now. If you're efficient with your focus room time, you could advance to cycling two in a matter of months."

"Bone meridian. Got it." I nodded. "I'll see what I can do. Thanks for the tips." I winked at her.

She chuckled. "Be careful with that. Most direct superiors won't take too kindly to junior cadets flirting with them."

"What? Flirting? Me? *No.* I couldn't put you in that position. Imagine what would happen if you got caught sleeping with one of your students."

Her chuckle graduated to a full on laugh. "That's enough from you. Get to your next class."

"Yes ma'am." I saluted. At her nod I spun on my heel and left the room, following the distant sounds of screaming children.

She seemed nice. It was some relief to finally meet someone who didn't insist on all the formalities, especially one who seemed to really care about the kids under her care.

Lucy's words echoed in my mind. *It's the ones that pretend to be humble you need to worry about.*

I groaned. Was it a ploy? Had she carefully calculated her casual manner to *get* something from me? The fact I had to even ask didn't bode well for my time on Fyrion.

It was with the nasty shadow of distrust lingering in the back of my mind that I arrived in what I can only describe as a dojo. A ring of benches lined the vast padded floor, across which the kids had already spread out and launched into a series of stretches. Racks of wooden weapons lined the walls, each lined with its own layer of padded cloth.

Three severe-looking men strode into the room at once, each clad in the same senior cadet uniforms as my prior instructors. Unlike my prior instructors, the kids all snapped to attention at their entrance. I followed suit.

"Cadet Rex, is it?" One of the instructors—a man with a long black braid, squinted at me. He looked me up and down with a derisive smirk and a sneer on his face, as if he'd expected a cultivator and found a mortal. "You look awfully... *humble* for a man named king."

Something about the air of superiority in the man's voice really got to me. "And you look awfully... actually, I don't know what your name is. Let's just say you look awful."

Actually, in hindsight, completely forget that thing I said about not getting mad. Sure, I wasn't gonna hold it against the guy that he'd insulted me, but I'd be damned if I let inner peace get between me and a witty retort.

The man snarled. "Do I need to—"

"Teach me a lesson? That's why you're here, isn't it?"

To my credit, I actually saw the punch coming this time. I still didn't dodge it because holy fuck that man was fast, but I *did* see it coming. Baby steps.

Standing at the edge of the dojo, the block knocked me back and over the bench behind me. Its corner dug painfully into my already-bruised upper back, but it kept my head from slamming into the concrete floor behind it.

"You would do well to learn some *respect*, mortal," the braided man sneered.

I kept quiet, too distracted running qi through my racing heart to manage a scathing reply. The energy's calming effects managed to stave off the worst of the fight-or-flight, but it didn't stop him from launching into a lecture.

"In his incompetence," the man paced as he addressed the children, "Cadet Rex has forced the sect's elders to prioritize his training over your own. Because his greater size and strength render him an invalid opponent to all of you, whenever it comes time to spar, one of Instructors Charleston, Davis, or myself will have to serve as his opponent rather than instructing the rest of you. His benefit is purely your loss. Am I understood?"

"Yes, Instructor Long!" the kids chimed in unison. A few of them flashed me angry glares.

Great. Day one and they'd already managed to turn the kids against me. And here I'd thought our lunch moment had meant something. Maybe Vihaan would still have my back. Nope, wait, he was scowling at me. Shit.

Then again, kids tended to like whomever was nice to them most recently. It couldn't be *that* hard to win them back, right?

Lucky for me, while my meditation skills had sorely lacked and my cycling skills completely mismatched my classmates', the limited combat training Lucy had given me proved remarkably effective, which was to say, my technique was only *four* months behind the group of ten-year-olds instead of *eight*.

While the rest of the class spent three straight hours practicing the same basic lunge ad nauseam, Instructor Davis wouldn't even let me hold a sword. He and I spent the entire session working on my stance, an apparently deeply specific bit of technique with plenty of opportunities for correction via a well-placed kick.

My muscles, still sore from the morning workout, protested alongside my bruised back and battered skull as the gaunt senior cadet forced me to drop in and out of the low-seated combat stance over and over again. It was boring, arduous, repetitive work, rife with sharp comments about my every flaw, which was to say as a vac-welder, I felt right at home.

The hardest part was refraining from informing Instructor Davis of which *particular* type of rotted fish his breath stank. Seriously, I think this man had some sort of medical condition, one of which he may have been aware, given how often he spoke right into my face.

I'd yet to successfully drop into combat-readiness without warranting a half dozen corrections when Instructor Long called the end of class. Even exhausted from the afternoon's training, each and every kid jumped to attention.

"Decent work today," Instructor Charleston announced, fiddling with his holopad. "I've sent out today's class rankings. Congratulations to Cadet Ria for taking second. Cadet Graham, do better next time."

A list of just over two dozen names popped up onto my holopad, a list on which I sat comfortably at the bottom. Of *course* they were ranking the ten-year-olds. Fucking cultivators.

I gaped as I watched tears well in the eyes of a blond-haired boy, presumably Cadet Graham. The list indicated he'd fallen just two spots.

Shaking my head, I slipped out of the dojo the moment the senior cadets dismissed us. I made a beeline for the nearest transport tube, waiting patiently on the platform until one of the public pods reached me. It thankfully arrived unoccupied. I wasn't sure I had it in me to deal with any more cultivators at the moment.

I spent the ride pondering the events of the day, the variety of abuses and questionable teaching methods I'd experienced. I understood wanting to instill a sense of competition in the kids, but it was no fucking wonder the rest of the sect was so cutthroat. I'd started the day getting hit with a cane and ended it with a lecture about how my presence *cost* my classmates.

By the time the transport pod finally pulled up to the inconveniently distant housing section D, I'd concluded that cultivators needed to spend a little less time contemplating the universe and a little more time contemplating effective organizational structure. Animosity did *not* breed productivity, however *competitive* you made people.

I ignored the derisive and evaluative gazes of the sect-members in the lobby as I waved to Arthur and mounted the steps to the third floor. They'd get used to me eventually.

I stopped off in my room just long enough to exchange my uniform for a towel and a bar of soap before I left for the washroom. I could call Lucy later. I had two hours before dinner, which should've been *just* enough time for what I had in mind, and I *don't* mean taking a shower.

After the way my first two days at the sect had gone, I really needed a win. I still had to talk to someone about ways to safely drink from the infinite sea, but that could be tomorrow me's problem. For now, it wouldn't be an issue.

I still had plenty of qi left to open my bone meridian.

10

I picked the third in the line of eight showers and reached in to turn the water on. A chill ran down my body as the first frigid droplets struck my arm, which I jerked away to give the stream a moment to purge the cool water before the hot could catch up. It felt like ages.

With near certainty I believed the other floors didn't have this problem, but since I was the only one using any of the third floor bathrooms, the water up here tended to *sit* in the plumbing for long periods of time. As I waited, I thought through my plan.

Opening a meridian outside of a focus room would surely draw suspicion, but my two hours per week in the qi-rich chambers made for too strong a bargaining chip to actually *use*. Unless I wanted to stink up my room and ruin the carpet, I'd have to cleanse the blocked meridian somewhere it'd be easy to wash the grime away. The showers just made sense.

Of course, I didn't have to run the water the whole time, but the last thing I wanted was some poor custodian walking in on me. Given the size of the settlement on Fyrion, the water I used wouldn't come close to straining the recycling system, so that wouldn't be a problem.

Anyone keeping an eye on me would just think I'd taken an abnormally long shower, which wasn't *strictly* inconspicuous behavior, but felt like exactly the kind of thing someone who'd had a public panic attack the day before might do. That was good enough for me.

I hung my towel on the exterior hook, pulled the faux-wood door shut behind me, and plopped my bare ass down on the shower floor. It felt *wrong* to just sit on the floor of a communal shower, but as the only third-floor resident, I could've argued all eight showers belonged to me.

The warm water washed down my back as I evened out my breathing and turned my focus inward. My qi sat in a pool at the bottom of my center, cool and dark and unmoving. I tugged at it, and it obeyed, strands springing up and spinning through my four open meridians. My heartbeat slowed, my blood cooled, my breathing deepened. I cycled for a few minutes, the outside world a distant dream as my focus solidified.

For the first time in my cultivation journey, I opened a meridian the right way.

Rudimentary as they were, Chrissy's exercises *had* been useful, at least useful enough to deduce what I'd been doing wrong. Instead of slamming a battery of qi into the blocked meridian, I formed the tiniest, sharpest sliver I could manage, and carefully, gently, pressed it against the base of my pelvis.

The pain began immediately. It was a constant, growing ache rather than the sudden spikes I'd grown accustomed to, one that slowly eroded at my concentration rather than shattering it completely. I pressed on.

Most cultivators start with their bone meridian for a pretty simple reason. If your bones stop working, it doesn't immediately ruin your breathing. It doesn't pause your heart and put you on a three minute timer for brain damage.   It doesn't outright knock you unconscious. Bones are wonderfully static objects, to the point that as I cleared out my bone meridian, other than a body-wide ache, I didn't notice anything particularly wrong.

Unlike heart failure or liver failure or kidney failure, bone marrow failure takes months or years to kill you. If I needed months or years to clear one meridian, I'd picked the wrong calling.

The width and speed of my qi grew alongside the full-body ache, washing away more and more of the spiritual gunk. My joints locked as my bones themselves seemed to swell and pulse and burn with the fires of a thousand stars, but the very qi that wreaked such havoc soothed and cooled and strengthened.

The pain vanished all at once. My cycling quickened as the last of the obstructions oozed out, widening and reinforcing the pathway as it healed the damage the cleansing had done. Moments later my eyes popped open. I checked my holopad. Only an hour had passed.

I grinned. It was a new record.

The smile wiped itself from my face as I got a whiff of myself.   Already the still-running shower had washed away the worst of the grime, but a thin layer of a foul-smelling oily substance still coated my skin. Thank fuck for that new record. I needed as much time as I could get if I wanted to clean myself up before dinner.

With a self-satisfied smirk, I pushed myself to my feet, reached for the bar of soap, and got to work.

———

I strode into the mess fifteen minutes late with a spring in my step. A few of the cultivators at the closer tables gazed at me with curiosity and disdain, but the vast majority of my sect mates failed to notice my entrance in the chaos of the thousand-person dining hall.

The scale of this place continued to astound me. I'd of

course been on larger stations, but never a single mess hall designed to feed a thousand people at once. It was insane. I couldn't think of a single reason every cadet in housing D had to all eat dinner in the same place at the same time, but it seemed like a logistical nightmare.

On the freighter that'd taken us to roofie, Brady and I had been assigned a set meal block and our choice of a dozen small cafeterias. Here, they had everything I could think of in one *room*.

"Newcomer!" Xavier waved me over to where he stood in line for curry.

I joined him. "You can call me Cal."

"Newcomer Cal! Congratulations on opening your newest meridian!"

I froze. How did he know? There was no way my holopad was broadcasting my physical status, and without cycling the open meridian didn't actually *do* anything.

Xavier slapped me on the back, clearly reading the confusion on my face. "You look like a man with five open meridians."

I blinked. "What... what does that look like?"

Xavier shrugged.

"Okay, um..." I sighed. "Thanks, I guess?" I glanced around the room. "Can they all see it?"

Xavier shrugged again. "I've never asked what they can or can't see." He suddenly leaned in, sticking his nose into the top of my head and taking a deep sniff.

I jerked away. "What the hell was—"

"Anyone who cycles their sense meridian within a few feet of you will smell that," Xavier explained. "Next time, use the shampoo."

"I used shampoo."

"Not *shampoo*, *the* shampoo. It's the only good way to get meridian gunk out of your hair. You can request some on your holopad. They don't charge for it because they don't want sect members walking around smelling like rotting meat on a pile of sewage."

"Thanks for *that* mental image." I shuddered. "I'll have to get some of that shampoo." I stopped to put a bowl of potato vindaloo on my tray. "In the future, if you notice I've advanced, maybe don't announce it for all the world to hear."

Genuine confusion flashed on Xavier's face. "Why not? Advancements are cause for celebration!"

"Just... do me this favor, okay?"

"Of course, newcomer Cal!" He slapped me on the back again, causing curry to slosh out of its bowl and onto my tray.

I skipped out on veggies after my particularly vegetal lunch, and scooped up a side of brown rice and some tofu for protein before joining Xavier in the search for a place to sit. Oddly enough, he didn't seem to have an immediate friend group to default to, which I supposed made some amount of sense. Knowing cultivators, it was because nobody wanted to befriend the guy at the bottom of the rankings.

Except, lucky for me, the guy second from the bottom.

For lack of direction, I scanned the crowd for the one other friendly face I'd found—using the word 'friendly' in its loosest sense. "Right there." I gestured with my tray. "There's some space at Charlotte's table."

Xavier seemed unenthused by the idea—a response I deduced both by his face and the fact he actually stopped talking—but followed as I set off. Curious eyes tracked us as we crossed the dining room, but nobody bothered us. It'd bugged me for a while, actually, the way nobody tried to bully us for our low ranking, until I'd realized the reason.

Nobody wanted to duel the bottom-rankers—they'd have nothing to gain and everything to lose. Since the sect required its members to accept challenges, if either Xavier or I challenged someone, they'd be forced to risk their position for no benefit.

So they gawked, they whispered, and they avoided us, but nobody dared single themselves out in their disrespect. I supposed in a way, I had so little status that even bullying me was beneath them. I wondered how long that would last.

The senior cadets and the elders, of course, had no such vulnerability. While I could *technically* challenge them, they were so far above me it would've been considered disrespectful to do so, and they'd be well within their rights to put me in my place. At least my immediate classmates would leave me alone.

Whatever Charlotte's table had been talking about ceased as we made our approach. In silence, five cultivators stared up at us.

"Hi Charlotte." I smiled at her. "Mind if we sit here?" I didn't wait for a reply before I plopped my tray down and took a seat. The moment my ass hit the metal chair, two of Charlotte's table-mates stood.

"Oh, is that... um... Francis?" the girl to Charlotte's left clearly bullshitted. "I should—uh—go catch up with him."

"I'll join you," the other standing cultivator added, pushing away from his seat and leaving the table.

The other two unfamiliar cadets simply stood up and left, either tagging along with the first excuse or simply not bothering to make one. Now alone with me and Xavier, Charlotte rubbed her eyes under her glasses and let out a sigh. "Great. Now I'm sitting at the loser's table."

I squinted as I watched the others leave. "Those guys are about as mature as the ten-year-olds in my class."

"They left for a *reason*, Cal," Charlotte said. "If you're seen hanging around bottom rankers, people will think you're weak. You'll have a harder time finding a skilled sparring partner, and lower-ranked members will see you as an easy opportunity to climb. I'll probably get at least two challenges because of this dinner alone."

I scowled. "That sounds like a shitty system designed to stop people from ever making friends."

Charlotte groaned and reached for her glass of wine. "What do you want?"

With questionably mean and unquestionably funny intent, I waited until she took a sip before I answered. "I want to give you one of my focus room hours."

She spat out her pinot.

Somehow, being Charlotte, she managed to do even this with poise and grace, collecting herself and dabbing at her mouth with her napkin even as Xavier and I broke out laughing.

"You're joking," she exhaled as she watched us cackle. "Of course you're joking. That was cruel."

"No, no, I—" I took a breath to force the laughter back. "I'm serious. Your reaction was hilarious, but I do want to give you an hour."

Her eyes shot open. "What? You can't. You need those. The entire purpose of—"

"Charlotte," I interrupted her. "Do you want it or not?"

"Yes," she answered immediately. "Of course I want it. I just need to know *why*. You're not going to gimp your advancement just because I helped you out yesterday. You started with what, four open meridians? If you give away any more hours, it'll take you years to open the other eight." She sat back in her chair. "What's so important to you that you'd trade away your most valuable resource?"

Interesting, I noted. She hadn't noticed my newly opened meridian. Was she particularly insensitive, or was Xavier particularly astute? I filed that little tidbit away for later.

"I need instruction more than I need qi," I answered

vaguely. "The kiddie classes are useful enough for the time being, and Xavier here can spar with me, but I need someone who really understands how things work around here."

"I understand—" Xavier started to say but Charlotte's glare shut him up. The gap in social skills between the two couldn't have been more apparent, and we all knew it.

"So, what? You want me to be your teacher?"

"I want you to be my friend," I countered. "If I have to frame it as an exchange of resources so it fits into your worldview, then sure, I'm offering you an extra hour in the focus rooms in exchange for advice and information, but really I just want to be friends. Friends that help each other."

"Deal," Charlotte didn't even take a moment to think. She didn't negotiate, didn't haggle, didn't press for any more information. She just jumped at the opportunity I'd offered.

Maybe I'd underplayed my hand. Ah well. I still had another hour to trade away, and that was just this week's budget.

"So," she set her wine glass down as she spoke, "what do you want to know?"

I asked the first question that popped into my head. "What's with the glasses?"

"I haven't needed them since I opened my sense meridian," she answered without hesitation. "I keep wearing them because I like how they make people perceive me—bookish, subdued, calculating."

"Calculating alright," Xavier muttered.

"Like you know what you're doing but aren't a threat." I nodded along. "That's smart. Manipulative, but smart."

She flashed me a dry look. "Anything else?"

"Tell me about the void horde."

"I was only twelve when it happened. Anyone else here

112

would know as much about it as I do."

"I didn't ask anyone else."

She sighed. "You can find the details on the local net. It's public info. A few cycles back, a horde of void beasts like we've never seen came after us. My father was critical in fighting them off. Nobody knows where they came from. Nobody knows why they wanted The Dueling Stars. We *do* know that in the past decade, void beast attacks have been coming more frequently. My father thinks it's just a matter of time before another horde shows up."

I blinked. That was news. Void beasts tended to follow the qi, so out in deep space they'd always been trivial to avoid. That something was driving hordes towards systems as weak as The Dueling Stars seemed important, but as someone who knew fuck all about anything, I was probably the last person that needed to be worrying about it. It wasn't like *I* could stop them.

"Is that why you're out here?" I asked. "Your dad wants you on the planet they'll come for last?"

Charlotte raised an eyebrow. "On the least defended outpost in the system?"

"Right." I looked at her expectantly.

"My relationship with my father has no bearing on your ability to prosper here on Fyrion," Charlotte finally answered, a sharpness to her voice. "Satisfied?"

"Not really, but that's okay." I took another bite of curry. "How well can you gauge my cultivation level?"

Her brow furrowed. "Is that a trick question?"

"No?"

"I can't. I've asked around. Nobody can." She gestured widely to the room around us. "I can tell you exactly how close to making copper each and every person on D-block is with a glance, but I get nothing from you. It's like staring at a corpse."

"Huh," I muttered. "You're the second person to tell me

that."

"Then why did you ask? You clearly know more about whatever technique you're using than I do."

I spared a sideways glance at Xavier. How the fuck was the overbuilt buffoon the only one who could guess my cultivation level? I guess it was a good thing nobody wanted to talk to the guy, at least as far as hiding my progress went. As far as maintaining a functional society, it was a very *bad* thing.

"Just curious," I said. "Always want more data."

Charlotte snorted. "You just wanted to know if I would lie. It'd be easy. Everyone knows you entered with four open meridians, and you obviously haven't opened another one on your *second day*."

I shoved another forkful of vindaloo-covered rice into my mouth, hoping that even if she cycled her sense meridian, the spicy curry would cover the lingering stench in my hair.

Thankfully, it never came to that. Charlotte downed the last of her pinot noir, set her glass delicately back on her tray, and looked up to me. "If there's nothing else, I need to go salvage what's left of my reputation. Cadet Wallace just walked in, and if he sees me with you he'll challenge me on the spot."

"Alright, alright, go on," I waved her off. Just as she turned and picked up her tray, I added, "See you at breakfast."

She let out an audible groan but still strode away without looking back.

"She's not very nice," Xavier said.

"So I noticed."

"Then why her?"

"I already have a *nice* friend." I patted him on the arm. "I need a devious one. There's good in her—otherwise she wouldn't have defended me yesterday—but she knows how to get what she wants. Lucy was right. This place is a viper's nest. I need someone who knows how to navigate it."

"Ha!" Xavier laughed. "I rise above their paltry machinations through sheer willpower and glorious combat!"

"That's funny," I said, pantomiming scrolling through my holopad. "According to this you've fallen *below* their paltry machinations. Right to the bottom of the rankings."

"That just means there's more work to be done." Xavier declared as he shot to his feet, the entire table shaking with the motion. "Care to join me in the ring, *sparring partner*? A cultivator's training is never done."

"Tomorrow," I told him, rising to my feet *without* moving the table. "It's been a long day."

"Of course, newcomer Cal." He smiled at me. "If you change your mind, you know where I'll be. If not..." He clapped my shoulder. "I'll see you in the gym tomorrow morning."

I lingered for a moment as I watched him leave, taking some solace in the momentary lack of gawkers. Apparently my sect mates had already begun to grow bored of staring at the newbie.

I realized as I moved to bus my tray that I really couldn't afford to be taking evenings off. Xavier was right. A cultivator's training really never *was* done. I knew I'd have way more spare time once I graduated out of the kiddie classes and moved on to the more freeform instruction the adult cadets enjoyed, but until then, I had to keep busy. Elder Lopez had put me on a clock, after all.

Then again, I doubted she'd thought I'd open another meridian on my second day.

The grin stayed stuck on my face as I left the dining hall behind and mounted the grandiose staircase to the third floor. Xavier and I could spar another time. Between my first classes, my bone meridian, and my deal with Charlotte, I figured I'd had enough excitement for one day.

Besides, I still owed a certain someone a phone call.

11

"For the last time, I'm *okay.*"

I paced circles around my dorm room as I spoke to the empty air, my holopad transmitting my voice with a half-second delay through Fyrion's comms network and into orbit.

"Cal, sweetie, you had a panic attack," Lucy's voice echoed clearly throughout the small room. "It's been less than a month since RF-31. Maybe you need more time."

"I need to get stronger," I countered. "I had a panic attack because I got in a fistfight with a cultivator above my level. I had a panic attack because for the second time my strongest punch barely moved him. I don't need more time. I need a stronger punch."

"Okay," Lucy said, the worry still apparent in her voice. "It's your decision, and I support you. Just… please let me know if it happens again, and if you ever need someone to talk to…"

I smiled. "You'll be the first one I call."

"Good. It's good they helped you, but I don't trust anyone down there to have your best interests in mind."

"I'm working on that. I'm already making friends with one of those boastful-types you mentioned, and I'm in the process of convincing someone a bit smarter that my interests align with hers."

"Oh? Tell me about them."

I went on to explain in depth my encounters with Xavier and Charlotte, the former's earnest eagerness for a sparring partner and the latter's self-serving interest in my focus room hours. Lucy agreed with my decision to trade the hours away, though she warned me it'd draw unwelcome attention if word got out.

Charlotte, at least, wouldn't let that happen. If I got kicked out of the sect, she'd lose her chance at more bonus hours. I'd just have to be careful to whom else I traded focus room time.

Lucy listened attentively as I ran through the day's events, from the rough but helpful meditation instructors to Chrissy's genuine care to Senior Cadet Long replying to my verbal swing with a physical one. She sighed at that last.

"You can't disrespect people like that," she chided me. "Right now, your low rank and my protection keep you relatively safe, but you have to climb eventually, and the longer I stay off-planet the less they'll remember my presence."

"He disrespected me first! I just responded in kind."

"He insulted you. He didn't disrespect you. There's a difference. 'Humble' could be considered a compliment or just a neutral observation. 'Awful' is *always* an insult."

"You didn't see his face."

"If his face was relevant, cultivators would be killing each other for the wrong *look*. We've been over this, Cal. The rules matter."

"The rules are bullshit."

"Language!"

"Sorry," I muttered. "I'll play nice."

"I didn't say anything about nice.   You'll play

respectfully."

"Respectfully…" I ceased my pacing and rubbed at the scruff on my unshaven chin. "I think I can do that."

From there I braced myself for the lecture to come and explained how I'd spent my afternoon. Remarkably, Lucy seemed oddly okay with it.

"Xavier's right," she said. "You should get some of that shampoo."

"Already ordered some. Should be here tomorrow." I opened my mouth to move the conversation along, but my curiosity got the better of me. "You're… just fine with the fact I opened a meridian alone in the shower?"

Lucy sighed. "I've realized there's not much I can say to stop you. The focus rooms are too valuable a resource to waste, and even if they weren't the elders would see how quickly you're advancing. At least you had some proper instruction this time. Next time, I hope you'll find someone you can trust to watch you. I won't be waiting outside with a medical cart."

I blinked. "When were you outside with a medical cart? My lungs?"

She didn't answer.

"Of fu—of course you were. You knew what I was doing and you knew the risks." I exhaled. "Thank you."

"I just want you to be safe," Lucy said. "Or at least as safe as you can be."

"I appreciate it. I really do. You've been absolutely amazing to me."

Her voice turned dark. "I've also been awful."

I sat and lay back on my bed, my legs dangling off until my knees bent and my feet touched the floor. "Tell me about him."

Lucy went silent.

"Your last passenger, I want to know."

"I…" Lucy's voice wavered. "I'm not ready to talk

about that."

"Okay." I let the word hang in the air for a moment. "Can I know his name?"

"Cedric. Cedric Stiathan."

"Cedric," I repeated the name, letting its syllables linger on my tongue. "I'm sorry."

A tightness clutched Lucy's tone as she spoke once more. "I'll let you get some rest. Call me tomorrow if you have a chance, alright?"

"I will," I promised. "Goodnight, Lucy."

"Goodnight, Cal. Sleep well."

The comms went quiet.

I lay unmoving for some time, mind caught worrying about Lucy and wondering about Cedric. I felt some kinship to the stranger, this mysterious cultivator whose inability to touch the very ocean of qi from which I drank had driven him mad. I pictured him alone in roofie's reactor room, a starving man surrounded by a feast he couldn't touch. I wondered if he'd sensed the void in those final moments, if it'd been the infinite sea that'd stolen away his sanity.

It'd very nearly driven me to despondency, and *I* could cultivate it.

The thought spun circles in my mind as I finally rose to cleanse my teeth and undress for bed. I fought to banish the specter, this unhealthy fascination with the madman who'd killed my brother, but even as my head hit the pillow, Cedric's twitching face sat lodged in my mind.

Sleep took over soon enough. I'd had, by all counts, a truly exhausting day. As in most things, Lucy had been right.

I needed to get some rest.

———

"If I wanted…" I inhaled sharply as I tugged back on the rowing machine. "…to find a particular technique…" I yanked back once more. "…where would I look?"

"The local net," Charlotte answered through a grunt as she finished a bench press. "Most of the sect's beginner techniques are there."

"Already looked. Where else?"

She scowled at me. "What are you… nevermind. You're not going to tell me. You should ask your sponsor."

I'd originally intended to spend the morning workout running, but after she'd hidden away in her room during breakfast, I needed the opportunity to speak with Charlotte. I took a quick break from my rowing. "My sponsor isn't a sect member."

"Your *benefactor* isn't," she said, "but you can't be a member without someone in the sect sponsoring you. The info should be on your holopad."

I scowled and scrolled through the holographic screen, bringing up my profile on the sect's local network. I sighed. "Shit. Elder Lopez."

"What's wrong with Elder Lopez?"

"She's doesn't like me."

"Of course she doesn't like you." Charlotte racked her weight and sat up. "You're an upstart mortal *and* a foreigner. You're taking up valuable resources just because some old ship asked for them. There probably isn't a single elder on all of Fyrion that *does* like you."

"I guess I'll just have to win her over with my rakish charm."

Charlotte laughed.

"See, it's already working on you!"

"You won me over with *bribery*," Charlotte said, pushing herself to her feet. She pulled the weights from her bar and returned them to their rack. "I'd say you should try that with Elder Lopez, but you can't give away *all* your hours." She turned away, leaving me behind to take off on a run around the massive track, but not before adding, "What use is a technique without the qi to use it?"

I watched her go, her pace far beyond what I could ever hope to match. "My thoughts exactly." With a spark of an idea and a grin on my face, I got back to my workout. By the time I'd finished rowing, I knew exactly how I'd spend the rest of the day.

Meditation class went about as boringly as one might expect from the words 'meditation class.' Senior Cadets Park and Stevens showed me some mercy compared to my first day, something my sore back deeply appreciated as I tried and failed to maintain my focus through their continued *distractions*.

I *felt* like I was making progress, but it was hard to quantify, and I had no way of knowing if I'd made it up or if it was only because the instructors weren't hitting me quite as hard. Either way, I let out a sigh of relief when the session finally ended and the instructors left the room.

The kids gave me the cold shoulder as I devoured the egg salad sandwich and potato chips I'd pilfered from the cafeteria that morning. They sat in clusters on the opposite side of the room, apparently no longer interested in the strange adult that had joined their class. Even Vihaan, the kind boy who'd offered me half of his lunch just yesterday, kept his distance.

I tried not to let it bother me, but truthfully the treatment stung. All it'd taken was a few words from Instructor Long to turn them against me. I figured I'd win them back eventually—Long wasn't exactly steep competition in the friendliness category—but for the time being I'd let them keep to themselves. For the time being, I had more pressing matters to worry about than the opinions of a bunch of ten-year-olds.

Chrissy arrived five minutes early again, and was kind enough to spend that time giving me a brief rundown of the most basic cycling techniques she taught. I couldn't ask for specific instruction for my newly-opened bone meridian without giving away too much information, but I could readily play the part of a new student desperate to catch up.

Once I knew everything the kiddos knew, I could just follow along with them. Thanks to my practicably undetectable qi, she wouldn't know I was working the same exercises as the others until I'd been there long enough to reveal my open meridians without raising too many questions.

I spent the three hour session mastering the basic cycling method and messing around with my newly opened meridian. Similar to my kidney, I couldn't easily feel the difference cycling qi through my bones made, but I figured reinforced bones would prove critical in a fight.

I made the furthest strides in combat class, by which I mean I took a literal stride. Apparently my training aboard Lucy let me skip an entire week's worth of learning how to stand and I could move on to learning how to take a step. The instructors still looked at me with resentment, but I could handle a few dirty looks. As long as they kept teaching me, I'd be fine. Hell, at this rate I'd place out of their class in a couple months and be done with them entirely. I held tight to that thought.

As the last dredges of afternoon valiantly held against the encroaching evening, I shared a crowded transport pod to Elder Lopez's office. I'm sure my fellow passengers resented how much exercise I'd had since my last shower, but my sore and exhausted self couldn't do much about that. I muttered an apology as I finally arrived.

I waited on the hard metal bench outside Elder Lopez's office for thirty minutes before her secretary ushered me in. I saluted the moment I stepped in the door.

A veritable shrine to false opulence surrounded me.

Faux-wooden panels covered the walls, the type designed to *look* as realistic as possible at the cost of giving off a faint chemical smell. Some people claimed they couldn't smell it, but any cultivator with a functional sense meridian would've found it overwhelming. I wondered if that was the point.

Gold trim decorated the veneer, off of which glimmered the yellow glow of the decadent chandelier. Rather than books or personal holos, natural treasures decorated the shelves.

Tufts of fur, bundles of feathers, pressed flowers and dried-out organs from spiritual beasts gave off thin streams of elemental qi, not enough to truly cultivate with, but enough to *feel*, and certainly enough to earn a small fortune in pill materials. I got the impression she meant it as a display of wealth.

The elder herself sat behind an oak desk, the only real piece of wood in the office. "Cadet Rex." She looked me up and down, disdain in her eyes. "Are you ready to share your qi masking technique with the Dragon's Right Eye?"

"No, ma'am," I answered, maintaining my salute and rigid frame as best I could.

"Very well. You may go."

I blinked. "Um, ma'am? I'm here for instruction."

"Really? Because I have two different senior cadets sending me complaints that you're taking up too much attention in the nine hours of instruction you already receive."

I gulped. Which two instructors? Long seemed obvious. Was the second one of his lackeys or from a different class? I dismissed the thoughts. "I need a technique. Something to anchor my spirit to my body."

The elder tilted her head. "Now that *is* curious. A part of your Way, I take it?"

"Yes, ma'am."

"I know of three such techniques." She kept her voice curt. "You already know what information I want in return."

"I'm sorry, I—uh—ma'am." I very charmingly corrected myself. "I'm sorry, ma'am. I can't tell you that."

"Then you may go," she repeated. She waved at me dismissively and looked down at whatever report she was reading.

"I'll give you a focus room hour," I blurted out.

That got her attention. She raised a manicured eyebrow at me. "So you're desperate, then. Desperate or stupid. Very well." She sat back. "I accept."

At her nod I pulled out of my salute to bring up my holopad. I had to go through four different confirmation windows to transfer my focus room hour, but the moment it went through Elder Lopez leaned in with a predatory smile.

"I know three techniques for anchoring a spirit to its body. None of them work below the bronze stage."

I blinked. "E...excuse me?"

"I said I'd share what I knew, not that it'd be useful. If you're so set on projecting your spirit, progress to bronze core. Otherwise, I recommend you leave your spirit where it is."

"But we had a deal!"

She scowled. "We had a deal, *ma'am.* You've already broken attention without my permission, and now you dare *question* me?"

"But I couldn't send you the hour without breaking—" I forced myself to take a deep breath. "I'm sorry, ma'am."

"That's better," she sneered. "You mortals need to learn your place. Then again, I imagine you're not so happy with it. Spirits don't get lost when they have something to come back to. You may go." She spat the dismissal at me.

I spun on my heel and stormed out of the office,

completely failing to hide the anger from my face. That bitch. I'd given her some of the sect's most valuable resource and *that* was how she treated me?

I exhaled. So my sponsor was awful. What did that mean? It meant I couldn't depend on her for instruction. For the time being that didn't matter; I had classes. Once I finished the kiddie classes and became a fully fledged sect member it'd be an issue, but I could cross that bridge when I came to it.

More immediately, I needed a way to safely drink from the infinite sea. I couldn't cultivate without qi, but the one and only time I'd drawn from that well it'd nearly washed me away.

My mind ran circles as I waited for the transport pod to take me back to housing D. Just because Elder Lopez had been useless didn't mean the other elders would be. Maybe I could wait until next week and offer an hour to one of them. Was that allowed? Lopez was my sponsor. I'd have to ask Charlotte about the politics involved.

I replayed the encounter in my mind over the ride back. It made sense that nobody had designed such a technique for beginners—most beginners weren't losing track of their souls. I wondered if Elder Lopez had given me access to the database entries for the bronze core techniques. Maybe I could adapt one of them.

The realization didn't hit me until I was already halfway up the stairs to the third floor.

Spirits didn't get lost when they had something to come back to.

She'd said it as a slight, but maybe the elder's parting words had been *exactly* the instruction I'd sought. The last time I'd touched the void, I'd just lost my brother. I'd lost my life. I'd been alone on an unfamiliar ship with a soul I didn't know.

I wasn't alone any more.

I had Xavier and Charlotte to a certain extent, but above all I had Lucy. Nihilist crisis or otherwise, could I ever bring myself to abandon her like that? What about Brady or the others on roofie? I still owed it to them to make their lives matter.

I didn't head for the showers. I didn't change out of my dirty clothes or cleanse the lingering stench from my hair with the newly delivered specialty shampoo. The moment I returned to my room I sat cross legged on the floor next to the window and sunk into my center.

I reached out to the world around me. I looked past the deafening onslaught of the planet's qi, past the metal walls and glass window, into the vacuum beyond.

An endless ocean stretched out before me, calm to a mirror sheen that reflected no light, for here was the realm of darkness. The realm of stillness. The realm of naught.

My spirit knelt at the water's edge, at the brink of cold infinity, and lowered its head.

I drank long and deep from the infinite sea, my center swelling with qi until it spilled into my meridians. No wave came crashing down. No riptide bore me away.

I drifted not upon the currents of nothingness. I strayed not from the island of existence on which I sat. This time, I stayed put.

This time, I had something to come back for.

* * *

Elder Maria Lopez, one of six bronze core cultivators on all of Fyrion, third in command of The Dragon's Right Eye's local operations, kept her face a mask of cold neutrality as the outsider stepped from her office. A shiver ran down her spine as the door closed behind him.

That man was not human. Not anymore.

She'd bought the lie at first, believed he'd somehow learned a technique to mask his spirit before he'd even opened all his meridians. Looking back, the idea was absurd.

What legitimate reason could there be for a beginner to practice such complete stealth? Maria didn't know of a single member in the entire sect with such flawless shrouding. Even as it'd fought her probe of his meridians, she hadn't truly sensed his qi, only its resistance. At the time, she'd salivated at the idea of such a powerful technique that someone with as little control as the outlander could learn. Now, she realized the truth.

It wasn't a technique at all.

It was an enchantment.

Either the soulship or whichever out-system master she served had cast a spell over Cadet Rex's core. It was the only sensical theory. It explained the completeness of his shroud in contrast to his lack of skill, it explained why he refused to share the technique, and it even explained the venerable ancient's interest in him.

Caliban Rex wasn't here for training. Whoever'd masked his qi would've made a far better teacher than anyone on Fyrion. He was a science experiment. The soulship had clearly remained in orbit to observe and relay data. The question was, which data?

Maria had two direct clues, both of which pointed in the same direction.

Caliban Rex was dead.

His benefactor had masked his qi to hide the fact it *wasn't his*. Either the soulship or her master had imbued a corpse with qi in an attempt to reanimate it, but even the *cadets* on Fyrion would've noticed the foreign qi if they could actually sense it, so the out-system cultivators had hidden their necromantic work for the sake of their unholy experiment.

But something had gone wrong. Whichever spirit they'd bound to the corpse—be it its original soul or one transplanted—had grown loose. No cultivator at Rex's skill level could project their consciousness. He'd so desperately sought a spirit-anchoring technique because he'd *needed* one.

Maria shuddered.

A more scientific mind might've marveled at the achievement, might've thirsted to analyze the bindings and enchantments in place. A human mind quivered in fear.

If the walking corpse could use his master's qi, what stopped him from stealing qi from sect members? Worse yet, if Rex's spirit *did* wander free, his body would make the perfect host for demonic possession.

Maria froze. What if he'd already *been* possessed? What if the experiment wasn't to reanimate a corpse, but to unleash a demon on a helpless sect and see what happened?

"Call Elder Ber—" She stopped. "Cancel that." Her holopad closed.

She couldn't bring this to Berkowitz yet. The head elder would laugh her out of her office just before scolding her for daring to speak ill of their visiting ancient. She needed more information.

The abomination's arrival couldn't have been an independent event. Too much else was going on. In the past month alone, three passing freighters and an out-system refueling station had gone dark. Reports from the recovery crews should begin trickling in over the next couple of days. The corpse claimed to have been a vac-welder. He must've come from one of those freighters.

Two nearby stars had also disappeared from the night sky, but while each was close enough to warrant concern, neither could be reached within a decade's travel. They seemed unlikely to be related. Void beast attacks happened.

Maria sent out a message to each of Rex's instructors, requesting they report on any odd behavior they noted in him or the students around him. She sent a similar request to the mortal staff in his housing complex. If he so much as *looked* at a sect member threateningly, she wanted to know.

Surveillance in place and salvage info still pending, Maria could only wait. In the meantime, she'd continue to play the part of the dismissive elder. She couldn't let Rex or the soulship know she was on to them, but she couldn't in good conscience *help* the insult to nature. It was in the sect's best interests that Caliban Rex remain weak, unable to pose a threat until she could gather enough evidence to prove her theory.

He'd just have to think she resented his drain on resources, that she didn't care enough about his progression to offer help. It'd mean making concessions, of course, but she could still bleed him of as many resources as possible in exchange.

And she certainly wouldn't complain about a few extra focus room hours.

12

"Are you sure this is a good idea?"

"I never said it was a *good* idea," I answered over my shoulder as I reached into the shower to turn it on. "I said it's my only idea. We've been over this."

Xavier leaned against the back wall, fully clothed. "I don't know, newcomer. I'm not trained in spiritual triage."

"Xave, I've been here a week. You can stop calling me newcomer."

Much as I'd like to pretend I'd needed that time to properly prepare for opening my skin meridian or to build trust with Xavier, in truth I'd only waited so my focus room hours would refresh. I'd spent both of last week's, and I needed the capital.

"Until someone newer arrives, you're the newcomer," Xavier countered. "You should really use a focus room for this. They have medical staff on hand. What if you run out of qi?"

I grinned and glanced inward at my near-overflowing center. "That won't be a problem."

Xavier sighed. "Are you going to tell me *why* you seem to have an endless supply of qi?"

"I would if I knew," I answered. "You've noticed by

now my qi works differently from yours. People can't sense it; it slows my breath and heart rate rather than quickening them; it cools me down instead of warming me up. In a lot of ways, it's the inverse of yours. While yours energizes, mine calms. While yours heats, mine chills. Where yours is scarce…"

"Yours is plentiful," Xavier finished for me. "How do I get some?"

I let out a sigh. "You don't. I had exactly the right epiphany at exactly the right time in exactly the right place, and even then I had to get remarkably lucky to survive. It'd be impossibly dangerous to replicate even if you weren't already…"

"Already what?" Xavier asked as I trailed off. "Already a cultivator? You think only mortals can—" He cut off as realization blossomed on his face. "You *are* a corpse, aren't you?"

I scowled and looked down at myself. "I don't look dead."

"But you *feel* dead," Xavier said. "That's what it took, wasn't it? Exactly the right time was exactly when your natural qi left your body. Someone drained you and then filled you up with this weird inverted qi. Who? Was it the soulship?"

"I'll have you know I reanimated *myself*, thank you very much," I mocked offense. "Seriously, I got lucky. I got *very* lucky. And even if I knew they'd survive, I wouldn't wish what I went through on anyone."

Xavier raised an eyebrow. "For infinite qi? Seems like a good deal to me."

A cloud of steam hazed the bathroom air, the shower water very much hot enough to use, but I couldn't very well end the conversation there. What was a few extra minutes of wasted water on top of the hours I was about to spend opening a meridian?

I looked through the steam to meet Xavier's gaze. "Every single person I've known for more than a month is either dead or so far away they may as well be. I'm struggling to keep up with a class full of ten-year-olds, my instructors actively resent my presence, and my neighbors can't decide if I'm a worthless mortal or a dangerous foreigner. My life isn't exactly—"

"And you get panic attacks," Xavier interrupted.

"Panic attack," I corrected, "singular."

Xavier sighed. "My apologies. If you say this qi of yours wasn't worth the price, then it wasn't. Whatever happened to you is yours to keep or share. I won't press you to relive it."

"Thanks." I swallowed. "Remember our deal."

"An hour in a focus room for my supervision and silence," Xavier rattled off. "Your secret is safe."

Despite his tendency to shout things to the high heavens, I trusted Xavier. There was an earnest sincerity to the man I couldn't help but admire, even when it got obnoxious. Hell, when I first told him all this, he'd called me a perfect sidekick for *his* great ascension. The good news was, legendary heroes didn't rat out their friends, so sidekick or otherwise, I could depend on him.

I nodded my thanks and stepped into the shower, tossing my towel over the door as I did. I kept a pair of underwear on for Xavier's benefit, happy to ruin the garment to spare him the terror of seeing my pasty ass. Originally I'd thought to close the shower door, but that would've defeated the purpose. He couldn't sense what my qi was doing, so he'd have to watch my body.

I evened my breathing and sank into my center. A brimming pool of perfectly still, liquid qi greeted me. One by one I pulled strands from the reservoir, feeding them into each of my open meridians. My heart rate slowed. My body cooled. My breaths came deeper and more stable.

As Chrissy's exercises and details in the sect's database outlined, I crafted a needle and thread from a tiny fraction of the remaining qi and slowly pushed it into the qi pathway at the middle of my back.

Expected pain washed over me as my skin cried out against me. Ants crawled down my back. Flames licked at the soles of my feet. Ice bit at my fingertips. Needles danced up my chest. Every form of protest my skin could manage, it assaulted me with as the cleansing wreaked havoc upon it. I pressed on. I'd felt worse.

The pain ended at my skin, after all. It didn't threaten to kill me. It didn't shatter my focus. It itched something awful, but compared to heart failure, compared to a qi-infused bone through my blood meridian, this was nothing.

No wonder they gave this meridian to the kids.

I was about two thirds of the way through bolstering the qi flow, deep in cultivation, all sorts of nasty gunk oozing from my pores, when an unfamiliar voice drifted into my awareness.

"What's going on?" the voice asked. It sounded boyish and full of false confidence, a combination that screamed *teenager* in my head.

"We're just—" Xavier tried to explain.

"Is he *opening a meridian*?" the teen cut him off. "In the showers? Threads, are you insane?"

Oh, that reminds me. Holy *fuck* did the cultivator world need my help. Not one of them had the faintest idea of how to swear. Threads? Seriously? *Threads*? Amateurs.

"Who are you?" Xavier asked.

"I'm Nick Vesper. I... joined the sect yesterday."

"A newcomer!" I didn't *see* it, but Xavier slapped the kid's back loud enough for me to hear. "Welcome! Remind me to challenge you to a duel as soon as we're done here."

Nick audibly gulped. "I should go get—"

"Nonsense! You clearly came to take a shower. You should shower."

I tuned their conversation out once I knew Xavier had no intention of letting the kid leave. I'd have to talk to him once I finished, but I could worry about that later. I couldn't stop now.

I pushed and I pushed, cycling faster and faster until the last of the impurities oozed out and the qi flowed freely. I don't know for sure how long it took, but I knew my watchers had been paying attention, because the moment my qi ran through an open skin meridian, the kid's voice echoed through the bathroom.

"Threads, is he okay?"

"I'm *fine*." My eyes shot open to find Xavier and a sixteen-year-old boy with curly, sandy blond hair both kneeling in front of me.

Nick gaped. "You look like a corpse."

"So people keep telling me."

"Not feel," Xavier said, "*look*."

I looked down at myself, still cycling qi through my newly opened meridian. Sure enough, my skin had gone deathly pale, nearing blue in some places.

Xavier touched my arm. "You're cold."

I scowled. "I'm sitting under a stream of hot water."

Xavier nodded. "And you're *cold*. Like a corpse."

"I'm pretty sure even corpses get warm when you run hot water over them."

"So you're more corpse-like than a corpse?" Xavier asked.

"A hyper-corpse," Nick added, as if that made any sense at all.

"What I am is fine," I said, standing up and ceasing my cycling. Before my eyes, color returned to my skin. "Guess

I'll need to be careful about cycling that one in public." I stretched my neck. "Unless I want to scare the shit out of someone, I guess."

Unable to get to my back from his position in front of me, Xavier slapped my shoulder. "A haunting visage indeed!"

Nick's eyes flashed frantically between me and Xavier. "You're just... okay with this? His meridian clearly didn't open correctly. He needs *help*."

"I'm Cal, by the way," I introduced myself, hoping to defuse the tension.

"N-Nick."

"Well, Nick, what I need is for you not to tell anyone what you've seen here. We're not breaking any rules—I checked—and I'm very clearly *alive*, but you're about to start the kind of rumor people don't easily escape."

"But I have to—"

I sighed. "I'll give you a focus room hour."

That got his attention. His eyes shot open as he sputtered for a few moments before managing a coherent, "Really?"

"Really. All you have to do is keep your mouth shut. If I don't get in any trouble, maybe there'll be more hours coming your way down the line, but that doesn't happen if I get kicked out of the sect, got it?"

I've never seen a man nod so furiously. "I got it."

I smiled at him. "Good. Now, if you two don't mind, I've got a meridian's worth of gunk to clean off and only an hour until dinner."

Nick skedaddled promptly, apparently forgetting the shower he'd originally intended to take. I understood. I wouldn't want to spend time in a bathroom that smelled like this one did either.

Xavier paused to flash me one more concerned look but didn't comment before he too took his leave, no doubt to track down and challenge Nick to a duel.

I shut the door behind him and showered in peace.

Nick's appearance had been unfortunate. I could handle losing my status as the third floor's only resident, but I hated having to bribe the kid. They'd only just refreshed and already I'd run out of focus room hours for the week. That meant if I needed information from Charlotte or instruction from Elder Lopez, I'd have to wait.

I resolved to talk to him later. I'd have an easier time trusting Nick if I got to know him, and even if he managed to escape the qi-sparse third floor, for the time being I had unique access to the sect's newest member. Maybe I could swoop in and make a friend before this place's cutthroat nature took hold.

My thoughts wandered on to my next problem as I lathered and re-lathered my hair with the specialty shampoo.

Cycling my skin meridian made me look like a corpse. Logically, I understood why it might lighten and cool my skin. Normal qi made people's skin warmer and brighter, of course mine made me pallid and cold. I just hadn't necessarily realized what *else* looked pallid and cold.

The only place I imagined it could be a problem was cycling class. I supposed I could practice the cycling methods that involved the skin meridian on my own time, and spend Chrissy's class working on other meridians, but I'd still have to cycle in front of her to advance to the next class. I let out a breath. I'd cross that bridge when I came to it.

I wrapped myself in my towel for the walk back to my room, tossing my ruined underwear into the garbage chute on the way. Moments later I emerged fully dressed and smelling faintly of lavender, an entire eight minutes early for dinner.

I opted to spend those extra minutes chatting with the

other friend I hoped to make—the mortal that manned the reception desk.

"Arthur!" I greeted him, leaning comfortably with an elbow on his chest-high circular desk. "I didn't know we had a new resident."

"My apologies, sir—Cal," he corrected himself. "I assumed you knew. I thought you and Cadet Honchel went upstairs together to challenge him as Cadet Honchel does all new recruits."

"Don't worry about it. I-uh-shouldn't have assumed privacy in that bathroom."

Arthur nodded. "If you and Cadet Honchel require privacy, it can only be guaranteed in his or your quarters."

"If we... what?" I scowled. "No. *No.* It's not like that. I'm not... Xavier isn't... actually, he might be. I wouldn't know. Wait, nevermind. Pretty sure the only thing Xavier's attracted to is himself. Don't worry. We're not—"

"It's alright, Cal." Arthur smiled warmly. "I know cultivation makes emotions run hot. You don't have to explain yourself."

"Right, but we're not—" I sighed. "You're not going to believe anything I say here, are you?"

"I wouldn't dare accuse a sect member of lying," Arthur said, his voice calm and political but his eyes gleaming with mischief.

I exhaled. There'd be no winning this conversation, so I opted not to play. "What can you tell me about the new arrival?"

"I know he's younger than most when they first join. That could work in his favor or it could isolate him. Whether or not he makes any friends will depend on how charismatic he is and how fast he progresses. He could thrive, he could flounder."

"That... is really useful insight. Thanks, Arthur. How come nobody else presses you for information?"

"Most cultivators assume they know better," he explained. "And those that don't wouldn't be caught dead spending time with a mortal."

"Eh, fuck those guys," I said.

Arthur let out a soft laugh before he caught himself and scowled at me.

I grinned. "Everyone's way too serious around here. Someone should do something about that."

Arthur paled. "Please don't."

I laughed, full and boisterous in contrast to his stifled chuckle. "Don't worry; I've got more important things to worry about than a critical humor deficiency." I let out a breath. "Like dinner! Dinner is more important. Take care, Arthur. Try laughing sometime!"

"Enjoy your meal, Cal. And don't worry." He winked at me. Seriously, he fucking *winked*. "Your secret's safe with me."

I groaned as I walked away. A benefit I hadn't realized I'd enjoyed back on roofie was that if your best friend was your brother, nobody accused you of boinking each other. I'd been here a week and already somebody had seen me and Xavier sneak into a bathroom together.

At least *that* rumor was ultimately harmless. I wouldn't have to hand out more focus room hours to keep Arthur quiet. On the grand scale of things, I figured 'people think you're fucking your friend' and 'people think you're a walking corpse' didn't really compare. The latter would've probably ended in me leaving the sect, while worst case the former made it a bit harder to ask women out.

I could live with that. Like I said, more important things to worry about.

All in all, I headed to dinner with my head held high. It'd been a productive day. Classes aside, I was down two focus room hours and up an opened meridian and a potential friend. I counted that as a win.

I found Xavier in the mess hall at our usual spot—which was really *Charlotte's* usual spot, at which she tolerated our presence. She'd been slow warming up to us, but progress *had* been made. Apparently even the daughter of the sect's savior was susceptible to bribery. Still, she let out a quiet breath as I sat across from her.

Moments later, a fourth tray landed on our table. I looked up to find a certain fresh-faced teenager standing over it.

"Can I, um…" Nick stammered. "Can I sit here?"

13

I learned more about my budding friend group over the course of that one dinner than in the entire prior week. I don't know if I'd reached some threshold of trust with Xavier or if Nick just had a talent for getting people to talk about themselves, but talk they did.

Apparently, once a cycle—the three-ish years it takes for The Dueling Stars to complete a single revolution around each other—the Dragon's Right Eye and the Dragon's Left Eye competed in some major tournament to determine who gets control of Ilirian, the system's only habitable world.

At the age of eight, Xavier had decided he was going to win that tournament.

It explained everything. It explained why he wanted to duel everybody; it explained why he trained so hard; it even explained why he introduced himself as the 'future champion of the Dragon's Right Eye.' His parents, both of which lived and cultivated here on Fyrion, had never dared shatter his dream, even if they knew how impossible it'd be for a nobody on the sect's weakest outpost to make it to tungsten, the cultivation level of the last several champions.

For his part, Xavier seemed to genuinely believe he could do it. He had no delusions about how long it would take or how easy it would be, but he'd decided on his goal and by the threads he was going to achieve it.

I couldn't help but root for him. Even with his tendencies for over-honesty and overconfidence, there was an earnestness to Xavier I deeply respected. He genuinely enjoyed things in a way I envied, and the pitfalls of his low ranking or regular defeats in the ring barely phased him. Xavier had a clear goal and a path towards it, disadvantages and complications be damned.

Nick, in contrast, seemed as if he didn't want to be there. Unlike Xavier, as one of the youngest in the sect's history to form a core and achieve full membership, Nick had an obviously bright future. The kid smacked of promise, enough that *he* probably wouldn't have much difficulty finding a spot on a better settlement than Fyrion.

Shit, Charlotte even warned the lad against hanging around with the likes of us, declaring the damage to his reputation too great for someone with so much to lose. He didn't leave.

Nick apparently wanted nothing more than to work on his parents' herb farm, a job that didn't require cultivation skill much beyond what he'd already achieved. His parents had disagreed, forcing the teen to stay with the sect and focus on cultivation until he turned eighteen.

Charlotte took offense at his outlook. She claimed he owed it to his family and to himself to pursue his obvious potential as a cultivator. Xavier asserted the opposite, arguing that Nick and Nick alone got to decide what mattered to him.

I spent the entire conversation thinking about Lucy's empty garden and how much I'd wanted to recruit a crew member who knew how to work with spiritual herbs. Nick was almost too perfect.

As we moved on to dessert, I brought the topic back around to future plans, particularly where it pertained to the three of them.

I had three friends and only two focus hours each week. The solution I decided on, which they each agreed to in turn, involved a set rotation. Charlotte, Xavier, and Nick would take turns taking any spare focus room hours from me. I guaranteed them at least one per week, with the second going to whomever was next in the rotation if I didn't need it to bargain for something.

The plan had a number of benefits. The extra hours in the qi-dense rooms would accelerate their growth, helping them keep pace with mine, while also incentivizing them to remain friends with me. None of them would betray me or my secrets if it meant slowing their own cultivation.

Given the content of the conversation, then, it came as no surprise when once Xavier and Nick had adjourned to go fight their duel, Charlotte leaned over the table and whispered, "I want to know."

I blinked. "Could you be more specific?"

"Why can't anyone sense your qi? Why are you giving away your focus room hours? Why don't you care about being stuck on the third floor?"

I exhaled. "Ah. *That*."

"Xavier knows," Charlotte said plainly. "I'd wager Nick knows something too. That just leaves me."

"I trust Xavier, and Nick knows more than he should and less than *you* want."

Charlotte let out a breath. "I'm not going to say you can trust me because those words don't mean anything, but you *can* trust that I wouldn't jeopardize my focus room hours for anything. You *can* trust that I'm going to find the truth one way or another. I just want to save myself the trouble of looking into you and you the trouble of trying to hide from me."

I let my eyes lock with hers for a few tense moments before casting my gaze around in all directions. I caught two different cultivators and a staff member with a mop all looking at me.

"Not here," I said. "Too many prying eyes."

Charlotte nodded.

We left the dining hall together, walking in silence back to the lobby and up the stairs to the third floor. As we mounted the steps, I stood ambiguously close to her, pausing to flash a smug wink over my shoulder at Arthur.

If he was going to think I was boinking my friends anyway, I figured he may as well think I was boinking *all* of my friends.

Charlotte noticed the gesture. "What was that about?"

"Oh, I'm just fucking with Arthur."

She paled a little bit less over my use of profanity this time. Progress! "The receptionist?"

"Yep," I whispered back. "He's got it into his mind I'm sleeping with Xavier, so I figured I'd throw him a curveball."

Charlotte didn't even falter. "Put your arm on my back. It'll sell it better."

Now *this* I could work with. It was brilliant really. I just had to redirect Charlotte's manipulative nature *away* from progressing her own agenda and *towards* just screwing around with people. Why befriend a scheming manipulator when I could befriend the ultimate prankster?

I shoved aside ideas of slipping hair dye into Instructor Long's shampoo to focus on the matter at hand as we crested the steps and slipped into my dorm room together.

The moment the door closed behind us, Charlotte stepped away and spun on me. "I want the truth."

"All business then, got it. Basically, I don't use the same qi you do." I explained it all, well, almost all. I left out the bits about roofie and Cedric and Lucy, cutting straight to the part about the vast reservoir of dark qi that seemed incompatible with the qi in all living beings.

Charlotte didn't question me. She didn't ask how I'd found it or if it could be replicated. She didn't accuse me of being a walking corpse. She didn't even comment on the sheer stupidity of opening meridians in the third-floor showers. When at last I finished my tale, she spoke exactly two words.

"I'm in."

I blinked. "What?"

"This plan, this secret, this conspiracy," she explained without really explaining, "I'm in."

"I repeat. What?"

Charlotte let out a long breath. "You've discovered something revolutionary, at least revolutionary as far as anyone in this system is concerned. You know what's out there better than I do. Anyway, you're right to keep it secret, and you're right to hide your progress. The elders would view you as a threat. Your plan is obviously to build a small group of people you can trust, give them focus hours so they keep up with you and feel indebted to you, and use them to help keep your secret. I'm in."

"Oh." That was easy.

"You're uncouth, you're inexperienced, and worst of all you're naive, but if what you just told me is true, and I'd wager it is, you're going places most cultivators can only dream of. I'll do whatever it takes to come along for the ride."

I raised an eyebrow. "Does that include trusting me?"

The corners of Charlotte's mouth tilted up into a slight grin as she moved for the door. "Let's not get ahead of ourselves."

With that she left, stepping past me into the hall before disappearing down the stairs. I watched her go, mind racing to try and figure out her angle. I came up blank.

I was still standing there, watching the steps when Nick's face peaked above them, a dark spot under his left eye. I flashed him a halfhearted grin. "Duel went well, then?"

Nick grumbled indecipherably at me.

"Yeah, me too," I replied as if he'd just made some interesting point.

I let him shuffle off down the hall and disappear into room three-eleven, taking note of his residence. It'd been nice of Arthur, I supposed, not to make Nick and I share a wall. Gods knew how loud the teenager snored.

I adjourned to my own sparse bedroom and called up Lucy for our nightly chat. True to form, she took immediate interest in Nick's wellbeing, forcing a promise from me that I'd look after him. I gave it freely.

When at last the comms went quiet, I went about my nightly routine of lying in bed and opening my spiritual senses to the qi around me. With every evening I grew more resilient to the qi's noise and heat, though even now, a week in, I still came away with a headache.

My last act before bed, without fail, was to push my senses just far enough to touch the infinite sea. It, too, I had to grow more comfortable with, and rather than a throbbing headache or racing heart, it left me with a calm spirit and clear head. Both ushered me to sleep.

I dreamt that night, as I'd found myself doing frequently, of Cedric. He'd look at me pleading with blue or gold or green eyes, whichever they'd been before the void-induced psychosis had turned them black. I never knew what he wanted from me, but there was always a desperation to his face, never the hunger or the cruelty or the muscle spasms that'd been there the only time I'd seen him.

I wrote it off as trauma. Threads knew I had enough to explain a few weird dreams.

The following morning, twin suns dawned on my first real day off on Fyrion.

On the subject of days off, and just *days*, for that matter, individual systems all had their own time measurements based on the local celestial movements.   I've already mentioned cycles in The Dueling Star system, for example. If you live in deep space or do much traveling between systems, though, local measurements fall apart, so we use circadian time. As a spacer myself, I still think in terms of that universal standard—twenty-four hour days, seven-day weeks, twenty-eight-day months, twelve-month years.

Since days on Fyrion technically only lasted eleven hours, we measured our days there in circadian time, existing almost completely out of sync with the rising and setting of the binary suns. Months and years, in contrast, held no meaning at all to the Dragon's Right Eye. They didn't care about the former, and preferred the aforementioned cycles to the latter.

All this to say, we got one day off a week, but every seventh week we had to spend that day fighting pre-scheduled duels. It bugged me to no end that they refused to make it every two months, so now I'm going to bug you with that little tidbit of uselessly frustrating information. Enjoy.

Anyway, I still had a few weeks before I had to step into the ring again, so after my morning workout and a breakfast shared with my three co-conspirators, I found myself playing ping pong with Arthur in the staff break room.

He spoke as he served. "You didn't sleep with either of them, did you?"

My paddle missed the ball entirely.

Arthur grinned. "Seven-two."

I chased the ball into the corner behind me. "How'd you figure it out?"

"I've been working this job for three cycles now. You think I don't know what's going on under my own roof?"

I tossed him back the ball. "She told you."

"I guess she'd rather screw with you than with me." Arthur served.

I managed to actually hit the ball back this time, but he returned it with the speed and ferocity of a hypersonic missile.

"Eight-two," Arthur chimed as I spun to chase after the ball once more.

Okay maybe I wasn't so great at ping pong. In my defense, I came from interstellar freight followed by a refueling station, neither of which had the square footage to spare for ping pong. Arthur'd been playing this very same table for the better part of a decade. Sure, I could start cycling and absolutely wipe the floor with him, but where's the fun in that?

"So I guess I don't have to try and trick you into thinking I'm boinking Nick, then." I served.

Arthur volleyed back. "I'd report you if you did. Nick's a minor."

I hit back at a hard angle. "You're right. That wouldn't be very funny."

He caught the angled shot with an easy backhand. "Is that really all you care about? Whatever's funniest?"

The ball slowed as I popped it up. "Would I be here if it was?"

Arthur tapped it back gently. "Here in the sect? No. Here in the staff room of housing D? Probably. From what I gather, you aren't even trying to get a lower room."

"I like it here. I think I'll stay until I outgrow Fyrion." I spiked the ball.

Arthur lunged for it, lobbing it up for me. "Outgrow Fyrion? From the bottom of the rankings? Ambitious, aren't we?"

"Don't worry. There's a method to my madness." I smacked the ball down. It slipped past Arthur's guard. "Three-eight."

"Is that why you're down here with me instead of spending your off-day doing something productive?"

I smiled and served. "Making friends *is* productive."

Arthur tapped it back. "Most cultivators prefer friends with actual influence."

I had to lean hard into the table to catch the ball and pop it back over. "You said yourself, you know what's going on under your own roof."

"So you want something from me." He smacked it hard, and the ball slammed into my side of the table and off into the back wall. "Nine-three. Game point."

I smiled sheepishly as I chased after the ball. "Let's say I wanted to bring some ice cream to the kids in my class. How would I go about doing that?"

Arthur blinked. "That's it? I'll do you one better. I'll introduce you to—"

I served hard and sharp while he was mid-sentence. He returned it flawlessly, rocketing off my side of the table.

Arthur flashed a wolfish grin. "Ten-three. Good game. As I was saying, I'll introduce you to Mindy."

"Who's Mindy?"

"Your new favorite person. Mindy's entire job is to deal with all the elders' special requests, at least the ones the mortal staff can handle. Means she has wide power to get shit done, and spends all day bored out of her mind until it's time to organize a four-course banquet on one hour's notice."

"That sounds stressful."

"Remarkably. But she's *usually* bored enough that she'll do pretty much any favor as long as you ask her nicely. Ice cream for a bunch of kids? That'll be the easiest phone call of her life."

"I'm sold. Where is she?"

Arthur shrugged. "Nobody ever knows where Mindy is. You don't find her. You call her." He raised his left arm and typed away at his holopad for a moment. Seconds later, a voice echoed through the room.

"What do you want?" Mindy sounded strangely relaxed for the abrasiveness of her words.

"Mindy! It's Arthur. I have someone I want you to meet."

A feminine moan came over the comms. "Excuse me," Mindy said, completely unabashed. "I'm trying out a new masseuse for Elder Berkowitz. She's *good*."

I glanced at Arthur. She certainly didn't *seem* stressed. Perks of the job, huh? "Mindy, I'm Cal. It's nice to meet you. I was hoping you could help me bring some ice cream to a class full of kids."

"Easy enough. When, where, and how many?"

"There's thirty kids. Any day's fine. I just need a portable freezer or cooler or something to keep the ice cream cold. I can pick it up and drop it off from wherever, as long as you let me kno—"

"It's done." Mindy said.

"Thanks, I really appreciate it. Just let me know where I shou—"

"A stocked cart'll be waiting for you by Arthur's desk tomorrow morning. Anything else?"

"Um… no. That's all. Thank you! The kids will really appreciate it."

"I'm sure they will. Don't give them my name. Nice to meet you, Cal. Next time, call me from your own holo. Goodbye Arthur!"

The line went dead before Arthur had a chance to reply. "So… that's Mindy."

"She… seems like she leads an *interesting* life."

Arthur laughed. "That's one way of putting it."

"So will we know when the ice cream is all set up?"

"Oh, it already is."

I blinked. "It what?"

"When Mindy says it's done, it's done. She probably typed out a message on her holopad while you were talking."

"Damn. She's good."

"You wanted one thing with an entire day's notice. On the Mindy-adjusted scale, you may as well have asked her to keep breathing."

A message beeped on my holopad confirming it'd logged Mindy's number. "I'll keep that in mind."

"So." Arthur cocked an eyebrow at me. "Ice cream for kids? Doesn't sound funny *or* productive."

"No, it's *nice*. Turns out I'm capable of more than just productivity and bad jokes. Who'd have thought?"

Arthur sighed. "If you were any other cultivator—if *I* were a cultivator—I'd accuse you of playing some angle."

"Good thing I'm not any other cultivator." I grinned and held up the ping pong ball, ready to serve. "Best two out of three?"

* * *

To be clear, I did *not* spend my entire day off playing ping pong. That came *after* I sat alone in a room for eight hours with a marginally declining headache from all the qi screaming in my ear. I *was* technically making progress, just not the kind of blazing, immediate progress I so preferred.

Anyway, true to Mindy's word, I returned from my workout the next morning to find a rectangular object obscured under a brown woolen blanket next to Arthur's desk. After bidding him good morning, I asked the obvious question.

"What's with the blanket?"

"You wanted it to be a surprise, right?"

"Right. Good point." I peeked underneath to find a simple battery-powered steel freezer on a set of wheels. At over four feet long, the thing was absolutely massive for the three-dozen ice cream bars inside, but I'd work. "Mindy's used to feeding more than thirty people, huh?"

"You don't want to know what kinds of things she's had to transport on ice."

I opened the freezer and stuck my nose in. "Smells fine to me."

"You *also* don't want to know what kinds of cleaning products she has access to."

I yanked my head out from under the blanket. "Don't ask questions. Got it."

I bid Arthur my thanks and set off for class, receiving my fair share of questioning looks as I wheeled the covered freezer in front of me.

I stashed it in the corner for meditation class. The kids kept glancing at it and whispering amongst themselves, but none dared peek within, and nobody willing enough to violate my excommunication asked me about it.

At the end of the three-hour class—in which, as it happened, I finally managed to keep my focus through one of Instructor Park's harder strikes—I gave the kids some time to eat their lunches before I made my move. Without immediately calling attention to myself, I slowly and deliberately pushed the covered cart into the center of the room. The slight squeak of the front left wheel slowly drew in more and more eyes as I approached, the children quieting one by one as their curiosity took hold.

By the time I came to a stop, silence had claimed the room.

"Hey everyone," I addressed my audience. "I think we may've gotten off on the wrong foot. I'm... newer to this cultivation thing than all of you, and I realize that means your instructors have had to pay me some extra attention.

I'm really sorry for that. I'm working really hard to catch up and pass out of your class so I can get out of your way, but that'll take a few months. In the meantime, I'd rather be friends."

"So." I clapped my hands together for dramatic effect. "As my way of saying thanks for putting up with me, I present to you... ice cream!" I whipped the blanket away with a great swoosh, the brown wool rippling through the air theatrically as I revealed the freezer beneath.

The classroom went silent.

"He's trying to bribe us," one boy said. "Don't listen to him!"

Damn, these kids were smart.

"We can still eat it," a girl countered. "We don't have to like him to have ice cream."

Yet a third child didn't speak at all, simply jumping to his feet and running up to the freezer cart. I wordlessly handed him an ice cream bar.

That opened the floodgates.

I spent the next five minutes frantically distributing frozen treats while simultaneously fending off the greedy little bastards who kept trying to slip in for seconds. The kids that actually looked at me did so with all sorts of facial expressions ranging from exaggerated anger to grudging acceptance to outright joy. I may not have won them all, but I'd won *some*. That was progress.

I'd finally finished distribution and begun unwrapping a bar of my own when a voice echoed from the doorway. "Ice cream, huh? Got any for me?"

I smiled up at Chrissy. "Only if you behave extra well for your cycling instructor."

She laughed and approached the cart. "I guess we'll have to work on our stomach meridians today, focus on processing all this sugar."

I grinned back at her. "Teach on."

True to her word, Chrissy led the class through a number of exercises for the one beginner meridian I *hadn't* opened. I still found plenty of opportunity to be productive, working through a few more complicated techniques I'd found on the sect's local network that could utilize my heart, lungs, and blood a bit more.

The moment her class time ended and Chrissy left the room, the kids swarmed the cart once more, ready to fight for the five leftover ice cream bars. I put an end to that, tying the brown blanket around my neck like a cape and declaring myself the grand defender of the ice cream.

We walked to combat class together, a giant mass of children crowding around me arguing why *they* should be the one to get seconds. I let them. At least they were talking to me.

That is, they *were* talking to me, when halfway down a long, windowed hallway, Lucy's voice blared from my holopad.

"Cal! Get to shelter. Get to shelter right now. I'm holding off as many as I can, but—"

The line went dead. The lights flickered and died. Red emergency lights flared up in their place. A siren screeched.

I stood there, frozen, surrounded by children, with a blanket-cape trailing along the floor behind me and a freezer cart ahead, when an announcement filled the hallway from a speaker in the ceiling.

"Please remain calm. A void horde has descended upon Fyrion. Please remain calm. Make your way to your nearest emergency bunker. Please remain calm."

In my defense, I managed to remain startlingly calm as I did the one thing you're not supposed to do when you get that kind of news while surrounded by children. At least I kept my voice low. I swear, none of them even heard me over the siren.

"Aw, fuck."

14

Void beasts come in all shapes and sizes with a few unifying characteristics. As the name would imply, they can all survive in a hard vacuum. They're all black as the infinite night, often visible to the naked eye only as a splotch of starless sky. Finally, they're all blind. They can sense qi and they can sense heat—two far more useful senses in deep space—but the visual world remains off limits to them.

That's where the rules end. Some void beasts travel in hordes, frantically devouring any source of qi they can find. Others float alone, massive leviathans that happily feed on whatever radiation comes their way. Yet others will drift in from whichever corner of the abyss they originate and conquer an entire system, swarming the local star and anything in orbit, eating and reproducing until there are so many of them that some number break off into a swarm of their own.

Every once in a while, a star somewhere in the galaxy will go dark, no supernova, no black hole, just darkness. *Usually*, a void beast colony is responsible.

That a void horde would come for Fyrion at all was a bit of an anomaly. Whichever mind controlled it would've had to have been smart enough to realize it couldn't overcome the cultivators in the inner system, yet stupid enough not to realize said cultivators would come for it the moment it attacked Fyrion. It was either some kind of weird fluke, or there was more going on than I realized.

Of course, at the moment, I thought about absolutely none of this. My thoughts ran more along the lines of, *shit shit shit, we have to get out of here.*

Calmly, of course. The nice voice in the ceiling *had* told us to remain calm, after all.

I realized then that all thirty of the kids were looking at me. Threads damn it. Why did *I* have to be the adult? Just because I had a cape on didn't make me a superhero. Welp, needs must.

"Take me to the nearest bunker!" I all but shouted at my holopad, glancing at the map that popped up and swiping audio navigation on. "Everyone, let's go!"

My stampede of children led the way, sprinting as fast as their short legs could carry them while I took up the rear. I cycled my heart, lung, and blood meridians as we moved, forcing my heart rate and breathing to keep calm and even. That alone staved off the worst of the panic, though I won't pretend I was thinking entirely clearly.

For instance, I kept pushing the fucking freezer cart. By all rights I should've abandoned it. Last I'd checked, ice cream was only of marginal utility in life or death crises, but at the quick jogging pace my young charges limited me to, the freezer didn't slow me down enough for my mind to even consider the idea.

My holopad beeped a direction at me and I echoed it to the children ahead. "Left at the fork!"

Only a handful of them made it out of the hallway before the window shattered.

It took a few moments for my eyes to make out the details of the jet black shape that burst through as the station's qi shields flickered to life to limit the loss of atmosphere. The thing was roughly the size and shape of a large dog, but wrong in every sense of the word. Its six legs bent in opposing directions, adding a weird twisting motion to its steps. Spiny chitin coated its torso, the bulk of its body scarcely wider than my neck yet three times as tall.

Rather than a canine snout or insectile mandibles, a three-pronged beak sprouted from its mouth, the right and left sides hooking up and the center hooking down. The simple act of this thing closing its beak over something would tear it apart.

It took a few moments for my eyes to make out the details of the void beast that burst through the window, but under a second to note that instead of feet, its limbs ended in sharp points.

One of which pierced a familiar child through the belly.

"Vihaan!"

I didn't think. I didn't plan. I didn't hesitate. I charged for the thing as it lowered its beaks for the kindhearted child, as drool dripped from its maw onto his face.

I would've preferred if my history of heroic acts had begun with the discovery of my signature technique, if I'd drawn a legendary sword and cleanly separated the thing's head from its body in a move with some bullshit name like The Meteor That Flies Across The Heavens. If only the void horde had waited until I'd gotten that far.

Instead, I rammed it with the ice cream cart.

Stainless steel met ebony chitin with a sickening crunch. Black blood dripped to the floor as the collision knocked the beast back, ripping its pointed leg from Vihaan's stomach and bowling it over. I pulled back and slammed the freezer into it once more, crushing its narrow torso and the organs within. I stomped the side of its head for good measure, caving in its brittle exoskeleton and shredding the gray matter in its fragments.

I fell to my knees over Vihaan. His eyes were still open, his face contorted in pain. I grabbed his arms and pressed his hands down onto his open wound. "I need you to press down on this. Can you do that?"

He gritted his teeth and nodded.

"Good, good. Okay. This is going to suck, but I have to take you to safety. Ready? And up." I heaved as I lifted him, cradling him in my arms like an infant as he held his injury closed as best he could. I stood and turned to the other children to find them gawking at me.

"We need to move! Left at the fork!" I shouted at them.

They listened.

Together we ran, a chaotic mess of kids swarming around me as I carried Vihaan through the halls of Fyrion. I called out directions as they came up, my eyes flitting up to the path ahead and back down to the child in my arms.

We'd taken a half dozen twists and turns before I realized three of the kids had banded together to bring the freezer cart along. I let them. It didn't seem to be slowing them down, and any amount of comfort it could bring to the kids would be worth it. The last thing I needed right now was an argument over leaving the ice cream behind.

My qi-cooled heart lifted as the bunker finally came into view. It sank again as three windows shattered in sequence behind us. "Faster!"

My imperfect focus slipped. Adrenaline took hold. My breathing quickened. My heartbeat sped. My hands shook.

The void beasts gave chase.

The six-inch steel door slid open at our approach. I stopped just outside, ushering the kids inside and yelling at them to hurry. Five of the vaguely dog-shaped monstrosities bore down on us, their pointed feet digging into and scraping against the linoleum floor. "Hurry up!" I shouted. "Inside, inside, inside!"

Vihaan and I were the last ones in.

"Close the door!" I called to my holopad, the kids, the door controls, the gods, anyone, really. I don't know which listened, but the bunker door slammed shut behind us. I didn't even have time to exhale before *something* crashed into the other side, scratching and clawing against it powerfully enough to echo past six inches of solid steel.

We held our collective breaths for tense seconds until the void beasts finally gave up and moved on. I exhaled, relief flooding me for the few seconds I could spare. We'd made it.

I spun away from the door to survey our surroundings. They weren't promising.

Apparently, our nearest emergency bunker spent ninety nine point nine percent of its time as an oversized broom closet. Mop buckets and cleaning supplies lined the walls. The only bunker-like aspect to it was the toilet in the back, wide sink, miniature qi stove, and cupboard full of basic rations and supplies. It was to that last I sent two of the children to search for a first aid kit.

"Make room." I gestured with my head for the crowd of kids to back off and clear some floorspace, upon which I stretched the blanket with my foot and deposited Vihaan. I paused to untie the knot around my neck to allow my former cape to lie flat before I leaned in. "How're you doing?"

Vihaan looked up at me with red eyes. "It hurts."

"I know it does, buddy. You're doing great. Just stay with me, okay? I need to take a look at your injury."

He nodded weakly.

I gently lifted his hand and lowered my nose to the puncture wound in his lower abdomen. It smelled foul.

"Shit," I cursed, letting the unintentional pun go unnoticed as I pushed Vihaan's hand back onto the injury.

"It's pierced your bowel." I looked up. "Where's that first aid kit?"

A woefully small tin box landed at my side. Inside I found some bandages, a packet of med gel, a bottle of isopropyl alcohol, and a few doses of various medications. I cursed again.

I couldn't seal up Vihaan's wound without addressing the hole in his bowel, yet I had neither the equipment nor the training to do that. Even if I *could've* muddled through it, the act of moving him from that hallway would've shifted the damaged bowel away from the entry wound. I'd have to root around inside him to find it again.

That wasn't happening.

I found a single-dose morphine syringe in the first aid box and injected a quarter of it just above the wound. It wouldn't be enough to fully remove the pain, but I didn't dare give the kid any more. I knew jack shit about narcotics dosing for minors, and with the local net down I had no way of looking up how much was safe to administer.

Next, I grabbed the alcohol and emptied the small bottle into the wound. Vihaan gasped and writhed and cried out, and I knew you couldn't disinfect a perforated bowel, but I prayed it would buy me a bit of time before the sepsis took hold.

"Is there an emergency phone in here?" I called out to the uninjured kids.

They responded with blank stares.

"A hardwired comm terminal?" I tried. "Something that would work with the network down?"

Still nothing. A few of them even shrugged.

I sighed and scanned the walls myself, searching through the painfully fluorescent light for anything that looked remotely like a way to call for help.

I came up empty.

"Okay. Shit. Um…" I trailed off. I was going to have to move him. With no way to call for help, I couldn't trust that anyone would find us anytime soon. Vihaan needed medical attention now—*trained* medical attention.

An idea struck.

"Nicki!" My eyes shot up to one of the kids whose name I knew. "There's a switch on the underside of the freezer. I need you to turn it off and take all the ice cream out. Can you do that?"

She didn't answer, simply darting right for the cart and feeling around the underside for the off switch. Unbidden, three others ran to help empty it.

As they worked I stuffed the wound with synthetic cotton and wrapped it with gauze to stop the bleeding, instructing Vihaan to maintain pressure.

"You still with me, buddy?"

He nodded.

"Good. Good. You're doing great. So great. Okay. I'm going to get you out of here, take you to a doctor. I need you to keep a hold of your qi. Don't cycle. Don't cultivate. Just hold it in as tightly as you can. Don't let any leak out. Can you do that?"

He flashed a frightened look.

"Okay. Just try your best, alright?" Ideally I would've had him cycle his blood meridian to reinforce his body against infection, but the class hadn't gotten that far. He'd have to depend on his natural defenses and hope to minimize the detectible qi he gave off.

Vihaan nodded.

"Perfect. Excellent. Vihaan, you're a wonder. Alright, I'll be right back." I leapt to my feet and walked over to the freezer, snatching the leftover ice cream off the ground much to the kids' chagrin. I knelt down to find the refrigeration unit at the bottom and held a hand over it. Sure enough, it still radiated heat. I iced it down with the half empty box of ice cream bars, melting the delicious treat for the sake of ridding the freezer's exterior of the last of its warmth.

Next I reviewed the map of Fyrion I'd thankfully cached on my holopad. Without comms I had no way of knowing how much of the station had been overcome, but I couldn't just wander randomly. I didn't trust that the transport network would still be running, so I threw together a hasty list of potential holdouts within walking distance.

Far and away the most likely candidate was Family Housing B, where sect members with young children lived. It would have the largest pocket of combat-ready cultivators on this side of Fyrion. That left us with a twenty-minute walk ahead of us.

A twenty-minute walk through void beast territory.

I returned to Vihaan's side. "Okay, everyone," I addressed the class. "I have to take Vihaan to a doctor. I need all of you to stay here until someone comes and gets you. Okay? It's dangerous out there, but you'll be safe in here. Understand?"

A girl raised her hand. "What about you?"

"Sometimes adults need to do dangerous things to keep people safe," I said. "But you don't. You stay here, got it?"

The kids all nodded.

"Perfect. You're all so brave." I leaned down to wrap the blanket around Vihaan, layering him up against what was to come. That done, I lifted him up and carried him to the open freezer, bending his knees against his chest so he'd fit in the tight space. I'd have to be quick. At least I didn't have to worry about the residual frost freezing him to death. The CO_2 buildup in the confined space would kill him long before that happened. If only he'd had an open lung meridian to help with that.

I left the freezer open as I pushed it up to the bunker door, pausing just before the exit to take a moment for myself. I dared not linger, dared not let the absolute insanity of what I was about to do sink in. Unarmed, undertrained, and without even a core from which to externalize my qi, I'd no hope of winning a fight against a void beast. Threads, I'd only defeated that first one because it'd been distracted drooling over Vihaan.

I didn't calculate the odds. I didn't itemize the dozens of ways this could get us both killed. I only knew that letting Vihaan die was not an option.

If I was going to flail against infinity, saving a child's life seemed like a hell of a good way to start.

"Nicki, you're going to close the door behind me, got it?"

The girl nodded firmly.

"Excellent. Thank you. Okay, Vihaan. Deep breath."

I heard a fierce little inhale from within the freezer. I smiled with false bravery. "And here. We. Go."

I cycled my blood, heart, lungs, and skin meridians, slowing my pulse and my breathing and chilling my body both inside and out. Keeping my focus, I swiped at my holopad and the door slid open. I pushed the freezer cart through.

The hall outside was clear, the pack that had chased us apparently losing interest in defended prey when easier targets abounded. The bunker door slammed shut behind me.

I turned right, back down the way we'd come, and set off. I walked with purpose, with long and solid strides rather than an outright run. I cared not for the sound or the smell of our passage—such things didn't exist in space —but I feared motion itself might draw attention. Any heat from the friction of the cart's wheels certainly would. I'd have to hope we didn't generate that much.

The gentle rumble of the wheels against the floor echoed eerily through the empty halls. The red emergency lights cast the space in angry tones that clashed with the uncanny peace of the lifeless passages. We passed a broken window, atmosphere slowly wheezing out through imperfections in the qi field that patched it. Hopefully the life support systems could replace the lost pressure.

We found our first corpse before our first void beast. I uttered a silent thanks that Vihaan couldn't see the rent flesh and missing organs and exposed bone as we passed. Even as the red light muted the gory scene, the blood and viscera and flesh all blending together into a mess of what looked like brown compared to the crimson world around it, I swallowed down bile. Man or woman, old or young, mortal or cultivator, not enough remained of the carcass to know. In the moment, I thought it would take decades to unsee that sight.

It took twelve more steps.

I froze as I pushed the freezer cart around the next bend to find three black shapes stooped over something red and wet. I heard the drip of lifeblood upon the floor, the rip of tearing flesh, the damp smacking of beak against beak. I smelled the gas and shit of death. I tasted iron in the air.

I gulped.

None of the void beasts looked up from their meal.

I pushed onward, swerving around to hug the far wall and keep as much distance as I could. My left shoulder passed but four feet from the closest beast's rear end. I refused to look, refused to watch the carcass's feet twitch as they chewed on its spinal cord, refused to see their narrow bellies engorge as they feasted.

They left me alone. With no qi they could sense and a body even cooler than air around it, I held no appeal to the void dwellers. Where they came from, they had plenty of cold and dead.

The qi and adrenaline running through my body kept my panic at bay, kept me from considering what would happen if they detected Vihaan's qi through the freezer.

I kept my eyes straight ahead. The soles of my shoes stuck against the floor with each step as I strode through the blood that had pooled upon the floor. The wheels of the cart left four thin red lines in their wake, a visible trail of our harrowing passage.

I fought back a sigh of relief as we turned from that hallway into the next, even breathing of the utmost importance until we found safety. Until that happened, I had to keep calm. I had to keep steady.

I had to keep moving.

* * *

Senior Cadet Alice Garret gripped the shaft of her pike with white knuckles. For two cycles she'd trained with the weapon, including even a spirit beast hunt on Ilirian.

She'd never faced down a blackblood.

Alice had been in class when the alarms rang, when the lights turned red and the comms went dark. In her mind she'd done her duty, escorting her pack of teenage students to the safety of the housing block, only to find that the housing block hadn't been as safe as she'd hoped.

There were too many people to realistically sequester them all in a bunker, too many to organize without functional comms. For lack of an elder, a senior member had taken command, ordering cultivators about to defend the altogether too many entrances to the housing block.

Instead of safety, Alice had found more duty. Instead of a team, she found herself the lone guard at the eastern, first-floor hallway. Senior Wallace had understandably directed most of their forces towards defending the higher levels where more of the void beasts had landed, but with only a dozen yards of visibility before the hallway turned and without even a partner to fall back on, Alice resented the choice.

Standing alone in a red-lit hallway in the height of a

void horde incursion made for a harrowing experience in and of itself.

A scream sounded in the distance.

Glass shattered somewhere in the maze of passages ahead.

Her breath seemed to echo down the empty hallway. Alice's heartbeat sped as her qi invigorated the muscle. It kept her jumpy and nervous, but ready to leap into action at a moment's notice.

She froze. Her ears, empowered by the qi running through them, caught two distinct noises in the distance: the eerie and dissonant whine of a squeaky wheel, and wet and sticky footsteps. The steps came even and rhythmic, not the desperate flight of a survivor but a calm and deliberate walk.

They were coming closer.

Alice tensed. She lowered her pike, ready to bring her main offensive technique, The Comet Falls, to bear on whatever monstrosity presented itself.

Instead, a skeletal figure in cadet's clothes rounded the bend, pushing before it a steel cart stained with black blood. A chill ran down her spine as the walking corpse approached. She'd never heard of void beasts with necromantic magic, but she couldn't deny the lifelessness of the *thing* that approached her.

Nor could she deny the spark of qi she sensed not in the undead monstrosity, but from the cart it pushed.

She pointed her pike at it. "Stop right there!"

To her surprise, the figure actually stopped. An unfeeling voice called out in reply. "Is the housing block secure?"

"It is," Alice growled, "and it'll remain that way. Release your captive and step away from—"

"Oh, thank fuck," the corpse swore. It—he, Alice supposed—leaned forward and opened the lid of his cart.

From inside she heard soft breathing and smelled blood and excrement.

She glared at him. "I said, release your capti—"

He charged her. "Medic!" he shouted into the air behind her.

Alice readied herself to strike, but hesitated as the life seemed to spring back into the corpse. She still sensed no qi within him, but color returned to his face and emotion to his voice.

"I need a medic!" he shouted again, desperation finally apparent in his tone.

Alice blinked in stunned silence as he barreled past her, unable to bring herself to strike down a man calling for a medic, however uncanny his appearance. She turned and watched him disappear down the hall behind her, fighting off the urge to follow.

All she could do was keep her vigil and hope she hadn't unleashed a demon on the mortals and children of the housing block. Anything else, she concluded, was below her pay grade.

* * *

I stopped cycling the moment I saw the look on the guard lady's face, mentally adding her to the list of people who'd seen me go all corpse-like. The last thing I needed was to scare the bejeezus out of the medic Vihaan so desperately needed.

"Vihaan?" I asked him as we raced past the guard. "How are you doing, buddy?"

He didn't answer, but I heard a ragged breath drift up from the now-open freezer.

I ran faster.

"I need a medic!" I shouted once more as the hallway spit us out into a cavernous room over twice the size of housing D's common room. I rushed past a gray-haired man barking orders at groups of scurrying cultivators up to where two sect members directed a team of mortals around a half dozen maimed and wounded.

A woman in a junior member uniform approached me.

I preempted her questions as I reached into the freezer to pick up Vihaan. "He's got a punctured bowel. I gave him a quarter dose of morphine and rinsed the wound with isopropyl. I didn't know what else to do."

"Lay him there," the woman ordered, pointing to a section of empty couch.

I obeyed.

"You and you," she jabbed her finger at two of the mortals, "with me." She looked up to face me, eyeing both the empty ring denoting my low rank and the dark bags under my eyes. "You did well. We'll take it from here."

I nodded mutely and stepped out of her way.

I sat on the floor as they worked, leaning against the side of the sofa by Vihaan's head. Time passed in a blur as I waited, exhaustion and fading adrenaline leaving me feeling hollow as mortals and cultivators alike hustled and bustled around the lobby or similarly sat stock still with vacant expressions. One of the nurses tapped me on the shoulder when they finished healing Vihaan. I didn't wake him.

The day dragged on. The medics began to flag as fewer and fewer injured came in. Someone brought me a wet towel to wipe the blood from my hands. It only kind of worked.

In time, the red emergency lights flickered out. A collective sigh of mourning relief echoed through the room in lieu of a victorious cheer. The comms came to life.

"Cal?" Lucy's voice sang like music to my ears. "Cal, are you okay?"

"I'm okay," I replied. I exhaled, listening, for a moment, to Vihaan's soft and rhythmic breathing behind me.

"I'm okay."

15

I awoke with a start to a hand on my shoulder. The lights in the lobby had faded to their nighttime tones, indicating the passage of time if nothing else. The ice cream cart was gone. I looked up to find one of the mortal nurses looking down at me.

"The lockdown is over," he said. "You can go home, now."

I blinked the sleep from my eyes and rubbed at the sore neck sleeping against the side of a sofa had left me. "I should stay until Vihaan wakes u—" I froze. I pressed my palms against the floor to look up and over the armrest at the couch behind me. It was empty. "Where's Vihaan?"

"He's fine," the nurse led, clearly hearing the worry in my voice. "His parents took him home."

"Oh," I said, slumping back down onto my ass. "Without waking me?"

"They were more concerned with Vihaan, and *you* needed the sleep."

I raised an eyebrow at the man who *had* just woken me up. "And I don't anymore?"

"That was seven hours ago. The cleaning team is here and need you out of the way."

"Oh. Oh! Sorry. I'll just..." I scrambled to my feet, taking note of the absolute mess of bloodstains I'd left on the floor. None of it was mine.

I wandered out of Family Housing B in a daze, stretching in every way I could think of in a vain attempt to alleviate the absolute havoc my sleeping position had wrought on my lower back. It wasn't until I made it to the transport station that I bothered to check the time on my holopad.

Three AM.

I sighed. It seemed the cleaning crew had waited until the absolute last possible moment to wake me. So much for my sleep schedule.

I decided, as an empty pod slid into the station, that I was happy they hadn't roused me when Vihaan left. I didn't think I'd have had it in me to relive the attack for a couple of concerned parents. I did my level best *not* to relive it as my pod shot towards housing D.

I waved to Wilma—Arthur's nightshift counterpart—as I crossed the empty lobby and mounted the stairs to the third floor. I made it three steps past the landing before I saw him.

Nick stood by the window, staring out into the starry sky.

I froze. For a moment, a frighteningly long moment, Nick vanished, and Cedric stood in his place. He turned to me, his eyes black as the day he'd killed me, and flashed a wide and menacing grin.

Then he was gone. Nick was alone.

My heart pounded. I fought back the urge to flee, recognizing the irrational response for what it was. Over and over I reiterated that fact to myself.

I'm not in deep space anymore. I'm not in deep space anymore. I'm not in deep space anymore.

It took a few breaths for the panic to die down, but it

did. I didn't run off. I didn't scream for help. Instead, I moved to join him. "Couldn't sleep?"

He didn't look away from the window. "It's like the universe hates us," he said. "It's not enough that the void would trap us on these rocks. It has to send monsters to hunt us even here."

I shuddered at the idea before rejecting it. "The void didn't send those things. I think they were escaping it."

"So the universe hates them too," Nick reasoned. "People say that nature abhors a vacuum, but I think they've got it backwards. The vacuum abhors nature."

"The void doesn't care," I said in no uncertain terms. "That's really all there is to it. It was here long before us and it'll be here long after we're gone. It makes no effort to support us, yet bears no grudge that we specks of dust have the audacity to exist. What more could you ask of it?"

Nick didn't answer.

"I think it's beautiful," I continued. "We fight and we learn and we build and we fix, all to keep out the cold. I've spent my entire adult life working as a vac-welder, working to hold the void at bay. I didn't stop hate or violence or greed or death. Those don't come from the void. They come from us. They come from *life*. All I could do was hold the line against encroaching apathy—a patchwork, dented, rusty bulwark against uncaring. That's the only real danger in the dark."

"But in the end, the void always wins."

"In a way," I replied. "We all spring from nothing and we'll all return to nothing in time, but that's not defeat. Emptiness isn't our enemy; it's the universe's default state to which *we* are the exception. I really think the only way we can *lose* is to stop caring. All life flails against infinity. To stop is to stop living."

"Flailing against infinity," Nick mused. "I like that."

172

"It's kind of becoming my catchphrase."

"Really?" Nick raised an eyebrow. "It's not a very good catchphrase."

I laughed. "No, I suppose it isn't. It's way too brooding." I reached out and placed a hand on his shoulder. "I'm going to go wash up. Get some sleep, okay?"

"Yeah, I will." Nick didn't turn from the window. "Thanks."

"Hey, don't thank me. Before the year is out you'll have a weirdly broody catchphrase of your own."

That earned me a smile. "I look forward to it. Goodnight, Cal."

"Goodnight," I echoed his sentiment as I turned and left, stopping at my room to exchange my bloody clothes for a towel before heading to the showers. By the time I emerged still feeling not quite clean, Nick was gone.

I lingered for a few moments as I made it back to my room, considering my sloppily made bed and the early hour. Sleep seemed impossibly distant. I needed time to think.

A flash of motion caught my eye from outside, drawing me to my bedroom window. Even at four in the morning, Fyrion bustled with activity as workers in vac suits scurried across the hull repairing the damage the void horde had inflicted. I didn't watch for long.

I donned a clean uniform and left my dorm behind, crossing the lobby and calling a transport pod without a second thought. Minutes later I emerged into a hurricane of laborers.

Baggy-eyed mortals hurried this way and that, carrying all manner of tools and parts for gods know what as they each went about their specific tasks. Those wakeful enough to notice the cultivator in their midst stopped to salute or offer confused and anxious looks. Others simply made way, hoping I wouldn't stop them from going about their work. None dared stand in my way as I moved through the busy staging area.

The nervous and unwelcoming glances I received clashed against my life experience. All too often I'd been the mortal keeping his head down as a cultivator passed by. Even now I often felt like that. The way these people looked at me... I shuddered.

Most cultivators didn't think me one of them. Apparently, neither did the mortals.

I tried to wait in line for a chance to speak with the foreman, but the queue seemed to evaporate around me as I approached. With a sigh I stepped up to the messy desk, looking past the five empty and two half-full coffee cups to meet the man's gaze directly.

"Whatever you want, get one of your valets to handle it," the foreman barked at me. "Half the station's leaking atmosphere; I don't have time for sect business."

"I'm here to help."

"This is a worksite, *sir*," he spat the honorific with more derision than I'd previously thought possible. "Not your chance to look for enlightenment. Go meditate on your own time. We have work to—"

I cut him off. "I'm a guild-certified vac-welder. Allcorp, class C."

He blinked at me. "Low-G?"

"Zero, but I can manage."

"Good enough," he grumbled. "You should've led with that." He twisted his neck to look back over his shoulder. "Gary! Get our cultivator friend a vac suit. I'm sending him out to breach eleven." He looked up at me. "Don't fuck up."

I smiled at him. "Wouldn't dream of it."

I didn't waste any more of his time, following a red-haired fellow—presumably Gary—over to a row of wall hooks sparsely populated by hanging vac suits. He wordlessly pointed at one and walked away.

True to my expectations, my loose-fitting cultivator pants bunched up uncomfortably around the crotch once I put the vac suit on, but the slightly-too-big suit helped alleviate the discomfort. Within minutes I had a hud in front of me, a torch in my hand, and a collection of sheet metal strapped to my back. I shared the airlock with four others, but as the doors opened and Fyrion's gray surface exposed itself, we all went our separate ways.

My first weld took longer than I would've liked as I grew accustomed to working in point-zero-eight G, but soon enough I fell into a familiar pattern, bounding from job to job as my hud directed me.

My mind wandered as I worked, a sort of meditative calm overtaking me. For a few precious moments the world almost felt normal again, at least until I finished a weld and realized Brady wasn't there to criticize it. At the very least, it felt good to work with my hands again. Even with the dwarf planet below me, it was the closest I'd been to a vacuum since roofie.

Most of all I spent the time mulling over the day's events, picking apart my every decision in the search for some lesson to be learned, something I could've done differently to spare myself—to spare *Vihaan*—the traumatizing experience. Time and time again I came to the same conclusion.

I had to get stronger.

Between today's attack and what'd happened on roofie, I couldn't escape the frightening truth that the galaxy was not a safe place. I had the tools at my disposal, the opportunity to develop into a power the likes of which the system—if not the galaxy—had never seen. I could contribute as a vac-welder. I could effect change as a cultivator.

I had to get stronger.

By Lucy's telling—which I trusted far more than anything sect leadership published—the attack had been far too coordinated for what it was. Whether it'd been by chance or on purpose that they'd come while her orbit had her on the wrong side of the planet was up for debate, but mindless beasts didn't randomly hit the comms and local net, not as precisely as today's horde had.

I couldn't begin to fathom what that meant. Had they come for Lucy? Had they come for *me?* That seemed unlikely. The void beasts I'd encountered hadn't even looked at me.

Only about a tenth of the horde had made it through Lucy and Fyrion's other orbital defenses. That a living being would so willingly throw its life at something like that astounded me, even knowing their propensity for violence and hunger. It absolutely reeked of some greater plot, one so far beyond me that it left me reeling.

I had to get stronger.

My holopad's alarm beeped seven o'clock. My hud flashed that I was due a break for rest and hydration. My body sluggishly agreed.

I stepped back into the airlock in silence. I ignored the curious glances of the mortal laborers as I went through the motions of peeling off my vac suit. I let them stare. I wasn't one of them anymore.

Images of haughty cultivators flashed through my head, of Elder Smith's derisive gaze, of Elder Berkowitz practically falling over herself to flatter Lucy. I'd never be one of them either.

I was something new. I was something different. I'd carve my own path through the endless night, and anyone who didn't like it was welcome to fuck right off.

I came away from my morning's labor with remarkably few answers, yet I felt all the better for it. Of it all, the only true conclusion I'd reached had come early, not in my contemplation but in my conversation with Nick.

The void didn't care. The living did. If I learned nothing else from my communion with the infinite sea, I prayed I could learn to do both, to wield cold apathy like a double-edged sword, cutting loose the petty frivolities of the living to better defend the hot passions of *life*.

Then and only then, as I wandered through the uncharted dark, could I find my Way.

* * *

"Elder Lopez?" her secretary's voice crackled over the intercom. "There's a Senior Cadet Alice Garett here to see you?"

Maria Lopez rubbed at the dark circles under her eyes. *Apparently* a void horde had shown up while she'd been in isolated meditation, cruelly robbing her both of her chance to gloriously lead the defense, *and* her night's sleep. Elder Lawrence—the self-important prick—had taken all the credit and left *her* to deal with the mess.

She'd be stuck signing off on requisition requests and casualty compensations for the next week, and that was ignoring the elder council meeting later that day to discuss what the attack might've meant for Fyrion as a whole. The few details she'd seen already seemed off, which meant she'd likely spend the entire evening listening to Elder Rajadendra rant about sabotage from the Dragon's Left Eye.

The thought was foolish, of course. Nobody could control the void hordes, not that Elder Rajadendra would ever accept that.

She groaned as the intercom beeped expectantly at her. "What does she want?"

"She says a walking corpse delivered an injured child to Family Housing B."

Maria straightened in her seat, pausing for a moment to

keep her voice disinterested and disbelieving. She couldn't have this cadet thinking she was worried. "A walking corpse?" She forced a sigh. "Let's get this over with, then. Let her in."

She picked up a random report from her desk as the cadet walked in, pretending to read it while the stocky woman saluted.

"At ease," Maria said without looking up. "You saw a walking corpse?"

"I did, ma'am," Alice replied. "It—*he*—brought a wounded boy out of void beast-controlled territory into Family Housing B for medical care. Healer Li said he probably saved the child's life."

Maria clenched her fist beneath her desk to keep from otherwise reacting. She answered with a dry tone. "How heroic of him." For the first time since her entrance, Maria looked up from her report to meet the cadet's gaze.

Alice Garett stood some five and a half feet tall, with broad shoulders and a healthy layer of muscle that loaned a sense of stability to her physicality that her voice belied.

Maria raised an eyebrow at her. "You are aware that Fyrion hosts a cadet who masks his qi, correct?"

Alice hid it well, but Maria caught the slight twitch of frustration her eyebrow made as she answered, "Yes, ma'am."

"And you're aware this cadet shares classes with a number of young children? Classes which might've been in session at the time of the incursion?"

"Yes, ma'am," Alice replied through gritted teeth.

"Do you suppose, in the midst of an incursion, you might've conflated your physical senses with your spiritual ones?"

"I know what I saw," Alice snapped before adding a too-late, "ma'am. His skin was pale and cold. He wasn't breathing. His heart didn't beat. He didn't come to life until he was already running me down."

"He ran you down?"

"Yes, ma'am," Alice regained some of her composure. "I was guarding the eastern first floor hallway into Family Housing B at the time."

Maria saw her opportunity and pounced. "It sounds to me like the two options here are that you got mixed up in the heat of the moment, or you allowed a product of necromancy past your guard unchallenged. Is that right?"

"Ma'am, I—"

Maria cut her off. "Here's what you're going to do. You're going to find everyone you told about this and let them know you were mistaken. You will refrain, in the future, from spreading dangerous rumors. If, in the process of my own investigation, I find merit to your wild claims, I will be forced to call a tribunal to evaluate your decision to let a *walking corpse* into a room full of mortals and children. Am I understood?"

Alice seemed to relax at her mention of an investigation, at least until the word 'tribunal' set her eyes wide. "Understood, ma'am."

"Good. You may go. Hope you don't hear from me."

To her credit, Senior Cadet Alice Garett held herself well as she spun on her heel and exited the office. Maria watched with cold eyes as the door closed behind her.

She tapped her holopad. "Show me Caliban Rex's class schedule." The relevant data popped up. Maria scanned it for the number she needed before issuing a second command. "Bring up the security footage outside classroom... B-eighteen. Yesterday at fifteen hundred."

A larger window sprang up from the holo projector in her desk, displaying a two-dimensional image of an empty hallway. Maria leaned in. She watched with rapt eyes as a crowd of children spilled into the hall, followed by a man pushing a stainless steel cart and wearing a woolen blanket like a cloak. Maria thought he looked absolutely ridiculous.

The surveillance system automatically tracked his progress, flipping from camera to camera as he led the gaggle of babbling brats towards their next class.

She watched as the black shape burst through the window, scowled as its foot impaled a dark-skinned child, counted the seconds before Cadet Rex reacted.

He took three. Maria filed that bit of information away for later.

She watched the strange cadet ram his cart into the void beast before stomping its head in—hardly an elegant solution, but an effective one. She took in every detail of the way he leaned in to pick the boy up, how he directed the class towards the nearest bunker, the way he nobly made sure they all made it in before following them to safety.

She'd have to contain this footage. The last thing Maria needed was the sect to herald the soulless abomination a hero.

No camera monitored the bunker itself—the presence of a toilet in there would've made surveillance a privacy violation by sect policy—but she looked on as the cadet emerged a different man.

A chill ran down her spine.

The surveillance cameras unfortunately lacked the detail for her to determine whether his heart beat or his lungs drew breath, but his skin had certainly lost all color, retreating back as if shriveling upon a corpse. With bony hands he pushed his cart, moving with a trancelike calm she'd never seen in the man before.

Convincing Alice Garett she hadn't seen a walking corpse may prove harder than Maria had hoped. She prayed her threat would at least keep the girl quiet.

Thoroughly unnerved by the image before her, Maria

chewed her lip as Caliban paused to glare with cold uncaring eyes at a half-devoured corpse before casually moving on. Her own stomach churned at the sight, at least until she sent a wave of qi through the relevant meridian to quiet it.

She realized she'd struck gold the moment the image flicked to a hallway in which three void beasts feasted on a dead mortal. Her mind raced with possibility as she imagined what kinds of unique or secretive techniques the outworlder might utilize to overcome what seemed to her to be overwhelming odds.

She wasn't prepared for him to do nothing.

Maria didn't move, didn't breathe, didn't blink as Caliban Rex swerved to the far side of the hallway and walked right by the blackbloods. He didn't so much as shiver at the horror a few feet to his left as he passed, seemingly unperturbed by the deadly beasts within arm's length.

More harrowing still, the beasts just let him past. They didn't twitch. They didn't try to defend their kill. They certainly didn't *attack*. Cadet Rex may as well have been invisible to the creatures for all they reacted to his passing.

Invisible, Maria realized, or *familiar.*

Could the void beasts have raised this corpse? That seemed impossible, but so too did their behavior towards Caliban. Maria found it more likely that Cadet Rex was hardly his benefactor's first experiment. She'd just have to add experimenting with void beasts to this mysterious necromancer's long list of crimes.

She scrolled forward through the rest of the video in the hope it'd reveal more as to the nature of Caliban's relationship with the blackbloods, but found instead his encounter with Alice Garett much as the senior cadet had described it. The moment he got to safety, life returned to Caliban. Nobody else even glanced at him with suspicion.

Maria's first step was to store a copy of the footage on her holopad and scrub it from the local net. She still didn't know enough to definitively declare the cadet a danger, and dared not risk anyone else stumbling upon her discovery. When she finally exposed him, it'd be she and she alone that got the credit for it. In the meantime, he had more to offer her.

She made a note to have her secretary schedule a meeting with the suspicious recruit and turned back to the footage she'd saved. Only as she pulled up the image of Caliban so calmly pushing his cart past three killing machines did Maria's eyes peel away from the screen to notice her hands were shaking. She forcibly stilled them.

She stared at the image for some time, clasping her hands tightly in her lap as she comforted herself with the reminder that the cadet hadn't hurt anyone yet. Perhaps he wouldn't. Perhaps his actions belied his monstrous appearance.

The way Maria shuddered whenever she looked at him disallowed such thoughts. Even she couldn't deny the sheer heroism he'd displayed, defending the children so, but a hero did her little good. For her purpose, she needed a villain. Caliban Rex certainly looked the part. She'd have to keep a close eye on him, be ready to intervene at a moment's notice.

If she spun it just right, wrung every resource she could out of him before being the one to save the day if he eventually went rogue, then maybe, just maybe, Elder Maria Lopez of the Dragon's Right Eye may've found her ticket off this gods forsaken rock.

Maria shoved the report she'd faked reading to the bottom of her pile. She'd yet to really start it before the incursion had dumped a veritable mountain of work on top of her, all of which took priority. Besides, with this new footage she'd found, Maria had far more promising leads on Caliban Rex to pursue.

RF-31 had probably just fallen to the void horde anyway.

16

I arrived to breakfast ten minutes late, my brow sweaty and my uniform creased from the vac suit. I received a few more of the curious stares than usual as I crossed the mess to fetch a tray and made for my usual table, but none of the louder attention I'd feared. Nobody confronted me. Nobody appeared frightened or hostile or interested in blaming me for the incursion.

As the sect's resident weirdo outsider, that last was a real concern.

"I didn't know you two were friends," I greeted Xavier and Charlotte as I joined them at their table.

Xavier slapped her on the back. "Charlotte here has offered to show me the Veleraeu family style!"

Well, she certainly knew how to make Xavier happy. The question was why she wanted to. I raised an eyebrow at her.

She shrugged. "If we're going to be in a cohort together, I figured it'd be better if we liked each other."

I stared at her for a moment before deciding I was just hungry enough to take her word for it. I'd slept through dinner last night, so the tray of eggs and sausage in front of me was the first thing I'd had to eat since yesterday's ice cream bar.

Given the choice between eating breakfast and being suspicious of my friends, I chose breakfast.

Charlotte looked me up and down as I shoveled omelet into my mouth. "You certainly don't *look* like someone who missed the morning workout."

I paused to finish chewing and swallowed. "I spent the morning outside, helping with the repairs."

Her eyes shot open. "You missed dinner immediately after a void horde attack, without messaging anyone to let us know you were okay, so you could *vac-weld?* Cal, you're not a mortal any more. That's not your job."

"I told Lucy I was... you're not in contact with Lucy. Right. You're right. I should've messaged you. I had other things on my mind, and I thought I'd be back for dinner. I didn't expect to fall asleep like that."

Xavier scowled at me. "You fell asleep? What happened?"

I sighed and leaned in, lowering my voice to stave off any eavesdroppers. "How much do you guys know about yesterday's attack?"

"A void horde came out of nowhere at around three o'clock," Charlotte rattled off. "Our orbital defenses handled most of it, but a few stragglers made it planet side. Reports show some eighty dead, double that injured, mostly mortals, but a few cultivators from Family Housing B and the classroo—" She froze. "You were in the attack."

"I killed one," I confirmed. "Immediately after watching it stab a ten-year-old boy through the stomach."

Xavier clapped me on the back hard enough I had to catch myself against the table. "A glorious victory!"

I blinked at him. "Did you miss the part about the stabbed ten-year-old?"

"Did you do everything you could to protect him?"

"Of course I did."

"And is he alive?"

I nodded.

He clapped me on the back again. "Then it was a glorious victory!"

"He's right," Charlotte told me. "You may be bigger and stronger, but you fight and cultivate at a preteen level. The fact you even *looked* at a type-six void beast and lived is incredible. That you *killed one?* It's almost unbelievable."

I faltered under the praise. "It wasn't that impressive. I just rammed it with the ice cream cart a few times then stomped its head in."

Xavier beamed. "You have a warrior's spirit!"

Charlotte squinted. "Ice cream cart? Why did you have an ice cream cart?"

I started from the beginning, my instructors' efforts to turn the class against me and my own to win them over. I told of asking Arthur for help, carefully leaving out any mention of Mindy. She had enough to deal with without unleashing Xavier and Charlotte on her.

I explained my panic as Lucy's voice had crackled its warning and the comms went dead, relived our mad dash down the hall and its abrupt and violent end. They listened in silence as I told of smashing through jagged chitin, of frantically grabbing Vihaan off the floor, of our desperate race to shelter. Curiously enough, it wasn't the blood that caught their attention.

"You *smelled* his injury?" Xavier asked loudly enough to draw eyes from other tables.

I glared the onlookers into giving up and lowered my voice. "Gut wound one-oh-one: if it smells like shit, that means shit's leaking. Shit in the blood means sepsis. It's not an exact test, but once you stop the bleeding, a good sniff is step two."

"Unless the patient is a cultivator," Charlotte said, "and thus perfectly capable of fighting off infection on their own."

"Yeah, well, mortals get injured too. Children get injured too. This shit's worth knowing."

Neither of them laughed at my admittedly stupid pun, but that's showbiz, baby. You win some, you lose some. They were, luckily enough, so stunned by the bad joke that they stopped talking. I took the opportunity to continue with my story.

"Anyway, I knew I had to get him medical attention, and I *knew* there were void beasts between us and it. Comms were down, so I couldn't call for help, and even if I could've, gods knew how long it would take them to clear out the beasts. I was unarmed, and a shit fighter besides, so fighting our way through was out. That just left sneaking past. *I* was easy. With the way my qi cools my body and is damn near impossible to sense, I figured I could slip right by."

Charlotte blinked rapidly in surprise. "And that *worked?*"

"I'm still breathing, aren't I?"

She shook her head. "That's *insane*. Some type-sixes can sense motion. Others can feel footsteps through the floor. Threads, just because humans can't detect your qi doesn't mean void beasts can't!"

"What was I supposed to do, just let him die? I took a calculated risk, and it paid off."

Xavier nodded along. "Makes sense to me. I've never known a blackblood to chase after a corpse, and you make a pretty convincing corpse. So after your heroic escape, you returned with reinforcements to clear the way to the children?"

"Not quite. I told you, I had no idea how long Vihaan would last, nor how long it would take to muster up enough firepower to fight a medic back to him."

Charlotte furrowed her brow. "So what did you—"

I grinned. "I brought him with me."

Charlotte went silent. Xavier figured it out.

He snapped his fingers. "The ice cream cart! They'd have trouble sensing his qi through that much steel, and there's no way any body heat leached out."

I winked. "Waltzed right past three void beasts. Could've reached out and touched one if I'd wanted."

Charlotte groaned. "You're insane." She glared up at Xavier. "You're both insane. Threads, you probably saved that child's life, but still..." She trailed off, staring into space for a few seconds before gazing intently at me. "You're either going to change the universe as we know it, or die from making some dumb decision before you make gem."

"That's the plan." I smiled. "The changing the universe part, not the dying part."

"You deserve a medal!" Xavier chimed in. "Accolades! Extra focus room hours!"

"If nothing else, Vihaan's parents owe you a debt," Charlotte added. "I'm sure they'd give you anything you asked for."

"I'll pass on all of that, thanks," I said. "Don't need to draw any more attention to myself. As it was I scared the crap out some poor woman. I *will* track down Vihaan's parents, though. I want to see how he's doing."

"And after all that you went and worked as a *vac-welder*?" Charlotte asked.

"After all that, I passed out leaning against a couch in the lobby. Slept through dinner. Slept through Vihaan's parents taking him upstairs. Slept through the cleaning crew covering every inch of the place *except* where I was lying. I managed to roughly approximate a full night's sleep by four in the morning. I actually ran into Nick on my way up."

"I'm not surprised he didn't sleep," Charlotte said. "His

little sister lost her left hand in the attack. Apparently the limb is so torn up it'll take years of cell treatment to regrow it."

"Yeesh." I grimaced. "No wonder he seemed so out of it." I didn't go into detail. Nick's early morning musings weren't their business, especially if he'd shared them in confidence. I wasn't too keen on sharing my thoughts either. "Hold up. Why are they regrowing it when a neural prosthetic would work just as well without the painful recovery time?"

Charlotte raised an eyebrow at me. "Because she wants functional blood and tendon meridians?"

"Oh. Right. Those run through the hands, don't they." I clapped my hands together to turn the conversation away from my dumb question. "Anyway, I've got the day off while they repair and clean up all the classrooms, so once we're done here..." I looked over at Xavier. "I'm going to need your help."

"Ooh, sparring or a meridian?"

"Meridians," I clarified, emphasizing the plural. "I figure I can get my stomach, tendons, and senses all in one go."

Charlotte gaped. "You *what*?"

"I don't know, Cal," Xavier said. "That's ambitious, even for me."

"I know it was a freak attack, but I felt so *helpless* yesterday. I don't like feeling helpless. I want to get my meridians open and my core formed so I can be fighting with qi as soon as possible. I've cleared three at a time before. Three *harder* ones, even. Muscles, spine, and brain will all take way more training, but the other three are simple enough. It's not like I'm low on qi."

Charlotte collected herself. "If you have the qi, I say do it."

I glanced at her askance. "That was a quick leap from

'you're going to get yourself killed' to 'open three meridians at once.'"

Charlotte sighed. "People put a lot of stock in the power of epiphany, but they forget that overcoming adversity is just as important. I'd wager that whatever happened to get you started was worth more than enough adversity to help with those first three meridians. After yesterday's adventure, your body's probably more ready to advance than it's been since. Normally people use this kind of thing to push their core to the next level, but *normally* cultivators don't see real adversity before they've cleared all their meridians. Some never do. If you can handle three meridians at once, now is the time to do it. Threads, you'd be wasting the opportunity if you *didn't*."

I looked to Xavier, but he just shrugged. "She's the smart one. If she says go for it, I won't cower away."

"Great," I said, shoving the last of my breakfast into my mouth. Still chewing, I stood and grabbed my tray. "Let's go."

Xavier followed me as I left, his long strides more than enough to catch up and keep by my side as we bussed our trays and headed back to housing D.

"I still can't believe you slayed a void beast and saved a child's life," he gushed as we walked. "You're a real, honest to goodness hero."

"The ice cream cart did all the real work. I just drove it."

Xavier laughed. "Still on the first steps of your Way and already your legend begins. They'll write books about you. They'll make holos!"

"We'll deal with my growing legend *after* I get to wielding my own magic."

Xavier scowled. "It's not magic. It's careful manipulation of the fundamental qi within all things."

"*Yeah*. That's *magic*."

"Don't let any elders hear you say that."

"Eh, they already think I'm an uncultured mortal."

Xavier let out a breath. "Let's focus on today's task before we start with next year's. Even if you succeed today, it takes months of preparation for the brain meridian alone, not to mention the others, and that's not even considering the monumental task of forming your seed core."

"Yeah, yeah, magic's a distant pipe dream." I waved him off as we crested the third floor stairs. We made straight for the showers. "Let's make it a bit less distant."

Xavier flashed a nervous grin. "Good luck."

I undressed and sat cross-legged in my usual stall, letting the warm water wash over me as I evened out my breathing and focused inward.

I had no idea if Charlotte's speech about overcoming adversity held any water, but my reserve of qi seemed to jump into action, springing about my center in tune with my surface thoughts. I didn't hesitate, sharpening it into the needle and thread I'd grown so accustomed to visualizing and directing its tip to the entrance of my stomach meridian.

My belly convulsed. Nausea washed through me. I fought back the urge to gag, to retch, to bid farewell to my breakfast. To be clear, trying this immediately after downing a plate of eggs and sausage and whatever else they put in those omelets was no mistake. I had done *some* research. Conventional wisdom suggested a full stomach to dilute the impurities I was about to vent into my digestive system.

I was about ready to tell conventional wisdom to fuck off and send my breakfast on its merry way when my qi completed its first loop. A second wave of nausea echoed the first, this one lower and nastier.

I should mention, everyone calls it the stomach meridian, but really it governs the entire digestive tract.

My stomach wasn't the only thing suffering; several yards of intestine joined the pain party.

I pushed on. Faster and faster I cycled the qi, thickening the strand into a cord into a true *flow* as more and more of the blockage seeped out of me. This being the meridian that it was, my pores remained mostly unscathed as the toxins took a... different route.

The meridian popped open all of a sudden, the pain and nausea giving way to the familiar sense of cool comfort. I hadn't the faintest idea what cycling my stomach meridian did, but given the way my others had acted, I guessed it slowed digestion and stretched the nutrients further. Rather than metabolizing and reenergizing quickly like most cultivators, I'd survive longer without a meal.

I stopped cycling for a moment to push my senses outward, squinting past the obnoxious background qi and Xavier's blinding core to reach for the back wall and the vacuum beyond. The infinite sea stretched out before me. I drank my fill.

Fully loaded and raring to go, I set my spiritual sights on my next target.

The tendon meridian was remarkably simple, enough so that I wondered why the sect waited until cycling two to open it. Sure, my entire body locked itself in place as my various bits of sinew tightened and held, but that didn't stop me. Sure, the competing forces yanking at my mortal muscles hurt more than any meridian I'd opened yet, but after the shit I'd been through, that didn't stop me either.

Actually, maybe that was why they didn't teach it first. Kids didn't exactly have a reputation for handling pain well.

I did.

Okay, maybe not *well,* and maybe not exactly a *reputation*, but I'd been through worse. Once you've crawled down a gangway with a dozen puncture wounds and as many broken bones, you see pain with a bit of a different perspective. It hurt like three hells and half, but my tendon meridian posed no problems.

Two down, one to go.

I took a moment to cycle, quickly cataloging the body-wide chill and otherwise lack of noticeable effect it had on my tendons. As it turns out, most people don't really perceive their tendons until they fail. Presumably my newly opened meridian would stop that from happening. I knew at the very least the tendon meridian was considered a prerequisite to opening the muscle meridian. Empowering one without the other held obvious dangers.

My pool of qi still more than sufficient, I didn't bother taking in more before directing my focus to the entrance of my sense meridian just behind the bridge of my nose. My reading on the sense meridian had left me somewhat perturbed.

The process of opening it seemed simple enough, yet most cultivators reported a painful recovery period as their bodies acclimated to the explosion of information. Some opted to open their brain meridians first to help process it all, but I didn't want to wait. Besides, when had my qi ever behaved the same as everyone else's?

The moment I pressed my needle of dark qi into the blocked channel, my visualization *blurred*. I saw two, three, four copies of my construct piercing through four identical meridians. I pushed them all forward.

Bright light flared beneath my eyelids. My ears rang with a thousand sirens. My nostrils burned with dryness and the oppressive scent of the toxins I'd purged thus far. My tongue exploded with heat and cold and an overwhelming mishmash of vile flavor. I edged on.

My spiritual senses flickered in and out, my qi and the meridian through which it struggled vanishing and reappearing blurrier and messier than before. Black gunk flowed from my tear ducts, down my ears, out my nose.

The image in my mind's eye blinked out entirely.

And then it came back, crisp, clear, and sharper than ever. Qi flowed freely through the open meridian. Tension drained my body. I'd done it.

My eyes flicked open and I took in the world around me, unbothered by the flood of sensory data. It all seemed muted, grayer and softer yet more detailed than I could've imagined. My unempowered brain failed entirely to process it all, leaving me to frantically pore over it consciously to pick out the details that mattered compared to the ones that didn't.

Nothing leapt out. Nothing overwhelmed. I looked at the world as if through a machine's eyes, taking in the hot water rushing down my back with the same intensity as the muffled conversations two floors below us. It was all just... information.

I cut the flow of qi and the world returned to life. My nose burned and my stomach roiled from the fetid grime that covered me. The warmth and pressure of the shower relaxed my muscles. Xavier looked down on me with both concern and uncertain pride.

I smiled up at him.

Xavier smiled back. "Charlotte's right," he said. "You're going to change everything."

I looked down at myself and back up at him. "Not before showering I'm not."

He laughed. "Clean yourself up, get some rest, then meet me in the lobby. Drinks are on me."

I nodded and smiled again as Xavier left and I shut the shower door. I checked the time. Five hours had passed, five hours for which I felt I owed Xavier some recompense. He'd been remarkably patient and a huge comfort given the risk I'd taken. If nothing else, I knew Lucy appreciated his presence.

Another ninety minutes had passed before I finally shut the water off and reached for my towel. I walked away with my head held high, my heart swelling with pride at my accomplishments over the past two days. Now would come the time for cycling, for acclimating to the changes my body had undergone and fortifying my newly-opened meridians.

I had a long way to go, a lot to learn, and an ungodly amount of practice ahead of me, but for today, if only for today, I was satisfied. I'd done it.

Only as I returned to my room and donned a clean uniform did I open my holopad to find two new messages had come in, one from Elder Lopez, and one from an Ananya Basu. I recognized the last name if not the first.

It was Vihaan's.

I fell back exhausted onto my bed as I scrolled through the missives. Both requested meetings. I exhaled as I drafted my replies.

Hopefully, at least one of them would have good news for me.

17

I awoke to my blaring alarm the following morning with a pounding hangover that lasted approximately forty seconds before I remembered I was cultivator now. I couldn't soothe my head directly, but I could run qi through my blood meridian to improve circulation and through my kidney meridian to fortify my liver. Together with a few healthy swigs of life-giving water, the headache didn't stand a chance.

I halfheartedly celebrated my newly realized ability to cycle while *drinking water.* It was a far cry from passing out of meditation class, but my focus *had* improved. It helped that my qi dulled the impacts of the outside world rather than intensifying them, a fact that felt an awful lot like cheating, but who was I to complain?

Still groggy if no longer in debilitating pain, I dragged myself out of bed and ran through the motions of changing into a less-wrinkled uniform and running a comb through my hair. I paused for a moment before the mirror, remembering something Xavier had told me as we'd downed our third whiskey too many.

Most cultivators' eyes changed at some point as they progressed to better reflect their affinity with their Way.

Usually it came in the form of a color change or slight reshaping of the pupil or iris, and usually not until well into the gem levels, explaining why I hadn't yet seen anyone with wacky eyes. What I *had* seen was the way cycling the sense meridian brought new vibrance to a cultivator's eyes, making their color really pop in a hauntingly intense way.

I'd assumed that cycling *my* sense meridian would do the opposite, mute the color of my eyes just as it paled my skin. According to Xavier, the truth was far spookier.

I evened my breathing and sent qi through my sense meridian, watching the world desaturate around me as I sifted through the flood of information. My heart skipped a beat then raced in panic. My sclera and iris had gone as black as my pupil.

I looked like Cedric.

I looked like a void psycho.

My breath hitched. My focus shattered. Color flooded back to the world and my eyes at once, the humanity returning to my face as I caught my breath and calmed my pounding heart.

This wasn't right. I wasn't insane. I wasn't murderous. I didn't ache for lack of qi. I had more than enough. Xavier would've said something if I'd truly looked like I'd gone VIP, right? I knew Fyrion didn't have all the posters up that RF-31 had, but he had to know at least *that* basic sign, right?

I let out a long sigh and focused up to take another look. This time, I was ready for the sight that greeted me. This time, I got a closer look. This time, I saw what I'd missed.

I had stars in my eyes.

I stared not into the inky abyss of Cedric's gaze, but the infinite promise of the night sky. Foreign constellations depicted new and ancient myths. Nebulae colored the edge of my periphery. Distant galaxies twirled their eternal dance.

In my eyes lay not insatiable hunger nor lifeless nothing, but endless points of life and light, countless fires burning hot against the inexorable cold, a million bulwarks of existence.

My alarm blared once more and I cut off the flow of qi, escaping the depths of my starlit eyes back into the real world. I mentally added my sense meridian to the list of ones I couldn't cycle in public, at least with my eyes open. It was nice to find one that didn't make me look like a corpse, but the change was still far too drastic to show off.

Mind still racing to figure out what exactly it all meant, I stepped out into the hallway and joined a bleary-eyed Nick on his way downstairs. Momentous progress or otherwise, I'd missed yesterday's morning workout. Unless I wanted to be branded a layabout, I couldn't afford to miss another one.

The last thing I needed was to give Elder Lopez another reason to think me a weakling before my meeting with her that night. I already had a feeling it wasn't going to go well.

* * *

I rubbed at the particularly nasty bruise Instructor Long had left on my shoulder as I waited patiently outside Elder Lopez's office.

"Excuse me?" I asked her secretary. "How much longer is it going to be?"

Okay, maybe I wasn't so patient, but in my defense, *she'd* summoned *me*, and I'd already been waiting for half an hour. With how many of the kiddos had—understandably—stayed home from class that day, the combat instructors had been especially... giving with their attention. I wanted nothing more than to eat dinner, lie down, and cycle until my body stopped aching all over, but instead I was here, waiting for Elder Lopez to let me in for the meeting she'd scheduled for *thirty minutes ago.*

The poor secretary only shrugged.

I sighed, debating for the umpteenth time just standing up and leaving. If she didn't want to respect my time, why should I respect hers?

I knew that wouldn't end well. Like it or not, Elder Lopez held authority over me, and given literally *everything* I knew about cultivators, disrespecting her might've been the last thing I ever did. So I sat, and I stewed, and I pictured the look on her face when I inevitably surpassed her. Given how quickly I'd been progressing, it wouldn't take *that* long, right?

"You can go in now."

I leapt to my feet, blinking the daydream out of my thoughts as I stepped into the elder's office. The foul smell of the faux wood veneer all over the walls assaulted my nostrils as I saluted and stood at attention for a bored-looking Elder Lopez.

She glanced up at me with disapproval. "I'm told you elected to skip yesterday morning's workout so you could play vac-welder with the mortals."

"Yes, ma'am. I was helping with the—"

"I'm told," she cut me off, "that rather than fulfilling your duty to this sect to grow stronger, you opted to do the work of mortals."

"The work needed doing and I had the qualif—"

"I'm *told*," she interrupted again, "that immediately following your failure to protect one of the sect's most vulnerable, you forwent the opportunity to help rectify your weakness for a few hours running around outside."

I blinked at her absurd reasoning. "I saved his life! I killed the thing that—"

"You will remember your manners," she snapped.

I swallowed back a retort. "Yes, ma'am. As I was saying, I saved Vihaan's life after he—"

"After *you* allowed a void beast to imperil it. You were one of forty-nine fully fledged sect members present at the time of the attack. You were the only one who oversaw a critically wounded child."

"Ma'am, I haven't been here for two weeks. I've never seen combat. I need more time to—"

She swiped her hand up and a video appeared from a holo projector built into her desk. I stared agape at an image of myself, stunned and horrified, as I froze up for a few seconds before rushing to Vihaan's aid. Elder Lopez ended the feed before I charged the void beast.

"Sheer luck saved that boy's life. Your hesitation gave that void beast plenty of time to end it. Your weakness allowed him to be wounded in the first place."

I spoke behind gritted teeth. "That isn't fair. I couldn't have—"

"And even worse, when confronted with your failure, you make excuses. Instead of working harder at improving yourself, you run away back to your mortal life." She shook her head. "Luckily for you, I'm more forgiving than my peers. Luckily for you, I've removed this security footage from the public logs."

I withheld a sigh as I realized where this was going. "Thank you, ma'am."

"Of course, I can't allow this transgression to go unpunished, nor, if you value your position here, should my kindness go unrewarded."

I exhaled. "If I give you a focus room hour, will you let this be?"

A thin smile stretched across her face. "The loss of focus room time does sound like a suitable punishment." She nodded. "I will allow it."

I had to shut my eyes to keep myself from rolling them as I pulled up my holopad and made the transfer. "Will that be all, ma'am?"

"For now," she replied. "Remember, your benefactor expects great things from you. So does the Dragon's Right Eye. I would recommend you spend less time drinking and cavorting with mortals and more time on your studies. You're dismissed."

I would've saluted again if I'd ever *stopped* saluting throughout the conversation. Instead, I simply turned on my heel and left the office, bristling over the encounter.

Blackmail I could understand. Saving potentially compromising video footage to steal resources made sense. I didn't quite understand why she felt the need to obfuscate it behind the thin veil of doling out punishment or whatever the fuck that had been all about, but the end result had been the same.

She'd wanted a focus hour. She'd gotten a focus hour. All the bullshit power plays and shitty fault-finding and disapproval were obnoxious, but meaningless. I hadn't done anything wrong. I hoped Vihaan and his parents would understand that. They were the only ones I really cared about, and given that they'd invited me to dinner rather than requested a meeting, I had high hopes.

I left it at that. Sure, the loss of the focus hour meant Charlotte would have to wait a week for her next turn at an extra hour, but that was hardly the end of the world. I'd even planned for such occurrences when I'd designed the schedule. It sucked that my direct superior wanted to be a self-serving asshole, but given what Lucy had told me, that was kind of the default state for cultivators. I'd live.

I was late to dinner that night, a product of the half hour I'd had to wait outside Elder Lopez's office. The others hadn't waited for me, an understandable decision given the way I'd completely missed the meal two nights ago. They did have the good grace to sit with me as I ate and listen to me gripe about Elder Lopez. Apparently I wasn't the only cadet who rather disliked the woman.

I retired early to cultivate and take my nightly audio call with Lucy. She agreed with my analysis, adding the insight that even in her corruption, Elder Lopez felt the need to maintain the appearance of moral superiority. It all just felt like silly posturing to me.

The next couple of days passed in a flurry as I exercised and studied and practiced cycling my new meridians in and out of class. Bit by bit my classmates returned, noticeably quieter and more reserved after our shared trauma. The instructors went easy on them, or at least *easier*.

I knew I'd technically met the requirements to pass out of Chrissy's cycling class, but I still lacked the fine control I really wanted, and it would've attracted attention if I'd done so so early. Besides, she was the only instructor I actually *liked*. I wasn't in a hurry to replace her.

The Basus, knowing my schedule for its similarity to Vihaan's, had been kind enough to schedule our dinner for an hour after combat class ended, leaving me plenty of time to get myself washed up and in a clean uniform. I spent the pod ride over reassuring my strangely frantic nerves, reminding myself that the kind of parents whose kid would give away his lunch to a hungry stranger couldn't be *that* bad.

The lobby of family housing B struck me as remarkably unfamiliar, seemingly a different space entirely than the chaotic room to which I'd delivered an injured Vihaan or the empty hall I'd awoken in. Cultivators and mortals went about their business. People milled about. Young children clung to their parents' hands. Teenagers scowled and slouched and stalked about. It looked… normal.

I followed my holopad's instructions up to apartment two-nineteen, where the metal door slid open to reveal four and a half feet of unadulterated cuteness.

"Mister Caliban!" Vihaan raced up to me and wrapped

me in a great hug.

"It's just Cal, buddy." I hugged him back. "Just Cal. How are you doing?"

He pulled back. "The doctors say I can come back to meditation and cycling class in two days, but I have to wait two whole weeks for combat class!"

"Well, you'd better listen to them. We wouldn't want you to hurt yourself any worse."

"He's right, you know."

I looked up to find two women standing side by side, one that mirrored Vihaan's dark complexion, and another with the same vibrant blue eyes. The former extended her hand.

"Ananya Basu," she introduced herself. "And my wife, Lisa."

I shook both of their hands. "Cal. It's a pleasure to meet you."

"Come in, come in," Lisa beckoned me. "Vihaan has told us so much about you."

"Hopefully more good than bad," I replied. "Some of our instructors have some… choice words about my presence."

Ananya smiled grimly. "Some of your instructors are bitter that they're stuck teaching beginner classes."

I laughed. "That explains so much." I followed them into a spacious, two-bedroom apartment decorated in all the usual trappings alongside a number of gorgeously crafted metalwork sculptures. Lifelike statues of meditating cultivators or wild animals seemed ready to jump to life next to abstract art pieces of sharp angles and delicate curves.

"These are brilliant," I commented as they led me to a marble table set for four. "Where did you find them?"

"They're Lisa's," Ananya answered. "She has a master's touch."

"You stop that," Lisa chided. "You helped with at least half of these." She wrapped an arm around Ananya's waist. "And you *inspired* all of them."

"*Mom,*" Vihaan complained. "You're being gross."

I laughed and rustled his hair. "You'll understand when you're older."

Ananya separated from her wife. "Can I offer you a drink? Dinner won't be ready for another few minutes, but in the meantime we have a bottle of Wechelian red we've been saving."

"I'd love some," I answered, having no idea what Wechelian meant. I assumed it was some vineyard on Iliria. I did my level best to hide my complete ignorance of the wine world as I sipped the aged burgundy. It was good. I said as much. "It's good."

"Mmm," Lisa replied as she took a sip of her own. "Yeah, that's the stuff."

I blinked, unsure of the etiquette for this type of interaction before realizing there probably wasn't any. I took another sip of my wine. "So... you two work with metal?"

Ananya smiled. "We met in the foundry and haven't left yet. Lisa's sculptures are the pride of the sect."

"And Ananya's weapons help keep us safe," Lisa inserted. "I just make pretty shapes."

"I think you mean *gorgeous* shapes."

"*Moms.*"

I chuckled. "It's hard work," I said. "I was a vac-welder before I became a cultivator, and let me tell you I *wish* I'd had the skills to work in the foundry."

"Vac-welding is important," Lisa argued. "Some of us *enjoy* continuing to breathe. In fact, I did my apprenticeship with—"

An alarm beeped in the kitchen behind me.

"That's the stew!" Ananya jumped to her feet and

scurried away from the table. Lisa followed, the two of them assembling plates of slow-cooked beef stew over rice with a side of roasted vegetables. I thanked them profusely as they placed the dish in front of me.

We had a truly wonderful dinner. The wine was tasty, the food was magnificent, and the conversation was lovely. Lisa told the story of how the two of them met when she'd accidentally used up a pile of scrap that'd belonged to Ananya, and promptly made it up to her by crafting a stunning silver necklace Ananya still wore to this day.

In turn I shared the tale of my ongoing cooking war with Lucy, my only story that even held a candle to any of theirs. Most of my best stories weren't fit for polite company, let alone the dinner table.

We left the subject of the void incursion alone, at least until the dinner had wrapped up and Vihaan had adjourned to his room. Only in the lad's absence did the conversation turn serious.

"Vihaan told us what you did for him," Lisa said, "the risk you took to save his life."

"I did what anyone would've done," I replied. "I was lucky, really."

"That's not the way he put it," Ananya countered. "You killed a void beast. You brought him to safety. You risked your life to get him to a doctor in time."

I instinctively looked to take a sip of my wine. The glass was empty.

Ananya stood. "You may've wondered why we waited so long to have you over."

I hadn't. I'd assumed Vihaan had needed time to recover. I nodded anyway.

She grabbed something from behind the counter and hid it behind her back as she returned to the table. "I needed time to make you this. I doubt we'll ever be able to repay the debt we owe, to *properly* thank you for saving our son's life, but I hope this will go some way towards showing our appreciation."

From behind her back she revealed a sword sheathed in faux black leather. Matching ebon grip tape wrapped its hilt, leaving only the gleaming silver hand guard and rounded pommel visible. I took it.

Ananya smiled. "Draw it."

I obeyed. The blade stretched just over three feet long, length enough to justifiably be wielded in one or two hands. Its edges were straight and on both sides, but its tip was aligned not with the center, but with one particular side, giving it a clear front and back edge. To my amateur eyes it seemed somewhere between a saber and a longsword, a strange design, but one that smacked of flexibility above all else.

I supposed that made sense for a cultivator with no discernible style. Either way, they were the experts, and I trusted they'd built the right blade for me.

Beneath the warm glow of the light fixture above us, the metal shimmered with a thousand swirling lines, the bright silver clashing with the dark streaks that ran through it. "It's beautiful."

Lisa grinned. "She has a master's touch," she echoed her wife's earlier words.

"I wasn't sure what fighting style you'd develop, so I went with a design that could fit into as many as possible," Ananya explained. "It's an alloy of steel and Fyrion silver, not the strongest sword I've ever made, but perhaps the most spiritually significant."

I looked up at her askance.

Lisa explained. "We took the steel from the freezer cart you used to save Vihaan's life."

I gaped.

Ananya nodded. "As a brute force implement it may fall short, but as a channel for your qi and extension of your spirit, you'll be hard pressed to find a better weapon."

"I—uh—thank you," I managed, looking them each in the eyes before the blade itself reclaimed my gaze, a blade forged by a parent in thanks from the silver on which we stood and the steel used to save her child's life. "This is amazing."

"You've earned it," Lisa said, "and so much more."

"If there's anything you ever need here on Fyrion," Ananya added, "just ask. We'll make it happen."

"This..." I trailed off as the blade's beauty caught my attention yet again. I sheathed it, a metal slot along the sheath's side opening up as it sensed the sword's proximity and guided the weapon home. "This is plenty. Thank you, really."

Lisa shook her head. "Thank *you*, Caliban Rex."

Ananya flashed a warm smile. "May it serve you well."

I offered three times to help them clean up the dinner they'd cooked me, only to find myself ushered out the door with a sword in one hand and a fresh-baked cookie in the other. As oven-warm chocolate chips melted over my tongue, I couldn't decide which was the better parting gift.

Actually nevermind. I had a fucking sword.

All jokes aside, it warmed my heart to find that Vihaan was okay. As much as I resented Elder Lopez's maneuvering or reveled in his parents' adoration, that was all that really mattered.

I made it back to my room that night with an indomitable grin on my face. Lucy may have been right about some cultivators. Some of them *were* self-serving, manipulative, dicks. But not all of them.

Some earnestly strove to be the best version of themselves they could be. Some would give away their lunch to feed a hungry stranger. Some just wanted to make sure that those they cared about stayed safe.

And some had just forged me the coolest goddamn

sword I'd ever seen.

That was good enough for me.

18

The following day—exactly one before my next rest day—
Arthur flagged me down on my way from breakfast to the
transport platform. Once I'd completed that awkward
half-jog-half-walk you do when someone's waiting for you,
I leaned over the reception desk to hear what he had to say.

"I have tomorrow off," he led. "Since I know you do
too, I was thinking *tonight* we go out for drinks. Celebrate
that heroism of yours."

I snapped my fingers and pointed at him. "Deal.
Caveat—you pick the place. It'll be nice to get away from
all these damn cultivators for a while."

Arthur exhaled in amusement. "You *are* one of those
damn cultivators."

"Not tonight I'm not. Tonight I'm just Cal, I'm a vac-
welder, and I am getting *hammered.*"

He smiled. "I know just the place."

"First round's on you!" I called over my shoulder as I
turned to go. Just because he's a mortal and I was a
cultivator didn't mean I wasn't just as near broke as he
was. I heard him laughing behind me as I boarded the
transport pod.

Class itself wasn't more or less boring and unpleasant

than I'd come to expect, but the prospect of a night out powered me through the long hours of silent meditation and Instructor Long's abuse. Gods it sounded nice to escape all the cultivator bullshit for an evening and just live my life like a normal gods damned human being.

I eagerly waved at Arthur as I returned from dinner to run upstairs, take a quick shower, and rid myself of the sect uniform that had regretfully come to define me over these past few weeks. I left my shiny new sword sitting on my desk as I threw on a T-shirt, leather jacket, and a black pair of those loose cultivator pants I'd inherited from Cedric. Damn were those comfy.

Fully de-sect-ified, I made it downstairs just in time to find Arthur greeting his evening-shift replacement. The elderly woman bowed her head at me. "Cadet."

Arthur raised an eyebrow. "Cadet? Where? I don't see any cadets here."

"I'll have your tongue for that you insolent swine! How dare you insult my illustrious—nah I'm just kidding." I flashed a shit-eating grin. "C'mon. Let's get out of here."

Arthur led me through the back, past the break room and its ping pong table into the back passage the staff members used. He pointed out the doors to the kitchens, laundry, life support, and various maintenance rooms as we walked, a quick and dirty guide to what housing D was *actually* like for those that worked there.

In a word: cramped. The hallway barely fit two abreast, forcing me to dip behind Arthur whenever we passed someone. The ceiling was low, walls lacking windows, the lighting pale and somehow both discomfortingly bright and insufficient to fully illuminate the space.

"This passage actually passes under the transport tunnels," he told me as we walked. "If I wake up early enough, I'll skip the pods entirely and just walk to work. It doesn't take much longer, and any amount of motion helps before sitting at a desk all day."

Despite his words, he led me up a narrow stairway to a dingy transport platform. Some four dozen mortals milled about, crowding the limited space as the shift change pushed the system beyond its capacity.

Arthur shouldered us through, weaving through the mass of people to get us just close enough to make it into the first pod to arrive.

In contrast to Elder Lopez's private pod with its plush chairs and center table, or even the sect ones I used every day, the staff pods lacked seats entirely. We crammed in like sardines, shoulder to shoulder, chest to back. A few handholds dangled from the ceiling to stop people falling over as the pod lurched into motion, but nobody touched them. The density of the crowd enforced stability on its own. The entire compartment quaked as it moved, its walls thinner, less stable, less insulated against the noise.

We stopped twice to allow a handful of passengers to exchange places with new boarders before the cramped staffing platforms gave way to a massive open one. We, alongside two thirds of our temporary traveling companions, disembarked into a cacophony of light and noise given name by a faded sign on the platform wall.

Droe Lane

"Welcome to the busiest, most important place on all of Fyrion," Arthur regaled me over the din of voices, laughter, and the echoing dance music drifting in from eight different directions. He led me down the steps onto a busy thoroughfare.

Someone, officially or otherwise, had disabled the overhead full-spectrum lighting, leaving only the colored glow of a thousand LEDs and neon signs to light the way.

Let me be clear, Droe Lane was *dark*. It reminded me of the back alleys between the nightclubs back home, away from the glow of the streetlamps and hidden from the moonlight in the shadow of the buildings themselves.

The kind of place you'd go if you were in the mood to get stabbed.

The entire street matched that aesthetic, well over forty feet wide and not quite packed but certainly busy with foot traffic. The chemical stench of cheap alcohol hung in the air like a fog, pierced only by the deeply unpleasant undertones of three different bodily fluids.

"Right now, we're smack dab in the middle of the three biggest apartment complexes on the planet," Arthur did his best to tour guide as we weaved around revelers, stepped over spilled drinks or dropped food, and avoided making eye contact with the scantily clad men and women plying their wares. "That makes it the go-to evening destination for half the city. Since most jobs stagger their off days, you'll see a different crowd of people here every night."

We passed by a man leaning against a dark wall with his eyes closed, audibly snoring, yet still upright. Three beer bottles lay at his feet. "Except for folks like Yorick there," Arthur added. "You know how it gets. Some people never leave."

Given the sudden seriousness of the subject matter, I withheld the "alas, poor Yorick" joke that leapt to the tip of my tongue. Now wasn't the time.

"So this place is like this every night?" I asked.

"What?"

"It's like this every night?" I repeated, but louder.

"Oh, yeah. Some of the locals treat partying like an art form. And some of them…" He trailed off as an exchange of shouts caught our attention from up ahead. A ring of people had gathered, through the heads of which I caught two men engaged in what seemed to be a fistfight.

Arthur pulled me away. "Don't engage. Don't get caught up. Best to keep moving."

I nodded along as we continued to walk, craning my neck to look back at the brawl behind us despite myself. From there I took to looking into the darker corners of Droe Lane, past the neon signs to the broken windows and flaking paint beyond. Arthur dragged me ever forward, fighting to keep me from lingering or otherwise thinking too hard about our surroundings, but even he couldn't keep me from stopping short when I saw *her.*

She was lying in an alley, her legs tucked into the two-foot-wide space between a bar and a dance hall, her torso sprawled out onto the sidewalk. Her glittery dress did little to hide the needle marks up and down both her arms. Her make-up had run where a now-dried stream of vomit trailed down her cheek. Three blood spots marked where the knife had entered her chest.

The other passersby seemed entirely content to ignore her, stepping around or even directly over the pale corpse without so much as blinking, without so much as deigning to allow this stranger's death to come between them and their evening of revelry.

Arthur grabbed me by the wrist and tugged me along. "They'll get to it in the morning," he explained. "There's always a few of them, each night."

I glared at him. "And you're just *okay* with that?"

He shrugged. "That's life. That's what happens when you borrow money from the wrong people."

The sheer nonchalance of it all, from Arthur, from the authorities, from *everybody*, cast a cloud over my mood even as Arthur finally pulled up at a place I'd charitably call "a charming dive." The Three-Legged Pony, as the screen in the window declared, had an almost cozy sort of grime to it.

Countless sets of names and initials and crude depictions of genitalia had been carved into every inch of the hard resin tables, crafting the perfect channels for every spilled cocktail to get trapped and keep sticky until the end of time. They were the kind of tables you tell yourself not to lean on, only to wind up doing exactly that without a care in the world by the time drink number four arrived.

The clientele seemed happy enough to keep to themselves, leaving Arthur and I to chat in the relative privacy of the cacophony of conversation around us while some kind of arrhythmic folk techno drifted in from the club next-door.

Credit where credit is due, the waiter—a middle-aged man with shadows under his eyes darker than this story— delivered our drinks mere minutes after we'd tapped our orders into our holopads. Arthur had some kind of dark and bitter spritz, while I got a tall glass of something the menu had simply called "the blue."

I have no idea what was in it, but damn was it blue. I'm talking toxic waste meets swimming pool blue. Threads, it even *tasted* blue. Well, like low-quality alcohol and blue.

By the time I'd downed my third one, I'd stopped tasting the alcohol. Then it was just *blue*.

It took until about that time for Arthur to distract me from the corpse we'd seen stuffed into a dark alley and move on to more pleasant conversation. We took turns picking out random strangers from the crowd and coming up with their increasingly absurd life stories, we shared jokes and dreams and embarrassing stories, and Arthur even let me in on some of the hot gossip among the housing D staff.

Twice over the course of the evening did Arthur—with the aid of my *incredible* pep talks—work up the courage to get up and approach some of the more obviously single women at the bar. I cheered him on but otherwise stayed put. I was here to have fun, not get my skinny ass rejected by some woman I'd never see again either way.

And it was fun. It was good, genuine, fun. The kind I

hadn't had since I'd come here. Since roofie. Threads had I needed it.

But you know what they say about all good things.

The Three-Legged Pony had only just started to wind down as Arthur and I closed our tab, but even as we pushed to our feet and wound our way to the exit, newcomers pushed their way in to claim the smattering of open tables.

Officially, the fun well and truly came to an end as we stepped back out into the chaos of Droe Lane to find two of the absolutely *widest* individuals I'd ever seen standing in front of us.

"Excuse me, fellas, you're in our way," I slurred at them.

Arthur froze.

The goon on the left, in faded jeans and a stained T-shirt that clung to the altogether too many muscles on his upper body, flashed a toothy grin. "Well, Humphrey, would you look who it is."

Goon two, presumably Humphrey, in a slightly less ragged version of the same gooniform, mirrored the smile. "Hello there, Arthur. Victor wants to talk to you."

"For the last time, I don't know where she went." Arthur's words came quick and pleading, a fearful color to them. Given the sheer mass of the duo in front of us, I understood where it came from.

"That's not what Victor says," goon one replied. "Victor says you helped her give him the slip."

"Well you can tell Victor I don't own my sister any more than he does," Arthur insisted, his hands visibly shaking.

"What do you think, Dennis?" Humphrey asked, finally giving a name to his fellow goon. "Do you believe him?"

"I think Victor wants to ask for himself," Dennis said.

I took that as my cue. "I think if Victor has a question he can come and ask it himself." Already I cycled qi through my blood and kidneys to clear as much of the alcohol out of my system as I could.

"Stay out of this, Cal," Arthur whispered sharply at me.

I ignored him. "Look, if meathead here and his partner…" I scrambled for a second scathing nickname. "…meatshoulders wanna talk, they can talk. If they want to stop us from going about our evening… that's another matter entirely."

Meatshoulders cracked his knuckles. "Looks like someone's got a mouth on 'em."

I raised an eyebrow. "You'd prefer I didn't have a mouth? How would I eat?"

As my mouth and I hurtled headlong into what I was pretty sure would be a losing fistfight, three thoughts crossed my head.

The first was that this was a really bad idea.

The second was that I couldn't just stand by and let them take Arthur to some dark alley, not after what I'd already seen that night.

The third was that I dearly wished I'd brought my sword.

"You'll be eating through a tube if you don't step aside," meathead—I mean Dennis—threatened.

"Wouldn't that be drinking? That sounds more like drinking."

Humphrey swung at me.

I was ready.

My skin went cold and deathly pale as I ran qi through my skin meridian, fortifying and solidifying it as I fell into one of the unarmed forms Instructor Davis had drilled into me again and again. *Technically* The Dragon's Grasp was designed as a desperate ploy against an armed opponent, but it turns out, it works even *better* when your foe doesn't have a weapon.

With my right palm I pushed his fist aside, lunging in to jam my elbow into his throat. He stumbled back, clutching his windpipe as he gasped for air. I didn't give him a chance to recover.

I advanced again, delivering a left-handed jab backed by the momentum of my step directly into his stomach. Still fighting for breath, his abdomen wasn't tensed for the blow.

He doubled over as I knocked the air out of him. With a hand to the back of his head, I slammed my knee into his nose. It broke with a sickening crack.

That's when I learned you can't just ignore one of your opponents.

Dennis's fist crashed into the back of my skull, sending black spots racing across my vision but failing to otherwise damage the qi-enforced bone. I stumbled forward, past the now-kneeling Humphrey, to build a bit of distance between the still-standing combatant and myself.

I turned just in time to block his follow-up with my face.

A year ago, such a strike would've shattered my jaw, knocked loose at least a couple teeth, and sent me sprawling to the floor.

Today, my head simply twisted to the side as his fist continued past.

I grabbed his overextended arm, at first intending to yank him off balance before realizing my fingers couldn't actually wrap far enough around his bicep to manage that.

So I shoved.

Dennis stumbled back, his right arm pinned to his chest as I pushed my advantage. With it out of position, he offered flimsy resistance as I stepped in for three quick jabs to the face. A black eye and a bleeding cheekbone later, I hooked my heel behind his ankle and kicked back, sending him onto his ass.

I exhaled.

I looked up at the crowd of onlookers, drinks and trays of greasy food in hand, as they stared at my corpselike appearance.

I turned to Dennis and Humphrey and uttered my final remark, loud enough for our audience to hear. "Arthur Kent is under sect protection. Do not approach him again."

I didn't get a chance to hear their replies before Arthur grabbed my wrist and pulled me into the night. At a near run he led me, further and further from the scene of the fight as I peppered him with questions.

"What was that all about?"

"My sister," Arthur growled over his shoulder as we sped on. "She used to work at one of the restaurants that asshole Victor shakes down. He's obsessed with her. She had to flee the city to get away. Now he thinks *I* can lead him to her."

"Threads, Arthur. Why didn't you tell me?"

"I didn't think it'd be a problem," he said. "Last week I told him I didn't know where she went, and I thought that was the end of it."

"Clearly not."

"Clearly," he snapped.

Only as we reached the busy transport platform did he finally stop. "Are you okay?"

I spat out blood, but a quick probe with my tongue confirmed my teeth were all where they were supposed to be. "I'll be fine. You?"

"Yeah. I just…" He shuddered. "You didn't have to do that."

"Yes, I did. Those dudes weren't gonna take no for an answer."

"You could've gotten yourself killed. You could've gotten *me* killed. Cal, you can't just go picking fights with —"

"I know I'm a cultivator now, Arthur." I cut him off. "But I didn't grow up one. You don't need to tell me how this works."

Arthur opened his mouth as if to speak again, but after a pause, let out only a sigh instead. "You're right. Thank you."

"C'mon." I patted him on the shoulder as I requested a pod with my holopad. Thankfully, one of the sect ones pulled up. It was empty. "Let's get you home."

We rode in silence, arriving within minutes.

I wanted to walk Arthur all the way to his door, but he steadfastly refused. He seemed confident enough that meathead and meatshoulders were the only goons at Victor's disposal, so I let him go. Those two wouldn't be coming after him again any time soon.

Still, I left Arthur with a message. "If any of them contact you again, you let me know. I'll deal with them."

Arthur gulped and hesitated for a moment, but did eventually nod. "I will. Thanks."

I smiled, hoping I'd managed to get *most* of the blood out of my teeth. "That's what friends are for."

As the doors closed behind him and the transport pod whisked me back to housing D, I reflected on the evening's revelations.

Droe Lane had certainly been… *different*, but in the end, none of it had been anything I hadn't seen before.

Cultivator or mortal, on Fyrion or back home, there would always be people who thought they could take whatever they wanted. There would always be Lopezes and Longs and Victors.

There would always be assholes.

If nothing else, I'd learned a lesson.

I was a cultivator now. That came with power, that came with responsibility, and that came with danger. By the time the pod doors opened to reveal the neat and sterile housing D lobby, I'd made to myself a hard and fast commitment.

From now on out, no matter where I went or who I went

there with, I carried a sword.

19

The next few weeks blurred past as I threw myself into my studies. Each day I awoke to my holopad's alarm at the crack of six—formerly five twenty-seven before I'd re-synced my circadian time to Fyrion's schedule—and joined Nick on the way downstairs for the morning workout.

Approximately two hours of weightlifting, agility training, and boring old cardio later, the four of us—who I'd in secret begun to think of as my crew—went to breakfast. Charlotte daintily dined upon strictly measured portions of unsweetened oatmeal, berries, and artificial meat grown with such low fat I considered it an abomination against nature and flavor both.

Xavier, in contrast, piled his plate high with anything from scrambled eggs to chicken apple sausages depending on his mood, always including no fewer than two waffles drenched in the appropriate quantity of maple syrup. I tended to follow his approach, stacking my plate with whatever looked tastiest that morning, more so in an attempt to get myself to eat than for lack of nutritional care.

Fat seemed to shy away from my body, leaving my wiry muscles well-toned but without anything resembling Xavier's bulk. More and more I found I had to force myself to eat, appetite staved off by the qi in my stomach meridian. Compared to the voraciousness I saw in the others, it made sense. Making sense, though, didn't mean I liked it.

That wasn't to say I didn't grow stronger—I readily tracked my progress as I lifted heavier and heavier weights —but nobody, I repeat, *nobody*, lifts weights exclusively to get stronger. We all care a little about how we look.

Nick, similarly, failed to bulk up, though certainly not for lack of appetite. The boy ate as much as Xavier and I combined, a miraculous feat at half Xavier's weight. It was never enough. A black hole seemed to reside within his belly, unceasingly hungry and unwilling to share its bounty with the rest of Nick's body.

Charlotte balked, at first, at Nick's absurd caloric intake, but Xavier simply slapped him on his back and concluded that even at sixteen, he was clearly still growing. I declined to weigh in, explaining it away as somewhere between being a growing boy and the cultivating prodigy his parents seemed to think him. All cultivators, bar myself, had supernatural appetites, after all. Why wouldn't an especially promising cultivator have an especially large appetite?

After breakfast my friends left to shower and go about whatever it was they did all day while I hastened on to my nine o'clock meditation class.

Far and away the least interesting of the classes, meditation was the first to which Vihaan returned. After the ice cream day fiasco, my classmates had moved from suspicious neutrality to grudging respect, no longer outright scowling at me, but making no effort to interact or otherwise make friends. That changed the day Vihaan returned.

They all watched as their wounded peer rushed into the classroom to wrap me in a great hug, listened at lunch as he told and retold a rather exaggerated version of my actions that day, and heard in no uncertain terms that I'd saved his life.

Apparently, saving his life wasn't enough to get him to call me anything but 'Mister Caliban,' but I'd take what I could get.

From then on I became an object of fascination for the children, unable to exist in their presence without answering a barrage of questions on everything from why I'd become a cultivator to my favorite dessert. I answered ice cream to both.

As for meditation itself, I made consistent progress as the days dragged on, maintaining my focus through more and more of the senior cadets' abuse. At least, after my work with Lucy, my posture didn't require correcting. I refused to cycle during class, feeling my qi's numbing effects would cheapen the training, but I knew that had I tried, I could've advanced to meditation two then and there.

I didn't.

Charlotte and I had already worked out a strict schedule for when I could reasonably pass out of each class without arousing suspicion. I had two months of meditation one to go.

After a lunch break filled to the brim with questions from curious classmates, Chrissy arrived to lead us in my favorite class of the day.

I realized, far later than I would've liked to admit, that many of her cycling exercises were designed to help improve a young cultivator's qi sense and work towards maximizing the percentage of the ambient qi they could pull into their core. My qi sense was already so sensitive that it hurt, and even a minuscule percentage of the ocean outside overwhelmed me.

Charlotte had implied that an important step in forming

your seed core was stretching out your center to fit as much qi as possible, but I was still three meridians shy of that part. All of my remaining unopened meridians weren't taught until cycling three, a class I wouldn't reach for another six months according to Charlotte's schedule, so little of what Chrissy was allowed to teach actually applied to me.

I mostly ignored her instruction, keeping out of the way as I built up my resistance to the local qi's migraine-inducing effects and practiced various illicitly obtained exercises targeting my spine meridian.

For all her talk about not trusting me, Charlotte hadn't hesitated to break sect rules and offer instruction on things she was absolutely not authorized to teach. The spine meridian, according to a few documents she'd sent me, governed the lower nervous system, including but not limited to instinct, reflex, and pain. The latter of which made it the fucking worst to prepare for, as most exercises involved teaching yourself to ignore your instincts, your reflexes, or your pain in anticipation for all three to go haywire.

If anything was going to give my desperate crawl down roofie's gangway into Lucy's airlock a run for its money, it'd be opening my spine meridian.

Theoretically, with my skin, bone, kidney, and stomach meridians open, I could've advanced out of Chrissy's class any day, but again, Charlotte's schedule held me back. I was happy to oblige. Chrissy was nice, and while incessant, my classmates had finally started treating me as a friend rather than a threat.

For those first few days after he came back, Vihaan clung inseparably to my side as we walked from Chrissy's classroom to the dojo. I made a point of hastening as we passed through *that* hallway.

Of them all, combat class proved both the most painful

and the most challenging as I either sparred with or suffered under the instruction of one of the three senior cadets.

The void horde attack had firmly placed the class's importance into my mind, so I bit back my glib impulses and took my lumps with an eye towards improvement. Some combination of my renewed diligence and Vihaan's extolling of my virtues managed to earn some respect from Instructors Charleston and Davis, but Instructor Long maintained I'd done an underwhelming job of something any true cultivator could've achieved far more easily.

I didn't like Instructor Long.

Of them all, combat class posed the biggest barrier to achieving Elder Lopez's deadline of catching up to the other cadets by the year's end. Rather than sandbagging my ability to hide my progress, I'd have to train hard to meet the necessary milestones. It didn't help that I needed to convince Instructor Long of all people of my skills, but I'd cross that bridge when I came to it. In the meantime, I started drilling with my new sword.

They didn't let me spar with it for obvious reasons, but I spent hours drawing and sheathing it over and over, until I could bring the blade to bear from its home on my back without conscious thought. The steel and silver's difference to the weighted practice swords threw my balance off entirely, forcing me to relearn the minutia of the basic swings I'd spent weeks practicing. It came easier the second time.

Xavier had absolutely gushed over the weapon when I'd first shown it to him, insisting I run through some forms with him then and there. By his judgment, I'd performed miserably yet demonstrated 'a hero's resolve to accept failure.' Threads that man had a confusing outlook.

On his advice, I carried the sword with me wherever I went, less for protection than to grow comfortable around

J.P. Valentine

the weapon. According to Xavier, true mastery required a cultivator's weapon to act as an extension of his body, both as a tool for dealing death and a channel for his qi.

In addition to my combat class, he gave me a list of forms to work through each night, dominating yet another hour of my already packed schedule. At least the AI that judged my accuracy with the forms just beeped how badly I'd failed rather than smacking me with a stick to make corrections mid-motion. It made for a less productive lesson, but a significantly more pleasant one.

Dinner each night varied on the whims of housing D's cooking staff, but it always included enough variety to keep everyone at least mostly happy. My only consistent dining behavior was to forego the salad in favor of something I'd actually enjoy eating, usually some kind of meat, starch, and roasted vegetable.

Only Charlotte and Nick partook of the nightly salad, the former as a part of a well portioned plate and the latter as the first course of four.

After dinner I had an hour to spend either sparring with Xavier, peppering Charlotte with questions and requests for more documents, or reading. Threads I did a lot of reading. I read about void beast classifications—they're entirely based on size, by the way. Any link between type and threat level is completely arbitrary. I read about cycling techniques, fighting styles, and pre-meridian exercises. I read about anything and everything that caught my interest, staying up long into the night before I finally called Lucy for our evening update before bed.

And so the days passed.

I spent my off days playing ping pong with Arthur, sparring with the others, and in ceaseless meditation, only allowing myself to relax in those late hours alone in my room with endless dense manuals and academic papers to read and the curiosity to wade through them.

The work never stopped. The training never ended. The nights blipped by in a matter of seconds before my alarm blared again and I set about once more upon the grind of repetitive, incremental progress. No revelations came, no mastery sprang from nought, no void beasts descended. I woke up, I worked tirelessly to improve in some small yet measurable way, I went to bed sore and exhausted. Rinse and repeat.

Six weeks into my stay on Fyrion, the twin suns rose on a day I'd been anticipating and dreading since my arrival: dueling day.

It began, as all important days ought, with breakfast.

"You guys should've *seen* the gym this morning," I greeted them, wiping sweat from my brow as I sat at our usual table. "Absolute ghost town. Would've thought people wanted to warm up before they fight."

"There'll be time before the first round," Xavier explained. "Better to save your energy for when you need it."

I shrugged and grabbed a chocolate chip banana muffin off my tray. "Not like I could win even if I wanted to." I sank my teeth into the muffin top, tearing away almost half of it in a bite so large I immediately regretted it.

Xavier scowled at me. "You should always desire to win. The ceaseless drive for victory distinguishes the cultivator from the mortal."

I swallowed, pausing to gulp down water to wash it down. "I'm pretty sure generational wealth distinguishes the cultivator from the mortal, but I see your point. Counterpoints: I don't need any of the rewards the sect grants for a high ranking, I won't waste time fighting off challengers if I stay at the bottom, and somehow winning when six weeks ago I only had four meridians open would draw way too much attention."

Charlotte nodded along. "He's right."

"I know," Xavier grumbled. "I don't like it, but I know."

I took another bite of my muffin.

Our conversation lulled for a few moments as we ate, each absorbed in our own pre-duel worlds, before a cacophony exploded through the vast mess hall as a thousand holopads beeped at once.

"Huh." I glanced down at the message. "Pairings are up." I discarded my now-empty muffin wrapper and moved in on some hash browns.

Xavier and Charlotte both similarly nodded and continued eating, leaving a bewildered Nick to gape at us while all around our neighbors pored over their pairings. "Y…you guys don't care?"

Xavier beamed. "A true champion accepts any challenge that comes his way."

Nick blinked. "Right. You, I get." He glanced over at me. "And you don't care because you're going to lose anyway." He turned his eyes to Charlotte. "But why are you not obsessively crafting battle plans right now?"

"I already have. I set my pairings up weeks ago."

Nick gaped. "You can do that?"

Xavier glared at her, his voice turning sharp. "No. You can't."

"*You* can't," Charlotte clarified. "The elders make the pairings, and most elders are willing to move things around a bit if the right person asks."

I raised an eyebrow at her. "And you're the right person?"

"Threads no, but I know who is." She opened her holopad, spinning its display to show off her three scheduled duels. She started at the top. "Benjamin Plithe, rank thirty-nine-oh-two is the son of Elder Plithe. He feels my father got too much of the credit for *his* grandmother's work during the void horde a few cycles back. I hired a dozen mortal staff members to talk about how great my father is as he passed by, just enough to remind him of the bad blood between our families, just enough for him to convince his daddy that he needs to put House Velereau in its place."

She lowered her finger to indicate the next name. "I chose Barbara Duff, rank forty-two-eighty-six, because it'd look suspicious if I only fought people ranked above me. She was easy. I just had to throw a sparring match against Xavier right as she walked by to convince her I would be an easy target. She ran straight to Elder Chang, her mother's best friend."

She moved on to her final match, her voice dripping with pride. "Last but not least, Lucas Ulrich, rank thirty-seven-nineteen. Two months ago, I let slip to Wendy Grant —known gossip—that I had a thing for him. Two weeks ago, I sent flowers to his girlfriend under Harris Brown— his best friend's—name, making sure the security cameras in the flower shop saw me do it. They all got in this huge fight—I think Harris wound up with a black eye—before they tracked the flowers back to me. Now Lucas thinks I'm a crazy stalker who almost ruined his relationship *and* his friendship, so he asked his godfather, Elder Smith, to pair us together so he could teach me a lesson. If all goes to plan, I should be in Housing C by the end of the day."

Nick stared slack jawed. Xavier bristled with disapproval.

I actually spoke. "That's insane."

Charlotte smirked. "That's the game."

"It's dishonest," Xavier snarled. "If you deserve a higher ranking, you'll win naturally."

"You think any of those three got their rankings by just being better fighters?" She shook her head. "The nice part about this trick is it only works on people willing to abuse their family connections."

"Then challenge them normally," Xavier said.

"He has a point," I added. "Why bother with all this when you can just challenge people whenever?"

Charlotte sighed, leaning in and taking on the tone of explaining the obvious. "If you specifically challenge someone several hundred ranks above you, it sends the message that you prepared a tactic specifically for them. That makes you look weak for your rank and thus paints a target on your back. But I couldn't have prepared for my matches today. I only got the pairings this morning." She winked.

"You think nobody's going to realize what's going on here?" Nick asked.

"These people don't know each other," Charlotte said, "and even if one of them began to suspect, nobody would ever admit to being played."

"It still feels shady," I said. "It's a lot of dishonesty for what, a room with a bit more ambient qi? Isn't the extra focus room hour enough?"

"Every edge, Cal," Charlotte replied like a mantra. "Every edge. We don't all have an infinite supply of qi right outside. The sect allocates its extremely limited resources to the most promising cadets. More resources means more success means more resources. The higher up you get, the bigger the feedback loop. If you want to reach the top, you need every advantage, every trick, every edge."

Every cultivator thinks it's gonna be them, Lucy's words echoed through my head. I exhaled. "Alright, well, as long as you don't use your mind control powers on any of us, I guess go ahead."

"It's not mind control," Charlotte scoffed. "It's an art. It's about finding out what people want and what they're afraid of and looking for opportunities therein."

"Social voodoo," I teased, "got it. Just don't use it on me."

Her face flattened, her gaze going cold as she spoke with a dead even tone. "Who says I haven't?"

I stilled. My eyes met hers, the hubbub of the meal hall around us fading into the background as tension mounted. My mind raced. Had she been playing me from day one? Had she *known* I'd give her focus room hours? Could she —

Her mask cracked. A sly smile stretched across her face. It shattered as she let out a laugh. "I'm kidding. Most people I manipulate come out the other side *really* disliking me. I'm going to make some enemies today. *You*, Cal, I hope never to consider an enemy."

"Yeah," I said, still unnerved at her social voodoo, "me too."

"Hey, Cal?" Nick's voice broke the moment. He gazed down at his holopad. "I think you should look at your pairings."

By the look on his face, I already had some idea what I was going to find as I opened the missive with my dueling schedule. Sure enough, there it was, right at round one.

0930, Ring 12: Caliban Rex v. Nickolas Vesper

"Well, hey." I reached across the table to pat him on the shoulder. "Congrats on your free win."

Nick gulped.

I recognized neither of my other two opponents, but a tap on their names brought up a headshot and some basic info. Both sat near the bottom of the standings. Both would probably whoop my ass if I let them.

Taking his cue from the rest of us, Xavier finally checked his own pairings to find yet another surprise. "The threads favor me! Look!" He shoved his holopad in Charlotte's face. "I've got my own match at housing C. No maneuvering required."

Charlotte squinted at the name. *"Darla Young*? She's six hundred spots above you. How did that happen?"

"It must have something to do with my meteoric rise."

I had to give it to the big guy, he *had* improved. I couldn't tell you what part the extra focus hour or bonus sparring sessions with Charlotte played, but in the six weeks since my arrival, Xavier had climbed over five hundred ranks, from the absolute bottom at five thousand and six up to forty-four ninety-three. I guess his habit of constantly challenging people to duels was finally paying off.

Charlotte groaned. "That'd be just like them, throw a rising star against a wall to either accelerate their trajectory or knock them down a peg. Darla's going to want to beat you bad. She needs to send a message."

Xavier clenched his fist enthusiastically. "I eagerly await this challenge!"

I couldn't help but grin. For all his weird idiosyncrasies and way of speaking, Xavier probably had a healthier mindset about all this cultivation stuff than any of us. I gestured with my head to the growing mass of people flowing out of the dining hall. "Shall we?"

We stood as one, wading through the rapidly emptying mess together to bus our trays. Only there did we part, Nick and I to join the masses on their way to the gym, Charlotte and Xavier to the transport platform to catch a pod to housing C.

But before we left, before Charlotte's scheme could come to fruition, before Xavier could run headlong into a wall named Darla, before Nick could pit himself against cultivators years his senior, before I could struggle to lose with as few injuries as possible, Xavier stopped us. One by one he looked us in the eyes, his brow furrowed in stern solemnity as he gathered our complete focus.

A big dumb grin stretched across his face. "Happy dueling day!"

Charlotte let out an exasperated breath. Nick blinked in

uncertain silence.

Something about Xavier's earnest enthusiasm rent clean through my rising trepidation, pierced my cynicism of the whole ranking system, obliterated any ounce of misanthropy that might've lingered in my mind. Here, amidst the schemers and the bullies and the nepotists, existed a man who honestly enjoyed the challenge, who truly wanted to better himself, who really was just happy to be there. It made me glad to call him friend.

I smiled back. "Happy dueling day."

20

"So what do you say we make a bit of a show of it?" I asked Nick as we followed the flow of people to the housing D gym. "Stage an epic battle at the bottom of the rankings, really give the gawkers something to talk about."

Nick audibly gulped.

"Alright, alright, no theatrics," I conceded. "But you should at least show off a bit. Do you have anything flashy that won't kill or injure me?"

Nick didn't answer.

"C'mon, work with me here! You've gotta have *some* cool way to kick my ass, right?"

Nick's voice wavered with a nervousness that struck me like a punch to the gut. "People are gonna watch?"

I stopped and pulled him aside, stepping to the edge of the hallway to let others pass as I spoke to him. I looked him in the eye. "You're gonna do great."

"Why can't we just spar like we normally do?"

I sighed. "We can if that's what you want, but I'd recommend against it. It's a ranked match on the one day qi attacks are allowed. If you fought me without even cycling, it'd look like you either didn't *want* to win, or *couldn't*."

I should explain the whole qi attacks thing. The short version is, the Dragon's Right Eye are stingy bastards.

The long version entails the expense involved in running the qi fields that surround the arenas during duels to protect onlookers and infrastructure from wayward techniques. Since the sect doesn't want to pay for it, they just keep a blanket ban on external qi use outside of scheduled dueling days. As a system it meant that cultivators more skilled with internal qi manipulation and physical combat prowess dominated the leaderboards.

It also meant today was my first chance to see some real magic. I was psyched.

Nick wasn't. His face seemed to pale even under the warm LED glow in the hallway.

"Look," I told him plainly, "it's gonna be a circus out there, and in no uncertain terms, *I'm* the clown. In case you haven't seen a circus holo, do you know what happens when a clown steps into the ring?"

Nick shook his head.

"Unless everyone involved makes a concerted effort otherwise, the moment a clown walks in, it becomes a clown show. Them's the rules. In about fifteen minutes, you're going to step into the ring with the clown. If you want people to take you seriously, we need to make that concerted effort."

Nick blinked at me. "I... um... what?"

I let out a breath. "Okay, forget the circus metaphor. What's your most badass technique? I don't care how powerful or effective it is, just how cool it *looks*."

"I guess I can—"

"No, no, no," I interrupted. "Don't tell me. It'll help me sell it. Whatever it is, just don't bang me up too bad, avoid the face, and win quickly. Make it look easy."

"Um... okay?"

I clapped him on the back, gentler but without the

enthusiasm Xavier managed. "That's the spirit. Now come on. Let's go put me in my place."

Nick flashed me a curious look but otherwise seemed to center himself. "Alright," he said. "Let's do this."

Startlingly quickly after that ghost town of a morning workout, the gym had exploded with activity. Familiar faces of housing D residents mixed with visitors from housing C swam through an ocean of people in civilian clothes. Friends and family, I deduced, cultivators too young or too old to compete for resources in the cadet program and thus free for the day to enjoy the show and support their loved ones.

I had no such support. Lucy, for obvious reasons, would have to watch my duels via holo, and I hadn't thought to invite the non-cadet connections I'd made thus far. I was sure Arthur or Vihaan and his family would've come if I'd asked, but it would've been a favor to me. Three quick, one-sided losses didn't exactly make for good entertainment.

If Nick's family had come, he didn't point them out to me.

Ring twelve awaited us as far away from the main entrance as possible, the least convenient of the arenas. Somehow its inaccessibility hadn't deterred the growing mass of onlookers, a mix of cadets with some free time before their first match and visitors from the city at large. They crowded the limited space between rings, some standing on the back-to-back benches in search of a better view.

The cadets all maintained bored expressions as they chatted amongst themselves, less than interested in Nick or me. They'd seen us sparring a dozen times before.

The visitors, in contrast, practically gawked as I passed, some likely sensing my lack of qi for the first time. Charlotte kept telling me it made people uneasy. They didn't look uneasy. They looked curious, excited to see what tricks the strange outworlder had under his sleeve, what tools he'd used to slay a void beast and save a child before even forming his seed core. The mysterious disappearance of that day's security footage hadn't helped.

I couldn't wait to disappoint them.

The audience parted for us as we approached, clearing our way to the steps up into the ring. A mortal official met us there. He didn't bother with niceties.

"Scheduled duel between Nicolas Vesper and Caliban Rex." He turned to me. "As the lower ranked participant, you have weapon selection."

I stashed my stuff at the base of the ring. "No weapons, please."

The man gave a curt nod. "Very well. Please step into the arena. A tone will sound as the qi field falls into place. Keep arms and legs away from the edge of the ring while the tone sounds. When it falls silent will be your cue to begin."

"Thanks." I flashed the man a smile as I mounted the steps up onto the padded floor of the arena. Nick followed, looking paler than ever.

The tone signaled the crowd to go quiet, a dull and droning thing that buzzed in my ear at a most unpleasant frequency. I took a moment, as the air seemed to shimmer around the ring, ever-so-slightly distorting the gymnasium at large, to wonder where the gong they used for unscheduled duels had gone. The tone was just so... anticlimactic.

I watched as the faint distortion in the air traveled up and overhead to come together in a dome at the ring's center. My eyes were still up there when the ring went silent.

I darted in, hoping to maintain the appearance of an actual challenger even as I cycled no meridians and crafted no battle plan. I made it shockingly far, almost thirty feet across the forty-foot ring before Nick made his move. He swung his hand out, pointing at me with his palm as he directed the technique. No blast of qi flew at me.

Instead, from a small leather pouch on his belt, a vine erupted.

Little more than half an inch thick and sporadically sprouting flat, pointed leaves, more and more of the plant emerged from the pouch. Rather than falling limply to the floor or climbing up the nearest surface, its length shot through the air right at me. I made a halfhearted attempt to dodge before it wrapped itself around my left ankle.

I tripped, catching myself on my palms as my momentum sent me skidding forward.

I wasn't on the mat long.

Nick swung his hand up, and the vine obeyed, yanking my left leg up. My three free limbs flailed about, scraping against the floor and fruitlessly reaching for the vine, but before long they found only air.

I hung suspended there for a moment, dangling from the vine's grip around my ankle, blood rushing to my head as I futilely swung about, before ceasing my struggles, craning my neck to look Nick in the eye, offering my best embarrassed look—an easy one with gravity pulling blood to my face—and uttered the words, "You win."

The gong sounded.

"Oh, there it—" I cut off as Nick's vine released me and I fell the three feet to the padded floor. By the time I looked up, the vine had fallen to the floor, desiccated and dead.

"Victor, Nicolas Vesper," the official droned.

Lukewarm applause washed over the ring as I pushed myself to my feet and followed Nick down the steps back to floor level. I placed a hand on his shoulder.

"That was awesome! I was expecting like an energy

pulse or something simple, and you conjured an entire vine! You should've told me you were a badass."

Nick blushed. "Um... thanks?"

"Seriously, that was super cool," I continued. "Where did you learn that?"

He patted the pouch on his hip, some amount of confidence finally returning to his voice. "It's a special seed my grandfather engineered. It grows explosively when you feed it qi, and will follow wherever that qi tells it to go."

"Nick, you can control plants. Do you have any idea how cool that is?"

"It's really not," he deflected. "Most cultivators can move fast enough to dodge it, and anyone with a bladed weapon can just cut the vine."

"Then reinforce it. Make it faster. *Practice.* That thing's a few poisoned thorns away from dealing some real damage."

"My parents keep the lethal varietals locked up," Nick said, "and to reinforce it I'd have to run enough qi through it to harden some on the edges. Maybe if I made bronze I could do that, but that's a big if."

"Nonsense. You'll get there."

"Yeah," Nick said through an exhale, sounding more deflated than inspired, "sure."

In the moments since our match, the crowd around ring twelve had dispersed by over half, leaving plenty of space both for the next two competitors to climb into the ring and for me to slip past them to grab my sword and other belongings from where I'd left them. "So," I said as I strapped the sheathed blade to my back, "where to next?"

Nick shrugged.

"Ring one?" I offered. "I want to watch a few actual cultivators fight."

Nick nodded and passively followed me back across the

busy gym towards ring one. We got there amidst the flurry of activity between matches, the crowd chaotic enough that we managed to snag a few seats on one of the benches facing the ring. A few minutes later, two cadets climbed into the ring, one local, the other unfamiliar enough I reckoned she could only have been from housing C.

As the buzzing drone rang out and the qi field activated, I reached for the super special tool I'd procured to keep people from noticing what my sense meridian did to my eyes.

A pair of sunglasses.

The aviators weren't perfectly dark, but their lenses tinted just enough that the blackness of my eyes didn't stand out. Better yet, anyone who saw me wearing them simply assumed they were holopad integrated and displaying some HUD rather than the simple pieces of darkened glass they were.

The glasses had been Charlotte's idea. Xavier's had been to just keep my eyes closed. I preferred being able to see.

The world flattened into a deluge of information, the hairs of the mortal official's eyebrows striking me with the same importance as the grip each cultivator held on their weapon. Without my brain meridian, I knew I'd never successfully sift through the sheer amount of data my eyes and ears provided, but with dedicated focus I could at least track what was going on in front of me.

Without my sense meridian, it would've all been a blur.

The match ended in under a minute, the girl from housing C distracting her opponent's guard with a flash of light then sweeping his legs with her quarterstaff to down him. The audience around me all blinked and rubbed at their eyes as the blinding light flashed, an experience from which my flattened senses protected me.

Well, that and the sunglasses. It turns out, those help

protect your eyes from bright lights.

We stayed put as the match ended and the ring cleared, waiting patiently for the next fighters to arrive. I had a bit of time before my next duel—again at ring twelve—and I was more than happy to spend it watching as many fights as possible.

After the speed with which the first match had ended, a good ten minutes passed before the next two cultivators stepped into the ring. They left their weapons behind, opting to fight hand to hand for their duel. Or qi to qi, I guess. The moment the droning buzz silenced, a pale white light blossomed around each fighter as they took similarly defensive stances. They traded blows, neither's fist making it past the dim aura around the other. A shield, then.

Approximately eight minutes of punching, grappling, and eventually wrestling followed as the pair each struggled to overpower the shield or break their opponent's focus while maintaining their own. It seemed clear from about minute four that neither of them knew any offensive techniques, at least none I managed to spot.

I'd just begun to consider braving the blinding light and deafening noise to look with my spiritual sense when a particularly frustrated-looking Charlotte stepped in front of me.

I should mention, one of the problems I'd come across with cycling my sense meridian was that once I'd managed to focus in on whatever I wanted to look at, sensory input I wasn't expecting tended to… fade into the background. Because my qi turned the world into a flood of more information than my brain could handle, little side details like, I don't know, your friend calling your name, struck with the same intensity as the man who farted thirty yards away. Only by blocking my view of the fight could Charlotte nab my attention.

"Sorry, sorry," I said, cutting the flow of qi through the meridian. "How'd it go?"

"I won, of course." Charlotte's voice came across as slightly snippy. "But Xavier took a beating."

I looked over to find the big guy sitting a bit to my left, holding an icepack to the back of his head. Whatever was wrong with it had to have been bad from the sheer fact he *wasn't* holding the pack to the front of his head.

Xavier's left eye had swollen shut, the entirety of it taking on a purple hue so dark it made *my* eye ache. Bits of blood streaked in various places where he'd incompletely wiped it away, all seeming to stem from a pair of cuts on his forehead. His nose sat crooked on his face, visibly broken and swelling to match.

"Holy shit, Xave, what happened?"

"I lost," he grunted.

"Darla felt she had to send a message with the upstart low ranker she paired her against," Charlotte explained. "He's lucky he got away with all his bones intact."

A knot formed in my throat. "You call that lucky?"

"I can still fight," Xavier said.

"Like hell you can. You're down an eye!"

Xavier just shrugged. "Only need one."

I shook my head. "Cultivators," I spat. "You're all insane."

Nick looked up at me. "You're a cultivator."

"*And* I'm insane. Point proven."

Charlotte sighed. Nick stared. Xavier grinned, revealing a gap where one of his front teeth had been. I grimaced. He'd lose an afternoon getting that replaced.

Charlotte glanced down at her holopad. "I'm up again soon." She nodded towards Xavier. "Make sure he gets to ring six. If he passes out, take him to the medics." She pointed across the gym to an area outside the running track, where a team of mortals had pushed away the exercise equipment to throw up a temporary infirmary.

"Will do," I said. "Good luck up there."

She raised an eyebrow at me. "Luck has nothing to do with it. A word of advice—most battles are decided long before the opening salvo. It pays to be the one doing the deciding."

I watched her saunter over to ring two, just to the left of the seats we'd found. Charlotte's opponent, Barbara Duff —the lower ranker she'd chosen to avoid suspicion—had a cut on her right cheekbone from her previous duel, little more than a thin red line to contrast with her short-cut platinum blonde hair.

She looked at Charlotte with hunger in her eyes.

Charlotte drew her rapier and looked back with disdain.

I gave up on trying to watch the duel as the crowd shifted to block my view. I didn't expect much from Charlotte's opponent, and a certain someone needed my support more.

"Alright." I looked to Xavier. "Ready to go?"

He mumbled something under his breath, leaning over with his elbows on his knees and his head facing the floor.

"Sorry, what was that?"

He kept going, continuing on in tones too hushed to pierce the hubbub around us.

"Xavier?"

He tapped his foot in a slow and steady rhythm, seeming to punctuate his sentences with the gesture. I noticed even his uninjured eye sat closed, his hands balled into fists.

He kept mumbling.

The foot-taps built, growing louder and more solid until they evolved into first gentle, then powerful stomps of his right foot against the ground. His entire body swayed with the motion. His lips moved with a fury. The stomps crescendoed but didn't speed up, keeping pace until, at the peak of their volume, Xavier clapped his hands a single time with sharp intensity, leapt to his feet, and said with a much more Xavier-like volume, "Let's do this."

I'd never before seen such determination, such solemnity, such *intensity*, on his face.

I smiled at him. "Give 'em hell."

Nick kept our seats as I scurried off after Xavier, struggling to keep up as he strode confidently through the crowd. Hot damn, whatever psych-up ritual he'd just done had certainly worked. Were it not for the slight limp to his step, I might've thought him entirely uninjured.

I didn't get in his way. I didn't offer any rousing speeches or battle plans. I simply stood ringside as Xavier opted for weapons against his higher-ranked opponent, grabbed a padded wooden battle axe from the rack, and climbed the steps into the arena.

I'd seen Xavier fight before. Threads, I'd fought him myself more times than I could count. He epitomized the Dragon's Fang style the sect taught, full of explosive aggression and decisive strikes. It suited his bulk and preference for the great axe perfectly, an overwhelming force that challenged its foes to meet it. Even within the style, Xavier eschewed the more controlled maneuvers in favor of unceasing assault, forcing the onus of strategizing and defending onto the opponent. His fights trended quick and decisive. Either you could stop his axe from cleaving you in two, or you couldn't.

I'd seen Xavier fight more times than I could count. I'd never seen him fight like *this*.

I watched him settle into the assault stance Instructor Long still insisted I couldn't do properly, listened as the buzzer droned, and slipped on my sunglasses so I could catch the finer details.

There weren't many.

The qi field arose. The tone ceased.

A well-timed pulse of qi through his muscle meridian sent Xavier launching forward, his axe raised and ready to strike. His opponent raised her buckler, crossing her short sword behind it to reinforce her defense and prepare a counterstrike at once. The shield glowed as qi ran through it, some kind of defensive technique I failed to recognize, one Xavier was set to run headlong into.

Except he didn't.

In what would've been a blur of motion to unenhanced eyes, Xavier adapted to his foe's defense. He shifted his left hand from the haft of his axe, redirected his footwork to carry him rightward, shot his free arm out to grab the top of his opponent's shield, yanked it aside, and delivered the padded edge of his axe directly to the side of her neck. He even stopped his strike midair half an inch from its target, demonstrating absurd control over the vast momentum of his heavy weapon.

A moment passed in perfect stillness before the poor girl even realized she'd been beaten. The brief seconds of shock lasted longer than the fight itself. The gong rang.

Xavier Honchel, former lowest rank in the entire sect, with one eye swollen shut, a limp in his left leg, and a broken nose, annihilated his higher-ranked opponent in under three seconds without even hurting her.

And the crowd had the audacity to look *bored*.

"Victor, Xavier Honchel."

"Let's go Xavier!" I cheered, seemingly the only one impressed by his feat. The onlookers returned to their own conversations, uninterested in quick one-sided bouts, upsets or otherwise.

Other than a single, feminine voice that shouted from somewhere further back. "Xavier!"

I blinked, failing to place the unfamiliar voice of Xavier's other fan, as the man himself bypassed the stairs to hop down from the ring directly. "Well fought." I patted him on the back as he stepped past me, weaving through the crowd towards the second voice. I followed.

"Xavy!" a four-foot-and-change blonde woman who looked to be mid-forties—which I guess translated to mid-fifties on the cultivator-adjusted scale?—ran up and cradled his face in her hands. "What happened to you?"

"Darla Young," he answered, letting the woman tilt his head this way and that as she inspected his swollen eye. "I faced defeat in housing C."

The woman's brow shot up. "You fought at housing C? Xavy, that's great!"

He smiled back at her. "May it be the first of many."

They both seemed to notice me standing there at once, turning in eerily perfect sync to look my way. I grinned awkwardly. "Hi there. I'm Cal."

"I've told you about Caliban," Xavier said. "Cal, this is my mother."

"Linda." She offered her hand. "Linda Honchel."

"Caliban Rex. Call me Cal." We shook.

The moment our hands parted she reverted her attention back to Xavier, a gesture I appreciated as I was too distracted wrapping my head around how someone Xavier's size could've come from a woman that tiny to make decent conversation.

"Has anyone looked at that eye? What about this cut? I'm sure nobody's looked at this nose." She ran a hand through his hair. "Is this a bump on your head? What hit you?"

"No, no, yes, a quarterstaff," Xavier rattled off his answers. "Mom, I'm fine."

"That's for the doctors to decide. Come on, you're seeing one right now." She grabbed him by the hand and took off towards the temporary infirmary.

Xavier craned his head over his shoulder to flash me an apologetic smile that flawlessly communicated the words 'ugh, I have to go.'

I held back a laugh. "Go on then, Xavy. I'm going to check in on Charlotte." I raised my voice to cover the growing distance to add, "Lovely to meet you!"

Linda called, "You too!" without looking back.

"Heh," I chuckled to myself, "*Xavy.*"

Shaking the humor of the diminutive from my head, I turned on my heel and headed for ring two, only to find the arena sitting empty as it awaited its next match. That option eliminated, I headed for the next most likely location.

Sure enough, there she sat at Nick's side, gazing intently at the ongoing duel in ring one. "How'd it go?"

"As expected," Charlotte answered, scooting over to make room between her and Nick. "I see Xavier's match didn't last long."

I sat. "He won in about three seconds. His mom's taking him to get his injuries looked at. Did you know she calls him Xavy?"

"Cute," Charlotte said, completely disinterested.

"You met his mom?" Nick perked up. "What was she like?"

I shrugged. "I don't know, motherly? Weirdly small. She must weigh, what, a *third* what Xavier does?"

Charlotte glared at me. "You met Xavier's mother and your first thought was about her *weight?*"

"No, my *first* thought was that she calls him Xavy. It took like three more thoughts to get to her weight."

Charlotte sighed.

"Look, all I'm saying is that Xavier is... well... *Xavier,* and his mom is tiny. It jumped out at me."

The end of the match in front of us rescued me as the gong rang out and the official declared a victor. Charlotte didn't comment, pulling up her holopad and typing with a fury.

I peeked over, catching a glimpse of her own copy of the sect rankings with detailed notes on every active entry. Even a few of the names aged out of the cadet program and thus ineligible for scheduled duels had little details neatly laid out beneath them, tidbits about everything from fighting style to relationship status to important family members.

I raised an eyebrow at her. "You take *notes?*"

Charlotte yanked her holopad back. "Of course I take notes. You never know what bits of information might prove useful."

"So that's how she does it," Nick breathed. "Meticulous notes."

"Ooh, what does it say about me?" I leaned in in an attempt to read more.

Charlotte closed her holopad, its holographic screen disappearing back into the implant in her forearm. She looked me dead in the eye. "It says you're either going to accomplish great things and elevate everyone around you, or get yourself killed. It says you have a long way to go. It also says you desperately want everyone to like you, even though you *know* that's impossible, so instead you turn every social conflict into a joke at the first opportunity."

She pulled up her holopad again, tapping out something with her right hand before spinning the screen around to reveal a picture of me with the phrase, 'gifted at making an ass of himself' written below it.

I sniffled and pantomimed wiping a tear from my face. "You know me so well."

She flashed me a pointed look. I smiled back.

The next match kicked off.

Our conversation ended as we watched the duel, then the next one, then the next one. A seemingly endless parade of cultivators climbed up to compete in housing D's top ring, their fights seeming to blend together as they implemented a mishmash of the sect's hallmark fighting style and their own family's techniques.

I didn't bother taking notes. I had no hope of contending with any of these people any time soon. I did make some effort to track any fighting style other than the Dragon's Fang in the hopes of finding something that suited me better than the sect's tradition, but without explicit instruction, I had little hope of picking up any new tricks.

It was out of boredom more than anything else that I looked with my spiritual senses. Truth be told I hadn't put much thought into what kinds of qi manipulation techniques I wanted to develop, both because I was still months away from developing a core, and because I couldn't trust that my qi would work in the same way as anyone else's.

Still, I opened my mind's eye to the cacophony of light and sound. The qi in the air was thicker than I'd ever seen it, a result of both the busy gym and duelists expelling qi for their various techniques. My head ached dully with the intensity of it all, far from the piercing migraine Fyrion had induced when I'd first arrived, but still an annoyance. I'd take an annoying headache over so-bright-I-can't-see any day.

The qi field obfuscated the view, but I could still readily track the cores of the competing cultivators, as well as those of various audience members surrounding me, and even the dim, natural qi in the mortal official. I'd long learned what living beings—cultivator or otherwise—were *supposed* to feel like.

For all I'd improved my tolerance for normal qi, I hadn't yet mastered the skill of looking through my spiritual senses and my mundane ones at the same time. As such, I failed to perceive the fight itself beyond the general positions of the competitors and the movement of the qi within their bodies. It was, to me, a novel way of watching a duel, but little more.

Until I noticed something odd.

One of the fighters pulled qi from their core and launched it in a simple—some might say brutish—burst to destabilize her opponent. I watched as the energy left her body, struck her foe, and dissipated into the environment, all as expected, but for a tiny mote of something *else* that drifted away, something cool, something dark, something *familiar*.

I tracked it as it rose, this little spot of calm amid a sea of light and noise. It wafted up, directly through the qi field, into the air, then out through the glass rooftop into the vacuum beyond. I blinked. That couldn't have been *my* qi, could it?

I shut my spiritual senses and glanced left to look at Nick, finding his head leaning against the top of the bench's backrest as he gazed, openmouthed and unblinking, through the skylight and into space.

"Nick, did you see that?"

He didn't answer.

"Nick? Hello?" I poked him.

He jerked back to reality. "Oh—sorry, I was-uh… meditating."

I looked askance. "Sure. Did you see that?"

"See what?"

I paused as I thought through the best way to explain it. I settled on a question. "What happens to qi after it's used for a technique?"

"It disperses into the local environment," Nick said like he was stating the obvious.

"All of it?"

"Yeah… or, well, not *all* of it. About a half a percent returns to the threads."

"Returns to the threads? What does that mean?"

Nick shrugged. "It disappears. It becomes one with the threads that bind the universe together. I don't know. I'm not a philosopher."

"Why would a philosopher know?"

"Because it's not the kind of thing a scientist or engineer would look into?" Nick offered.

I scowled. "But philosophers don't *know* anything. I think that's kind of the point."

"Are you going somewhere with this?"

The gong rang out as the duel in front of us ended. I exhaled. "Not sure. Maybe." In a desperate bid to escape the unseemly act of philosophizing, I excused myself from the conversation. "I'm going to go back over to ring twelve, get there a bit ahead of my next match. Want to come?"

Nick shook his head. "I'm fighting in ring eight soon."

I glanced over to Charlotte, who'd remained absorbed in her notes thus far.

She didn't even look up from her holopad. "I'm going to watch Nick. He at least isn't beyond help."

"Thought as much. I'll catch you after. This shouldn't take long." I looked back to Nick. "Give 'em hell."

"Yeah," he muttered, "sure."

I sighed as I slipped through the crowd. Clearly neither my pep talks nor his dominant win over me had done much for Nick's confidence. Goddamn Xavier and his goddamn need for medical attention. He was the only one any good at this kind of thing. I couldn't imagine a single thing Nick needed more than that hype-up ritual Xave had used before his last match.

After a few minutes of weaving through the busy gym, I reached the comparatively vacant seats around arena twelve. A girl with the same inch-long heavily curled black hair as the image of my next opponent was doing stretches ringside. I approached.

"You Cass?"

She didn't look up from her lunge. "I am. And you're Caliban."

I grinned and extended a hand. "Call me Cal."

She didn't shake it. "What do you want, Cal?"

"To talk. To apologize. I know I'm not an opponent anyone wants. I'm sorry you have to fight me. I thought we could figure out a way to make this work out as well as possible."

That got her attention. She stepped up out of the lunge, and turned to scowl at me. "You want to fix our duel?"

"It's hardly fixing if the conclusion's foregone. You have a core. I don't even have twelve open meridians. You're going to crush me one way or the other. I just figured..."

She sighed. "You don't want me to hurt you."

"I'd prefer if you didn't. At least not the face."

"Okay."

I blinked. "Okay? That's it?"

"Yeah, sure. Honestly, weak as you are, it's weird they have you fighting at all. If I didn't know better, I'd say someone in local management has it out for you."

"Yeah," I said, my mind immediately leaping to Elder Lopez. She *had* taken every opportunity to point out how weak I was. "That sounds about right."

"Anyway, you're being nice about it, and it's not like you challenged me. As long as you don't do or say anything that'll require I teach you a lesson, I can take you down painlessly."

"What is it with everyone and teaching people lessons?" I asked. "It feels like a weird choice of euphemism for beating the shit out of someone."

That earned me a smile. "It is, isn't it? Then again, that mouth of yours makes it sound like you still have something to learn."

"Oh, I have loads to learn. I just don't think debilitating

injury makes for great education."

"And yet it works."

"Obviously not. I'm still talking, aren't I?"

She cocked an eyebrow at me. "Maybe you should stop."

I opened my mouth to counter before realizing that just about anything I said would've proved her right. "Good point."

I let her return to her stretching as I stepped aside to do a few of my own, letting my mind wander over my earlier discovery. I'd need more data, but I was *pretty sure* that'd been my qi I'd seen emerge from that cultivator's attack. Did all techniques work like that? Would mine, once I'd progressed far enough to actually externalize my qi? What did it mean? Did anyone else know what it was, or did they all believe that half a percent just... disappeared?

The cultivation world's penchant for hoarding information made that last question remarkably difficult to answer. That Nick had directed me to philosophy rather than science implied at least *most* people didn't know. The obvious next step would be to try and take in that discharged qi, if only to confirm it was like mine and not something else entirely, but there'd been so little of it I questioned the possibility of such a thing.

It felt like I'd taken an important step towards understanding my strange qi, yet I still found myself with more questions than answers.

The sound of the gong rescued me from my musings as the match before us came to an end and the fighters cleared out. You all already know the whole pre-duel procedure, so I'll cut to the chase.

The fight was over before it began. The tone ended, Cass rushed forward, I made a halfhearted attempt at sidestepping so it'd look like I was taking the duel seriously, and a second later I found myself face-first on the mat with both my arms bent behind my back.

"Victor, Cass Denika," the official droned.

I stood up and respectfully offered my hand. "Well fought."

She shook it in a single, not-quite-friendly motion, turned on her heel, and left the arena. I followed suit.

Deciding my second loss of the day could not possibly have gone better, I set off towards ring eight in a sparklingly good mood. The schedule really hadn't left me much of a break, but with any luck, I could catch the back end of Nick's match before I had to return for my final duel.

The nasty thing about luck is it tends to fuck with you.

I heard the yelling before anything else, a single voice, masculine and hoarse with the act. Moments later I emerged from the crowd to see for myself.

"—barrassment. An embarrassment! After all the resources we dumped into you, all the pills, the extra hours, the private tutors, *this* is what you have to show for it? How dare you?"

The man himself stood with his back to me, but I didn't need to see his face to know who he was. All I needed was Nick, standing cowed and staring at the floor in front of him, clutching a horrifically swollen arm and visibly fighting back tears.

Two women flanked the shouter, one that matched him in age that silently scowled down at Nick, and a teenager, a girl who looked maybe a year or two younger than Nick. Her right arm ended in a bandaged stump instead of a hand.

Worst of all, as this all unfolded, Charlotte stood uselessly aside, typing furiously into her holopad. She was taking fucking *notes*.

"You're pathetic," Nick's father continued his tirade. "A useless threads damned leech given every resource he could've wanted and wasting it all in his own laziness."

Nick pleaded, "I just want to come home."

"Until you get your act together and start behaving like an actual cultivator, you don't have a home to come back to," the man spat. "A layabout son and a crippled daughter. What did I do to deserve this?"

I decided enough was enough and moved in to diffuse the situation the only way I knew how: by making it about *me*.

"Hi." I flashed a friendly smile, physically placing myself between them and Nick. "I'm Cal. You must be Nick's family."

Nick's mother blinked several times in surprise. His father stared dumbfounded by my interruption. His sister collected herself first.

"Oh! You're the one who saved that boy during the void beast incursion," she said, a painfully familiar look of relief on her face. She took my right hand in her left in a surprisingly well-practiced opposite-hand handshake. "I'm Martha."

"Ah, yes," Nick's father growled, failing to introduce himself, "the *mortal*."

"People *do* seem intent on calling me that, yes," I answered. "And you are…?"

"Stay away from Nick," his mother snapped, her voice stern and disdainful. "The last thing he needs is weak friends."

"Mom!" Martha interrupted. "He saved a kid's life!"

"A mortal could've saved that boy's life," the mother said.

"Again with the *mortal* thing," I said. "You people *do* realize I can cultivate, right?"

"That's enough. Come, Martha," the father snarled. "We're leaving. It reeks of failure here."

He turned and stormed off, leaving his wife and

daughter to scurry after him. I watched them go, waiting for them to disappear into the crowd before I turned to Nick. "Are you okay?"

Nick sniffled and shook his head. "My arm is broken. I'm going to have to forfeit my last duel."

That wasn't quite what I'd meant, but I wasn't about to push the issue. "That's okay, that's okay." I wrapped an arm around his shoulder. "C'mon, let's get you to the infirmary."

Charlotte fell into step with us as I ushered Nick away. I waited until after I'd handed him off to one of the medical staff before rounding on her.

"What the hell was that? You just fucking *stood* there."

She set her jaw. "It's not my place to interfere with other people's families. It's not *yours* either."

"It's my place to look out for my friends."

"You think you're doing him any favors defending him like that? Nick has to fight his own battles, otherwise he just looks even weaker. If Nick isn't meeting his father's expectations, his only recourse is to start."

My voice dropped, cold anger lowering it to a tight and even tone. "Did you see me defending him? I'm not *clueless*, Charlotte. You might be better at reading people, at getting them to do what you want, but some of us have a fucking *soul*. Whatever you have written in that notepad of yours, I know *exactly* how men like that operate. He's angry, and he's always going to be angry. It's better he's angry at me."

"Cal, whatever you think, you don't know them. You don't know what Nick's family is like, and you have no right to mess around with it."

"I know his *type*," I muttered, scarcely louder than a whisper. My holopad beeped at me. "Shit. I've got to get to my third match." I looked across the infirmary to Nick. "Stay with him, will you? He shouldn't be alone."

"Yeah, of course," Charlotte said. "Good luck up there."

"Thanks." I turned and strode away, weaving through the crowd towards ring twelve one final time. My mood had soured. I hated that Nick had to deal with that, hated the ways cultivation brought out the worst in people, hated myself for not stepping in sooner. I should've known Nick's lack of confidence came from *somewhere*.

I wanted to scream. I wanted to hit something. I wanted to punch that asshole square in the nose. Had I been a capable fighter, that might've been a good state of mind to have going into a duel. Instead, I found myself fighting off the foreboding notion I was about to get myself into trouble. I was good at that.

I spotted Xavier up in ring three as I passed, his nose and eye covered in white bandages. His mother cheered him on as he relentlessly battered his opponent's defenses, his bare knuckles dripping blood as he wore down the man's qi barrier.

I offered a shout of support for him, but didn't linger, daring not show up for my duel late. The last thing I needed was to give Elder Lopez more ammunition against me.

Ring twelve had its regular crowd of gawkers looking to watch the battle for the bottom, but most had seen my last fight, so none seemed particularly enthused. I hoped this next one would prove just as boring.

The look on my opponent's face was my first sign otherwise. The man sneered at my approach, managing to look down his hooked nose at me despite our equivalent heights.

"Edgar?" I greeted him, flashing the friendliest smile I could manage given my current mood. "I'm Cal. Nice to meet you."

He spat on the floor in front of me. That couldn't be a good sign.

"What do you want, mortal?"

I bit back my retort, resolving to at least *try* to play nice. "To apologize," I said, taking the same tact that'd worked with Cass. "I know you have nothing to gain by fighting me, and I'm sorry you have to waste one of your scheduled duels doing it. If you can end things quick and painlessly, I promise not to turn this all into some big joke."

"Your presence is a joke," Edgar growled. "You have no right to sect resources, but you take them anyway. Those focus room hours could be going to cultivators who deserve them, who fought for their place here, rather than an upstart mortal with a powerful friend."

It took some doing not to laugh at that one, given where my focus room hours were going, but I couldn't tell *him* that. Instead, I let out a sigh. "Look, all these people are at ring twelve hoping for a clown show. We can give them that, if that's what you want, but I think it's in both our best interests to keep it civil and get this over with. How's that sound?"

"Like a coward, begging for mercy."

"Okay," I said, trying to sound like it was. "Clown show it is."

I left my sword and sunglasses at the same spot by the stairs I'd used twice before and climbed into the ring, prompting Edgar to follow me up. We faced off on opposite ends of the forty-foot arena as the official announced our match.

I had the privilege of first strike as the tone buzzed and the qi field arose. In those moments before the duel technically began, fighting might've been barred, but nobody—and I mean *nobody*—had the power to stop me running my mouth.

"Out of curiosity," I said with my voice raised so the audience could hear, "do you actually believe *I'm* the reason you're so low ranked, or am I just the only one weak enough for you to take your anger out on?"

Edgar cracked his knuckles. "It's high time someone taught you a lesson."

"Ooh, what kind of lesson? Is it algebra? I hope it's algebra. I've always been bad at algebra."

The tone silenced.

I cycled my bone meridian in the hopes of avoiding the worst of it, wishing, for a moment, I'd managed to open my spine meridian so I could've done something about the pain. C'est la vie.

Edgar darted in faster than I could've hoped to counter and threw a jab at my midsection.

I doubled over, cycling my lungs to recover the wind knocked out of me. "Oh, when you said 'lesson' you actually meant 'violence.' My mistake." I righted myself. "You know, the only lesson violence teaches is how to be violent."

A right hook caught me in the ribs, thankfully soft enough not to break anything, though probably unintentionally. The asshole didn't know I had my bone meridian open.

I hit the mat either way, spinning from the force of the blow to catch myself on my hands. From the floor, I kept talking. "Is that why you're like this? Daddy spanked you one too many times and now you think violence is the answer?"

He kicked me, the toe of his boot digging into my side. I felt skin tearing beneath my uniform.

"Get up," he snarled at me. "I'm not finished with you yet."

I pushed myself upright. "Oh, you're trying to *finish*? So it's a sex thing then. You get a little chub whenever you make someone bleed? You know there are clubs for that. I've heard down in sector three there're people who'll even pay you for it."

He went for another body shot, sending me stumbling back clutching my midsection. As I ran up against the qi barrier, I spared a glance into the crowd. They stared up at us with wide eyes colored by a mix of revulsion and glee.

I always strive to entertain.

"Shut your mouth before I shut it for you."

I shook my head. "Edgar. Ed. Eddie-boy. You should know, I'm a goddamn savant at not shutting my mouth. Loads of people have tried to shut me up—including myself. It never seems to stick."

He stalked across the arena, his ire apparent yet still leashed tight enough to keep his composure. I figured I'd snap that leash soon enough.

"Your words are just that," he said. "*Words*. Crazed ramblings of a jumped-up mortal."

"Your punches are just that," I aped him. "*Punches*. Like an angry child that didn't get his way."

He swung for my face. A horrible *crunch* echoed through my skull as his fist collided with my nose, rocking my head back and knocking it into the qi barrier. A bright flash filled my vision for a moment as the blow rattled me.

Blood poured from my broken nose. It hurt like a bitch, but I'd had worse. "Oh, Eddie-boy, not the face. What will your mother say? You know she cherishes my boyish looks."

"Shut up." He hit me again, this time across the jaw. The bone held, but I felt my cheek shred against my teeth and my gum rupture. Blood pooled at the back of my throat.

I coughed. "Has telling someone to shut up ever really worked? You realize trying to silence someone tells the world you're afraid of what they have to say."

"I said shut up!" he shouted and struck my nose again, pain flaring through me as he pounded the already smashed flesh. My knees buckled, but he grabbed me by my shirt collar to hold me upright.

"You know, now that you've said it a second time, I think I actually will. We've been at this a while now. Are you getting close? Is this doing it for you? I can take my shirt off if you want."

"Shut up, shut up, shut up!" The blows rained down as he yelled, my jaw, nose, my temple. His grip on my shirt kept me from hitting the floor, kept me in range.

My words slurred as I spoke this next bit. "Ah, shit, Ed. I forgot the safe word. What was it again?" I turned my head to the side and spat out blood. I looked him in the eye—or at least where I thought his eyes were; I had too much blood in my own to actually see—and flashed a shit-eating crimson grin. "Oh, that's right. *Clown show.*"

I never heard the gong. I never heard the official declare Edgar the victor. I felt only a burst of pain from my temple, saw the world go black, and awoke on the padded floor.

Not quite ready to lift my own head, I wiped my eyes on my sleeve. Only the left one opened.

The qi field was down. The audience stared, agape. I caught Edgar storming off in my periphery. Charlotte, Nick, and Xavier stood ringside, the former scribbling down notes as the latter two blinked. Nick looked sick.

Xavier leapt up onto the ring to help me to my feet, pulling my arm up over his shoulder and supporting me down the steps and back to ground level. The four of us walked together to the infirmary.

"So," I broke the uncomfortable silence, "you guys saw that, huh?"

"We saw enough," Charlotte said, her voice cool.

Nick gulped. "What *was* that?"

"That was the clown show I told you about."

"Much as I applaud your courage in the face of pain, why disrespect him? You've made an enemy today, and taken more injuries than you needed," Xavier asked.

"He disrespected me first," I answered. "And believe me, this'll save a lot of suffering down the line."

Nick raised an eyebrow at me. "What? That man *hates* you now."

"Cal's right," Charlotte said. "Everyone here can crush him in a fight. The only leverage he has is the threat of making them look bad while they do it."

"I needed to send the message that 'teaching me a lesson' doesn't work. My round two opponent came away clean because she was nice about it. Edgar stormed off looking like a petulant child because even as he beat the shit out of me he couldn't make me stop taunting him."

"I still don't get what that accomplishes," Nick said. "Just because Edgar lost his cool doesn't mean others will."

I shrugged. "Edgar was going to beat me up anyway. All I did was make it clear he wasn't teaching me a lesson or proving his superior ability. Sure, maybe by running my mouth I've made a few more people want to punch me, but if that didn't prove how little punching me achieves, I don't know what will."

Charlotte nodded along. "Being paired against the lowest rank in the sect isn't a flattering experience. Cass's and Nick's fights with Cal were so boring, nobody will remember them. Edgar made such a spectacle, people will be talking about him and Cal for days. Whatever *deeply understandable* joy someone might get from hitting him, they'll have to weigh against the social repercussions of being seen emotionally invested in *Cal*. Even if they look calm, if Cal's taunting them, any real damage they inflict will look like he got under their skin. The only winning move is to play nice."

"Besides," I said, looking up at Xavier's bandaged face, "that nose splint looked so good on you, I just *had* to get one of my own."

I could feel the tension drain from Xavier's shoulders as he barked out a laugh. "You have a warrior's spirit, my friend."

"And a warrior's nose too." I smiled up at him. "I take it you won your third match?"

"A glorious victory that propels me ever closer to greatness."

"That's great!" I said, well past commenting on Xavier's... Xavierness. "So that's me oh-three, Nick one-two, and you two-one. Charlotte?"

We stopped at the back of the line for medical attention.

"Undefeated so far, with one match to go. When I win, I'll be promoted to housing C."

Xavier beamed. "I like that confidence!"

"Well," I said, "fair warning, but if that happens, injuries or otherwise, we're *going* to celebrate. I know just the spot."

"Do you have a table reserved?" Charlotte asked. "The bars get busy after dueling day."

"Don't worry." I winked. "Arrangements have been made."

She eyed me suspiciously, but didn't press the issue. "If you say so. Are you going to be alright here? I need to go prepare for my match."

"Go, go." I waved her away. "Give 'em hell."

A smirk crossed her face. "Always." With that she left, disappearing into the crowd to step into the ring with a cultivator she'd tricked into challenging her.

I looked back and forth between Nick and Xavier. "Should someone go with her? She's about to fight a guy who thinks she tried to ruin his relationship."

"I'll go," Nick said, casting weary eyes across the temporary infirmary. "I've had enough of this place."

Xavier kept by my side as the medic patched me up. It was a long process. Between setting and splinting my broken nose, sealing the various gashes across my midsection, forehead, lower lip, and inner cheek, hemoneural stimulation to cure my concussion, and a patch over my eye soaked with some chemical or other to bring down the swelling, my holopad had beeped with the confirmation of Charlotte's victory long before I ever got up off the exam table.

Before I could leave, the doctor shoved a bottle of capsules into my hand. "For the pain," she said. "If it's not enough, you can get something more powerful at your local clinic. We don't distribute the strong stuff here."

I glanced down at the pill bottle. "Why not?"

"The cadets like to go out drinking after their duels," the doctor explained. "Had enough incidents of people ignoring our warnings and mixing meds with alcohol, so now we don't hand out anything that reacts poorly."

"Huh," I said, pocketing the painkillers. "Good to know."

Xavier and I both thanked the woman profusely as we left in search of Nick and Charlotte. We found them waiting by the exit, Nick with his broken arm and Charlotte with the audacity to not even look *tired*. Damn her.

"So," I greeted them, "how's it feel to graduate from being a D-bag to a filthy C?"

Charlotte faltered. "Excuse me?"

I grinned. "Soon enough you'll get through being a son-of-a-B and become a true A-hole."

The consternation showed on her face. "Ignoring... whatever that was... it feels great. A long time coming."

"Does this mean we get to eat at the housing C mess?" Xavier asked. "I hear they have a chocolate fountain."

"Dreams of chocolate for later, big guy." I patted Xavier on the back. "Tonight, we have grander plans." I led them down the hall to the transport platform and boarded a pod, typing in our destination via my holopad to avoid spoiling the surprise. I was pretty sure Charlotte had already guessed it, but at least she had the wherewithal to *pretend* like she didn't know.

"So this place of yours," she said as the pod lurched away from the platform and into the dark tunnels below the city, "how'd you find it?"

"Oh, right place at the right time," I kept my answer vague. "Or wrong place. Depends on whom you ask."

I caught Nick's eyes lighting up as we whizzed past the transport station at Cadet's Row, where most of our peers would spend their evening.

Xavier didn't figure it out until our pod stopped not in the depths of the city, but at its fringe. "Threads," he swore, excitement dawning on his face, "is she—"

I cut him off as the door slid open. "In light of the day's events," I began my speech as I stepped out onto the platform, "in celebration of two of us surviving our first dueling day, of Xavier's tenacity in his ongoing climb up the rankings, and, of course, Charlotte's promotion to housing C, I've arranged something that's been far, far too long coming.

The others followed me out of the pod, stopping short with knowing grins on their faces as they took in the massive hangar in which we found ourselves, as well as its lone occupant, a small, matte white skiff with an off-center orange stripe along its length, and the designation LC-81535 painted upon its side.

"Everyone," I told them, "I'd like you to meet Lucy."

21

"A skiff?" Charlotte's voice echoed through the cavernous hangar. "The soulship's a *skiff?*"

"Her name is Lucy," I said pointedly, "be polite."

Charlotte froze. "Wait. She can hear us?"

"Of course she can. She's right there." I nonetheless raised my voice as I added, "Hi, Lucy!"

"Cal!" Lucy's response resounded from across the room. "What happened to you?"

"The learning process." I stroked my chin in mock thoughtfulness. "At least that's what people keep calling it. I couldn't tell you what I've learned for the life of me."

Charlotte snapped to attention, her right hand leaping to her brow and holding there like her life depended on it. "My apologies, venerable ancient. I meant no disrespect."

Without turning his head, moving his mouth as little as possible, Nick asked under his breath, "Wait, should we be saluting?"

Xavier mirrored Charlotte's gesture without hesitation.

I raised a hand to my mouth to hide my laughter.

"None taken," Lucy said. "You must be Charlotte. It's a pleasure to meet you."

"Likewise, ma'am."

"Xavier, Nick," I introduced them, gesturing unnecessarily to each. From our nightly calls, Lucy already knew Nick was the teen and Xavier the giant.

"It's an honor, venerable one," Xavier echoed Charlotte's formality as Nick struggled through a sloppy left-handed salute.

"It's good to finally meet," Lucy replied. "I've heard so much about you all."

"Only the worst of it," I said, taking off across the hangar towards the open ramp. I'd never actually seen Lucy in g-dock before, departing roofie and arriving on Fyrion through a zero-g gangway. It made for the best view I'd ever seen of her as a whole.

She stretched some forty feet long from tail to tip, with a familiar long window running along each side. It was tinted dark enough that I couldn't see in.

Four cylindrical qi drives made up the bulk of her propulsion, each some five feet in diameter and twelve long. They sloped sleekly inward to join seamlessly with her hull, the fifteen feet of interior width scarcely enough to support more than one or two passengers for any trip longer than a few hours. Two triangular wings tripled her width, not remotely a large enough span to support atmospheric flight, but she had vertical boosters for additional lift.

Her nose came to a rounded point, a further aerodynamic edge for her original purpose of ferrying passengers from a ship or station in orbit down planetside.

The pulse cannons on the underside of each wing stood out like a sore thumb, a weapon of war grafted onto a ship that'd never been built for combat. I wish I'd had a chance to see her use them against the void horde. I knew she'd killed far more void beasts than anyone else that day. Someone—either her or some local ground crew—had washed the black blood off her.

The loading ramp led us directly into the viewing deck at her front, where the meeting table had arisen from the floor to hold a set of flutes and a bottle of champagne in an ice bucket.

Charlotte kept her eyes respectfully forward as she boarded. Xavier failed at such, keeping his neck straight but allowing his eyes to dart back and forth to take in every little detail of the constrained space. Nick outright gaped.

"Welcome aboard," Lucy's voice greeted us warmly. A strand of qi wrapped around the champagne bottle and lifted it from the ice. "I understand congratulations are in order."

"Thank you." Charlotte bowed her head politely.

"Ooh, ooh, let me," I said, stepping up to the table and wrapping my hand around the champagne. With my other, I reached up over my right shoulder. "I've always wanted to try this."

Nick blinked. "Cal, is that a good ide—"

I drew my sword.

"No, no, hold it like this," Lucy interrupted, qi tilting the nose of the bottle up and away from my friends. "It's a single motion. Let the contours of the bottle guide you. Okay, now back slowly, then forward quick. Ready?"

With an audible *shing* I slid my blade down the bottle's neck and into the lip, snapping its tip clean off. Glass clattered down against the metal floor as I hurriedly righted the bottle before any more foam could spill out. I looked back at the others with a big stupid grin on my face. "That was *awesome*."

Charlotte scowled. "There are *less* messy ways to open a bottle of champagne."

Xavier matched my grin. "Also less fun ones." He slapped me on the back, causing yet more champagne to slosh out of the bottle in my hand and onto the floor.

I poured him the first glass.

"So what happened to losing gracefully?" Lucy asked as I doled out beverages.

"You know grace has never been my strong suit," I replied, handing Charlotte her glass. I pointed an empty flute towards Nick in a wordless offer, but he silently held up a hand to decline. Through it all I kept talking. "I *may* have goaded him on a bit, but I swear it was for a good reason. Besides, what kind of person just *decides* to beat the shit out of someone like that?"

Before I'd even put the bottle down, my holopad popped up with a request for biometrics. I swiped yes without even thinking, readily sharing the data with Lucy. As she quietly read through it all to confirm the medics hadn't missed anything in patching me up, I took a sip of my champagne and turned to the others. "Time for the tour!"

I gestured widely to the room around us. "This is the viewing deck slash meeting room slash passenger area. It's great for staring off into space or strapping yourself down for dockings and departures." I turned left and strode down the narrow hall, pointing down to the compartments beneath the window. "This is storage." I pointed in sequence to the doors to my left, specifically leaving out the one that led belowdeck. "That's storage. That's storage. That's mechanicals." We stopped where the hall turned back around the other way.

"And here's the cultivation room." I led them into the ten-by-ten space with its padded floor and the column containing Lucy's fusion core. A pillow and neatly folded blanket sat conspicuously visible by the wall, implying I slept there.

Lucy really was the best.

"So," I turned to the others, fighting to keep the smile from my face. "What do you think?"

The others froze. Xavier raised his champagne glass to his mouth to avoid the responsibility of answering. Nick actively avoided eye contact. I could practically read the words "that's it?" on their faces, words they'd never dare utter in description of a soulship—at least not in her presence.

Charlotte actually braved a response, tactfully dodging my question. "Is the… other hallway the same?"

"Pretty much." I shrugged. "Unless you have a thing for life support system design, there's really not a lot over…" I trailed off in my best impression of someone having an idea. "Or… actually, it's not that interesting, but I *guess* I could show you… this way."

I stepped past them back into the hall, veering right down the side we hadn't yet walked. I explained more doors. "That's air scrubbing. That's storage. Storage again. Mechanicals. And the soulspace." I kept my voice as casual as possible as the door slid open to reveal the hardwood floored hallway beyond, one that stretched far longer than Lucy herself.

I strode right in. The others didn't follow. I made it three steps before I caught Charlotte cursing under her breath.

"By the threads…"

Okay, it wasn't *much* of a curse, but I still counted that. A wide grin crept across my face.

Lucy broke first. It started as a giggle, bright and soft and joyous, then grew until waves of resonant laughter seemed to roll off the walls themselves. That was about when I joined in.

"Oh, threads," I managed through fits of laughter, "the looks on your fucking faces."

"Language!"

"Sorry," I said, the smile on my face somewhat belying my apology. I managed to collect myself, even as Lucy kept laughing. A moment passed. She didn't stop. I raised an eyebrow. "It wasn't *that* funny."

"Sorry, sorry," Lucy fought to gather herself. "It's been some time since I've played a joke on someone."

"The pillow was a nice touch."

"I thought so."

Through it all, Nick, Charlotte, and Xavier gaped at us—or rather, me, since they hadn't quite figured out how to look at Lucy.

Charlotte narrowed her gaze. "Did you two plan this?"

"Oh, for weeks," I said. "Do you have any idea how hard it was to *not* tell you guys all about this place?"

Xavier stepped inside. "I can't believe it. I'm in a real pocket dimension. On a *ship!*"

Nick's eyes widened. "How big is this place?"

"Big enough." I smirked. "C'mon, time for the *real* tour."

"Don't dawdle," Lucy warned us. "Dinner will be ready soon."

"Got it," I said with a snap of my fingers. "Okay, first up, we have..." I trailed off for dramatic tension as I led them through the first door on the left. "The sparring room!"

Xavier practically ran past me, weaving through the rows of exercise equipment to get a better look at the sparring ring that dominated the space. He fiddled with the control panel on its side. "Qi fielding, hit recognition... AI holo training?!"

"That's how I learned everything I knew before I made it to Fyrion," I explained. "The data set's... more than a little limited, but that's something we can fix."

"If you'd be kind enough to demonstrate your fighting style, it would be a huge help," Lucy said.

"Of course!" Xavier reached for one of the wooden axes on the rack beside the ring.

"Not now, big guy," I waved him off. "Dinner soon, remember?"

"I'll do you one better," Charlotte said, typing away on her holopad. "I have the full manual for the sect's style, and my own analysis of the Velereau style." With a swipe, she sent the data over.

I faltered. "Charlotte, that's incredible. Thank you."

"You're the golden goose, Cal," she said. "Every edge."

I sighed at the pragmatism of her gift.

Nick, meanwhile, had completely ignored our talk of data sets and AI combat training to stare slack jawed through the wall-spanning window opposite the entry. "Is… is that a *swimming pool?*"

"Moving on," I said with a mind towards Lucy's instruction not to dawdle, "next up we have the guest bedrooms."

I kept us moving at a reasonable clip as I guided them through the five bedrooms, past the various life support systems, and on to the next particularly impressive space.

Nick came alive the moment he laid eyes on the garden.

I stepped out of his way, the eagerness on his face absolutely adorable. "Go on," I prompted him.

"This is amazing," he said, gazing out at the barren dirt. His eyes darted back and forth across the space's various features. "Are those precision-wavelength grow lights? We've been trying to get our hands on those for *years*." He pulled up his holopad, connecting it to the room controls with a few taps. "Distributed drip watering? Do you have any idea how expensive that is to install? *And* qi re-circling? *Threads*, the things you could grow here."

He knelt, reaching his hand into the loam. He grabbed some, rubbed it between his thumb and forefinger, raised it to his nose, then pressed it against his tongue.

I wrinkled my nose as Nick tasted the dirt.

He didn't seem to mind, too wrapped up in his own

world. He looked up to the ceiling. "Where did this soil come from?"

"Terc-9," Lucy answered.

"I've never heard of it."

"I'd be surprised if you had. It's a few thousand lightyears away."

Nick blinked. "Oh. Right."

"Alright, that's enough gawking," I said. "We ought to help finish up dinner. Can't let Lucy do *all* the work for us."

"Too late," Lucy said. "The table's already set."

"Damnit," I sighed, physically grabbing Nick by his uninjured arm and pulling him away from the garden. "I swear, I'll help next time."

"Not if I have anything to say about it," Lucy boasted. "And believe me, I *do*."

I nonetheless led the others to the combined kitchen, dining room, and sitting room, sparking yet another round of wide-eyed shock at the luxury of the decor. The fireplace in particular earned its fair share of impressed looks, launching Lucy into a well-rehearsed explanation of the carbon-cellulose recycling system.

While she was distracted, I opened the wine.

I distributed glasses of the thirty-year Bordeaux—made from actual grapes!—to Charlotte and Xavier before again offering one to Nick, qualmless about pouring alcohol to a sixteen-year-old who could simply cycle his blood and kidney meridians for a few moments to clear up its effects.

He declined anyway. "No, thank you. It interferes with my meds."

I blinked. "Did you go to a second clinic? You know the temp one at the gym doesn't give out meds that conflict with alcohol."

"Not those, it's a… I have a neurochemical deficiency. It's nothing, really. I'm just on a thienobenzodiazepine to deal with it."

"You're on a what now?"

Charlotte's eyes sharpened with realization. "An antidepressant," she muttered. "Nick, you could've told us."

"Why? So you could've written it down in your little notepad?"

I gulped, taken aback by the sudden sharpness in Nick's voice. "It's okay. He's telling us now."

On his side of the table, Xavier murmured, "That explains the appetite."

My heart stopped. Depression *and* heavy appetite? It almost sounded like...

I'm not in deep space anymore.

Xavier misinterpreted my blank expression. "What?" he asked. "Antidepressants make you hungry."

I took a big sip of my wine.

Lucy, absolute angel that she is, chose that moment to distract us by simultaneously delivering four bowls of soup to the table, a creamy green affair that I couldn't begin to guess the contents of. It was goddamn delicious, though.

Joviality returned quickly to the conversation under the mood-lifting effects of good food and better wine as we recounted to Lucy the events of our various duels and she in turn regaled the others with a detailed account of her fight with the void horde.

By the time we'd finished our entrees of steak, potatoes, and some kind of roasted root vegetable I'd never seen or heard of before—it tasted like cinnamon, brown sugar, and chili—I was almost entirely too full for the final course.

Almost.

Xavier reached across the table to top up our wine glasses from the second bottle of the night as Lucy served one of the few universal constants between the culinary cultures of the different star systems: chocolate cake.

"I swear by the very threads that bind the universe," I began as I finally put down my fork, "no matter what peaks I reach, what corners of existence I explore, what bonds of mortality I may one-day slip, I will *never* get tired of Lucy's cooking."

"I've been at it for a very long time," Lucy deflected my praise, "and I have the ingredient collection to match."

"Shhh." I held a finger to my mouth. "Take the compliment."

"Thank you, Cal."

"Thank *you*," Charlotte countered. "That was amazing."

"Thank you, Lucy!" Xavier echoed.

"Oh, don't thank me. What kind of hostess would I be if I didn't feed you?"

"May I have some more hot water, please?" Nick asked, gesturing at the empty teacup from which he'd been drinking some kind of tea he'd made himself. The dried root he'd put in it had left him looking a bit out of it, leaving me to question exactly *why* he'd opted for herbal painkillers instead of chemical ones.

I leapt to my feet, but Lucy was already on it. Instead, I moved for the ingredient terminal and requested a bottle of brandy from storage. Grasping my prize in one hand and three glasses in the other, I signaled the others to abandon the dining table and join me in the plush sitting area around the fire. Xavier and Charlotte took the couch, sitting suspiciously close to each other, while Nick and I each got a chair.

We sat back, five of us in total, three sipping brandy and one a cup of potentially psychoactive herbal tea, and let out a collective sigh of contentment. For a moment, the conversation lulled as we quietly enjoyed our drinks, the soft leather upholstery, and the crackle of fire. Just as the quiet began to linger a little too long, I broke it.

"On nights like this, Brady and I used to play a game with the other crew members, kind of a way of getting to know someone beyond the surface-level, small talk stuff. It works best intoxicated and late in the evening. The rules are simple. On your turn, you pick someone and ask them a question they have to answer completely truthfully. Then it's their turn, and they ask a question."

Xavier lowered his glass. "I don't get it."

Charlotte giggled, a gesture which struck me as particularly disturbing given how unfunny that'd been. "That's 'cause some of us don't share our hopes and dreams at the drop of a hat."

"Okay, so other than Xavier who always tells the whole truth anyway, does everyone understand?"

I got a chorus of nods all around.

"Perfect." I rubbed my palms together. "I'll start. Charlotte, why are you on Fyrion?"

Charlotte blinked and rubbed at the bridge of her nose, displacing her glasses in the process. "Right for the throat, huh?" She sighed. "My father has a deep-seated disdain for the cultivators born on the Right Eye, says they're all softies who've had everything handed to them. Up until about two years ago, that included me."

I blinked. "He called you that?"

"No, but he implied it. He started out on Grune, not *quite* as qi-starved as Fyrion, but nothing like the Right Eye. To this day he believes that's why he was the one to save the sect all those cycles back—none of the pampered idiots that got the most resources had any real fight in them. He's not entirely wrong."

"So he wants you to earn your place like he did? Why are you all the way out here instead of Grune, then?"

"I lived in orbit of the Right Eye for nineteen years," Charlotte said. "I formed my core there. If I wanted any hope of proving *anything* to my father, Grune wasn't going to cut it."

Nick raised an eyebrow. "What happened to 'every edge?' Leaving the Right Eye for a place like this is a hell of a disadvantage."

"Like I said, my father wasn't entirely wrong. Overcoming adversity is essential to growing as a cultivator. If I spent my entire life on the Right Eye, knocking back pills and studying under private tutors, I wouldn't be chasing anything. Out here, it's me versus the world. I have to fight for every scrap of advantage I can get, watch my back because I don't have powerful family members around to make my problems go away. It may take me longer to gather the qi I need for each bit of progression, but I'm a better *cultivator* for it."

Charlotte took a sip of her brandy.

I stared at her for a moment, words eluding me. I wasn't sure what answer I'd expected—anything from being disowned to exiled as some punishment—but I hadn't fathomed she'd come here *by choice*. It just seemed so... *not* Charlotte.

I guess sometimes, people surprise you.

"Okay." Charlotte tried to straighten her glasses but only ended up pushing them crooked in the other direction. She leaned in *very* close to Xavier, who seemed to neither mind nor notice her proximity. "Xavier," she started, slurring the consonants and elongating the vowels of his name, "how is it that from the depths of housing D, all the way on Fyrion, with no real backers, no special techniques, no advantages of any kind, you honestly believe you're going to champion the sect one day?"

Xavier shrugged. "I just know. I've always known. I used to watch all the holos of old tournaments with my dad when I was little, and from the moment I saw them I knew I was going to be up there one day. I know I've a long way to go, and I'm going to have to work harder than anyone else to make it happen, but it's *going* to happen."

"He's ambitious," Nick mumbled, "I'll give him that."

"All the great legends started somewhere. Mine starts *here*."

"That's sweet," Lucy said. "It can be good to have your head in the clouds as long as you don't lose track of the ground on which you stand."

"Lucy!" Xavier exclaimed. "I almost forgot you were here. Your turn. How did you and Cal meet?"

We both answered at the same time.

"She saved my life."

"I left him to die."

Xavier blinked. "What?"

Lucy sighed. "In order to save my own life, I abandoned Cal on RF-31 with a victim of void-induced psychosis. By all rights he should've died. He *did* die for about four and a half minutes."

"By some definitions I'm still dead," I added.

"Your jokes sure are," Nick mumbled.

"I came back to find him miraculously still alive, albeit punched full of shrapnel and without a qi signature. I nursed him back to health, guided him through the process of cleansing his punctured meridian, and watched in awe as he went on to open two more right there on the operating table."

I nodded along. "Made a damn mess of that bed."

Lucy continued, "I swore I'd repay him for all the suffering he'd endured, both at my abandonment and at the hands of the cultivator I'd brought into his home."

"And then we came here," I said. "Shortly after I almost killed myself opening my lung meridian without any real idea what I was doing. You all know the rest."

Charlotte squinted. "But why were you at RF-31?"

"Oh no," Lucy said. "You already had your turn. It's mine now. Nick, forgive me if this is too personal, but I'm curious why you seem to show so little interest in growing as a cultivator. You clearly have a lot of talent to form a core so young."

"I always hated class," Nick answered without a thought. "Meditation is *boring*, and combat just felt so pointless. The higher-tier cultivators were always gonna do most of the fighting anyway. I pushed myself to progress because I thought the sooner I formed my core, the sooner I could stop going to those stupid classes. I just wanted to work in the gardens, you know? Not everyone needs to be super ambitious. Some people can just... be *happy*."

Nick didn't seem particularly happy to me, but I knew exactly whose fault that was. I really felt for the kid, especially since practicing herbalism on Fyrion would've meant going to work for his father. I hoped, once he came of age, he could join us on Lucy.

The conversation lulled for a moment as everyone sipped their drink and mulled over the discussion so far. Nick in particular seemed to zone out, his eyes glazing over as he stared into the fire.

"Nick," I gently prodded him, "it's your turn."

"Cal," he said, his voice trailing off. "Cal," he said again. "Caliban. That's a weird name. Why is your name Caliban?"

"It wasn't always," I explained. "My dad considered himself a history buff, used to watch documentaries and read articles about it in his spare time. After my parents separated, whenever Brady or I were acting out, he'd shout at us, call us Grendel and Caliban, two ancient monsters from the Mausoleum era. He thought he was being clever. See, Grendel's mother was famously a monster, and Caliban's was a witch. It was his way of insulting our mom."

Xavier blinked. "That's awful."

I shrugged. "I never minded it. Kept the name, didn't I? Brady didn't, for obvious reasons. I mean, seriously, Grendel's a shit name."

"Language," Lucy softly chided.

"Yeah, sorry." I raised my glass to my mouth. "My father was a lot of things. Pretentious, spiteful, self-important, but what he wasn't, was wrong." I downed the last of my brandy. "My mother was a monstrous witch."

Nick, of all people, broke the tense silence, his voice little more than a whisper over the crackling fire. "It's okay. My dad's an asshole too."

Lucy didn't comment on his language.

A moment passed. I gazed across the coffee table at Nick, struggling to read the pensive expression on his face.

He pushed himself to his feet, a bit wobbly but stable enough, and declared for all to hear, "I gotta piss."

My eyes lingered on the open doorway after he disappeared down the hall, my intoxicated mind absently musing over the evening's revelations.

Xavier's voice pulled me from my thoughts. "Um… Cal? A little help?"

I turned to find Charlotte fast asleep and snoring, her face smushed against Xavier's chest in a way that pushed her glasses up at a comically askew angle. A strand of Lucy's qi freed the unnecessary lenses from her face with immaculate tenderness as Xavier tried to maneuver himself out from under her.

I stopped him. "No, no, she's your problem now. Either wake her up or get her back to D-block."

Xavier looked up at me, then down at her, then up at me again, before shrugging with one shoulder so as to avoid rousing the slumbering Charlotte. In a single, gentle motion, he pulled her up and over his shoulder, putting her into a fireman's carry. He promptly moved for the exit, turning his back—and thus Charlotte's face—towards me.

I stood up. "Isn't there a more comfortable way to…"

I trailed off as Charlotte—clearly awake—silently raised a finger to her lips to shut me up.

Xavier whirled around to face me. "What was that?"

"Oh-um… nothing," I managed, still working out what exactly I'd just seen.

"Okay," Xavier chimed, turning back to the door. "This way, right?"

"Yeah, that's it."

Xavier walked off. I followed all the way to the upper deck, only stopping at the ramp down into the hangar.

"Thank you both," Xavier whispered. "I had a lot of fun tonight. It was nice to meet you, Lucy!"

"It was nice to meet you too, Xavier," Lucy replied. "You get home safe, alright?"

"Goodnight, Xave," I bid him.

He echoed my sentiment and turned to go. Charlotte winked at me as he carried her off.

"Be careful with that one," Lucy muttered.

"I don't know," I said as I watched Xavier ever-so-carefully bring her into a transport pod. "I don't think *I'm* the one who needs that warning right now."

"I think they're sweet."

I shook my head. "It's not going to end well. He's too earnest for her. Anything happens between the two of them tonight, she'll have him wrapped around her little finger by the next dueling day."

"Then he'll learn an important lesson," Lucy said plainly, "the kind that has to be learned the hard way."

"Yeah. I suppose you're right." I paused as a thought struck. "Where did Nick end up?"

"Good question. Let me just…" Lucy's presence vanished for a moment as she retreated into her soulspace, only to return a moment later. "Cal, there's something you should see."

I found him in the garden.

He lay in the dirt, flat on his back, his left arm sprawled out to the side, his right crossed over his chest, still in its sling. He stared up at the grow lights with unfocused eyes.

"Hey, Nick," I greeted him, "you doing okay?"

"I'm… good," he said in that slow and deliberate way high people talk.

"Why are you in the garden?"

"I like it here."

"Okay," I said, withholding judgment. "I think it might be time to get to bed, huh? It's been a long day, and the workers are going to want this hangar back."

Without budging, without blinking, with but a hint of moisture in his eye and a quiet solemnity to his voice, Nick spoke a set of words that I knew, more than any story told or question answered that night, to be the truth.

"Do I have to go back?"

My heart broke a little in that moment, looking down on the most promising cadet Fyrion had ever seen, happier here, lying in the dirt, than among the cultivators who so lauded his potential. I ached at the words I had to speak, for all I wished to take him away from it all, to save him from the pressures of his family and the loneliness of his success, I knew I couldn't.

Uncouth mortal I may've been, I hadn't yet stooped to stealing minors away from their parents. At least in student housing he wouldn't be around his father, for better or for worse.

I knelt at his side. "I'm sorry, buddy, but yeah, you do. I'll come with you, okay? Can you walk?"

"Yeah," he said, suddenly curt. "I'm fine." He pushed himself to his feet and dusted himself off, leaving *most* of the soil behind.

I walked with him back across the hardwood floors and out to the upper deck, hovering a hand behind his back just in case he stumbled. Uneven as his steps were, he kept upright without difficulty.

"Goodnight, Lucy," I bid as we reached the exit ramp. "Thanks for coming down to see us. And for dinner."

"Of course," she replied. "Any time. It was good to talk to you in person again, and I'm glad I got to meet your friends."

"Yeah." I smiled. "They're a lot, but they're mine."

"*You're* a lot," Nick retorted.

I patted him on the back. "That I am, Nick. That I am."

"Goodnight, Lucy," Nick echoed.

"Goodnight, boys. Get home safe."

For the second time in as many months, I disembarked Lucy for the dreary reality of sect life. This time, rather than a derisive elder and a head full of optimism, I stepped into the transport pod with a broken nose, a black eye, and a depressed teenager high on herbal tea.

I took some comfort in the knowledge that even after what felt like the longest day of my life, for all the duels and the discoveries, tomorrow the routine, the training, the *progress*, would all start up again. Even injured, drunk, and worried both about the teen at my side and whatever the fuck Xavier and Charlotte were up to, I wore a smile on my face for the entire ride back to housing D, because unlike Nick, I didn't *have* to go back.

I wanted to.

22

"This is the last one." Nick slid a small linen-wrapped bundle across the dinner table, more cloth than content. "If you can handle this one, you should be ready for tomorrow."

"Thank the threads for that," I said, swiping the package and slipping it into my pocket. "And thank you."

"You're welcome," Nick said. "When you're writhing on the floor later, remember you thanked me."

"Oh, come on. I handled the last one well enough, didn't I?"

Nick raised an eyebrow. "Charlotte?"

"Let's see." She pulled up her notes. "Last time, you called him cruel, an asshole, a sick bastard, a revolutionary sadist, and the shittiest drug dealer in the known universe."

"Okay, that last one was a joke, though," I countered. "And I completed the cycling drills, didn't I?"

"This one's worse," Nick told me. "It's bred to hit at least as hard as the real thing, but because of variance on the single-plant level, it skews harder." He glanced down at the half serving of grilled chicken on my plate. "If you manage to keep that down, I'll be impressed."

"I have to do this eventually, one way or the other," I said. "Tomorrow's my shot to do it as safely as possible."

The plan was simple enough. According to Charlotte's schedule, tomorrow I'd finally "open my bone meridian." That is, I'd actually show up to my focus room hour, open my spine meridian, and then tell the sect I'd opened my bone meridian. It was a trick that'd only work the once, because there'd be no masking the muscle spasms or complete lack of consciousness my muscle or brain meridians would cause, but the spine and bone meridians looked similar enough that we figured I could fool the mortal staff members.

It was all very complicated, but the sect *had* to think I was progressing if I wanted to meet Lopez's deadline, and I couldn't very well clue them in that I was going *way* faster than should've been possible.

Further on I'd have to come up with a different way to fake opening meridians on a less conspicuous timeline, but Nick was already working on that. It helped to have a drug dealer—I mean herbalist—in your back pocket.

Nonetheless, Nick's warning turned my stomach enough that I put down my fork.

"Alright then," Charlotte said. "Everyone ready?"

Nick nodded. I pushed myself to my feet. "Let's do this."

Xavier didn't answer, his eyes fixed on the remnants of his dinner.

I sighed. The two of them had been like this all week. I still didn't know what exactly had happened after Charlotte had feigned sleep to get Xavier to carry her home, but I knew *something* had. Better yet, from the way Charlotte acted entirely normally yet Xavier turned bright red and refused to so much as look at her in front of us, I could tell they'd agreed to hide whatever it was.

I found it endearing how absolutely abysmal a liar

Xavier was. It pained me to acknowledge that Charlotte was probably going to hurt him. Relationships are fucky like that sometimes. But hey, with any luck, the whole process would count as overcoming adversity and he'd get a nice boost to his cultivation out of it.

At the very least, he'd learn something. Hopefully, she would too.

I kept my thoughts focused on Charlotte and Xavier as we walked together back to my room on the third floor, if only to distract myself from what I was about to do. The four of us crowded into my dorm, Xavier leaning against the wall, Charlotte sitting on the bed, and Nick kneeling in front of me as I sat cross-legged on the floor.

I unwrapped the cloth parcel to find a single leaf, deep green and about twice the size of my thumb. Its elliptic shape and firm stiffness left its rounded edges sharp, not enough to cut the skin of my finger, of course, but enough to press in rather than bending away. If I hadn't known better, I might've thought he'd plucked it from any random shrub.

"It's like the second one," Nick explained, referencing an earlier step in my progression up the pain ladder. "Chew it, but don't swallow. I'll let you know when you can spit it out, okay?"

I gulped. "Let's get this over with."

I popped the leaf into my mouth. It tasted bitter and pungent with an unexpected sweetness that I found not entirely unpleasant, at least until I began to chew. It was tough, near leathery in its fibrousness as my teeth failed to punch through it. As I folded it over on itself with my tongue and ground away at it, I stabilized my breathing, cleared my mind of external influence, and visualized my center.

My pool of qi awaited me, calm and dark and cool comfort against the storm to come. I kept chewing.

It started slow, a faint tingling at my extremities. I kept chewing.

The sensation spread, traveling up my arms and legs into my torso. I kept chewing.

The feeling grew stronger, tingling to burning, itching to stabbing. I kept chewing.

From *somewhere else*, a voice reached me. "You can spit it out now."

I didn't hesitate to obey.

I could wax poetic about the creeping tide of agony that threatened to wash me away, about each individual nerve in my body crying out in desperate need for mercy I couldn't give, about the way it seemed to scoop out parts of me to throw to the sharks. No language, spoken or dead, contains the tools to truly convey the experience of total nerve pain.

It was revelatory, a glimpse at the depth of human experience even through such a narrow lens.

It was transformative, a momentary eternity of such intensity that the universe itself seemed to change before my eyes.

And by the gods did it fucking hurt.

The proper next step would've been to refocus on my breathing, keep my breaths even enough to cycle through each of my open meridians one at a time.

The actual next step was to breathe at all. My throat didn't like the idea.

I started slow, a thin thread of air that left my lungs screaming for more, but the rest of me was screaming too at the moment, so they were easy to tune out. It proved just enough to restore some flickering image of my center, just enough to run cool qi through my lung meridian.

Suddenly, that minuscule drip of precious oxygen seemed plenty.

My control solidified.

I kept my lung meridian going as one by one I cycled the others to prove I could. Next came simple qi manipulation, forming various shapes out of the liquid energy in my center, a line, a ring, a figure eight, a sculpture of Lucy, a bust of myself.

As I let that last fall away and return to the pool below, I collapsed back onto the soft carpet.

"Cal!" Xavier's voice resounded in the tight space. "Cal, are you okay?"

"He's not breathing." Panic tinged Nick's voice.

"He is," Charlotte corrected, her tone cool and calm. "Barely, but he is. He's cycling his lungs." She raised her voice to address me directly. "Congratulations, Cal."

"Fuuuuuuuu," I replied rather eloquently given the circumstances.

"On your first attempt!" Xavier boomed. "Well done, Cal! The indomitability of your spirit will shake the stars!"

I let out a groan in thanks, long past questioning Xavier's weirdly intense compliments. At least my position lying on the floor denied him access to my back. I didn't think I could handle one of his back-slaps at the moment.

With dedicated focus I retreated to the infinite sea, reaching my spiritual senses past the bright cores of my friends and into the vacuum outside. The cold numbness of uncaring met me, a welcome solace in the reminder of the insignificance of my body and its pain.

I wished, for the umpteenth time, that I could've opened my meridian afloat in these dark waters, but fine control proved antithetical to perceiving such vastness. I found it difficult to do much of anything out here save escape the mundanities of existence. It served me well as a refuge in which to wait out the effects of Nick's poison.

By the time I returned to the tiny island in the great dark that was the dwarf planet Fyrion, my torment had faded to a dull ache.   I blinked my eyes open to meet three concerned and congratulatory looks.

I grinned up at them.

"I'm ready."

* * *

The crimson glow of the Dueling Stars shined through my window as my holopad blared me awake, casting my room in sunset tones that nobody *here* would ever attribute to a sunset. Oh the cost of life on a planet with no atmosphere. By their place in the sky, it was midday on Fyrion. By the clock on my holopad and weight of my eyelids, it was three AM.

Excitement and anxiety worked in tandem to banish the grogginess from my mind as I shuffled out of bed and into my uniform.

The common areas of housing D sat all but abandoned, occupied exclusively by those others unlucky enough to have focus room hours so inhumanely early. I waved to Astrid—the sweet old lady who manned the reception desk for the night shift—as I passed by other bleary-eyed cultivators coming or going.

When the transport pod arrived to take me to the focus rooms, I found a man in laborer's clothes passed out inside, the stench of alcohol wafting off him. I let him sleep.

The focus room facility itself resembled a luxury spa more than anything else. Calming music drifted softly through the air alongside incense smoke and the faint smell of lilies. Dim LEDs reminiscent of candlelight lit the expansive waiting room, the serenity of the space clashing with the busyness involved in managing the seventy-plus cultivators who came and went every hour.

A teenage girl worked the reception desk at which I found myself.   "Hi there," I greeted her.   "I'm Caliban Rex."

"Caliban," she elongated each syllable of my name as she typed into the terminal before her. "Scheduled for three-twenty-four. You can take a seat. We'll let you know when your room is ready."

"I'll be opening my bone meridian today," I lied.

She blinked at me. "Oh. Okay. One moment." She pulled up something on her holo screen. She read aloud, "As this cultivator's parent or guardian, do you acknowl—wait. Sorry. You obviously don't need your parents. You said you're opening a meridian?"

"Yep," I cheerily confirmed.

"Okay... um... I guess..." She returned to the script, pausing as she edited out bits of it. "Do *you* acknowledge and accept the inherent risks of opening meridians, including but not limited to injury, permanent stunting of one's cultivation, and death?"

"I do."

"Great. Sign here and here." She swiped a pair of liability waivers over to my holopad.

I signed them.

"Excellent. A technician will be by shortly to fit you for qi monitors."

"No monitors, please."

She blinked. "No... monitors. Okay. Um..." Her eyes darted to each side, visibly searching for a more senior staff member to deal with me. None presented themselves.

I smiled apologetically.

"Okay, let me just... oh, here it is!" She sent me another form. "Sign here to confirm you've been offered safety qi and vitals monitoring and chosen to forego them, aware of the inherent risks of opening meridians, including but not limited to injury, permanent stunting of one's cultivation, and death." She thankfully rattled off that last a bit faster than the first time.

I didn't bother to read the waiver before I signed it.

"Perfect. Okay. You're all set to open your…" She glanced down at the info she'd recorded. "…bone meridian. You can take a seat."

"Thanks." I flashed her another smile as I stepped out of the way of the toe-tappingly impatient cultivator in line behind me.

I didn't sit. As comfortable as the plush leather armchairs seemed, I couldn't bring myself to recline with a glass of cucumber water minutes before embarking on something as painful and dangerous as opening my spine meridian. I thought to retreat to the infinite sea to calm myself, but I needed to remain aware lest I miss when they called my name.

Instead, I made a nuisance of myself pacing around the waiting room, earning a few dirty looks from those waiting more peacefully before my holopad beeped with a message directing me to wing three. I obeyed.

"Mr. Rex?" a man with his holopad out greeted me. "Right this way."

"Call me Cal," I said as I followed down the long hallway to a door marked sixty-three. I stepped inside.

The focus room itself resembled an even smaller version of Lucy's core room. Soft synthetic leather padded the floor, within which sat a drain for ease of cleaning. It had no decorations, no distractions, and only a single window that led into an observation room, no doubt where worried friends and family would wait while someone Vihaan's age underwent the meridian cleansing process.

The staff member nodded towards it. "I'll be in there, ready to administer medical aid should it be warranted. Since you've chosen to forego both qi and vital monitoring, I'll only intervene should you call for it. Do you understand?"

"Yep." That sounded perfect to me. The last thing I wanted was him running in to administer CPR the moment

I started cycling my lungs or heart. Threads willing I wouldn't need to cycle either of those, but you never know.

"Very well. There's a locker there if you wish to stow your uniform, as well as a robe you can wear to the showers. Good luck."

I bid him thanks as he adjourned to the observation room, leaving me alone in what felt a little too much like a padded cell. With a sigh I stripped down to my undergarments, tossing my clothes haphazardly into the locker before taking a seat on the floor, my back to the window. "Alright," I muttered to myself. "Let's do this."

I visualized my center easily enough, finding my pool of qi exactly where I'd left it. Without further ado, I formed the familiar needle-and-thread shape, directed it to the meridian entrance at the base of my spine, and got to work.

The pain exploded through my entire body at once rather than the slow build of Nick's various herbs, a difference I'd expected yet that startled me all the same. My focus flickered as my breath hitched, but I recovered quickly.

The sensation was different, coming in fits and starts as it chaotically leapt from the now familiar full-body agony to complete numbness and back again. I tuned it out, focusing exclusively on my breathing and the forceful flow of qi through the clogged passage. It was almost easy. Weeks of practice didn't count for nothing.

It ended as quickly as it began, abrupt and anticlimactic. For all the build-up, all the training, I'd almost expected something to go horribly wrong.

I guessed sometimes, the system worked. Of course, I still had two meridians left to potentially kill myself trying to open. I may have come a long way from nearly asphyxiating in Lucy's core room, but I still had plenty of peril waiting on the path ahead.

For now, though, I reveled in my success and

experienced for the first time the sensation of cycling my spine meridian. It felt... odd.

From my reading I knew it governed pain, sensitivity to temperature, and reflexes, the latter of which I'd have a hard time testing on my own. I dug my fingernails into the palm of my right hand to test the former.

It felt... cold, like four icicles pressing into my skin, distinctly noticeable yet entirely unlike anything I'd expected. It wasn't entirely pleasant, but it also wasn't the screaming distraction it'd otherwise been.

In contrast, the air around me stifled like a swamp, oppressively hot and humid against my skin as every bit of heat and moisture amplified in my mind.

I cut off the flow of qi.

The world returned to normal. I sighed. It seemed the more meridians I opened, the further I distanced myself from other cultivators. I'd never heard of such oversensitivity to temperature or humidity. I prayed I'd get used to it.

The beep of my holopad tore me from my trance and into the fetid stench of the focus room. The full hour hadn't yet passed, but they'd need extra time to clean up the mess of toxins I'd expunged. Crinkling my nose against the smell, I flashed the staff member a thumbs up and pushed myself to my feet. He smiled back through the window.

At his instruction I left my clothes where they lay and wrapped myself in the startlingly soft gray bathrobe hanging in the locker above them. Clad only in it and its pair of matching slippers, I adjourned to the showers, my spirit afloat with the glow of victory.

For all the weirdness, the unanswered questions, the unpredictable behavior of my qi as it interacted with my body, I'd taken one more crucial step on the inexorable march of progress, one critical milestone towards forming my core.

As the hot water of the shower washed over me, a single thought echoed over and over in my head, crescendoing until it manifested as a set jaw and the kind of slyly confident grin best grinned in private.

Ten down, two to go.

23

I returned twice to the focus rooms over the following five weeks, each time equipped with a different specialty herb Nick had tailored for my specific purpose. The process proved remarkably simple: I chewed on a few leaves to reintroduce impurities into my system, then cycled my blood meridian to force them back out through the appropriate avenue.

To fake opening my skin meridian, that meant an hour spent sweating black gunk. For my stomach meridian, it took a different route. At Nick's recommendation, I fasted a few days before that one to clear the way.

Simulating the *pain* of meridian opening turned out even easier. I just had to expand my spiritual senses beyond myself to glimpse the qi around me.

Oh boy did that suck.

I felt as if I'd fallen into a star, submerged in blinding light and scorching heat and ear-shattering *noise*.

I withdrew within the second, a migraine already taking root in my mind. Unbidden I let out a grunt of pain, one I'm certain helped sell the illusion of actually using all that qi to advance my cultivation.

Over each of the two hours I spent there lying to the sect

about my progress, only a handful of times did I reach for that deafening inferno. Accustomed as I might've grown to Fyrion's ambient qi, the planet-wide enchantment only left some ten percent of the world's qi production spread about its entire surface. The other ninety percent it divided evenly between the seventy-seven focus rooms.

A rough, *rough* estimate accommodating for the difference in surface area between the focus room and *the entire planet*, put the qi inside at about a hundred and forty *million* times as dense as that outside. And Fyrion was just a dwarf planet. I couldn't imagine the intensity of the focus rooms orbiting the stars themselves.

Actually, fuck imagining. I was pretty damn proud I managed to stay *conscious*, migraine or otherwise. The thought of trying to acclimate myself to that much qi didn't even cross my mind. It wasn't like I'd ever have to fight someone *inside* a focus room, right?

Anyway, by the time my official sect record considered my bone, skin, and stomach meridians open, I understood why everyone valued focus room hours so highly. Threads, divided evenly between the four people taking up mine—Nick, Charlotte, Xavier, and, sporadically, Elder Lopez—the extra hour meant an entire twenty-five percent more qi than they'd otherwise get.

No wonder Xavier and Charlotte were shooting up the ranks.

More importantly, I had my own advancement to attend to. Ranking be damned. Just over three months into my time with the Dragon's Right Eye, I'd finally steeled my focus, honed my combat prowess, and "opened" enough meridians to move on from my introductory classes into the intermediate ones.

I just had to prove it.

* * *

Exam day morning, my holopad chimed as I navigated the

crowd of sweaty cultivators from the morning workout to the cafeteria for breakfast. I answered.

"Mindy! We all set for today?"

"You're set," the reply came muffled, followed immediately by a distinct smacking sound.

I scowled, not that she could see it over the comm line. "Are you eating?"

She took another bite. "New sushi place just opened down on Hatcher's Row. I'm making sure it stands up to Elder Langham's exacting standards."

"You're eating *sushi?* It's eight AM."

"It is? Huh. No wonder they were closed."

My stomach churned at the sound of her swallowing and shoving something else into her mouth before she kept speaking.

"Anyway, I'm calling to let you know your spread's good to go. Crew'll be there come noon."

I blinked. "Crew? I just wanted a—"

"Excuse me? Yes, the pH on this is off by point—"

She hung up.

I exhaled, scooping a smattering of berries into my half-serving of oatmeal before making for our usual table. Absent Charlotte, who usually didn't bother making the trip back to housing D for breakfast, Xavier and Nick had already dug in, ravenously making headway into their large and massive portions, respectively. Even now my heart skipped a beat seeing Nick wolf down so much food, but I'd long learned to deal with that particular panic response.

I wasn't in deep space anymore.

"Just got off a call from Mindy," I greeted them. "Looks like lunch is going to be a bigger affair than I expected."

"Oh no." Sarcasm dripped from Nick's voice. "Not more food. Anything but that."

Xavier glared down at my meager breakfast. "You *do*

realize you actually need to eat, right?"

"I *am* eating," I said, forcing down a spoonful of oatmeal.

Xavier scowled. "Cal, you have fewer calories there than you burned on the track today. How can you expect your muscles to grow if you don't feed them?"

"I *am* eating," I repeated myself, my tone sharpening.

Xavier exhaled and dropped the issue. "You ready for today?"

"As ready as I'm gonna get," I answered. "Meditation will be a cake walk if I cycle my spine, cycling's just a matter of showing Chrissy that my sect file shows I have the right meridians open, and the AI puts me at eighty-four percent accuracy with the Dragon's Fang movements. I only need seventy-five to move onto combat two."

Nick looked up from his second omelet. "Excited?"

"*Extremely.* I'm gonna miss the kiddos, but progress is progress. I'll tell you, I'm *not* gonna miss my combat instructors. Senior Cadet Long has hated me from day one."

Xavier nodded. "You do have a talent for aggravating people."

"Only assholes," I countered. "It's not *my* fault they're so fun to mess with."

Xavier sighed.

Nick set down his fork onto a cleared plate and pushed himself to his feet. "Alright, I'm back to work. I'm close to a breakthrough on this apple variant; I'm sure of it. Good luck today."

"Thanks," I said. "Good luck with your seeds."

Xavier waited until Nick was out of earshot before speaking again. "I'm worried about him."

"Really? He seems fine to me."

"He spends all day cooped up in his room working with those seeds of his. He doesn't come out. He doesn't talk to people. He doesn't work to improve himself."

I shrugged. "Just because you don't see it doesn't mean he isn't improving himself. There's more to life than fighting. If he wants to focus on his craft, that's perfectly reasonable."

Xavier shook his head. "He's not well, Cal. He's skilled at hiding it, but he's not well."

I paused a moment to stare at Xavier. To this day I hadn't a clue how he knew the things he did. He seemed to alternate between complete obliviousness and deep insight, missing obvious social cues—*cough cough,* Charlotte hitting on him—only to suddenly know for certain the emotional state of a random passerby. Of the entire sect, he was the only one who could gauge my cultivation level, and he did so at little more than a glance.

I think that might've been why he was so incessantly honest. What he did or didn't know about a person was so divorced from what they wanted him to, he'd never learned what thoughts he was supposed to hide.

"Okay. I trust you. What should we do?"

"What else *can* we do? He's already seeing a doctor about it. Best I can think of is to be there for him. He needs friends more than anything."

"Yeah," I muttered. "I'll find some time for that after my nine hours of classes, two of working out, combat practice, cycling practice, and preparation to open the two deadliest meridians." I sighed and glanced down at my holopad. Time to go. "Speaking of…" I stood. "Dinner at C-block tonight?"

Xavier nodded. "Good luck."

My mind reran the conversation in loops as I bussed my tray and made for the transport platform. Much as I worried for Nick, I fundamentally lacked the time to spend with him. Charlotte and Xavier didn't have to plan around a busy class schedule, but with Charlotte already gone to housing C and Xavier pushing dangerously close to a promotion himself, they'd have a harder time fitting Nick in around their own training. At least I lived next door to the kid, for all that meant when he rarely left his room.

Painfully appropriately, I found my attention yanked back to my own world as I stepped for the last time into the beginner classroom. Senior Cadet Park was off talking with a parent, so I made straight for her counterpart.

I found him tapping away at his holopad. He didn't look up. "What do you want, cadet?"

I saluted. "Senior Cadet Stevens, sir, I'd like to test out of this class."

He snorted. "If you say so, but I'll have to caution you against it. Your numbers just aren't there."

I blinked. "My… numbers?"

He swiped at his holopad. "You average an impulse rating of forty-seven before your focus breaks. The minimum threshold for meditation two is sixty."

"You guys are *measuring* this? Why is this the first I'm hearing about it?"

Stevens raised an eyebrow at me. "Did you think we were just hitting you with sticks at random? The Dragon's Right Eye does have *standards*, you know. Standards you don't meet."

I sighed. I'd been hoping this wouldn't look too suspicious. "I'd like to try anyway if that's alright."

He shrugged. "Your bruises. The test is simple enough: make it through the class period without losing focus. We'll be hitting you harder than you're used to. That okay?"

I nodded. "Let's get this over with."

Most of the kiddos had already taken their seats by the time Instructor Park called for the class to begin. I caught Stevens whispering something to her as I sat cross-legged on the padded floor, her eyes flashing to meet mine for a moment's surprise.

Fighting back the sinking feeling Elder Lopez would hear about my sudden burst of progress, I evened out my breathing and descended into my center. Without any real idea what units they used to measure the force of their blows—not that that info would've meant anything to me either way—I worried that the numbing effects of my cycling wouldn't counteract the increase in intensity. I'd tested them before, of course—to great success even—but if the instructors were going to be hitting me *that* much harder... I just didn't know.

I supposed I could, if I'd wanted to, hide in the infinite sea for the duration of the test. My focus would've survived outright torture so sheltered in those dark waters of uncaring. I chose not to. If I lacked the focus to test out the right way, I clearly still had more to learn from meditation one, Charlotte's schedule be damned.

Lacking the capacity to cycle more than a few meridians at a time, I opted for my blood, senses, and, of course, my spine. I'd have loved to harden my skin against their blows or reinforce my lungs to help maintain my breathing, but they'd notice if my breath slowed or skin turned corpse-colored. I got away with empowering my senses to drown out the distractions in the deluge of information because the instructors couldn't see my eyes go all starry night with their lids shut.

I needn't have worried.

I didn't even notice the first strike, the icy sensation of spine-muted pain vanishing behind the overwhelming flow of data from my nose and ears. The second caught my attention with the same intensity as Nicki's heartbeat two spots to my left.

Minute by minute the hours ticked by, the morning class as boring as ever as I distracted myself tracking the senior cadets' movements by sound alone. Each breath, each step, each thwack of their cane I noted, the pair not even attempting to maintain their surprise against a sense meridian they'd never guessed I'd opened.

When at last the period ended, my eyes flicked open to find looks not of shock or congratulations, but of scorn.

"Cadet Rex," Stevens spoke with venom on his tongue, "I'm issuing you a request for your current blood chemistry data. You will accept it."

My holopad popped open with a biometric data request. I squinted at it. "You think I cheated?"

"You took strikes rated at more than double your previous threshold without even flinching," Park snapped. "Of course you cheated."

Shit.

"Well, I didn't," I replied, sending over the relevant data. I rubbed at my bruised midsection. "Why'd you go so high above the requirement to advance?"

"You're hardly the first cultivator to cut corners," Stevens snarled.

Of course I'm not, you ass. Who in their right mind would want to stick around while you beat them with a stick?

I didn't say that, however much I might've wanted to. Instead I simply shrugged. "I didn't take anything, if that's what you're asking. I improved. I *made progress.* Isn't that the point?"

Stevens looked up from his holopad over to Park. "His blood's clean. Should we check his urine? He's got his kidney meridian open."

Park shook her head. "That's not how he did it, then. No way someone at his level could've completely eliminated all traces of narcotics from his blood in three hours, and the effects would've worn off halfway through either way."

"So what now? We let him get away with it?"

"Threads no," Park said. "Report it to Elder Lopez. Let

it be her problem."

I bit back my sigh of relief at that. I knew exactly what Elder Lopez would do about it, and it had little to do with investigating me for cheating. I made a mental note to tell Charlotte she wouldn't be getting an extra focus room hour this week.

A look of annoyance flashed across my face as I stood and addressed my soon-to-be former instructors. "Is that all?"

"Pending our meeting with Elder Lopez, that's all," Senior Cadet Stevens said. "You're dismissed, Cadet Rex."

Despite his words, it was the two of them that left the classroom, no doubt headed directly for the Elder's office. I waited until they were gone before I too made for the door, albeit for a much more delicious purpose.

Sure enough, I poked my head into the hall to find two folding tables, four thermal carts for hot, cold, and frozen foods, and three mortals in black slacks and white button-downs emblazoned with a small logo and the words *Roseleaf Catering Co.*

I grinned. "Come on in."

The kids watched with wide eyes as the caterers filed into the classroom. Being the *considerate* classmate I am, I'd let their parents know in advance they wouldn't be needing lunches today, so most of them already knew something was up, but clearly hadn't expected full on catering. That was fair. *I* hadn't expected full on catering.

I addressed the classroom. "Some of you may've noticed me talking with the instructors just now. That's because—pending a few hiccups—I've finally tested out of meditation one. This afternoon, I intend to do the same in cycling and combat. Unless something goes horribly wrong, this is the last day of classes we'll share together."

A few of the kids, Vihaan included, gaped at the news. Most of them weren't listening. It was actually kind of cute, watching the way their eyes followed the caterers as they set up the tables behind me.

"So for our last day, I asked my friend to put together a pizza party. She-uh—" I glanced back at the caterers and frantically waved one down before he could deposit a collection of wine bottles onto one of the tables. "She went a bit overboard, but you all deserve it. You've been great classmates, even after I showed up and took away your teachers' attention. After-uh... everything we've been through together, I can honestly say you've grown important to me. Thank you for welcoming me. Dig in."

Okay so it wasn't the most *eloquent* speech, but the smiles on their faces as they stampeded past me to get to the pizza. Overkill or otherwise, Mindy had at least had the wherewithal to request mostly plain cheese and pepperoni, relegating the handful of gourmet pies to a corner where I and a few of the more adventurous ten-year-olds tried the gamut.

My favorite was spiced with masala and a blend of three cheeses I'd never heard of before. I think if I really pushed myself, I could've *maybe* pronounced one of them.

As the kiddos settled in and enjoyed their lunch, I kept off to the side for a moment's peace. I was gonna miss these kids. They were loud and obnoxious and, well, *kids*, but barring Instructor Long's attempts to paint me as a villain, they were the only ones in this entire godsforsaken sect who hadn't fallen into petty politics and maneuvering.

How many more years would they have before this place turned them against each other?

"When you said you were going to bring them pizza I didn't expect... this."

"Chrissy!" I greeted the cycling instructor. "Please, help yourself. My-uh... friend went a bit overboard organizing all of this." Per her request, I oh so tactfully avoided sharing Mindy's name.

She grabbed a slice of some blue cheese monstrosity I hadn't enjoyed. "I take it this means you were successful with your stomach meridian?"

"I was," I told her, not *technically* lying.

A warm smile stretched across her face. "Congratulations, then. You're ready for cycling two."

I blinked. "That's it? You don't want to... I don't know, check?"

"Should I? What would you possibly have to gain from lying?"

"Right. Good point. I guess I thought there'd be more of a test. The meditation instructors even accused me of cheating."

She raised an eyebrow at me. "Did you?"

"No, of course not."

Chrissy shrugged. "Then it's not a problem. Congratulations, Cal. You've earned it."

I smiled. "Thanks."

She directed the kids to return their plates to the caterers as the three mortals packaged up their supplies and cleared out. I took the opportunity to pull Vihaan aside, kneeling before him and drawing the sword from my back.

"I should've done this the moment I got it, but we're going to be seeing a lot less of each other soon, so now seemed like the time." I laid the weapon over my knee. "This sword is as much a part of your story as it is mine. It seems only fair that you should be the one to name it."

Vihaan's eyes went wide as he looked down on his mother's stellar craftsmanship. "Really? I get to name it?"

"Really."

He placed a hand on the flat of the blade, Fyrion silver alloyed with the very steel of the freezer cart that'd saved his life. He took a moment, staring at it and chewing his lower lip in thought, before he finally spoke. "Shiver."

"Shiver?"

Vihaan nodded. "That's all I did. It was really cold in there."

I smiled at the sweet simplicity of it. "Shiver it is then." I placed my hand over his upon the cool metal and put on my most solemn voice. "I hereby dub thee, Shiver, slayer of void beasts, deliverer of sanctuary, defender of the ice cream."

Vihaan let out a giggle. I counted that as a win.

"Okay, everyone! It's time to turn our thoughts inwards," Chrissy instructed.

Vihaan answered to Chrissy's call to attention, turning away and taking a seat on the padded floor. I returned Shiver to its sheath on my back, my muscle memory long trained to find the specialized slot that made the motion possible.

I shuffled back and took a seat of my own, opting to spend my last class period with Chrissy actually following along with her guided exercises. For obvious reasons I didn't need help preparing to open my kidney meridian, but every bit I could improve my control or stretch out my qi pathways to increase capacity would prove useful. My... unique access to qi made that latter both particularly easy and especially important.

Three hours of repetitive, focus-intense cycling later, I bid Chrissy one final thanks and joined the kiddos for a last walk down the windowed hallway to combat class.

With a knot of trepidation building in my throat, I made straight for the head instructor and announced my intentions. "Senior Cadet Long, sir." I saluted. "I'd like to attempt to test out of this class."

He laughed in my face, a loud and sharp and derisive thing that seemed to punch through the air between us. "No."

I blinked. "Excuse me?"

"I said no. You're an upstart mortal that lacks the skill,

discipline, and drive to succeed as a cultivator. It would be a stain upon this sect's integrity to allow you to advance further."

I fell out of my salute. "That's absurd. I work as hard as anyone here, and I've made *good* progress."

Long's face hardened. "You're robbing *children* of valuable instruction so you can play at warrior. I refuse to reward such behavior."

"Then let me go! The sooner I test out, the sooner you don't have to deal with me. I've reached over eighty percent accuracy with the forms. Sect guidelines only require—"

"Sect guidelines leave the final decision to the lead instructor," Long snapped.

"C'mon, Bao," Instructor Davis came to my defense using Long's first name. "He has been working hard. Give him a shot."

Long glanced over to Davis then back at me, a thin smile taking shape on his face. "Very well, cadet. If you can perform all ninety-nine steps of the Dragon's Fang to my satisfaction, I'll allow you through."

That didn't sound good.

I looked to Davis for help.

He offered none.

I bit back a groan, my mind racing for alternatives to going along with Long's idea, but I found none. He'd offered exactly what I wanted. I gulped, nodded, and stepped directly into the obvious trap. "Okay."

"Okay, what?"

"Okay, sir. Thank you, sir."

As Instructors Davis and Charleston pulled the class away to begin the day's lesson, I stepped to an empty corner of the dojo and took on a neutral stance.

Long stood to my side, his hands clasped behind his back. "Begin."

In a single, rehearsed motion, I lunged my left foot forward to lower my stance and reached with my right arm for Shiver at my back, turning my upper body to form a smaller target for the imaginary enemy before me. The Dragon Prepares. I smoothly transitioned into the second step, drawing my sword and twisting my upper body as I advanced with my right foot, the force of the motion bringing my sword between me and my foe. The Dragon Raises His Claws.

I never got to the third step.

Something slammed into my wrist halfway through the step, knocking the blade from my hand and sending it clattering against the floor. I stopped short.

"Your grip is weak," Bao Long snarled, hands already behind his back once more. "Again."

I swallowed my retort and knelt down to collect my sword and return it to its sheath. With a nod I resumed my neutral starting position and reentered the first step.

At least this time I saw him move.

Halfway through the first lunge, Long kicked forward, sweeping my back leg out from under me with supernatural speed.

I caught myself on my hands just shy of my face slamming into the padded floor.

"Your footwork is unstable," Long spat at my prone form. "Again."

"You cycled for that! I could've had perfect footwork and I would've fallen."

"I said, again, cadet." Long spoke through his teeth.

I scowled and pushed myself upright. "Yes, sir," I growled.

I was ready for him this time, but no amount of preparation could bridge the gap between ten open meridians and a fully-fledged copper. At least I managed to cycle my spine to deal with the pain.

His fist met my stomach faster than I could even tense for it, doubling me over as it drove the breath from my lungs. His left elbow slammed into my back, knocking me again onto my stomach, where this time he pinned me under his foot.

"You're weak. You're pathetic. You're an insult to every cultivator who trained their entire life to earn their place here."

I gasped for air, what felt like several hundred pounds of force pressing me into the floor as breath eluded me. "Elder... Lopez," I wheezed.

Long laughed. "Oh, yes. Elder Lopez told me of your little arrangement. One year to graduate all three beginner classes before you're removed from the sect. She also so kindly reminded me of the authority afforded me as your instructor."

I pulled qi through my lung meridian to ease my breathlessness as I parsed his words. They didn't make any *sense*. Why would Elder Lopez turn against me? I was feeding her focus hours. She of all people should've wanted me to stay.

Shit. If Lopez was behind this, that meant I couldn't turn to her to fix it. What about Instructor Stevens' accusations of cheating? Did those come from her too? Was this just another attempt to wring more focus hours out of me, or something more?

There was too much I didn't know.

Long continued his tirade as my thoughts raced, but I didn't listen. It was the same "cultivators good, mortals bad" tripe he'd been spouting since the day we met. The fact I very much *was* a cultivator didn't seem to mean much to him.

By the time he finally lifted his foot and allowed me up, my outrage had cooled from the blaze of indignation to the icy chill of resentment.

I left class early, furiously tapping away at my holopad to schedule a meeting with Elder Lopez. Her secretary sent me a time six days from now. I groaned.

I didn't like not knowing where I stood. It grated on me, the unanswered questions, the duplicity, the unfairness of it all.

I'd always known there were people at the Dragon's Right Eye that wanted me gone. Threads, Long had been one of them since I first set foot on this godsforsaken planet. The day's only revelation was that they'd finally come up with a way to get rid of me.

I had nine months left, nine months to form my core, to deal with Long, to pass through three levels of combat classes. Oddly enough, that first seemed the easiest of the three.

Perhaps it would help with the others.

For all the lingering pain in my stomach and wrist, for all the roiling frustration, all the indignity of being pinned to the ground like an animal, I returned to housing D with my head held high.

Stevens could throw his accusations. Long could yell his slurs. Lopez could play her games. None of it mattered. Nothing mattered. At the end of the day I'd outpace them all. At the end of the day my flails against infinity would ripple out wider than theirs ever would.

Even now, sore and beaten and exhausted from the day's developments, years behind my opposition and without the connections to contest them, I didn't stand alone. I didn't lack for tools at my disposal.

And I still had a few tricks up my sleeve.

24

"He did *what?*"

Xavier's axe slammed into my practice sword, sending the wooden blade flying from my grip. It bounced across the padded floor and over the edge of the dueling ring.

I help up my hands to admit defeat. "He refused to let me pass. Said as my instructor it's up to him, and he intends to keep me in combat one until my year's up and I get kicked out."

"Have you spoken to Elder Lopez about it?" Charlotte asked from her vantage on the sidelines.

"I think she's behind it. Long mentioned her, and when I tried to schedule a meeting she put me off."

Charlotte met me at the edge of the ring and handed up my wayward sword. "Even the strong of your blade can't meet him. Stop trying to match his attacks. You're never gonna out-Xavier Xavier."

I nodded at her advice and reclaimed my weapon.

"Have you considered going over her head?" Charlotte continued, returning to the subject at hand.

"To Berkowitz?" Xavier asked. "Good luck getting a meeting."

"Maybe Lucy could," I said, only half paying attention

as my mind scrambled for a step in the Dragon's Fang that could counter Xavier's aggression. Unfortunately, the style tended to answer aggression with *more* aggression. "Elder Berkowitz seemed a bit enamored with her."

"That's not what I meant," Xavier said. "She's off-world. Won't be back from her hunting expedition on Ilirian for at least a few months."

"Wait, really?" Charlotte pulled up her holopad and frantically tapped away for her notes on Elder Berkowitz. "Threads, you're right. She left three days ago for a spirit beast cull. Return expected in eight months."

"Welp, so much for that option." I looked up to Xavier and raised my sword.

"Aaaaand, fight!"

I took a different tact, slipping into The Dragon Lies in Wait for two heartbeats then twitching ever-so-slightly forward in an attempt to throw him off before transitioning into The Hidden Claw, a roundabout strike designed to catch an opponent off guard.

Xavier read me like a book, ignoring my feint and bringing up the haft of his axe to bat away my strike before it got anywhere near him. The maneuver forced his blade away from me, but that didn't stop all two hundred and fifty pounds of him from barreling into me.

I landed on my back.

He extended a hand. "Tricks either work once, or zero times. Don't depend on them."

I groaned as he helped me up. "I can't match you for strength or reach, and you know the style better than I do."

"Understanding one's weaknesses is the first step to finding one's strengths. Understanding one's opponent's weaknesses is the first step to finding victory."

I blinked at him askance but he offered no elaboration. I turned to Charlotte. "Can you translate that to Standard, please?"

"Xavier's very good at what he does, but what he does is simple and predictable. Since you can't take advantage of his qi weaknesses, you have to use his aggression against him. Have you thought about just leaving?"

"Have I what?" I paused for a moment as I parsed the cognitive whiplash of the subject change.

"You came to Fyrion because you needed instruction, right? Once we get you through the process of forming your core without killing yourself, you're done. I've already given Lucy the full manuals for both The Dragon's Fang and the Velereau family style, and it's not like you need the focus rooms."

"Charlotte!" Xavier snapped. "He can't just *leave.*"

I shook my head. "I may not need the focus rooms, but you guys do. If I left the sect that'd mean staying with Lucy, but Fyrion doesn't have a long-term berth for her. It'd either be just the two of us up in orbit for weeks on end, or we'd have to leave Fyrion altogether. I don't want to abandon you guys down here."

"You should at least consider it," Charlotte said. "Don't limit yourself for our sake. We'll be fine."

Xavier glared at her.

"*You* will be fine, but I can't leave Nick. Xav's gonna make it to housing C any day now, then I'll be all he's got. Nick's already done so much for me. The least I can do is stick around until he comes of age and can escape his situation."

"Cal's staying," Xavier said with a finality to his voice. "Doing otherwise would mean letting Long win."

"Alright," Charlotte conceded, understandably not *too* keen on my departure herself. "That takes us back to step one: dealing with Long."

"That's easy." Xavier shrugged. "Just duel him."

"I'd prefer to keep my head attached to my shoulders, thanks."

"Cal's right. Long already hates him. He'd consider a challenge a grave insult."

"Then win."

Charlotte and I shared a confused look before turning in sync to gape at Xavier.

My incredulity broke through first. "He's a *Copper*."

"To hell with his tier, he's one of the sect's top cadets. Threads, non-cadets included, Long's rank two-twenty-nine. Cal only has nine months."

Xavier's gaze met mine with stony solidity, an icy certainty discoloring his normally boisterous voice. "I know you can do this, Cal."

A chill ran down my spine. I shivered in spite of myself. "Okay."

He rapped his knuckles against the shaft of his great axe. "Again?"

Charlotte let out an aggravated sigh. "You two are going to get each other killed."

I nodded. "Again."

I settled in to The Dragon Lies in Wait for a second time as Xavier returned to his side of the ring.

As he charged in, I slipped into something... *different*. The motion came unnaturally from the Dragon's Fang's base defensive stance, but the half-remembered step came so imperfectly to my body that any dissonance in the transition fell by the wayside.

I twisted my elbow in and lowered the point of my blade, adjusting my footwork twice in the seconds I had to keep up my balance.

Xavier swung, a crossed overhand strike I'd seen him throw a thousand times.

I didn't meet it. I didn't try to match with a strike of my own or even think to fend off his assault. Nor did I leap to the side in some attempt to dodge his overwhelming force. Unimpeded, Xavier knew how to redirect an attack.

So I impeded him.

I swung my wrist up, angling my sword towards the floor just as Xavier's axe met it. His blade slid readily along mine, altering its course by a handful of degrees before leaving contact. My own weapon's downward point allowed his axe head to slip free rather than slamming hard into my crossguard, maintaining the axe's forward—and downward—momentum as I narrowly sidestepped and pulled my blade back to meet his neck.

Of course, Xavier's bulk just batted the blunt edge of my practice sword away, but even as he came to a stop and turned around, a red imprint remained across his throat.

"Brilliantly fought! Caliban, your prowess grows by the day!"

I caught the remnants of an endeared smile on Charlotte's face before she caught herself. "That was sloppy but the right idea. Minimize contact, disrupt just enough to gain a positional advantage, then go for the throat."

Xavier clapped me on the back. "Well done!"

"Where did you learn that?" Charlotte asked. "It didn't look like an improvisation, and I don't recall ever seeing it before."

"It's one of Cedric's," I answered, "the um… Lucy's previous passenger. She has some old holos of him practicing that I trained against on my way here."

"Do you know what the style's called? Where it's from?"

"No and no. Lucy probably knows more, but she's tightlipped about her past, especially where Cedric is involved. Why?"

"It suits you," Charlotte said. "You should consider incorporating it more into your style."

"But I need to master the Dragon's Fang to test out of— shit. You're right. I'm never going to beat Long at his own style, and if I can only advance by dueling him anyway, I don't *need* to perfect the Dragon's Fang."

Charlotte pulled up her holopad. "I'll ping Lucy with a request for her files on Cedric's fighting style. I'll have to go through them to pick out how to best incorporate it, but that should only take a day or two. In the meantime, enjoy your afternoons off. It's not like Long is going to teach you anything useful."

"Bah!" Xavier burst. "Afternoons off? There're duels to be fought!"

I grinned at him. "Right you are, big guy." I raised my practice sword. "Shall we?"

I didn't win again.

Bout after bout Xavier bested me, exploiting the glaring flaws in my technique to barrel through my defense with masterful aggression. I improved in bits and pieces, solidifying my footwork and growing more comfortable with the maneuver, but my inexperience shone through.

Still, I bore my bruises proudly as I walked away from the training session. I had a plan in mind, another secret weapon in my arsenal, and, after three long months of slamming my head into a wall, at long last, I'd won a sparring match.

Threads knew I had a long way to go. Two meridians to open, a core to form, and an entirely new set of moves to meld into my fighting style, but damn did it feel good.

I mean, hey, if we don't celebrate our victories, what's the point?

I opted not to comment when Xavier oh so subtly stayed behind as I left the housing C gymnasium for the transport home. He and Charlotte would share their relationship when they were ready, however abysmally they'd hidden it so far. At least Xavier had stopped avoiding eye contact with her in my presence, even if he kept a conspicuously measured distance.

On this particular evening, it meant I walked alone up the steps of housing D to the third floor, where I found Nick standing by himself at the hall window, staring out over Fyrion's barren expanse and the starry sky beyond.

I stepped up to what had become our unofficial meeting spot and joined him in his stargazing. "We missed you at dinner tonight."

"I was working."

A second passed in silence as I waited for Nick to elaborate. He didn't. "This apple variant of yours?"

He nodded. "I want..." He trailed off for a moment before taking a different tact. "If it's possible for a human to swap out normal qi for yours, it has to be possible for a plant, right?"

"I... wouldn't know. I guess so. It'd probably be a lot safer to experiment with a plant than on people."

"But I have to find your qi first. I can't know what I'm doing if I don't."

"I don't know how feasible that is. Sensing it, I mean. The stars kind of had to align for me to manage it, and I think working with normal qi makes it harder. All I can tell you is that it's out there." I let out a breath. "Maybe I can help with your plant? Outside isn't the only source of dark qi."

Nick's gaze remained fixed on the distant gray horizon. "Yeah. That... that would be nice."

The conversation lulled once more.

We stood in silence for a few pensive minutes, caught up in our own worlds, before Xavier's words of worry from that morning floated to the surface of my mind. I looked over at Nick. "Penny for your thoughts?"

"What?"

"It's a—right. You don't use pennies here. Credit for your thoughts doesn't have the same ring to it." I shook my head. "What's on your mind?"

"Oh. It's nothing. I just..." He blinked, just once, for the first time since I'd joined him. A crack showed in his armor. "Is this really all there is?"

"How do you mean?"

"I mean, look. We're living in an air bubble on a wasteland, fighting each other for scraps. What's the point? Win enough and you can fight stronger people for bigger scraps? There has to be more than that."

"There's always more," I said. "You just have to find it. Four months ago, I was content to live my life out on roofie. I had oxygen to breathe, food to eat, and friends to talk to. I only really went looking for more after that was taken from me."

I paused and took a breath. "That's a lie. Roofie was the more that I found. It took Brady and me leaving home to find it." I turned to him, but he didn't meet my gaze. "I know your parents suck. I know you don't like it here. The good news is, in a bit under two years, you'll be free to leave. There's a whole galaxy out there, Nick, and once you turn eighteen, you can see as much of it as you want. Two years may seem like forever, but it's not, and I'll be here to wait with you. Charlotte and Xavier need to keep moving up the ranks for their cultivation, but I don't."

I touched his arm, forcing him to turn and look me in the eyes as I added, "I'm not going anywhere. I promise."

Okay, maybe I shouldn't have said that with Instructor Long's shenanigans hanging over my head, but after my progress in the ring, anything felt possible. A part of me acknowledged the precariousness of my position, realized that I was saying what Nick needed to hear, but truthfully, I meant it. I couldn't abandon him. I just couldn't.

"Okay. Um... thanks." Nick pulled away and returned to his stargazing.

"So how about tomorrow, just before dinner?" I strategically picked a time that would allow me to drag

318

him down to join us for dinner rather than eating alone in his room. "You can show me what you've done so far and maybe I can help out with those apple seeds of yours."

"Yeah. Sure. That sounds good."

"Perfect." I stepped back, patting him on the shoulder with half the expertise and a quarter the force of Xavier's back-claps. "I'm going to get some sleep. It's been a long day. Make sure you do the same, eh?"

"Yeah," Nick muttered, his gaze still fixed on the night sky. "I will."

I lingered for a few breaths in the hallway, watching him as he stared out the window. He reminded me of myself in far too many ways, ways I'd have preferred never to relive. As I slipped away into my dorm and readied myself for bed, I could only hope that Nick would heed my words. He had a rough patch ahead, one I'd barely survived myself, but one that would, eventually, end.

All I could do, between meditation and cycling and training with Xavier and studying with Charlotte and opening my meridians and developing my fighting style all the other thousand pulls upon my attention, was find time to help him through it.

I owed him that much. I owed myself that much.

Just two more years.

25

I skipped out on weight training the following morning for just a fifteen-mile run, my own futile attempt at giving my sore and bruised muscles a chance to recover from the prior day's abuses.

Listen to me. *Just* a fifteen mile run. Less than a year ago I could've *maybe* managed three before collapsing to the dirt rasping for air like I was dying of the fucking consumption. It amazed me how quickly I'd acclimated to this all, how readily I'd accepted that my mortal limits no longer applied.

I'd gone from spending most of my time in zero g to running two-hour half marathons in a matter of *months*. Even as I cooled down and plodded back through the hall to join Xavier for breakfast, I marveled at the insanity of it all.

I knew it wasn't enough. I knew I had months of hard training ahead if I wanted to catch up to Instructor Long in time. Threads, I'd already decided to push up the opening of my muscle meridian to try and buy myself more time to make copper after I formed my core.

But at the very least I could appreciate how far I'd come, even if my thoughts of pride came to a screeching halt as I reached the breakfast table.

"No Nick this morning?" Xavier asked through a mouthful of bacon.

"I haven't seen him," I replied as I set down my plate, a comically large dish for the single bran muffin it bore. "He seemed… out of it last night. I don't know. I'm going to spend the afternoon helping him with his apple project."

"Good," Xavier said. "That's good."

I glanced down at my muffin but couldn't muster the will to pick it up. "It's good he has something to focus on. Back when I was his age, pushing for my vac-welding cert got me through a lot of stuff."

"Don't give up your entire afternoons. We'll need time to train."

"I know, I know. And I need to spend more time with the electroshock machine if I want to open my muscle meridian before dueling day. *And* I need time to meditate on what qi techniques I want to develop."

"*And* you need to eat your breakfast," Xavier added.

I snatched the pastry off my plate and took a bite, chewing the admittedly tasty muffin as spitefully as I could.

Xavier smiled. "I'll talk to Charlotte about borrowing the machine again."

I swallowed. "Thanks."

Oh, right, I should explain the electroshock machine. There aren't really herbs—or at least not easily accessible ones—that can simulate the effects of opening the muscle meridian. Instead, pretty much all cultivators use a fairly simple device that basically electrocutes your muscles into seizing in a similar way. Most sect members have scheduled time with it baked into their cycling class, but since that doesn't come until cycling three and I wanted to advance *now*, I had to get one through other means.

Fortunately, one of the cycling three instructors owed

Charlotte a favor. Or a few favors. Or maybe some blackmail was involved. The story seemed to change each time she brought it up. Anyway, as long as it wasn't during class time, I could borrow a machine whenever I needed. Tonight, and for the next few days if I wanted to make this work, *I needed*.

The conversation lulled as I worked through the rest of my muffin and Xavier wolfed down his regular morning feast, us both caught up in our private thoughts as the cafeteria buzzed around us.

He still had half a plate of scrambled eggs in front of him by the time I finished and finally stood. I patted him on the shoulder as I left, only a *little* envious that he could take his time while I had to hurry off to class.

Truth be told, the structure was nice, especially seeing how aimlessly the fully fledged sect members milled about housing D. Still, I yearned for more time in the day, an advantage I wouldn't achieve until I escaped the metal stages altogether and a jade core reduced my body's need for sleep.

But that was for the future. Now, my main worry was getting to my new meditation class. Other than her assistant's message scheduling a meeting several days out, I hadn't heard a peep from Elder Lopez about Long's behavior *or* Park and Stevens' accusations of cheating. However that latter got resolved—presumably through focus hour bribery—I had no intention of returning to meditation one.

I strolled into a classroom well over twice the size of my previous one. As the door shut behind me, a group some hundred strong of kids ranging from twelve to seventeen turned to gawk at my presence. Of them, I spotted one familiar face.

"Caliban!" Nick's sister wove through the mass of students to approach me. "What are you doing here?"

"Learning, presumably." I smiled at her, fighting with an iron will to keep my eyes from glancing down at her missing hand. The bandages were gone, leaving a red and angry stump where the regrowth treatment had begun its work. "It's good to see you, Martha."

"Yeah-uh, you too. Nick didn't tell me you were joining this class."

"Nick's been... wrapped up in his work." I kept my answer diplomatic. "Some seed he's been fiddling with. I'm supposed to help him with it tonight, actually."

"That sounds like him. How's he been? I haven't heard from him in..." She scowled. "It feels like months."

"He's seen better days—you know his situation probably better than I do—but he's got friends. We're looking after him."

"Good. That's... good." She paused, visibly failing to find words. "Well, um, welcome to meditation two."

"Glad to be here." I smiled again and gave her a nod as a dark-skinned woman with bags under her eyes and a cadet's uniform—a copper going off the insignia on her chest—approached me.

"Cadet Rex, I take it? I'm Senior Cadet Buundi. I understand there are some qualms about your placement in this class."

"I did too well on my exam to test out of meditation one. The issue should resolve soon. I promise you, I do deserve to be here."

"I'll be the judge of that. This way." She directed me away from the entrance and around the various circles of chatting teenagers to an open spot by the left wall. "Meditation two works a bit differently than your other classes. Rather than working on maintaining focus in spite of external distractions, our goal here is to get you to the point where you can keep control of your internal qi while still interacting with the world at large. You'll only be done once you can fight at full capacity while manipulating your qi."

"Sounds simple enough." I'd already managed basic actions while cycling. Threads, Vihaan never would've survived the void horde attack if I hadn't been able to walk and cycle at the same time. There was probably a reason they insisted on mastering shutting out distractions before starting on multitasking, but I'd yet to stumble into it.

"You may've noticed the age range we accommodate here. That's because there is no meditation three. Once we're done with you, you're done. I understand Elder Lopez has given you until the end of the year. It'll be hard, but if you apply yourself—and if you are as ready for this as you say—I think you can do it. We'll be here to support you."

My eyes followed her nod to take in the twelve other Senior Cadets that had already begun to organize the class into sections. It seemed the large class size and wide spectrum of skill levels necessitated more instructors than any other class. "I appreciate that. I won't let you down."

"No," Buundi said, her voice suddenly sharp. "You won't." She gestured down at the empty stretch of floor along the wall. "We'll start with simply walking for today. I want you to cycle your bone, stomach, and skin meridians while you pace across the room, touch your hand to that wall, then return. Got it?"

I swallowed back the knot in my throat. "Seems easy enough," I lied. I couldn't cycle my skin, not without the whole class seeing me go pale as a corpse. I settled on my kidney instead, hoping to reach the same challenge level without revealing my qi's unsettling effects. Since she couldn't sense my qi, she'd have no way of detecting the change unless she prodded me with a stick or something. I inconspicuously looked Instructor Buundi up and down to confirm she did not, in fact, have a stick on her.

Shoving out the noise and motion of the class around me proved of little difficulty, leaving me the simple task of something I'd been doing for months. Once I'd made it across the classroom and back without dropping my focus, I faced Buundi with a smile. "How's that?"

"Good. Now do it again."

Thus began one of the more boring class periods of my time on Fyrion. At least in meditation one my mind had been free to wander. Here I had to keep rapt attention on my cycling as I paced back and forth and back and forth and back and forth.

I made it almost an hour before slipping up, losing track of my position in the space walking headlong into the wall. I sighed.

"Fifty-four minutes," Buundi read off her holopad. "Again."

I realized then the difficulty lay not in walking and cycling at the same time, but in the mental endurance to keep such ironclad focus for hours on end. I barely made twenty minutes on my second attempt.

By the end of the three-hour class period, my original fifty-four minute streak remained my longest, an unsurprising result according to Buundi. I found the practice to be an entirely new kind of exhausting, one that left me drained long before my instructor was done with me.

I posted up in the corner for lunch, content to avoid intruding on the class's complex teenage social web, up until Martha sat down to join me.

I tried and failed to mask my fascination as she expertly went about unpacking her meal with one hand, her right arm hanging limply at her side as she avoided making contact with its tender end. From what I'd heard, the cell treatment to regrow a limb—especially one as complicated as a hand—took years of near constant pain. I couldn't imagine going through that at her age, especially in such a toxic environment.

She noticed my staring as she lifted her sandwich to her mouth.

I blinked and averted my eyes.

"It's alright," she said, waving her stump through the air. "You get used to the looks."

"Yeah," I muttered, glancing out to catch several of the other students gawking at me, "I know the feeling. They get bored of it eventually."

"Or they find something new to stare at." Martha let out a laugh. "I guess I should thank you for that."

I mock bowed. "Always happy to provide spectacle. Making a scene is something of a specialty of mine."

"I know. I saw what you did last dueling day."

I grimaced. "That was... a necessary evil. I'm hoping I don't have to repeat it next week."

"Oh, you mean you *don't* want to get beat up again?"

"Something like that."

Silence reigned for a few moments as we chewed our respective lunches, only for Martha to swallow and blindside me with an abrupt change of subject. "Tell me about the void incursion."

I blinked, my eyes unintentionally darting to her missing hand and back. "What-um... what do you want to know?"

"You saved a kid's life, right? Tell me about it."

I exhaled. "Okay, well, I was walking with the class from cycling to combat..."

She nodded. "Yeah. So was I."

Shit. That's right. She would've been right down the hall from me when she lost her hand. "Right, so... you know what it was like. Alarms blaring, lights flashing, void beasts crashing through the windows..."

Martha didn't interrupt me further as I retold the tale,

leaving out the details of how I evaded the void beasts' notice. Everybody already knew my qi was undetectable—officially because of some technique I'd learned—so that cover story bought me some leeway.

"...and then, you should've seen the look on her face when I rounded the corner with that freezer cart. This one cadet, guarding a hallway entirely on her own, faced with me trailing blood along the floor as I ran at her yelling for a medic." I let out a gentle laugh as I relayed the moment, a brief glimpse of levity in an otherwise desperate story. "From there I made it to—" My holopad buzzed. "Damn, time for class. We have to finish this up tomorrow."

"Yeah," Martha said, her eyes soft and out of focus. "We do."

"Well, it was nice chatting with you," I said as I packed up the remnants of my lunch and pushed myself to my feet. "I'll tell Nick you said hi, okay?"

"Yes!" Martha seemed to collect herself. "Tell him I miss him."

I smiled at her. "That I can do. See ya tomorrow."

"Bye, Cal!"

I waved goodbye as I left the classroom to embark upon the incredibly brief walk to cycling two across the hall. My heart sank as I stepped inside to find a table set out with well-measured portions of an uncomfortably familiar herb.

"You must be Caliban," the lone instructor greeted me, a man whose hair had somehow gone gray despite the youth in his face. He seemed late twenties to my inexperienced eye, putting him right at the end of his time in the cadet program.

"That'd be me."

"I'm Quentin. Glad to have you join us," he said. "We're just beginning the section on opening the spine meridian."

"Great," I lied, nervously eyeing the table of herbs. "Is

that what the leaves are for?"

"It is. I've got an extra dose for you all lined up."

I bit back my sigh. I'd known this was going to happen eventually. As I climbed the levels of cycling class, the instruction fundamentally had to shift from the basics of cycling to specialized prep for opening specific meridians. It was just my luck that I'd joined in time for the pain training.

I chewed the leaf as was expected of me and settled in to sit cross-legged on the padded floor as my classmates did. For perhaps the first time since I'd come to Fyrion, the others suffered more than I did.

Before the pain could even take hold I started running qi through my spine meridian, neutralizing the herb's effect entirely. While my teenage classmates gritted their teeth and struggled to keep their focus against the simulated nerve damage, I spent a quiet class period fortifying and widening my various meridians ever so slightly, taking in qi from the infinite sea as needed.

The instructor flashed me a curious look as the class came to its end, but I didn't bother addressing it. Whether he thought me suspiciously talented or somehow a cheater didn't matter. Nothing mattered. I'd sit in class and follow along and "open my meridians" on a schedule the sect would believe until I finally graduated. Unlike combat class, the requirements to pass out of cycling were clear.

Either you'd opened the necessary meridians, or you hadn't.

Rather than continuing on to my third class of the day, I headed straight for the transport platform to return to housing D. I stopped by the empty cafeteria to bus my lunchbox before moving on to the gym. I found Xavier waiting for me, a new bruise across his left cheek.

"Did you win?"

"Not this time," he replied, not questioning how I'd

known he'd fought a duel. He did that every day. "But my prowess grows greater with every loss, my thirst for victory more indomitable with every defeat."

"That's good." I brushed right past Xavier's overdramatic phrasing. "Any word on Charlotte?"

"She's getting you that machine. She said something about tracking down a replenishment pill?" He shook his head. "I'm not sure what one has to do with the other, but I know Charlotte's core doesn't need replenishment."

"Huh. So we've jumped from extortion to bribery then. I… guess that's preferable?" I gestured over to the nearest empty sparring ring. "Shall we?"

Xavier took on a somewhat more instructive role than he had in the past, coaching me on imperfections in my technique and other such adjustments in much the same way an authorized combat instructor might've. Even if he himself still had a long way to go, I knew of nobody who dedicated so much of their daily life to mastering the Dragon's Fang, and Xavier had more than enough of a head start to be leaps and bounds better at it than I.

That didn't stop him from absolutely wiping the floor with me each bout, but those periods between fights where he actually *instructed* me added a new sense of progress to our regular practice.

I left after only two hours, tired and sore as ever yet far from finished for the day. A wonderful hot shower and a clean uniform later I found myself standing in Nick's doorway looking into what might've been the most crowded room on Fyrion.

Every surface other than a foot-wide path across the dorm and the bed itself bore a stonework pot from which sprouted *something* green. He'd hung blankets over the two windows to regulate the illumination level, leaving a mismatched collection of programmable grow lights the only way to see.

Upon his desk sat a scope of some sort, a machine I didn't recognize, and a stack of dirty dishes so precarious that I hesitated to so much as look them.

The room was dark and cluttered and messy and stank of soil and fertilizer and sweat and old food, but I waded through it to join Nick behind his desk, leaning with my hands against the back of his chair to look over his shoulder as he explained the project in front of him.

"This is the seed in question." He gestured to a white tray with its own attached light and magnifying lens. I squinted through it.

"Looks like any other apple seed."

"That's because it is. A salazar's snap to be specific. It's a popular varietal among botanists because it takes splices well and has a qi matrix that's both stable and scalable. It doesn't do anything *special*, but it's one of very few plants that can thrive in low-qi environments *and* contain high quantities of qi if given the opportunity. Supposedly, there's a two-thousand-year-old salazar's snap tree in the imperial gardens at Taz-9, planted by the first Augur of Pulma during the…"

I let him talk. It was more words than I'd gotten out of Nick in the past week, and he seemed genuinely enthused to share. Truth be told I couldn't care less about the long and storied history of his preferred breed of apple— threads, I didn't even recognize half the names he rattled off. It didn't matter that I wasn't learning anything or that we weren't getting any work done.

Whatever I'd said, I hadn't *really* come here to work.

Some twenty minutes of in-depth explanation on the finer details of intercellular qi transference later, Nick picked up a second seed with a pair of tweezers and set it beside the first. "And *here's* the problem."

I blinked at it. "It's identical to the first one."

"You would think that," Nick said, raising his hand to

reach for a switch on the side of the mounted magnifying lens. "Until you look inside." He flicked the switch, and the first seed came alight, a warm, steady glow emanating from its center. The second seed remained unchanged.

"This one," Nick gestured with his tweezers to the glowing seed, "is alive. It's dormant, but it still has germ qi it inherited from its tree." He pointed to the other. "This one is dead. It's gone through the exact same treatment as the living seed, except I've drained it of its qi in roughly the same way we'd have to to replace it with yours."

I nodded along, understanding so far. "And you can't re-add qi to a dead seed?"

"Exactly. If you try..." He dropped his tweezers and shuffled around through a pile of disorganized tools to grab what looked like little more than metal stylus. He touched its tip to the second seed, and a bright flow of qi materialized beneath the enchanted lens.

The seed exploded.

Well, maybe *exploded* is too intense a word for something so small. It made a nice popping sound that brought a smile to my face.

My grin didn't last as I realized exactly what I'd just watched. "That looks... a lot like what happens when you try to absorb someone else's qi."

"Wait, you mean like—" Nick shuddered. "No, no, no. It's nothing like that." He waved the stylus in my face. "The injector cleanses the qi that runs through it. That's not the issue." He blinked. "Okay, well, that's not the *only* issue. I just realized if we want to use your qi, we need an injector that can depersonalize it. Have we looked into how your qi interacts with enchantments?"

I snorted. "We aren't even entirely sure how it interacts with *me*. Enchantments are somewhere on the list between external techniques and how it interacts with normal qi."

Nick sighed. "It'll have to wait until you have a core,

either way. So much to do, so much to learn."

"Alright. How can I help?"

"Outside of forming your core? You can teach me to sense your qi."

I raised an eyebrow at him. "Anything *feasible?*"

"Yeah, you can read up on the theory. *Arlo's Principles of Qi Inheritance* would be a good place to start."

"Great," I said, typing the name of the text into my holopad. "I'll come back tomorrow to get started on that. In the meantime…" I grabbed his arm. "It's time for dinner. Charlotte and Xavier are waiting."

"Alright. I need to clean up here a bit. Why don't you go down and tell them I'm on my way."

I looked at him askance. "You sure?"

"Yeah. I'll be right down."

"I'm gonna hold you to that," I said, reaching past him to grab an armful of plates from the stack dishes he'd amassed.

"I won't be long." He turned back to his desk as I waded through his jungle of potted plants for the door, only to stop as Nick spoke once more. "And Cal? Thanks."

I looked back, flashed him a smile and a nod, and stepped out into the hallway. As I made my way downstairs and into the cafeteria to first bus the plates then join the others for dinner, I got the distinct impression Nick had been thanking me for more than my meager contribution to his project, for more than agreeing to read up on the topic, and certainly for more than carrying out a few dirty dishes.

* * *

It took two hours, between our group dinner and an especially long evening call with Lucy to fill her in on all the details of my new classes, before I could settle in with the absolute mess of cables and electrodes that was the electroshock machine. Just putting the damn thing on proved a task unto itself as I provided it access to every relevant muscle in my body.

It bears clarifying that, just like all the other meridians, the name "muscle meridian" isn't entirely accurate. That's what happens when you let a bunch of spiritual scholars that've been dead since before mankind discovered basic anatomy name shit.

Several muscles actually fell under the purview of other meridians, most obviously the heart, which had its own, but also the diaphragm, various intestinal muscles, and a whole slew of others. It might've been more true to call it the *skeletal* muscle meridian, but that would've gotten in the way of the whole one-word-name thing we had going on.

Anyway, all that to say I *wasn't* about to run a bunch of volts through my heart. I'd already opened that one.

Having been at this since I'd opened my spine meridian weeks ago, I required no assistance nor supervision as I sat on the floor and got to work.

While I'd cycled my lungs to keep my breathing even through other meridian openings, the muscle meridian mandated an ironclad focus on the tendons and bones. The latter because, as it turns out, mortal muscles are perfectly capable of snapping unreinforced bones. It's the brain that stops them. I'd have to keep qi running through my bone meridian to keep that from happening once the cleansing process sent all my muscles haywire.

Cycling the tendon meridian was even more important. It'd both prevent the seizures from rupturing all my connective tissue, *and*, if I didn't fuck it up, would help restrain my seizing muscles.

The training was about as unpleasant as you'd expect repeated electrocution to be, with the upside that it simulated the spasms and pain of opening the meridian at the same time. Outside of that, it mostly entailed cycling my bones and tendons while simultaneously running through the same set of qi manipulation exercises I'd used to practice for my spine.

It made for a long and grueling process of constant failure and tiny, incremental improvements, the exact kind of deeply repetitive task that seemed to define the act of cultivation.

I finished my practice for that night, spent a half hour meditating to decompress, went to sleep, and did it all again the next day. Workout, breakfast, class, lunch with Martha, class again, combat training with Xavier and Charlotte, an hour with Nick, dinner, a call with Lucy, and back to the electroshock machine.

I didn't play games. I didn't watch holos. I didn't read books. I found no time for leisure in the depths of my fervor.

I *improved*.

I made it to ninety minutes walking back and forth across the meditation classroom. I took great strides towards incorporating Cedric's moves into my fighting style. I learned more about the cellular biology of apple seeds than I'd ever wanted to.

But most importantly, on the fifth night of my new routine, one day before my scheduled meeting with Elder Lopez, I made it through the barrage of electricity with my focus intact. I completed the exercises; I cycled my meridians; I didn't budge.

I was ready.

26

Martha Vesper chewed the inside of her cheek as she moved through the faux candle-lit hallway to the reception area ahead. The calming music and scent of incense in the air did little to calm her nerves.

Her parents and personal tutor walked behind her, flanking her on either side as they both showed their support and cut off her only avenue of retreat. She was going through with this one way or another.

The two lesser qi absorption pills she'd already taken churned in her nerve-addled stomach. She'd have to cleanse herself of their byproducts later, but today all that mattered was getting together enough qi for what she needed to do.

At the age of fifteen, Martha had long fallen behind her brother's record-setting pace, a fact her father had no intention of letting her forget. At least now that Nick had squandered his advantage, refusing to fight his way up the ranks, in theory the comparison fell more in her favor.

In practice it left her the sole scion of her parents' expectations. She'd swallowed more expensive pills, drank more exotic teas, chewed more spiritual herbs than she could count, leaving her in a constant state of simultaneous explosive growth and painful recovery as she repaired the havoc such treatments wrought on one's spirit.

Threads, they'd even siphoned their focus hours to her, actively forfeiting the upkeep on their own cultivation to further accelerate her advancement. Their copper cores would wither and weaken, eventually falling to tin if they kept this up, all so she could have the extra focus hour a week that all sect members received once they aged out of the cadet program. Between the two of them, it doubled her qi input.

Martha hated it.

She hated having that unfair advantage over her peers. She hated constantly being dragged out of bed at odd hours to go cultivate. She hated the realization that she only received such gifts because Nick had rejected them.

Most of all she hated the power it gave them over her, the power to dominate her training, her time, her *thoughts*. There'd been a time in Martha's life when she'd considered herself her own person, an individual fighting her own battles even as her parents urged her ever forward.

They'd since freed her of that delusion. How could she give anything but her all after what they'd sacrificed, what they *continued* to sacrifice, in her name? How could she seek leisure, explore her own wants, make *friends*, when every minute spent outside of meditation or combat training was a minute squandering her parents' gifts?

A familiar twinge of pain brought her back to the present, a sharp cramp in the space between the knuckles of her right hand. Martha sucked air through her teeth and sent a thread of qi through her spine meridian, but it did little good. Sure, it settled the constant ache at the injection sites into a dull warmth, but the spirit couldn't dampen nerves that weren't there.

She wanted to scream. She wanted to cry. She wanted to shout that maybe, just maybe, the loss of her hand should've bought her some leeway, some mercy, rather than the relentless drive to make up for it, to overcome, to use this adversity as if her trauma were little more than a currency to be spent.

But she didn't.

Martha could understand why Nick had made the decisions he had. She could even respect his courage to reject their parents' sacrifice.

But she couldn't, under any circumstances, follow suit. She wasn't that brave. She wasn't that certain in her wants. She wasn't that weak.

So, her stomach churning, her phantom hand aching, and her nerves a jumble, Martha Vesper let her mother speak for her as they reached the front of the check-in line.

"Hello. My daughter would like to open her muscle meridian today."

* * *

I pushed open the door to the third-floor bathroom with my left hand, my right occupied holding up the towel around my waist. Halfway down the hall its corner had slipped off my bony hip, coming untucked and nearly falling to the floor before I caught it.

Strictly speaking, there was nobody there to see me accidentally expose myself, but Elder Lopez's stunt with the footage of my encounter with the void beasts had left me deeply aware of the dormitory's security cameras. The actual bedrooms and bathrooms maintained their privacy, and I doubted anyone was actually *watching* the housing D third-floor hallway, but you never know.

Nick and Xavier were already waiting for me inside, leaning against the wall facing the showers.

"Are you sure you're ready for this?" Xavier asked. "You have a warrior's spirit, but this feels... rushed."

"He's cleared the trial run, hasn't he? That sounds like ready to me."

"Sure, but only once," Xavier countered, a disquieting uncertainty to his tone. "The muscle meridian can be unpredictable. I went through a dozen trial runs before taking my attempt."

Nick shrugged. "I didn't."

"Of course you didn't," I said. "What kind of child prodigy takes his time?"

"My parents had me try for it as soon as I could cobble together the qi. You've got the qi."

I flashed a grin. "That I do." I slung my towel over the hook on the door and stepped into the shower, sending a pulse of qi through my skin meridian to inoculate me against the frigid water that rained down in the first few seconds after turning the knob. It was a frivolous use of qi, but why cultivate if I couldn't use it to be frivolous?

Xavier raised an eyebrow at me as my skin flashed deathly pale then crept back up to its regular, sickly pallidity. He didn't comment.

All the way up on the nearly abandoned third floor, the warm water took a few moments to arrive. It soothed my sore and nervous body quite effectively. Pleasant as it felt, Nick and Xavier hadn't come to watch me enjoy a nice hot shower, so I went straight to work.

Cross-legged, straight-backed, hands folded in my lap, I sat directly on the tile floor, bare and unequipped, ready for the challenge to come.

I'd wondered when I first researched this process why nobody bothers to restrain themselves before making all their muscles go haywire. The answer is circulation. Since the tendon and bone meridians are both absolutely necessary to survive the procedure, nobody at this stage in their cultivation—including me—had the capacity to also cycle their blood or heart.

Any physical restraints carried the fundamental risk of cutting off circulation when pulled upon with the full force of a seizing muscle for extended periods of time, a risk someone in the throes of opening a meridian wouldn't necessarily notice until it was too late. Apparently, in ye olden days, cultivators with all ten fingers were considered prodigies.

Okay, that last bit may or may not have been pure myth, but it sounds cool, doesn't it?

Anyway, seated at my usual soggy perch, with my two guardians to watch over me and warm water running down my back, I evened out my breathing, sank into my center, and got started.

* * *

Martha forcibly stilled her bouncing knee as the two techs fitted her for qi monitors. Ten times she'd been through this process, and ten times she'd shivered with discomfort as hands clad in latex gloves pressed the cold silver sensors onto her exposed skin.

Luca, her personal tutor—another "gift" she'd inherited from Nick—stood over her, a glass of water in one hand and a blue pill bottle in the other. "Three of these next," he explained, handing over a set of matching red and white capsules nearly half the size of her pinky.

Martha took them without question.

"Okay, now this one." A white tablet with dull brown specks.

"Excellent. Now, we're going to have to put on the qi bridge before you can take the paralytics." Without looking away, he raised his right hand, snapped three times, and waved someone over. "You're going to want your spine meridian for this one."

Martha sullenly nodded and obeyed, running qi through her most used meridian as she raised her right arm for the approaching tech. She shut her eyes before it happened, but not in time to avoid seeing the pair of two-inch probes, each nearly a quarter inch thick at their base, that would have to sink into her flesh to bridge her severed tendon meridian.

How she hated that thing.

It was a crude, inefficient solution that would hemorrhage qi over long-term use, but it'd work for long enough to keep her body intact through the next hour.

Every challenge is an opportunity, she reminded herself as heat and pain flared down her arm, even muffled behind her active cycling. *Every challenge is an opportunity. Every challenge is an opportunity.*

It certainly didn't feel that way, especially not as she opened her eyes to see the enchanted metal stuck to the end of her arm where her hand should've been. The tech wrapped it with bandages to stem the bleeding at the two entry sites. It was her third time equipped with the device. It hadn't gotten easier.

"Okay, now here's the paralytic." Luca shoved another tablet into her hand, this time a dusty yellow one the size of her fingernail. "It won't help with the seizures but will stop you from overcorrecting them. Remember, this isn't about keeping tense. It's about keeping *still.*"

Martha took it. She knew her parents had gone through the regimen with Luca and opted for anything and everything with even the slightest chance of helping.

"Great," Luca said as she took one last gulp of water and handed him the glass. "Now get into position before it takes effect. You have..." He glanced at his holopad. "Thirty-eight minutes. You've got this."

He patted her on the shoulder, a contact against which her instincts tried to flinch, but her body failed to react. Threads, that paralytic worked fast.

She kept her spine going as she sank into her center, holding the pain in her arm at bay as she pushed her spiritual senses outward into the room around her.

The air felt alive.

Warmth and life and joy danced across the focus room, a wondrous mist of everything good in the world. Martha breathed it in.

Time to get to work.

She opened her center and *pulled* upon the qi in the air, exerting her hard-trained will upon it. It resisted.

It danced away, sprang to far walls, expanded to fill the space as best it could. Martha wrestled with it, ironclad effort that bit by bit drew in the vital force and contained it within her spirit. Here, the qi absorption pills earned their keep, the chemicals within attracting the energy into little eddies which Martha readily reaped. By the time she had enough, sweat dripped down her brow.

Next, she pushed.

With practiced technique she formed a sphere of intent around her center, trapping the qi within. In and in and in she forced it, fighting tooth and nail against its tendency to spread, to move, to *escape*. It struggled against her and she struggled back, unyielding in her endeavor to further constrain and condense until—

Drip.

A single drop fell to join the shallow puddle at the bottom of her center, a bright and prismatic liquid that glimmered like a diamond and exuded life-giving warmth.

Now for the hard part.

* * *

I began by reaching my spiritual senses out past the edge of the shower, past Nick's and Xavier's blinding cores, and through the back wall into the vacuum beyond. The infinite sea awaited, cold and dark and overflowing as ever. I tasted but a drop, topping off my qi reserves.

It condensed to join my own pool easily enough. It only wanted to sit and exist, content to bend or move or flow as the world around it saw fit.

Next, I set about cycling my bones and tendons,

fortifying them both and tightening the latter as I'd practiced so many times. I allowed myself a few moments to settle into the action, letting the minutes tick away until I felt comfortable diverting some attention. I'd set aside three hours for this attempt, plenty of time to open the meridian and get cleaned up.

Nick and Xavier probably would've preferred if I didn't waste too much time, but I knew they wouldn't want me to rush.

Only once I was good and ready did I form the familiar needle-and-thread shape, press it to the meridian entrance just above my left glute, and begin to push.

Immediate tension shot through me as my muscles spasmed in protest. Massive soreness sent waves of aching up my back, as if I'd somehow managed the perfect full-body workout and now paid the price.

Except I couldn't sit still. I couldn't relax or rest as over and over again I tensed and seized with no pattern or rhythm. Black ichor seeped from the wiry cords of tissue, wreaking havoc as it passed both into my bloodstream and through my pores.

I kept going. Of course I kept going. The experience was a bit more… intense than I'd expected, but I could handle it. I'd passed the trial run after all.

I could feel myself rocking back and forth as I quaked, the hard ceramic beneath me grinding painfully against my tailbone with the motion. I shut it out.

The water ran down my back.

My right leg kicked out, my foot traveling just an inch along the shower floor before my gridlocked physique reigned it in.

I was moving. The uneven twitches across my body sent me sliding across the wet tile.

Still I pushed, splitting my focus three ways as I ran qi simultaneously through three meridians, two freely, and

342

one against the resistance of two decades of built-up grime. I isolated my senses, segmenting the soreness from the warmth of the shower from the ache in my tailbone from my internal qi, defending myself from distractions as that cleansing thread wormed ever forward.

It'd almost completed its first loop when the unthinkable happened.

My imperfect stillness and my inching motion across the shower floor sent the ball of my ankle across the metal drain grate at the perfect angle.

Pain, sharp and sudden and insidious shot through my foot as the drain sliced into it, sharp enough to break skin, dull enough to tear it. It took under a second to notice the injury, to parse the sensation of rent flesh and flowing blood before I could dismiss that too as a distraction from the task at hand.

But a half second was enough.

A second burst of agony bloomed, this time from a tendon in my lower back weakened by my momentary lapse. Before I could think, before I could stop, before even panic could reach my mind, a muscle, no longer contained by the bone to which it'd been bound, seized.

I shot backwards.

My head hit the wall.

I heard a terrible crack.

And the world went dark.

* * *

Before she could begin, Martha first had to forfeit the mercy of her spine. It proved harder than she'd expected, stopping the flow of qi and allowing the pain of the device stuck into her arm to return, an exertion of will unto itself rather than the simple cessation of effort it should've been.

Any other day she might've considered that an excellent sign of both progress and readiness to tackle her brain meridian. Today, it meant only more work.

She pushed past the torment easily enough. Even inexperienced with the bridge as she was, pain in her hand had been Martha's only constant over the last few months. More or less of it made little difference.

Next, she meticulously divided her qi into three pools, carefully rationing her limited supply between the two meridians that would need constant feeding and the one that would claim the rest. Without a moment to spare, she set the first to cycling at once.

As in her practice, qi flowed unsteadily through her tendon meridian, seeping out where it left and reentered her body at the probes embedded in her flesh. She'd overcome it then and she'd overcome it now.

Her bone meridian similarly ran below capacity, picking up impurities left behind by the various pills abrading against them. That also, was nothing new.

Martha didn't drop a beat before collecting up what remained of her qi, crafting her purging formation, and getting to work.

She barely twitched as the seizures set in, her reinforced skeleton taking the brunt of the force as the paralytics stopped her from trying to fight it. Impurities fell away freely from the walls of her meridian, loosened by the expensive meridian cleansing pill her father had provided.

Martha snaked her qi thread through the clogged meridian with well-rehearsed restraint, pushing solidly and consistently against every bit of resistance without rushing to finish or dragging to reduce the ache.

The focus tonic she'd downed at breakfast kept her mind on task, away from her churning stomach and mounting headache, neither of which, as far as she knew, were side effects of opening the muscle meridian.

At every step in the way, Martha worked with practiced perfection. Her qi rations were measured, her attention unwavering, her technique flawless in its execution.

So it came as a surprise when a micro-movement in her lower forearm muscles pushed the qi bridge ever so slightly out of place. It rebounded immediately, the flow through her tendon meridian recovering in under a second.

But a half second was enough.

Burning, jagged agony exploding in her right shoulder. She compartmentalized at once, reasserting her focus and halting the progress of qi through her muscle meridian. The spasms didn't stop, but they lessened as the qi remained unmoving within the partially opened meridian. She'd trained for this.

The shouts reached Martha's ears through the glass that separated the observation room. She sat tight, even as her arm flailed wildly and painfully around her.

Help was on the way.

* * *

Xavier Honchel shifted his weight between his feet as he tried and failed to argue away the sinking feeling that'd lingered in his stomach since he'd awoken that morning. The foreboding instinct made no sense. Cal was going to be at his side when he fought as champion of the Dragon's Right Eye, so it stood to reason the outsystemer wouldn't die today.

Unless Xavier found a way to bring him back from the dead. Wouldn't that make an enthralling tale! Through sheer grit and determination, the hero defies the gods to pluck his dear friend's soul back from the very threads themselves!

He entertained himself with the possibility as the minutes ticked by, pleased with the distraction from the looming impression that something wasn't right. He trusted Cal would be okay. Cal had a warrior's spirit, after all.

Nick's third forlorn exhale of the afternoon pulled him from his reverie.

"Fret not, young newcomer," Xavier replied to Nick's clear statement. "However distant it may seem, through perseverance, all battles shall end in glorious victory."

"I-um... what?"

"You were saying..."

"I wasn't saying anything," Nick snapped. "I was *breathing*. I'm allowed to breathe, right?"

Xavier blinked. Why did people tell him things they didn't want him to respond to? "Uh... of course. Apologies. I thought you meant to—"

Crack.

Xavier spun to the source of the noise. He saw Caliban slide down the shower's back wall, water running down his chest as his crossed legs slid forward across the floor. Next, he saw the cracks in the tile behind him.

Finally, he saw the blood.

Xavier surged forward, falling to his knees at Cal's side and snaking his left arm under the foreigner. He effortlessly siphoned qi from his tin core through the necessary meridians to more than overcome Cal's apparent impulse to flop his lower back around like a fish. Wrapping his hand around the base of Cal's skull, he held his bleeding head away from the wall, away from further damage.

"Caliban! Caliban, can you hear me?"

No response.

He reached with his right hand for Cal's eyes, tugging open their lids to find two unfocused orbs beneath. "Threads, he's unconscious. Nick! Call a transport!"

"That's... that's a lot of blood."

"Nick! A transport! Now!"

"I—yeah. Yes. A transport."

Xavier didn't look up to watch the kid swipe at his holopad. Instead, he carefully ran a finger along the back of Cal's head, finding blood and shards of ceramic that'd stuck there, but no soft spots. "His skull's not fractured. Thank the threads he kept his bone meridian up, but there's a chance he's bleeding in his brain. How's that transport?"

"It's-um... eleven minutes out."

"Eleven minutes. Okay. C'mon Cal. It's only eleven minutes. You can make it eleven minutes."

* * *

Within seconds Martha had four pairs of hands on her, restraining her arm, securing the qi bridge, injecting deadening agents into the relevant muscle. She'd lose muscle tissue over this.

"It's okay," Luca told her. "It's okay. We talked about this. You did well. We're going to implant an emergency patch to repair the tendon. That'll mean killing off a good chunk of your deltoid so the medics can work. It won't be pleasant, but it's the safest way to continue. I need you to keep cycling. Can you do that?"

He knew full well Martha couldn't respond, not through her focus on cycling through the pain, and *certainly* not through the paralytic. She simply obeyed.

She heard metal tools clanging together on a tray, felt another needle inject ice into her shoulder, and braced herself as best she could. At least for this, they could afford the severance of body from spirit that numbing agents inflicted. That bit of muscle wouldn't be a part of her much longer.

Martha experienced little more than pressure and heat as they cut into her and applied their patch. They wiped the blood from her back, patched up the millimeter-wide hole through which they'd threaded their tools, and walked away as if they hadn't just condemned her to yet another long and painful recovery. Threads, it'd probably be months before she could even move her arm again, a *year* before she'd fully regain her strength.

But Martha didn't break.

She didn't collapse, she didn't wallow, she brooked no cracks in the dam she'd long built up. Not a single tear dared well within her emerald eyes.

Martha kept straight. Martha kept her focus. And, once she received confirmation from Luca, Martha got back to work.

* * *

"—And then I reversed into The Dragon Rears Its Head before he could raise his quarterstaff in time, and earned another glorious victory!"

Xavier rambled. About anything and everything that came to his mind he rambled—mostly tales of his glorious victories. He had a lot of those.

Cal wasn't listening. Cal was unconscious. Cal was *still* unconscious. On he rambled.

"Nick, how long has it been?"

"Twelve minutes."

"You said it would only be eleven!"

"Well, now it says they're eight minutes away."

"Threads be—" Xavier shook his head before he could utter the curse. "Run downstairs. Tell reception they're coming and where we are. I don't want them getting lost."

Nick froze, eyes wide as dinner plates, then bolted from the bathroom.

"C'mon, Cal," Xavier spoke to the twitching form in his arms. "Just eight more minutes. Just eight more minutes."

He paused and took a breath.

"Have I told you about my glorious victory against Wesley Blum?"

* * *

The seizures stopped all at once.

A brief shiver of warmth and wonder ran down Martha's back as every muscle in her body thrummed with energy and power, practically begging to leap into action at a moment's notice.

Every muscle except one.

She cut off the flow of qi, allowing the liquid light to fall from her three meridians back into her center. Scratch that. She wove up another thread and ran it into her spine meridian, finding some semblance of relief from the pain in her stump and shoulder. Funnily enough, both still hurt. Next came her blood and kidneys to cleanse herself of the paralytic, finally freeing her to move again of her own volition.

By the time her eyes flicked open, two mortal techs were already approaching with bandages, antiseptics, and a syringe of intradermal sealant. Luca followed.

"You did well," Luca told her as the techs got to work removing the qi bridge and closing the two holes its probes had made. "It's a shame about your deltoid. We'll have to reevaluate your training schedule to accommodate for regrowth treatments and physical therapy. I'll schedule a surgery to remove the dead tissue tomorrow, and we can work from there. Your combat training will take another hit, so you'll have to work extra hard to…"

Martha tuned him out. His halfhearted praise meant little to her, especially undercut by his immediate thoughts on her newest disability.

A knot forming in her throat, Martha turned her head to look over her damaged shoulder, past the dark blue flesh, at the window to the observation room. Her parents stood within.

No pride looked back at her.

Her mother refused to meet her gaze, eyes flitting down or to the sides, looking anywhere and everywhere that wasn't at Martha. Her father had no such qualms.

With frigid eyes he looked upon his daughter, his legacy, the vessel in which he'd entrusted the entirety of his bid to flail against infinity, twice crippled in the span of a few months.

He bore a look Martha had seen upon his face but once, absent his customary ire or exhaustion or disappointment. It'd harrowed her then, even directed upon someone else. Here, she felt its full force.

It was neither the pills in her stomach nor the stench of purged toxins on her skin nor even the weight of the setback she'd just experienced that set her off, but the heart-wrenchingly hopeless sorrow in his eyes.

With a newly opened meridian, with her tutor standing over her making plans for the future, with five minutes left in her allotted focus room time, Martha vomited on the floor in front of her.

Then even her father looked away.

* * *

Xavier's anxiety had reached its peak by the time three paramedics and a gurney crashed through the bathroom door. The woman in front dashed right up to Cal.

"How long has he been seizing?"

"He's been unconscious for nineteen minutes," Nick answered from the doorway, carefully dodging the question.

"And he's been seizing this whole time?"

Xavier nodded.

She wrapped a hand around each of Cal's bony ankles, one soaking wet and the other slick with blood. "Randy, Joe, get his arms." She looked to Xavier. "Keep on his head. That he's been non-responsive this long isn't a good sign. How's his skull?"

"Okay, I think."

She shook her head. "You cultivators... Let's hope we can get a needle into him." She waited for her subordinates to arrive and support Cal's back and take over Xavier's job restraining his arms before she spoke again. "Alright, let's get him out of here. Three, two, one, lift!"

Xavier did little more than keep Cal's head up and away from the walls as the paramedics expertly lifted him from the slippery tile and moved for the gurney. A few tense seconds later, they had him on the cushioned surface, strapped down to limit his back's continued wild bucking.

They got moving immediately, one paramedic checking him over while another injected him with medication and the third pushed the gurney. Nick and Xavier followed them down the hallway.

"Jaw's clenched tight. Probably hasn't bitten his tongue off, but I can't get a guard in there. Joe! Where's my scanner?"

"In the pod."

"Alright. We'll have to settle for baseline biometrics for now. You've got his pad?"

"Confirming now," the other paramedic, Randy, said as he tapped away at Cal's holopad.

"Is he going to be okay?" Nick tried to ask.

"Too soon to tell," the woman answered. "I'll need a scan to see how bad his brain is swelling. Do you know what happened?"

"He slipped and fell," Xavier lied. It wasn't even a good lie. He absolutely reeked of meridian grime, but the mortal medics wouldn't dare question a sect member. They were smart enough to figure out how to treat him. Xavier just needed to control what went into the report.

The paramedics didn't respond.

They burst from the elevator into the lobby to an already growing crowd of onlookers, cultivators with apparently nothing better to do than gawk at the medical emergency in their midst. Xavier snarled at them for their laziness. At least nobody got in the way.

One of the paramedics—Joe, she'd called him—waved Nick and Xavier back as they loaded Cal into the transport pod. "No ride-alongs. You can see him in trauma center three once he's out of surgery."

Xavier didn't argue. Nick wasn't even looking at the man.

Only once Cal's gurney was secured to the specialized mount inside the ambulance pod did either of them speak.

"Holy shit."

"Nick!" Xavier glared at the kid. Mortally wounded or otherwise, Cal really was a bad influence on the lad.

"No, look!" He pointed into the pod.

Xavier squinted, craning his head to get one last look at Caliban before the door closed between them.

"The seizures stopped," Nick explained.

"That's good. The meds are taking eff—" Xavier cut off. Meridian-opening seizures didn't respond to medication.

"He's been seizing this whole time and now he's stopped. Do you think that means…"

"By the threads." There upon the transport platform, his uniform soaked in water and blood and meridian gunk, adrenaline coursing through his veins as he watched the emergency pod whisk his friend away, Xavier smiled.

Nick's eyes widened. "While *unconscious?*"

Xavier clapped him on the back. "I told you he has a warrior's spirit."

27

"Cadet Rex? Cadet Rex, can you hear me?"

My eyes blinked open to a bright light shining into them. I groaned.

"I'll take that as a yes."

The light flicked off and vision slowly clarified to reveal a sparsely adorned hospital room complete with sunlight blaring in through the window to my left and refracting off the polished linoleum floor right into my eyes. Before me stood a middle-aged woman in a pale green medical apron, currently in the process of typing into her holopad.

A window to my right revealed an open hallway, through which various patients and personnel went about their business. Xavier, Charlotte, and Nick looked in with concern on their faces. I flashed them a weak grin.

"How are you feeling?" The—I squinted at her badge—*doctor* asked.

Hmm. Good question. "What happened?"

"We'll get to that. How are you feeling?"

"Thirsty. My head hurts. And-um…" I paused to do a quick inventory. "My lower back is sore."

She nodded, continuing to tap away as she spoke. "There's some water to your right. Don't drink it all. Your

353

mouth is probably dry, but we've been hydrating you intravenously. Headache is normal. Are there any dark or blurry spots in your vision?"

I shook my head.

"That's a no," she stated the obvious. "Can you wiggle your fingers and toes for me?"

One by one we went through a slew of tests to confirm I hadn't fucked up my nervous system, tests that *should've* been redundant with the biometrics from my holopad, but I guess it paid to be sure. Mostly I just wanted her to leave so I could check my meridian. Unfortunately, only once the doctor was good and satisfied did she move on to her next question.

"Do you remember what happened?"

"I hit my head. I-um…" I trailed off, hit by the realization that I probably *shouldn't* tell her I'd been opening meridians in the third-floor showers. Luckily, Charlotte had my back.

I glanced past the doctor to find Charlotte's holopad pressed to the window, three words written upon it in massive font.

SLIPPED IN SHOWER

I blinked, reverting my gaze to meet the doctor's. "I was showering after class and I slipped."

She nodded along. "Good. We found a laceration on your ankle that seemed to have come from the fall, a severe contusion in your brain we had to treat surgically, and a ruptured tendon in your back from the ensuing seizures. You're lucky to be alive."

"Don't I know it," I muttered darkly, more to myself than to her. "I'm okay, then?"

"We're going to keep you here another night to be safe, but right now, all signs point to full recovery. We'll have you up and getting beaten to a pulp by your peers again in no time."

Huh. A doctor that wasn't too fond of all the dueling. Who would've thought?

I smiled at her. "Thank you."

"Just doing my job," she replied, closing her holopad and turning to go. "I'm going to let your friends in, now. That alright?"

"Yes, thanks."

She just nodded and left, leaving the door open for the others to enter. As they did, I silenced them with a raised finger.

First things first.

I sank into my center, finding my qi waiting patiently where I'd left it. My heart pounding in trepidation, I gathered up a thread of the liquid darkness and directed it into my muscle meridian.

I didn't seize. No pain wrenched through my body.

A sense of cool solidity spread through me, as if my flesh had turned to iron, immovable and unstoppable. It took a force of will, greater than I'd expected, to spur my muscles into motion, but once I did they moved with a quiet power that sent chills down my spine.

I cut off my cycling and returned to my friends. I could play with it later.

"It worked." I let out a sigh of relief. "My—"

Charlotte shushed me and stepped back to close the door behind her.

I lowered my voice. "My meridian's clear. No damage."

Charlotte nodded. "We thought as much. Nick said he saw you stop seizing as the medics loaded you out. What happened?"

"The fucking drain happened. I should've seen it coming. My muscles twitched in just the right way to slice my ankle against the drain. Surprised me enough I lost focus for half a second."

"That'd do it," she said. "You were lucky. It takes a

good instinct to keep cycling after getting knocked out like that."

Xavier beamed. "You have a warrior's spirit."

I smiled gently. "Thanks Xave. And thanks for helping me. Both of you." I looked to Nick too. "Gods know what would've happened if I didn't have you supervising me. I take it you're the ones who called the paramedics?"

They nodded in tandem, Xavier enthusiastically and Nick shyly.

"Seriously, thank you. You saved my life."

"That's what we were there for," Xavier said. "You *were* paying us to watch you."

"I know, I know. Still." I let out a breath. "How long was I out? What all did I miss?"

"Two days," Charlotte said.

I blinked. "I missed dueling day? Hell yes! I should have brain surgery more often. How'd you all do?"

"Two-one, two-one, oh-three," Xavier rattled off, pointing at himself, Charlotte, and Nick respectively.

I stared at him. "Does that mean…?"

He grinned, wide and proud. "I'm moving to housing C this afternoon."

"Xave, that's great! Congrats! We'll have to celebrate. Maybe I can get Lucy to come down and—Lucy! Did someone talk to her? She's probably—"

"I messaged her as soon as I heard," Charlotte butted in. "We're keeping her updated. She knows you're awake, that you're okay, and that you'll call her when you're ready."

"Okay." I exhaled. "Thank you. Is there anything else I missed? Anything I need to…" I trailed off as before my eyes Charlotte reached for Xavier's hand and intertwined her fingers with his. "Holy shit."

"Cal!" Charlotte chided.

"I know, I know, I just… if I'd known it'd take a

traumatic brain injury for you two to admit you're dating, I would've bashed my head into a wall weeks ago."

Xavier blinked. "You knew?"

"Of course I knew. You're a terrible liar. That's what I like about you." I looked to Charlotte. "It's you I'm surprised about. What all do you remember from that night we got drunk last dueling day?"

Charlotte froze. Like, full on deer-in-the-headlights *froze*. "Did I-um... do something I should know about?"

I laughed, remembering the image of her drunkenly shushing me as Xavier carried her home. "Let's just say your secret never stood a chance."

Charlotte blushed. She actually *blushed*. Red cheeks and everything.

"Anyway, I should probably talk to Lucy. Doctor says I'm not getting out of here until tomorrow, so we'll have to hold off celebrating Xavier's promotion until after he's already moved. Is there anything else I need to know?"

Nick finally spoke up. "We're-um... we're glad you're alright."

I smiled at him. "So am I. Imagine how boring it would get around here without me to make a mess of things?" I chuckled to myself, making approximately one of us. "Thanks, Nick. That means a lot."

They shuffled back out to reclaim their seats in the hallway and offer some privacy, an unnecessary gesture but one I appreciated all the same.

Lucy picked up the instant I hit the call button. "Cal! Sweetie, how are you? I heard you... slipped and fell."

Lucy, you angel. "I'm okay. And the doctor's gone. No one can hear us."

"Oh, good." She lowered her voice nonetheless. "And your meridian? How bad is it?"

"It's fine. It's *open*. Apparently I finished clearing it while I was out."

"That's... Cal, that's outstanding. You did it! That's... oh threads, that's such a relief. I worried you'd face permanent consequences. You wouldn't be the first to sever a meridian like this."

My mind jumped to the disclaimer I'd had to sign to "open" meridians in the focus rooms. *Including, but not limited to, injury, permanent stunting of one's cultivation, and death.* I didn't like the sound of any of those. Particularly not death. "I was wondering about that actually. I'd messed around a *little* with some exercises for subconscious cultivation, but never particularly seriously. Too many other things to work on. Do you have any idea *why* I managed this?"

Lucy let out a breath—or, more appropriately, mimicked the sound of letting out a breath, what with the whole *no lungs* thing. "My knowledge of the human spirit is limited to what I've overheard, but I think your rapid progress had something to do with it. Normally I'd be the first to advocate for taking it slow and avoiding risks, but in this case, you may have only survived because you've opened so many meridians so quickly. I think you've—for lack of a better word—*taught* your spirit how to complete the process by doing it so many times in so few months."

"Huh." I ran through the idea in my head. Correct or not, it certainly *sounded* good. "That actually makes sense. So you're not mad?"

"I'm not mad. I wish we had the funds to purchase pills for you, but anything in our price range might well have done more harm than good."

Skipping right past the complexities of interstellar exchange rates, between my time on the freighter and then roofie, I'd saved up a few hundred credits—the currency the entire Eternity's Maw sect and thus all its subsidiary systems used. For reference, that was enough to cover incidentals like the odd night out or new outfit, but if I'd had to pay *rent* to stay on Fyrion, I would've been in trouble.

Lucy didn't have much use for money. People usually jumped at the chance to load her up with fuel and supplies once they realized she was a soulship. *Cedric* had had money, but while I had taken a good amount of his stuff, I didn't have any legal claim to it. His money in particular remained locked up in his account, presumably until his next of kin—wherever the hell *they* were—realized he was dead.

Long story short, I wasn't *quite* broke, but I wasn't exactly in line to buy expensive pills.

"I'm just happy you made it through," Lucy continued. "You took my advice and had friends watching over you, and it sounds like it made the difference. I'm proud of you. Maybe you could've done a few more test runs, but no amount of practice is going to make cultivating not dangerous."

"That's… thank you. You're right about the test runs. I should've done more. I wanted to open the meridian before dueling day and my meeting with—shit!"

"Language."

"Right, right, sorry. I missed my meeting with Elder Lopez. I waited almost a week for that chance to see her."

"You'll have another opportunity."

"Yeah. Gods know how long it'll take. You think she knows why I didn't show? If she thinks I just forgot…" I shuddered.

"I'm sure it'll be fine," Lucy reassured me.

"You're probably right. I just hope she isn't too angry with me."

* * *

Elder Maria Lopez couldn't have been more pleased.

After months of dead ends, empty reports, and an absolute dearth of new evidence, her surveillance of Cadet

Rex finally had a new lead. She'd begun to grow impatient.

Not for a moment as she'd watched him play the part of the diligent student day in and day out had she fallen for his charade. His motives may've remained unclear, but long periods of normalcy didn't invalidate the evidence she had, the footage of him, unbreathing and with the pallid skin of a corpse, walking unmolested past a trio of void beasts. Threads, he'd even come to her asking after a way to secure his spirit to his body!

However many of her sect members he'd fooled, Maria knew. Something *necromantic* was going on.

Unfortunately, industriously training, attending classes, and making friends didn't quite fit her undead abomination theory. There had to be more. More secrets, more schemes, more cracks in his facade.

But none had shown, so Maria'd done what Maria did best.

She'd applied *pressure*.

That pompous upstart Long had made the perfect tool, his disdain for mortals an excellent handle with which to wield him. Bigots were *so* easy to manipulate.

Maria had had enough experience not to bother thinking Caliban might show his true colors the moment Long pushed him, and the fact he'd used her name had tipped her hand more than she might've liked, but she could maneuver out of that little implication.

For five days she'd watched. For five days she'd waited. For five days her hopes of pushing Cadet Rex to do something desperate dwindled.

Until her contact in the trauma center informed her that Cadet Rex had been admitted for severe head trauma, presumably from slipping in the shower.

She didn't believe that for a second.

Which led her to today, with at last another lead and the

perfect excuse to further delay meeting with the cadet in question. Threads, she could even use his absence to wring another focus room hour out of him! She couldn't have planned it better.

Maria scrolled back through the security tapes, unfortunately limited to the hall outside. It'd have to do. She watched the two male friends, Cadets Vesper and Honchel, step into the bathroom, followed shortly by a towel-clad Rex. She scrubbed through a half hour of nothing before Cadet Vesper bolted back into the hall and down the stairs, only to return minutes later with paramedics in tow.

What had they been doing in there for so long? Why had Vesper and Honchel been uniformed and Rex undressed?

A brief delay later, she watched the medics roll Rex out on a gurney, strapped down and spasming from the head trauma. Maria leapt back and watched it again. And again. And again.

Threads, it looked like a fall. She watched the way he moved, the looks on his friends' faces, the mess of his injuries. Over and over she analyzed that tape, searching for something, anything out of place, anything to bely the story she'd—there! In the linens of the gurney, washed away and obscured by the water and the blood, Martha spotted it.

The telltale black of cleansed impurities.

He was opening a meridian. Why there? Why with those two? *How* was he opening a meridian after showing an almost willingness to part with his focus room hours?

Her second question answered her third.

They were giving him qi.

It all made sense—the secrecy, the veil over Rex's qi, his close relationships with some of the sect's most vulnerable. It explained the uptick in instances of void induced psychosis, the disappearing ships, the abandoned refueling stations.

Whoever had created Rex wasn't just experimenting with necromancy. They were experimenting with vampirism. Rex must've been the answer. After dozens of failed attempts leading to the uptick in void psychosis, his mysterious master had turned to necromantic practice to create something that could take in the qi of others, that could *steal* power without being destroyed.

And now they'd sent it to Fyrion, a fertile ground of weak cultivators that nobody really cared about.

Maria was giddy.

The theory fit almost *too* well. She had no direct evidence, of course, but it would come. All she had to do was be the one to stop him when he showed his hand, and she'd have her ticket off this godsforsaken rock. It was the perfect opportunity, one for which only she was looking, one for which she needed only wait until the time came.

Cadet Vesper had even floundered since coming to meet Rex. Sure, his other two lackeys had made astounding progress up the ranks since his arrival, but if Rex was feeding *Maria* focus room hours, it stood to reason she wasn't the only one. Perhaps he drew more heavily from Vesper.

She could work out the details later. For now, she reveled in her discovery. It explained everything in a neat little package that provided her exactly the opportunity for advancement she was looking for. The evidence would arrive eventually.

And even if it didn't, Maria had ways of *making it.*

Yes, things were coming along nicely. She couldn't have been more pleased.

* * *

I waved the others back in with Lucy still on the line, wanting neither to hang up nor make my friends wait for us to finish. They all greeted her politely enough, though Charlotte in particular came across stilted and uncomfortable. Even now she struggled speaking to a millennia-old soulship with anything resembling familiarity.

"I've heard you've earned a new housing tier?" Lucy asked. "Congratulations, Xavier."

"Thank you. It is but a step on the eternal climb towards glorious victory."

I snorted. "That means it's about time for another celebration."

"I'll coordinate with the harbormaster," Lucy said, "but it may be a few days. There's a queue of food freighters from Ilirian because something went wrong with the latest silver shipment."

"That's fine," I said. "We don't need a full hangar, either. They've all had their chance to revel in your beauty."

Charlotte nodded. "A normal bay will do."

"Aaand, sent. We'll see what he says. They're usually quite accommodating."

"Well, you *are* very impressive." I laughed.

The conversation drifted on from there, the morning passing in comfortable companionship as Xavier relayed—in detail—the stories of his successful dueling day. Nick kept understandably quiet about his three losses, while Charlotte spent more time explaining why she'd targeted the opponents she had—including the intentional loss to avoid suspicion—than going over the actual duels.

The suns had long passed beyond the frame of my window by the time the talking wound down. Lucy hung up to go talk with the harbormaster, and the others inevitably had to return to their own days.

"Are you sure you don't need anything?" Xavier fussed. "I could stay and spar with you."

"I'm pretty sure sparring is the last thing I should be doing. I'm fine. I could use some meditation time, actually. You've all been great, really. Thanks. Now go pack. Xavier's moving today, remember?"

They smiled and waved and said their goodbyes and get-well-soons, only to stop at the door as I remembered an idea that'd been itching at the back of my mind.

"Hey, wait," I flagged them down. "I actually have one more question."

Charlotte stopped with her hand on the doorknob. "Yes?"

"Well it's just... now that I opened my muscle meridian while unconscious, does that mean I'm ready for my brain meridian?"

28

I wish I had an interesting story to tell about clearing my brain meridian. After all that excitement, it feels wrong to just open my final meridian without a hitch, doesn't it? Anticlimactic, even.

Sometimes life doesn't make for interesting stories though—or even boring stories for that matter.

In this particular case, I waited a few days after my discharge from the hospital to make my attempt, used a *different* shower than the one I'd almost killed myself in, plopped down, descended into my center, pushed a thread of qi into the entrance of the meridian in question, and promptly fell unconscious.

That's pretty much it.

Unlike the spine's pain or the muscles' seizures, the main difficulty in opening the brain meridian was training your spirit to do it while you were out cold. Since I knew I'd already *done* that thanks to a teensy bit of severe head trauma, I was good to go.

Unfortunately, this time around I can't even treat you to the in-depth description of the process because I was, well, *unconscious.* I woke up a half hour later with enough meridian gunk in my hair to seriously consider shaving it all off.

It wasn't until after I'd sent Nick and Xavier on their way and shut the shower door to wash up that anything worth relaying happened.

I cycled it.

Time slowed down. The world broke apart into a series of inputs and outputs, losing a layer of abstraction as my mind processed the sheer *data*. My thoughts sped and grew clinical, divided by some spiritual wall from my instincts and impulses, my desires and ideals.

And then I added my sense meridian.

My eyes went dark, iris and sclera black as the night sky and as full of stars.

Hot water didn't stream down my back. Distinct drops, eight degrees above my body's temperature, struck me at a point-three radian angle before breaking apart, sending droplets splashing in all directions, colliding with the walls or the floor, or flowing in a complex yet predictable path across my bare skin.

I stood and I watched and I listened. I calculated the viscosity of the falling water, tracked its temperature as its warmth leached into the tile walls, simulated the splatter of each drop before it even hit the floor. None of it mattered, of course. Nothing mattered. But I found the exercise no more or less interesting, no more or less worthwhile, than anything else I could've been doing.

My holopad beeped. I glanced down at it. Seven o'clock. Dinnertime. I'd been standing in the shower for two hours.

It took but a moment, but I had to parse through the reasons to finish up. My body required sustenance. If I didn't eat, I would eventually waste away. If I wasted away, my friends would be sad. Preventing that would constitute "good." In the absence of a compelling argument in either direction, the general consensus among society took precedence—perhaps they knew something I didn't. The general consensus stated that one should do "good." Ergo, I should finish my shower and head down to dinner.

I cut off the flow of qi.

My heart sped. My blood rushed. I gasped for air.

What the hells was *that*?

From what I'd read, the brain meridian was supposed to sharpen your thoughts, slow down perceived time, and hone your ability to pick out relevant information.

Mine had done one of those things. Threads, how was I supposed to win a fight if I had to keep reminding myself I didn't want to *get stabbed*?

I'd have to practice with it. I'd been able to reason using previously established information—namely the bit about following consensus, something I'd concluded while adrift in the infinite sea—so maybe I wouldn't have to *remind* myself of things, but needing a logically sound reason for everything felt like a nightmare.

I got the impression I had an awful lot of meditating in my future.

For the time being, I forced the worries from my mind as I hurriedly scrubbed myself clean and dried off.

I made one last stop before finally departing the third-floor bathroom, a momentary pause as I threw away the last of the anti-meridian-gunk shampoo. It landed in the bin with a satisfying clunk.

I grinned.

Twelve down, none to go. Next stop: forming my core.

* * *

After a long and deeply enjoyable meal spent receiving congratulations from Nick and Xavier while relaying every detail of my brain meridian's weirdness to a furiously tapping Charlotte, I walked with the happy couple up to the transport platform. As they waited for a pod to bring them back to housing C, Charlotte took every opportunity to talk me out of my own destination.

"I really don't think this is a good idea," she said. "The other cadets already think of you as an upstart mortal. You're only going to prove them right."

"The other cadets can think what they want. I'm the only one here who wasn't handed a spot by my parents."

"You're also the only one that hasn't been training every day since birth," Charlotte countered. "You can't keep falling back on your qi supply to carry you. Eventually, you're going to need people to respect you."

I scowled at her. "People do respect me."

"*Cultivators*, Cal. You need *cultivators* to respect you. At the rate you're going, soon enough you're going to outgrow Fyrion. You're going to outgrow *me*. My social network will only get you so far, and you're going to have a hard time getting the materials you need to advance if nobody in power respects you."

I shrugged. "I'll cross that bridge when I get to it. I'll always have *some* clout through Lucy, and theoretically I'll eventually get to the point where my cultivation speaks for itself. I obviously can't hide it forever, just until I'm strong enough to scare off anyone who wants to take advantage. In the meantime…" My holopad beeped as a pod pulled up. "Ope, that's me. You two have a good night."

"G'night, Cal!" Xavier bid in return.

Charlotte just sighed.

I ignored her theatrics as the pod door closed behind me and took off down the transport tube. I gazed out the window, watching station after station blur by, the platforms growing dirtier, the city more crowded, its residents more destitute. Twenty minutes later, I emerged in a familiar work bay.

I almost didn't recognize the place. Instead of the mess of laborers running about every which way, the mortals moved about in casual efficiency, chatting amongst themselves as they geared up or peeled away their vac suits to hang them on the wall hooks. It appeared I'd caught them at the shift change. Perfect.

Those who noticed me flashed me surprised looks or fell into messy salutes as they spotted my cadet uniform. I tried to wave the first few off, but word spread through the staging area faster than I could contain it. By the time I reached the foreman's desk, not a right hand in that room sat anywhere else but upon its owner's brow.

The foreman—or forewoman, as it were—greeted me far more politely than the man I'd spoken with last time. "How can I help you, sir?"

"Don't—" I gestured downward with my hand. "Don't salute. Please."

She lowered her hand, glaring at the workers around me. They followed suit, returning to their tasks even as they failed to hide their gawking.

"So what can the southwestern exterior maintenance division do for you, sir?" the forewoman asked. "I'd warn you, this is a place for work, not for seeking enlightenment or picking fights."

"Good. I'd like a job."

"You-um… excuse me?"

"Part time, of course. I'm only free between eight and midnight each day." I pulled up my holopad and swiped over my credentials. "I'm a certified zero-G vac-welder with four years' experience. Since my schedule is tight, I'll accept below entry-level pay, which you'll give me, because working alone I can outperform a full team of three."

Her eyes darted back and forth as she scanned through my certification and work history. "This is all… I've heard of you. You worked on the void incursion repairs?"

"I did."

She glanced up at me with narrow eyes. "And now you want... a job."

"I do. Part time. Working alone."

"If you say so, I mean—ah, yes, sir."

"You're going to have to stop calling me sir if you're gonna be my boss."

"Yes si—er, um—" She glanced back down at her holopad. "Caliban."

I grinned. "Call me Cal. Can I get started then?"

"Sure. Just sign this and this." She swiped over a pair of boilerplate employment contracts, terms auto-edited as per our conversation. I gave them a cursory reading before sending them back.

"Great, you're all set. Oy! Garry!"

I flinched as her shout caught me off guard.

A half-dressed man with the top of his vac suit hanging off his waist ran over.

"Get Cal here into a suit. He's working the back end of second shift." The forewoman turned back to me. "Welcome aboard."

I could feel heads turning to track me as I followed Garry to one of the benches that lined the wall, picked out vac suit number eighty-six, removed it from its hook, and suited up. Garry didn't speak a word throughout the process, communicating entirely through grunts and gestures up to and including the point I stepped into the airlock.

Something about the hiss of air draining out, the artificial gravity fading away, and the iron walls of Fyrion vanishing beyond my periphery sent a wave of relief crawling up my spine. For a few beautiful moments, my fears and ambitions and hurdles ahead fell to nothing. For a few beautiful moments, I gazed upon the gray wasteland around me and found strange comfort in its barrenness. For a few beautiful moments, I looked at the sky.

And then I got to work.

Through all my life, I'd never quite put my finger on why I'd found the dull repetitive act of vac-welding so calming. I figured it lay in some combination of the simplicity of following directions, the rhythm of trekking to an impact site, making repairs, and moving on to the next one, and the ability to do it all on autopilot, keeping the busybody parts of my brain active and leaving the rest to wander as it may.

It'd taken becoming a cultivator to realize what I was doing. In the unbreakable silence of a vacuum, undisturbed but by the guiding arrow to my next task, surrounded on all sides by the cold embrace of the infinite sea, I meditated.

By the time my HUD led me home, I felt better than I had in months. I thought more clearly, my spirit sat soothed, and I came away a few credits richer for my efforts.

The other workers left me alone as I returned my gear to storage and hung my vac suit on its hook. I didn't bother trying to strike up a conversation or escape their curious stares and quiet whispers. I waved goodnight to the forewoman, stepped into the transport pod home, climbed the steps to the third floor, and had my best night's sleep in months.

* * *

And so the days passed. Three dueling days and the weeks between disappeared in bleary-eyed exhaustion and interminable, zealous *work*.

I knew the fervor with which I pushed myself was neither sustainable nor healthy, that I hurtled wildly towards a burnout the likes of which I'd never imagined. I did it anyway. I could rest when I advanced. I could rest once I'd met Lopez's one-year deadline.

I could rest once I'd defeated Long.

Until then, I would train.

I awoke each morning to my holopad's alarm, a torturous thing that sent me stumbling from my bed and into uniform for the morning workout. I exercised on my own as Nick slept in and the others didn't bother with the trip from housing C, leaving me alone with my ponderings as I lifted weights and ran in circles, all the while cursing in frustration whenever my holopad beeped to correct my technique.

I broke fast with Charlotte and Xavier more often than not, taking the time to join them rather than eat alone or hope against hope Nick would make it out of bed in time for breakfast.

I took a transport pod directly from housing C to the family district, arriving at meditation class for my daily three hours of walking back and forth. As the weeks flew by, I advanced from simple pacing to navigating basic obstacles to performing the combat forms I'd so tirelessly trained myself in. I yet lacked the ironclad focus to fight an entire duel—reacting to the opponent, crafting a plan, taking hits, et cetera—but considering most students took several years to reach that point, I found my progress more than adequate.

A number of those class periods I spent working through the cold lens of my brain meridian, practicing the untaught art of acknowledging the constant calculations without allowing them to distract me. Faster and more efficient though it made my thoughts, running my mind at such speed came at a cost, one I paid in exhaustion come the session's end.

Mental endurance became a cornerstone of my morning class, joining fortitude and focus at the foundation of an effective spirit.

Lunch with Martha fit neatly into my routine, us both misfits in our own right among the oversized class. Her right arm now lay continuously in a sling, apparently a result of some injury she'd undergone while opening her muscle meridian. I wished I could've commiserated with her over it, but I dared not reveal the extent of my progress to anyone I didn't *need* to.

I felt for the girl, I truly did. From what little I'd seen of Nick's interactions with his parents, she was under a lot of pressure, pressure that would've been difficult enough *without* both a missing hand and a non-functional arm.

She hid it well, all smiles and laughs and I'm okays, but every once in a while, when her shoulder bumped into something or she lost her focus too early in a meditation exercise, I caught her staring at the wall with unfocused eyes, a momentary crack in her facade through which a glimpse of soul-rending exhaustion could slip through.

Whenever I saw it, a part of me wanted to rush over and give the kid a hug. Another part wanted to commit unspeakable violence upon her parents. Always, by the time I reminded myself neither option would've been appropriate, Martha's mask was firmly back in place.

Maybe I wouldn't whisk Nick away the day he turned eighteen. He clearly wasn't the only one that needed saving.

Misguided notions of rescuing overburdened teens from abusive parents aside, lunch each day did have to end, leaving me to push on through my second class of the day.

In contrast to meditation two, cycling two proved more and more useless as time passed. As my classmates worked their way along the path towards opening their spine meridians, I took up the practice of purging the pain herbs from my system by cycling my stomach, blood, and kidneys so I could spend the class period working on my own.

Charlotte had, at risk of expulsion were she caught, given me a number of qi manipulation exercises designed to hone control and intake in preparation for core formulation, a stage for which I worked tirelessly day in and day out.

The promise of magic made for a good motivator.

So I practiced precision and detail and complexity in my internal constructs, growing more and more adept at warping the liquid darkness within me to my will. I found it easy, too easy, almost. It took some effort to nudge my qi into motion, but it obeyed readily. I didn't have to wrestle with it or otherwise assert control over the energy, a difference that made all three of my confidants deeply jealous.

After class I'd spar with Charlotte and Xavier, alternating between fending off his overwhelming offense and withstanding her meticulous control.

I discovered that what little I knew of Cedric's style suited me particularly well, the steps' focus on economy of motion a natural fit for my qi's preference for stillness and fluidity of movement. Like the infinite sea in the face of existence's imposition, I gracefully flowed around incoming attacks, moving as little as necessary to dodge and deflect and build a positional advantage until it came time to deliver the winning blow.

Or, well, that was the idea.

In practice my clumsy attempts to incorporate bits and pieces of one style into another put my muscle memory in conflict with itself, leaving me as likely to trip over myself or step *into* Xavier's axe as outmaneuver it. In a way, adding Cedric's moves was like starting from scratch as I relearned which steps to make when. At least I was starting from scratch down a path that would offer tools I could wield against Long.

I'd never beat him at his own style. I just might beat him with *mine*.

Charlotte refrained from adding any of her own moves

to the mix, both for simplicity's sake and because nearly all the Veleraeu steps were designed for the empowered rapier the family favored. They'd be of little use to me.

Of my two instructors, which I worked with—or if I worked with both—largely depended on whether or not they were speaking with each other that particular day, a fact that seemed to change with the frequency of a metronome.

By my count, they broke up with each other fourteen times in that five month span, miraculously winding up back together within a few days. Absurd as I found it, Nick informed me that it wasn't rare in unmarried cultivators—something about imperfectly controlled qi heightening emotions. Presumably they'd eventually either separate for good or settle down, especially as they advanced their cores and grew more accustomed to reining in their qi's effects.

Personally, I laughed at the ridiculousness of it all. Annoying as their constant on-again-off-again might've been, it seemed preferable to the dangerous levels of nihilistic apathy my own qi had a tendency to inflict.

It thus struck me as absolutely insane when, upon Charlotte's blisteringly early promotion to housing B, the two of them *moved in together*. Oddly enough, that seemed to lessen the frequency of their breakups.

After combat training came my hour working with Nick, using the word "working" as loosely as possible. Mostly the time consisted of reading through dense texts on the spiritual science of germination while Nick tinkered feverishly at his desk. I tried and failed several times to keep up with what he was doing, each time running headlong into a wall of botanical jargon so impenetrable it could've held off the vacuum of space.

Since I still couldn't externalize my qi, we ran a few tests trying to use the minuscule amount of dark qi that escaped as a byproduct of light qi usage, but Nick couldn't sense it, and while I could absorb that percentage point that "returned to the threads," I lacked both the experience in qi manipulation and the knowledge of extramundane molecular biology to accomplish Nick's goal.

Despite my attempts to convince him I'd manage it eventually, that I'd form my core soon enough, Nick grew increasingly frustrated with the project. A few weeks in, his questions shifted once more from the properties of my qi to how he might learn to sense it. Worse yet, he refused to be dissuaded.

I can't say for certain when Nick made up his mind that he had to find the infinite sea, but two months after I joined his research, he stopped assigned reading, stopped actively explaining things, and descended deeper into his own thoughts.

With alarming frequency I'd open his door at six pm to find him lying in bed, unmoving and silent but for his barked instruction to leave him alone. On other nights I'd return from work to see Nick standing in the hall, his eyes glossed over as he stared out the window at the starry sky.

I'd join him for a few quiet moments on those late occasions, offering words of advice if he asked or silent companionship if he didn't. If nothing else, I could remind him he wasn't alone.

I never lingered long at that window, my own meditation long finished for the day.

I spent my vac-welding shifts musing over all manner of life's mysteries, the details of which I'll withhold for the time being lest this turn into a painfully amateurish manifesto. I started from a place of icy logic, establishing firm—or at least firm sounding—reasons why I should continue living, strive to better myself, do good, avoid evil, that sort of thing.

I read philosophy, not out of curiosity, but necessity,

building a logical framework from which my emotionally stunted brain meridian could make decisions.

Most of all, I pondered the universe and my place in it. I mused on what it was I wanted and why I wanted it, for what I toiled day in and day out, for whom I trained and learned and fought.

In truth, this proved the most difficult step in my advancement, the last and highest hurdle in my preparation.

If I were to declare some piece of the great dark my own, to drink from its unending depths to bolster *my* spirit, fortify *my* body, build *my* core, to assert my existence upon the vast nothingness and wield its power in my futile struggle against infinity itself, I had to know *why*.

Because a full five months after the opening of my brain meridian, eight into my time on Fyrion, and with only four more before the deadline loomed, I finally sat down to do exactly that.

29

I bounded across the rooftops of Fyrion, leaping over peaks and valleys in the contiguous mass of metal that separated the city from the vacuum beyond. The dwarf planet's gravity had taken more than a little getting used to, but now months into my vac-welding work, I needed neither the reflexes of cycling my spine nor the stability of cycling my muscles to expertly traverse the uneven terrain.

I kept high, staying to tops of the multilevel buildings and vaulting across the often-thirty-foot gaps where only a hallway or single story connected them. In low-G, everything moved in slow motion, the rubber treads at the base of my vac suit going several seconds between contacts with the metal, bringing an almost leisurely rhythm to my journey.

My destination loomed ahead, a behemoth of glass and steel that towered over the city around it. At some thirty stories tall, Gyaro Spire housed and officed the city's middle class: well-to-do mortals. Executives of various industries too low on the hierarchy to live off-world, yet high enough to afford luxurious apartments with sweeping views of Fyrion's gray wastes, the non-cultivators cared little for the reduction in ambient qi so high off the ground.

I shared that apathy.

More importantly to me, unlike Fyrion's actual tallest structure, Gyaro Spire sat on the opposite end of the city from the constant flow of ships into and out of port. The planet's lack of atmosphere might've halted the noise from all those launches, but it certainly didn't stop the docking framework from shaking like all hell.

No, it was Gyaro Spire for me.

I pulled the one piece of equipment I'd brought with me from its hitch on my belt, and leveled the maganchor as I neared the spire's base.

A maganchor is exactly what it sounds like: a magnet for anchoring things. It's basically an electromagnet with a handle, a toggle switch, and a few tie-off points used in zero- or low-G environments to secure equipment and climb structures. Today, it would do the latter. And also the ladder.

Anyway, it took under a minute to scale one of the vertical support beams right up to the top, where the spire's, well *spire*, sloped inward until it peaked at the flat foundation for a broadcast antenna. It left me with only about three feet of clearance before the drop off to a thirty-story fall, but that was enough for me.

For safety's sake, I hitched the maganchor back to my belt and engaged it against the antenna to my back, just in case something went horribly wrong and I started seizing or fell unconscious or whatever. And hey, this way if I died during the process, I wouldn't traumatize some poor rich kid by falling limply past their window.

Prepared as I was ever going to be, I sat down cross-legged on the roof of Fyrion's second-tallest structure, took a moment to appreciate the entire city and gray expanse beyond stretched out before me, shut my eyes, and focused inward.

I had done—and this is a technical term—an absolute

fuckload of reading prior to this. Sources agreed the act of core formation to be the first true step in a cultivator's journey, the moment they forged all that they were into all they could be, the defining milestone in finding their Way.

No pressure.

Liquid qi sat still within me, filling my center near brimming where it pooled in quiet shadow. Silencing my doubts, my fears, my trepidations, I spun up a thread and got to work.

I started with the blood meridian, the first I'd opened all those months ago while Lucy had removed the piece of Cedric's rib that'd pierced it. My body temperature dropped. My blood ran cold. I pumped more and more qi through the channel, far more than I could've hoped to back with Lucy, back before half a year of fortifying and stretching and training its capacity.

Next came my heart. My pulse slowed to a crawl as my heart rate plummeted, pumping with newfound efficiency and strength.

The last of my qi went to my kidneys, the third and final meridian I'd opened on Lucy's ventilator. My body tore through any lingering toxins, primed and ready to resist venoms that would've sent me to the threads mere months ago.

For a moment, I breathed. At three meridians, I'd come against the limits of liquid qi. My center sat empty, depleted as its energy now ran elsewhere. To continue, I needed more, more than my center could hold, more than *I* could hold, and with yet no way to externalize my qi, if I failed to form my core, there'd be no getting rid of it.

No getting rid of it alive, that is.

Seriously, you do not want to fuck around with qi overflow. Remember what happened to Cedric after he took in qi that didn't belong to him? Think along those lines.

I reached outward, past the narrow boundaries of my vac suit into the void beyond. The infinite sea awaited me, vast and imposing and endlessly calming in its reminder of my own insignificance. Suddenly the risks didn't matter. Nothing mattered.

With barely a thought I let that frigid tide wash over me, and stepped past the point of no return.

Newly replenished, I set right to work. I added my lungs to the mix, fighting off memories of asphyxiating on the floor of Lucy's core room, an important lesson in the dangers of cultivation. My breaths slowed and deepened, purging more CO_2 with each glacial exhale.

Then I reached my arrival at Fyrion, that first meridian I'd opened alone in the third-floor shower. My bones hardened, growing marginally denser with each bit of qi I fed them.

My skin grew pallid and icy as I cycled it too, the first meridian I'd cleansed under Xavier's watchful eye, its effects enough of a shock to scare Nick half to death. I wondered how my time at Fyrion might've differed had he not walked in on us at that moment. I wondered how his might've.

I reached for more qi and the universe obliged, flooding my center a second time with enough power to turn me into a fine red mist. I pushed on.

The next set I'd opened all at once in the immediate fallout of the void beast incursion. My metabolism dropped as I cycled my stomach, ready to wring every molecule of nutrition from the sustenance I sent its way. My tendons strengthened against damage, reinforced against the hyper-natural forces inflicted by and upon a cultivator's body.

My senses sharpened and flattened at once, the world around me exploding with detail my unempowered brain failed to parse. My eyes went black, sclera and irises taking on the inky tone of my pupils but for the glimmering stars and planets and distant galaxies that appeared within.

Three more to go.

I drank once more from the infinite sea.

The lingering soreness from yesterday's workout faded to a slight chill as I cycled my spine meridian, honing my reflexes and dulling the edge of existence at once. Weeks of agonizing training flashed through my mind, pain the likes of which I'd never feel again, not that it mattered. Nothing mattered.

Strength rippled through my body as I ran qi through my wiry muscles, finding power in stillness and a sense of solidity even in my gaunt figure. An unexpected shudder rolled down my back as I recalled that horrible moment where I'd lost control, the *crack* I'd heard before losing consciousness in the shower.

Last but not least, I cycled my brain. Suddenly the deluge of data from my empowered eyes and ears and nose and touch made *sense*. I found patterns and truths and ideas hidden in the chaos, and saw but a tiny glimpse of the perspective shared by the greatest among the gods.

All-knowing, uncaring.

For the first time in the minuscule blip of my existence, I cycled all twelve of my meridians. I juggled more qi than ever before. I tasted power.

Yet the infinite sea remained, undiminished, undisturbed, unstirred by even the greatest height I'd ever reached. Cold and dark and apathetic, that ocean of power in which I swam, on which I sailed, of which I drank, drowned me in the meaninglessness of it all. No milestone, no purpose, no ideals would survive the inexorable onslaught of eternity. None of it mattered. Nothing mattered.

But maybe someday, I could forge something that did.

To that end I opened myself to one final wave from the infinite sea, one last influx of that quiet power that filled my center to brimming even as qi coursed through my every meridian. Now for the moment of truth.

In inverse order, I ceased my cycling.

The edges of my center strained against the pressure as I emptied my brain meridian into it. I held on through sheer will, forcing the qi to condense, to thicken, to stay put.

Then I emptied my muscle meridian. Then my spine.

One by one I added to the reservoir, fighting with increasing vigor against both the power within me and that without, for even as I flailed against infinity, the great dark imposed its endless question.

Why?

I had to know. In finding the infinite sea, in learning to cultivate its vastness, I'd embarked upon a path the likes of which I'd never heard. I had to know where it led. I had to know what it meant. I had to know what it could do. I emptied my sense meridian into my center.

Why?

I had to beat Long. I had to prove that I deserved my place here, that he by right of birth bore no imperium over those less fortunate, to look upon his snide face as he realized he'd been bested by the mortal he despised so much. I added my tendon meridian.

Why?

I had to support my friends. They'd all given me so much of their time and knowledge and companionship. To repay them with anything but success would be a betrayal. I owed them. Above all I owed Lucy, who'd taken me from death's door to a life of magic, of power, of purpose. I ceased the flow of qi through my stomach.

Why?

I had to protect those who couldn't protect themselves: Nick, depressed and alone in his forest of potted plants;

Martha, twice-crippled and still beneath the thumb of her parents' expectations; Vihaan, shivering and bleeding out where a void beast had run him through. I stopped cycling my skin meridian.

Why?

I emptied my bones.

Why?

I emptied my lungs.

Why?

I emptied my kidneys.

Why?

Why?

Why?

For myself. Because too many times I'd come up short. Too many times I'd found myself at the mercy of others, of chance, of the threads and their cruel sense of humor. Too many times my lack of power had left me the victim, victim of bullies, victim of void beasts, victim of a VIP, twitching violently as he drained from me my very life-force. I emptied my heart.

Why?

For roofie. For Cedric. For Brady. For those whose lives had been cut short, whom I'd left behind in that floating graveyard out in space, whose entire impact on this world lay on me, on how they'd changed me, on how I'd change the universe. I emptied my blood.

But none of this matters. Nothing matters.

Perhaps. Perhaps not. But if ever there was a way to prove otherwise, to pierce eternity with the vibrant spear of purpose, this was it. The dimmest hope of reason made worth the endless struggle against the self, against the spirit, against infinity.

Even in the dark one might find beauty.

Even in the cold one might glean meaning.

Against the stronghold of my will the qi roiled, crashing

in waves upon my resolve in its bid to disperse, to escape, to return to the great uncaring from whence it came. With as much fervor as I kept the latter out, I kept the former in.

Harder and harder I pressed, restraining the condensing qi with all I had and all I was. Into it I poured my hopes, my fears, my petty wants. I poured in my worry for Nick, my pride in Xavier, my respect for Charlotte.

I added my love for Lucy, my sorrow for Cedric, my curiosity over their mysterious past; my drive to improve, my wonder, my nightmares of a black-eyed man standing over a pallid corpse; my disdain for the Longs and Lopezes of the world, for the parents Brady and I had worked so hard to escape; each and every one of the seventeen men and women that'd died on RF-31.

Only once my every ounce of love and hate and everything in between had joined the fray could they overcome the uncaring, could they reject the shadow of infinity, could they lay claim to the power within me.

My qi solidified.

The pressure ceased.

There, floating in the middle of my center, about the size of a cherry tomato, was a sphere the color of burnt charcoal surrounded by thin, pale wisps of gaseous qi like gray smoke off a smoldering fire. Even cold and quiet and unimposing as it seemed, I could *feel* the energy thrumming through it, the new heights of power newly within my grasp.

My tin core, the seed from which I'd grow the foundation of my cultivation, the beginning stage of true advancement, and the first step along my Way, had finally taken shape.

And I couldn't wait to try it out.

30

I slammed my head into the sitting-area table. The reinforced resin against my forehead made a rather satisfying thud, even as I let out a groan. "It's not *working*."

"Then try again," Charlotte repeated for the umpteenth time. "You know how this works, Cal. You do it over and over again until you figure it out."

With a well-executed—if I do say so myself—overdramatic sigh, I pushed off against the edge of the table to bring my head up and send me collapsing into the booth's plush backrest. The housing D lobby was fairly busy at the late afternoon hour, but Arthur had been kind enough to snag us a table while I was still in class. Xavier and Charlotte both had made the trek over from B-block, sparing us all the attention my presence would accrue somewhere the neighbors hadn't already gotten bored of me.

"Yes, ma'am, Senior Cadet, ma'am." I doubled up on the honorifics as I referred to Charlotte as my favorite thing to call her in the two months since she'd made copper. It hadn't gotten a rise out of her then, and it *certainly* didn't now, but that's showbiz, baby.

I forcibly unclenched my jaw and shut my eyes, ignoring the vision of my core that sprang to view to focus instead on the world beyond my skin. I thankfully didn't have to peer far enough to be blinded by Xavier's or Charlotte's blazing cores, but the ambient qi of Fyrion still shone an unwelcome distraction into my mind's eye. I ignored it too.

Next, I visualized the sigil for force palm, a fairly simple shape of two loops and a pair of skewed crossing lines. I'd long memorized the form to ridiculous precision, well aware how even the slightest inaccuracy could severely alter the technique's effects if not ruin it entirely. I wagered that's where Charlotte imagined my failure.

But I never even got that far.

With the sigil locked firmly in position just above my upturned right palm, I pulled a thread of qi off my core, ran it along my tendon meridian to get it to my hand, and *pushed*.

It didn't make it to the sigil. Well, *some* of it did, in exactly the same way that if you exhale in the same room as a balloon, *some* of your breath will wind up inside, but you could be damn sure that balloon wasn't inflating any time soon.

Instead of flowing directly from my body into the technique, my qi dispersed the moment it left my body, spilling out in all directions like a gas line with no pressure behind it. It was like trying to *throw* confetti at someone. No amount of effort was going to make it go very far.

Still I tried and still I failed, pouring out more and more qi with every attempt only for it to dissipate and drift away into the infinite sea without actually *doing* anything.

Can you believe that? All this time spent building up to the point where I could do magic, and it didn't even *work.* That was some bullshit.

"It's okay, Cal." Xavier reached across the table to put a

hand on my shoulder. "It took me almost a year before I mastered my first technique. Keep at it, and I know you'll get there."

"No, no, it's not *mastery* that's the problem." I shook my head. "It just doesn't *work*. Here, show it to me again."

Xavier shrugged and held out his hand, emulating the force palm as I watched, wincing, through my spiritual senses. Sure enough, the qi sprang straight from his hand into the sigil, completing its motion and dissipating into the atmosphere alongside the tiny burst of dark qi all techniques seemed to generate.

I sighed. "Okay, so, it *looks* like the problem is my qi. Your qi wants to do things. It practically jumps from your body into the sigil, races around, and dissipates. Mine just wants to sit. It's like trying to push a wave onto shore. It doesn't matter how well I visualize the technique if qi won't even *go in*."

"Then find a way to make it," Charlotte said as if it were that easy. "Sticking to your wave analogy, manipulate the tides, lower the shoreline, dig a canal."

"Okay, the analogy isn't *perfect*," I admitted, "but you get the point." I looked down at the sigil, still drawn up on my holopad. "Maybe it's this technique. Maybe I need something better suited to my qi."

"Ah, yes, it's *the technique's* fault." Charlotte laughed. "Cal, if I had a credit for every cultivator who's said *that*, I wouldn't be bargaining for favors."

Xavier scratched his head. "Maybe he's right. Cal's qi has never worked the same as ours. Why would it work with the same techniques?"

"Sure, that's *possible*," Charlotte countered, "but that'd mean Cal has to come up with his own sigils for *everything*. Without even a rudimentary understanding of what *would* work with Cal's qi, we're either flailing in the dark or sitting around waiting for divine inspiration."

"Divine inspiration?" I jumped on the curious phrase. "What's divine inspiration?"

Charlotte exhaled. "It's where most techniques originally came from. If you pay sharp attention to the world around you and meditate on and on over whatever little detail catches your eye, *sometimes* a technique can just... come to you."

I snapped my fingers. "Just like that?"

"Just like that." Charlotte didn't echo the gesture. "On the face of it, it's far and away the best way to learn a technique. You can reach a level of mastery that usually takes years of training in a matter of moments, and you'll *understand* the technique way better than anyone who just memorizes the sigil, but it's not remotely consistent. There are stories of cultivators spending decades of their lives watching the way rabbits hop or something equally stupid and never getting a technique out of it. There are *also* stories of inspiration striking out of nowhere and cultivators generating techniques from the most trivial observations."

"So I just have to meditate? That sounds easy enough."

Charlotte threw her head back in frustration. "Cal, stop it. Chasing inspiration is a fool's errand. You'll end up wasting half your life contemplating something silly just for the chance at *maybe* getting a technique out of it, a technique you can neither choose nor predict. That guy who watched rabbits hop? Thirty years later he discovered a technique for *making your hair softer*."

"That exists?" I ran a hand through my hair. "That exists and we're starting with *force palm*? I want the fuzziness sigil!"

Charlotte let out a noise somewhere between an exasperated groan and a scream into the abyss, complete with forward collapse onto the table. Even worse, *her* forehead landed softly on her arm, denying us all that satisfying *thud* sound I'd come to appreciate. Her and those damn glasses.

I chuckled. "Seriously, though, divine inspiration may be my best bet. I have *no idea* why this isn't working, which means nowhere to begin figuring out what *could* work. If I could manifest a new technique, at least I'd have something to go off of."

"Just don't waste too much time on it," Charlotte said. "You have more important things to worry about. There are four months left before Lopez's deadline, which means four months before *you* need to either fight Long or leave the sect."

"I'm not leaving. We've been over this."

Charlotte nodded. "In which case, you need to focus on two things: sparring Xavier, and advancing to copper. Any duel with Long is going to be unscheduled, which means no qi attacks allowed anyway. What *will* be allowed is his superior mastery of the Dragon's Fang, and his superior *everything else* if he's a stage higher than you."

"But I want to do *magic*."

"It's not magic," Xavier corrected. "It's a practiced externalization of your qi."

"C'mon. I worked so hard to get this far. I can't just *give up* on learning gods damned magic."

Charlotte scowled at me, though whether for the content of my comment or the foul language within, I couldn't guess. "An external qi technique isn't going to help you fight Long. You're going to have a hard enough time preparing if you *don't* waste precious hours praying for inspiration."

"But what if it *does* help me fight him?"

"Cal, external qi attacks are banned outside of dueling day," Xavier reminded me. "If you try to use one…"

"The sensors won't pick it up," Charlotte finished as realization dawned. "You can't get caught because nobody can sense your qi *anyway*."

"Well, Nick's working on that but I don't fancy his odds."

Xavier leaned in and lowered his voice, speaking in a whisper sharp enough to shave with. "Cal, that's cheating. You can't cheat in an official duel."

"He's abusing his power to get me kicked out of the sect! How is he not already cheating?"

"That doesn't make it okay."

"Actually, I'd say it does," Charlotte leapt to my defense. "It's not about rank. It's not about winning resources from other members unfairly. It's about staying in the sect *at all*. Cal *should* win, and he should do so by any means necessary."

"No," Xavier said flatly. "It's not happening."

"*Every edge*, Xavier. Every edge."

"Cal will win fairly or not at all."

"Guys, guys," I intervened in an attempt to stop the argument before it could pick up too much momentum. "It doesn't *matter*. I don't actually have any functional techniques, remember?"

"I can't believe you're this stuck on it." Charlotte kept on arguing. "You'd rather let Long win than break the rules he's been abusing this entire time?"

"Why are losing or cheating the only options? Caliban has a warrior's spirit, and I know he can do this. I believe in him."

"Except there isn't a reason to take that risk! All I'm saying is that *if*, by some miracle, inspiration strikes and Cal comes up with a relevant technique, he should use it to secure his place here—a place he *deserves*."

"He should use it to *cheat*. That's what you just said. That he should *cheat*."

"Because in this instance, it's justified."

"Cheating begets cheating. It erodes one's character, it

makes a mockery of the systems on which we base our lives, and it is never, *ever* justified." Xavier pushed himself to his feet. "That's it. I'm done." He stormed out of the lobby, nearly knocking some poor housing D-er on his face in his anger.

Charlotte just watched him go.

I blinked, eyes darting back and forth between the hall to the transport platform and Charlotte sitting across from me. "Is... um... is everything alright?"

"Yeah. He'll be fine by this evening. He's just..." Charlotte sighed. "*Xavier*. You never really know what silly hill he's going to die on next."

"Really? That seemed... pretty predictable to me. He romanticizes dueling and hates things that undermine it. Threads, I could see that fight coming the moment you stepped in to defend the idea."

"Every edge, Cal," Charlotte repeated. "I get why he wouldn't like cheating, but you'd think he'd see reason."

"Xavier has his own reasoning. You know that. What I don't get is why you aren't listening to it."

"*He's* the one who isn't listening to—"

"If either of you were listening to the other, nobody would've stormed off," I interrupted.

"It's just so *stupid*." Charlotte planted her head in her hands. "It's a pointless argument about what to do in the case of *divine inspiration*. Do you have any idea how absurd that sounds?"

"The word 'absurd' lost all meaning to me a while ago. Let's just assume that anything can happen, up to and including divine inspiration, divine motivation, divine experimentation, and, because why the hell not, divine hydration. Even the gods have gotta get thirsty sometimes, right?"

Charlotte just stared at me.

"What? That was funny. I'm funny."

"Assuming you *don't* pull a technique out of nowhere in a matter of months, we really should talk about other steps. You're making good progress with incorporating Cedric's steps, but none of that's going to matter if you can't make copper in time, ideally with a week's leeway to practice at the higher stage."

"Okay, but copper's easy right?"

Charlotte twitched, like, actually *twitched*. Her left eye and the corner of her mouth both jerked ever so slightly towards an expression of abject rage before returning to neutral, all in under a second.

"Easy for you, maybe." She masterfully suppressed any trace of anger in her voice. "For most of us, it's one of the hardest."

"Right, right, but it's also the simplest. I don't need to craft a focus or reforge my body or replace all my blood with apple juice or whatever. I just have to whip up enough qi and go to town."

Charlotte's hand returned rather firmly to her forehead. "Please refrain from referring to core advancement as *going to town*. Yes, copper is the only stage that's gated exclusively by qi access, and *yes*, in your case that makes it easier than any of the others, but it's not that simple."

"Why not? It seems pretty simple."

"Because it can't be! It takes years of preparation, hours and hours of focus room time, of scrimping and scraping and *fighting* for every scrap you can get, every pill, every natural treasure, *every edge*. And then you'll be…" She trailed off as her brain caught up with her mouth. "Gods damnit. You could do it today, couldn't you?"

"Language." I aped Lucy's tone of voice, flashing my best shit-eating grin as I enjoyed my hypocrisy. "And should I? Do you think that'd make learning a technique easier?"

Charlotte exhaled and rubbed at her temples. "I hate

you. Just… know that I hate you."

I grinned. "Noted. Actually, though. Do you think hitting copper would help get divine inspiration?"

"You're not getting divine inspiration. Give it up," Charlotte chided. "And I wouldn't push it. I guess if you…" She paused in clear thought. "Sorry, this isn't something I've had to consider before. Most people can't just immediately jump to copper the day after they make tin."

"But I *could*."

"I'd hold off. Wait a week, maybe a bit more. Your body's probably still undergoing changes from forming your core. It's probably best you let it, give yourself a chance to get used to it before you push forward again."

I nodded. "I can do that." I looked down at my hand, clenching and unclenching it as I watched. "It kind of already feels normal. Like, I *know* I'm stronger, faster, tougher, all that stuff even before I start cycling, but it still feels like *me*."

"Good," Charlotte said. "With any luck, it'll never stop feeling like you. Waiting a few days to hit copper isn't going to kill you."

"Alright, alright. I'll wait until my *next* day off. In the meantime, I think we should revisit my graduation schedule."

Charlotte narrowed her eyes at me. "How do you mean?"

"I just need to fake two more meridians before I can test out of cycling, and I'm pretty sure I could pass meditation *now* if I pushed it. Yeah, people will think I'm a prodigy if I graduate that fast, but that might work in my favor. If-slash-when I beat Long, it'll be better if I already have a reputation as some kind of genius. The alternative is…"

"They accuse you of cheating," Charlotte finished. "Another point in Xavier's column." She shook her head.

"It'll look fishy either way, and I guarantee Long isn't going to take the loss well, but you may be right. You'll even have more time to train if you're not stuck in class all morning."

"Exactly! So let's see… I'm waiting a week or so to push for copper, setting aside my next three focus room hours to fake opening two meridians and forming my core, and practicing for the meditation two exam."

"And working on force palm," Charlotte added. "Like it or not, figuring it out is still your best chance at ever learning a technique. Mess with it. Experiment. I know trial and error isn't very exciting, but it's the only way you're going to figure out what isn't working."

"Yep, yep," I said, pantomiming typing notes into my holopad as I spoke. "Trial and error my way through the problem. I'll get right on that." I lowered my holopad to look directly at her. "In the meantime, could you clarify something for me?"

"Of course." Charlotte straightened in her seat. "That's what I'm here for. What's unclear? The qi regulation into the sigil? The classifications of different types of techniques? The synergies inherent in a well-rounded arsenal?"

"Yes, well, I was wondering…" I leaned in, resting my elbows on the table and clasping my hands together with my fingers intertwined. "What would be the best thing to meditate on for divine inspiration?"

Charlotte groaned.

I smiled back at her.

Xavier may've stormed off, and Nick may've hidden away nowhere to be seen, and my first attempts at magic may've fallen painfully flat, but none of that felt insurmountable. Charlotte and Xavier would inevitably patch things up before the day was out, Nick finally had a use for me now that I could externalize my qi, and as for the magic, well, apparently I just needed to find the right *inspiration*.

How hard could that be?

31

One day and precisely zero flashes of divine inspiration later, I awoke to something far more troubling: a missed call.

Okay, maybe that on its face isn't *that* troubling, at least until you account for the realization that the call came from Arthur—someone who'd called me a grand total of twice—at approximately four-thirty-two in the morning. Confused, groggy, and so far only a little bit worried, I took the obvious next step. I called him back.

Call failed.

That got me to sit up. I scowled at the message, mind scrambling for a reason the call might've failed. Arthur's shift at the reception desk started at six. He should've been downstairs by now, chilling behind his desk with little to do *but* answer calls. Maybe he'd taken a personal day? The kind he'd call me at four in the morning to warn me about?

I dismissed that thought before I even finished it. Either Arthur had some kind of family emergency, or those goons had finally stepped over the line. By the time I'd worked my way out of bed and into my uniform, a nasty feeling had settled in my stomach.

I grabbed my sword on the way out.

My next clue appeared the moment I mounted the stairway down to the lobby, from the top of which I had a clear line of sight to the reception desk. No Arthur. Wilma, her scowl even deeper than usual, stood in his place, her eyes dark and baggy, remnants of a night shift that'd left its mark. I made right for her.

"Wilma! Wilma, Wilma, Wilma. How are you this fine morning?"

"What do you want?" She half-growled-half-slurred the words, like an angry alcoholic or a very tired rottweiler.

"Where's Arthur? Isn't it his shift?"

"He never showed. I'm stuck here waiting while they find a temp to replace him."

I furrowed my brow. "That doesn't sound like him. Did he say what happened?"

"Not to me, not to Saul."

Saul's the building manager. He's not important.

My heart rate sped. "He didn't call in?"

"No." Wilma snapped. "If he did I'd have given him a piece of my mind. Do you know where he is?"

"I don't," I answered, swallowing back a knot in my throat. "But I think I might have an idea. Thanks, Wilma."

She grunted at me.

Fighting back my urge to ridicule the use of a grunt in lieu of actual words, I left the reception desk behind, tapping away at my holopad as I made for the transport platform.

Xavier, at least, actually picked up. "Hello?"

"Xavier! Where are you? Actually, nevermind. I need your help. Arthur's missing."

"Arthur...?"

"The receptionist," a feminine voice groggily drifted over the comm link.

"Oh, good morning, Charlotte," I greeted her, opting not

to wonder how exactly they'd gone from storming off yesterday to waking up next to each other today. "You're together. That's perfect. I need your help tracking him down."

"Why do you need our help tracking down your receptionist?"

"They're friends," Xavier said.

"I *know* they're friends," Charlotte hissed. "Friends don't *track each other down.*"

"I think he's in trouble," I explained as a transport pod arrived and I stepped in. "He called me at four AM this morning, didn't leave a message, and now I can't get through to his holopad. Worse yet, he's AWOL from work. Poor Wilma's been stuck here something like eleven hours. I think those guys from the bar might've pulled something."

"Cal, that was half a year ago," Charlotte said. "He was probably out late and overslept. He can't have been sober if he thought you'd answer his call at four in the morning."

"That's why I want you to check his place. Maybe he's there. Maybe there's something—or someone—that can tell us what happened. I'm heading to the Pony, see if I can pick up a trail there."

"We're on it!" Xavier committed before Charlotte could protest.

I grinned. "Thanks, guys. I really appreciate it. Arthur appreciates it!"

"Try not to get yourself killed," Charlotte warned. "There are dangerous people down in—"

"Oh, whoops, looks like my pod's arriving. Thanks for the help, bye!" I hung up before Charlotte could lecture me further. If my hunch was correct and this *was* about Arthur's sister, I'd scuffled with these guys before. Based on my prior experience, it wasn't exactly the most *professional* outfit.

Droe Lane was an entirely different place during the day. Sunlight banished the evening gloom, reducing the glare of the few beat-up screens and neon signs still plugged in to little more than a dull glow. The dissonant mess of adjacent nightclubs leaking their music into the street had vanished entirely, leaving a sense of eerie quiet as workers cleaned up the prior night's revelry.

The foot traffic too had transformed. Gone were the partiers and the prostitutes and the chem dealers, replaced by the horrid trundling specters of the hungover on their walks, shameful, prideful, or both, from wherever they'd spent the night. Had I an idle mind, I might've enjoyed guessing which had found beds and which had spent the night somewhere less... intentional.

The starkest change to Droe Lane in the light of dawn wasn't its populace or its clubs, but its *filth*. No more did a mass of pedestrians or evening murk disguise or distract from the grime of the place. The remnants of a dozen dropped meals and spilled drinks littered the street, a veritable minefield of mess just waiting for a misplaced shoe. The air reeked of vomit and urine, whether from the street itself or those that still walked it, I couldn't tell.

Dark stains and chipped paint characterized the buildings more than anything else, their unkempt facades obscured no more by the glare of their signs and backlit screens.

The city itself was hungover, and like any addict, it'd take but a few hours to clean itself up and get right back to it.

The Three-Legged Pony was no exception. Its door hung open, allowing exit for the—I counted three—patrons who yet slumbered at their tables. A middle-aged woman stood outside, wiping down the window with a rag that may have once dreamt of being white, but lived a reality of unflinching gray.

"Excuse me." I approached her. "I'm looking for a man named Arthur Kent. Yea high, medium weight, short, black hair. You seen him?"

She didn't even look at me. "Nope. I haven't seen anything."

"Are you sure? What about two taller gentlemen, buzz cuts, arms the size of my thigh, about twelve brain cells between the two of them?"

She didn't answer.

"What if I told you their names are meathead, and meatshoulders? No, wait, those are their nicknames. Their name names are Dennis and Humphrey."

The woman froze for a moment before continuing her window washing. "You can tell Victor I didn't see anything."

"Lady, look at me. I'm a cadet with the Dragon's Right Eye. You really think I'm working for *Victor?*"

She finally turned to face me, lowering her rag-carrying hand into the pocket of her apron as she sized me up, most notably the rank icon on my breast. The hollow circle denoted me as somewhat of an anomaly—a cadet that hadn't formed his core. The insignia was, of course, *wrong*, but she didn't know that. The only question was whether she concluded I was a special case, or that the uniform was fake.

I cut to the chase. "Look, my friend is missing, and I think this Victor guy had something to do with it. Where can I find him?"

She shook her head. "I didn't see anything."

"Yes, yes, I know you didn't see anything. You've been clear on that front. But you either know Victor, or you know enough about him to be scared of him. Does that include where he might be?"

"I'm sorry, sir. I can't help you." She turned back to her task.

I squinted at it. "That window is clean! Look, I just need to know..." I sighed. This wasn't getting me anywhere. I wasn't going to talk her out of being afraid. I did have another option, but it was one I loathed to implement. Unfortunately, the ticking clock left me little choice.

I put on my aviators, leaned in close, and cycled my sense meridian. "I get it. Victor's a scary man. He has goons. I'm sure you pay him a tidy sum to keep this place safe. The thing is, I'm pretty sure Victor's taken a friend of mine, a friend I would very much like to see again. If you're afraid of what Victor will do if you talk..." I lowered my sunglasses to reveal my black and star-filled eyes staring directly into hers. "Imagine what I'll do if you help him keep my friend from me."

"Gordon Street," she whispered the name. "There's a flower shop. Victor works out of the back."

I returned the dark lenses to my face and flashed her a smile. "See, that wasn't so hard. Thank you kindly."

"You won't—" She gulped. "You won't tell Victor I..."

"Don't worry," I said as I turned to go. "Victor won't be the one asking the questions."

I left her with that, heart pounding in my chest as I mentally fawned over how *badass* that felt. Yeah, I felt kind of guilty about threatening that poor woman, but there was no getting around that Victor had already done the same. Only way to get her talking was to convince her I was just as scary, something my scrawny ass had never actually managed before. Ten points for spooky space eyes.

I rode that high for about eight steps before I had to pull out my holopad to look up where the hell Gordon Street actually *was*. As it turns out, spooky space eyes: badass. Confidently walking off in the wrong direction: not so badass.

Xavier called as I navigated Droe towards where it met

with Gordon. I walked as we talked. "Anything at his place?"

"He's not here," came Xavier's reply. "Cal, this place is a nightmare. Arthur's entire apartment is smaller than Charlotte's *bed*."

"How did you *think* the mortals lived? Square footage is pricey. Anything leap out at you?"

"Wednesday is laundry day," he answered. "There are five sets of dirty—"

"Xavier!" Charlotte's voice interrupted. "Priorities. The door was kicked in. Either someone searched his place—"

"Or he was taken," I finished. "Shit. Okay. I think I have a lead on where. Something about a protection racket running out of a flower shop on Gordon Street. I'll bet that's where Arthur is."

"A flower shop? They're extorting people from a *flower shop?*"

"It's more intimidating with the two goons out front," I answered as the shop in question came into view. Sure enough, Dennis and Humphrey flanked the entrance. "In Full Bloom, on Gordon," I confirmed the name.

"You're there?" Charlotte asked. "Cal, wait for us. We'll be there in fifteen."

Right on schedule, a muffled yet distinctly identifiable scream echoed from somewhere beyond the storefront, one not of rage or terror, but of agony and desperation. Neither of the guards even flinched. "No can do," I muttered into the holopad. "It sounds like they're working him right now."

"They've had him for four hours, Cal. He'll make it another fifteen minutes."

"He might." Another scream rang out. I wrapped white knuckles around Shiver's hilt. "But I won't."

"Cal—Cal, listen to—"

I hung up. One of a very small group of people on

Fyrion who'd been nothing but friends to me was being tortured in there, and I'd be damned if I waited around outside any longer than I had to. Besides, I'd gone up against tweedle-dumb and tweedle-dumber before, and while this time they saw me coming, I wasn't the same fighter today as I was back then.

And this time I had a motherfucking *sword*.

"Meathead! Meatshoulders! Fancy seeing you here," I announced my presence as I approached, arms out and palms up in a friendly gesture.

"He came!" Dennis snapped at Humphrey under his breath. "I told you he'd come."

"And I told *you*, this time I'm ready." Humphrey pulled up his T-shirt to reveal a piece of black metal shoved down his pants.

I stopped short, still some twenty feet away. "A slug thrower? Seriously? You're gonna punch a hole in the hull with that thing." I made a point of lowering my gaze to waist level. "Then again, with where you're keeping it, the hull might be the least of your worries."

Simultaneously hilarious and convenient as it might've been, Humphrey managed to avoid shooting his dick off as he tore the gun from its ill-advised holster. He *didn't* manage to get a shot off.

Not before I did.

I pulled enough qi from my newly formed core to cycle all twelve meridians at once. My skin hardened and turned deathly cold and pale. My bones indurated, my thoughts quickened, and, most critically, my muscles thrummed with *power*.

The world moved in slow motion as I rocketed forward at superhuman speed, my footsteps falling into the familiar step I'd drilled over and over again for closing in on a distant enemy: The Dragon Descends.

In hindsight, the goons never stood a chance.

Humphrey's pistol still pointed at the floor by the time I reached him. His arms, easily triple the size of mine, moved like putty in my hands as I yanked one to the side and wrenched the gun from the other. Grasping it by its muzzle, I resisted the instinct to slam the butt of the pistol into the bruiser's head. Asshole or otherwise, he didn't deserve to have his skull caved in.

Of course, my qi-chilled mind didn't really care what he did or didn't deserve, but the math worked out in his favor. Anyone else probably would've gotten away with it, but my position at the sect was tenuous enough to slot murder firmly in the "bad idea" category.

So I dislocated his shoulder instead. It was startlingly easy. I simply tugged on the wrist I already held in my left hand, sending him tumbling to the ground as a distinct pop reached my ears.

Dennis hadn't even moved. His brother in goonhood had gone from drawing his gun to laying on the ground with his arm bent in the wrong direction before *he'd* even had time to take a step.

I raised an eyebrow at him beneath my aviators. "You heard him. This time he came prepared."

Something about my corpselike skin, skeletal features, and voice entirely devoid of emotion scared the absolute bejesus out of Dennis. Well, either that or the fact I'd dispatched his colleague in under two seconds.

He ran.

I squinted at him as I watched him sprint away, oh so nobly leaving Humphrey alone with me and his dislocated shoulder. "Damn," I muttered. "I didn't even get a chance to use my *sword*." I glanced down at Humphrey. "You up for a round two?"

Humphrey groaned.

A second scream echoed from somewhere inside the flower shop.

I tossed the magazine from Humphrey's weapon in one direction and the pistol itself in the other on the off chance Dennis had taken all twelve brain cells with him and Humphrey got it in his head to follow me. For good measure, I stomped on his left forearm, leaving a nasty bruise as I crushed the implanted chip that drove his holopad. Victor would receive no warning from him.

I moved for the entrance.

The door was locked.

Was.

Okay, sure, I suppose *technically* it remained locked even after I knocked it from its hinges, but come on. It wasn't even difficult. With qi still running through my muscles like an ice flow, all it took was the base of my palm slamming against the hollow aluminum to tear the screws right from their holes. The door landed a few feet from its frame, leaning nearly upright against an innocent orchid and a lily that was looking at me all shifty-eyed.

I stepped around it.

In Full Bloom reminded me in a lot of ways of Nick's dorm room, a veritable forest of potted plants crowding up a cramped and gloomy space. At least this place had the excuse that the lights were off. I didn't bother turning them on. The artificial daylight blaring in from the street more than satisfied my qi-enhanced eyes, even behind the dark lenses I wore.

The shop was empty. No henchmen rushed me, no ringleader tortured my captive friend, and no friendly old lady tried to sell me flowers. I scowled. *Somebody* had to have heard me break the door down, right?

I vaulted over the counter, shattering a terra cotta vase in the process, and made straight for the door marked *employees only*. This one they hadn't bothered to lock, saving me both the effort and element of surprise as I burst through to find... nothing. A tiny back room complete with sink, wire shelves of sod and supplies, and little else greeted me.

I surveyed the space, drinking in the little details in a torrent of information as I made sense of it all. In the near blackness of the unlit room I searched, standing stock-still as my eyes flitted from wall to wall. The sink caught my eye, a deep and rectangular thing built large enough to fit multiple pots or vases or watering cans or whatever flower shops needed water for. I'd seen the like before in a janitor's closet back on roofie.

Except this wasn't that. Its spout was at the same level, and its basin was roughly the same dimensions, but instead of ending at the bottom of the sink to expose the plumbing beneath, the basin's walls extended all the way to the floor. I knelt down and ran a finger along its base. Sure enough, it wasn't actually attached, sitting ever so slightly above the cold concrete.

I pushed.

With a muffled *crack* confirming that I'd broken some mechanism or other, the entire sink receded into the back wall, exposing a metal ladder down into some dark passage. I hopped right in.

I landed with a gentle clang onto a catwalk of sorts, some kind of suspended walkway comprised of sheet metal attached to the ceiling. It extended far into the distance to both my right and left, well past the point at which the gentle curve of the tunnel broke my line of sight. Behind me, a metal wall closed off that entire side. Ahead, a matching one lasted for all of twenty feet in each direction before disappearing, exposing the empty air beneath the catwalk.

From the right, a deep rumbling reached my ear, rapidly crescendoing as its source drew nearer. The catwalk itself quaked beneath my feet and a rush of air blasted across my face.

And then it passed. The noise faded, the shaking ceased, and I realized exactly where I was.

The transport tubes. Victor had his very own access point to maintenance tunnels for the gods damned *transport tubes*. Threads, he could probably get anywhere in the city from down here. A scream sounded to my left, muffled no more as it echoed through the empty passage. A voice followed.

"I am not a patient man, mister Kent. Now are you going to tell me where my dear Clara has gone, or do I need to get serious?"

"She's not your dear," Arthur growled. "And I've already told you. She's *gone*. Offworld and not coming back."

"Yes, yes, you've been clear about that. Offworld *where?*"

I rounded the corner to find two men, one wielding a pair of pliers, the other tied to a chair, in the middle of a catwalk that crossed over the tunnel proper. Victor did not look remotely as intimidating as he sounded.

The ghastly pale glow of the cheap LED lamps fell upon a small and pudgy man, no more than five foot five yet easily over two hundred pounds. Greasy hair more gray than black circled a bald spot atop his head, leaving him looking more like everyone's least favorite uncle than the head of a protection racket.

"You heard the man." I announced my presence in the inhumanly even tone my barely breathing lungs produced. "She's not your dear."

"Cal," Arthur breathed with audible relief.

"What do you want?" Victor asked. "The sect has no business here."

"Neither does he." I nodded towards Arthur. "And yet here he is."

Victor didn't move. He didn't speak. He stared at me in

silent stillness as if evaluating the situation, coming up with a way to talk himself out of this.

But he couldn't hide from me. I heard the pounding of his heart. I saw the little twitch in his eye. I caught the tension in his right arm as it moved ever so slowly behind his back. The faint rumble of an approaching pod echoed in the distance.

By the time he burst into action, Shiver was already in my hand. Before his knife could even reach Arthur's throat, I was upon him.

"Come any closer and I—"

The threat died on his lips. His arm fell limp into Arthur's lap, severed at the elbow before it could deliver on its promise of violence. Not even the roar of the transport pod below us could mask the man's scream.

Victor fell to his knees and clutched his stump to his belly, stemming the bleeding as best he could.

I looked down upon him, this fat, greasy, weasel of a man, and pulled the sunglasses from my face to reveal the black and starry eyes beneath. He gazed into them transfixed, adrenaline and horror clashing with an unexpected wonder on his face.

As the roar of the transport faded into the distance, I delivered my message. "This man and his sister are under sect protection. Do you understand?"

Victor nodded.

"Good. You'd better get going then. You don't have long before the blood loss starts to take effect."

Victor scrambled to his feet and took off, racing desperately away until he disappeared around a corner. I let him leave. Hopefully the threat would stick, and if it didn't I supposed I could always come back. Killing him might've been simpler, but it *also* might've gotten me kicked out.

I slipped my glasses back on to cover my eyes as I

turned my attention to Arthur. "Can you walk?"

"I... I think so."

"Good." Three swipes of my blade sent the cords binding him falling to the catwalk. "Let's get you out of here." I grabbed his wrist to help him up, bypassing his mangled hands in the process. He shivered at my touch.

I called in a medical transport as we walked back towards the flower shop. I climbed the ladder first, reaching down to again pull Arthur up by his wrist. We made it out to the street just in time to find Charlotte and Xavier browbeating a frightened Humphrey, who, in my absence, had managed to make it to his feet and lean against the storefront.

"Cal!" Charlotte greeted me. "Are you okay?"

"Of course he's okay! He has a warrior's spirit!"

"He's white as a ghost and covered in blood."

"Not mine," I explained. "Medics are on their way. Victor did a number on Arthur's hands."

Charlotte paled before my eyes as she glimpsed the damage. "And Victor is...?"

"Gone. No doubt he'll be back extorting again with a shiny new prosthetic in a few days, but he'll leave Arthur alone."

"Good. Good." She looked me up and down. "You should go."

"Charlotte, I can't just leave—"

"We'll take it from here. If the medics see you like this, there're going to be questions."

I exhaled. She was right. Why did she have to be *right?* "Okay." I wiped Shiver on my thigh—what was a little more blood when you're already covered in it?—and returned it to its sheath. I turned to Arthur. "You'll be alright?"

He swallowed and nodded. "I'll—I'll be fine. Th-thank you. If you hadn't come, I don't know what I would've—"

"Best not to think about that." I stopped him. "And you're welcome." I gestured down to my sect uniform. "What's the point of all this if we can't protect our friends?" I looked to Charlotte and Xavier. "Take care of him."

And with that I left, striding right down Gordon Street with a sword on my back and somebody else's blood down my front. Only once I'd turned the corner, disappeared from Arthur's line of sight, did I cease the flow of qi through my meridians.

Color and warmth and horror returned to the world. I stumbled as the coppery stench of blood reached my nose, no longer a single detail in a panoply of scents as it overpowered my unenhanced senses. My heart pounded. My stomach churned. For a few moments I stopped short, strongly considering giving up on that morning's breakfast.

But then I kept walking.

Arthur was okay.

He'd need a few days to recover physically and probably a few years to recover emotionally, but he would, in time, recover.

I was okay.

My nausea would pass, and though I had a brand-new traumatic experience to heap onto the pile, I knew it wouldn't slow me down.

Everything was going to be okay.

If anything I felt vindicated, justified in working myself to the bone day in and day out to advance my cultivation, hone my skills, and grow all the more lethal in the process. For all I wanted to learn and to prove myself, for all I waxed poetic about flailing against infinity, *this* was what it was all about: the power to protect those I cared about, to change things for the better even in what tiny ways I could.

For the first time in my already long and arduous

cultivation journey, I'd come against those that would do harm, and actually been able to *do* something about it. Even harrowed and bloodstained and sick to my stomach, I couldn't deny the other emotion welling up within my chest: pride.

I'd done good. I'd helped my friend. And sure, it might've been against a bunch of mortals who hadn't stood a chance, but I'd finally tasted that glorious victory Xavier never shut up about.

I think I could get used to it.

32

"I still can't believe Xavier beat me to copper," I muttered to myself as I stacked a handful of apple seeds with a pair of tweezers.

"How are you still on that?" Nick asked without looking up from his genetic resequencing tool. "It's been two weeks."

"Shit." The tower of seeds I'd assembled collapsed—four high, just shy of my record.

Nick let out a sigh. "Some copper you are."

"I'm trying, okay? Divine inspiration isn't easy to come by."

The handful of months since Arthur's kidnapping had passed almost painfully quickly, a haze of exhausting routine broken up exclusively by my advancement to copper mere hours after Xavier's. We'd celebrated both achievements in one epic night of drinking, dancing, and, most importantly, karaoke—a tradition *I* intended to continue whether or not Charlotte was altogether too good of a singer for it.

The advancement process itself had been... honestly, kind of boring. I guess the exciting part was that I'd managed in weeks what had taken every single cultivator

Fyrion had ever seen *years*. Xavier himself, late bloomer that he was, had spent half a decade tempering his focus, perfecting his ability to scrape together every minuscule mote of qi from his food, his environment, and his focus hours just to build up enough to push for copper, a skillset that would serve him well along his Way.

I'd taken one sip from the infinite sea and gone to town.

Yes, it was unfair. Yes, if I expended a single modicum of thought it was obvious I had no right to expect I'd beat Xavier to copper. That didn't stop my competitive side from lamenting the fact. And hey, I may've had a lot of it, but at least his qi *did something*. Mine just sat there.

I pulled my thoughts inward to gaze at my upgraded core. It didn't look much different.

It had grown some thirty percent larger, the exact opposite of what most cultivators experienced as they condensed their qi to push to copper. With the infinite sea at my fingertips, I'd already more than reclaimed that lost volume. More noticeably, dull brown flecks had appeared, tiny spots of metallic color along the charcoal sphere. I imagined they'd grow larger and more plentiful as I climbed the metal tiers.

Bronze, however, wouldn't be so easy. I'd have to craft a focus out of natural treasures and something spiritually significant to me personally. I already had an idea for the latter, but the former would mean waiting for a chance to join one of the hunting excursions on Ilirian. Threads knew how long that would take.

"Okay." Nick's voice pulled me from my thoughts. "This one's just about ready."

I leaned over in my seat—a stool we'd pilfered from downstairs—and peered through the magnifying lens at the seed in question.

"On the count of three," Nick told me, frustration still clear in his voice. "One... two... three!"

Through the enchanted glass I could see a tiny spark of dormant qi leave the seed. At the same moment, I pushed a flow of my own qi into it. Most went elsewhere, billowing out in all directions as my qi tended to do, but by virtue of going everywhere, some *did* end up inside the seed.

Just not enough.

Three seconds later, Nick let out a resigned breath. "And it's dead." He tossed the seed in the trash with the other failures.

"Sorry. I'm trying."

"You're stacking seeds on top of each other," he snapped. "Cal, this is *important*. You need fine control. Any tin should be able to do this."

"I'm not any tin."

"You're right. A year ago you barely knew what cultivating *was*. It's no surprise you can hardly control your qi."

"Nick, it's not that simple," I tried. "You know my qi doesn't—"

"No. I don't know. That's the *problem*, Cal. You have a preteen's understanding of how any of this works, and because nobody can sense your qi, nobody can tell you what you're doing *wrong*."

I took a breath. "I'm trying," I repeated. "Do you want to take a break?"

"No." He pulled another seed from the pile. "We'll go again."

That was the other major development since I'd first formed my core. As time went on, Nick grew increasingly certain in his belief that my inexperience was the only reason our attempts kept failing. He probably wasn't *entirely* wrong, but I hated that he couldn't see the problem for himself. Fine control became a whole lot harder when the task at hand was pushing out a cloud of qi and hoping the exact right amount ended up inside the seed rather than in the air around it.

Of course, it wasn't *all* for nothing.   Pitiful as my attempts at externalization may have been, the qi *inside* my body worked wonders.   It turns out, all that cycling and fortifying and whatnot really works. My qi pathways were wider than ever, and now at copper I'd begun experiencing a number of benefits even without cycling.

It was actually sort of a problem.   The sect officially thought I'd just reached tin, and all my peers in housing D still saw me as the weak mortal at the bottom of the rankings. I'd spent the last three weeks purposely gimping my morning workouts to maintain the illusion.

Dueling day had certainly gotten interesting, though. As a copper, I thoroughly overpowered the tins my sect rank paired me against, none of whom used their one advantage—qi attacks—for fear of disrespecting their weaker opponent. Nobody wanted another clown show.

Instead I got to play this fun game of pretending their punches hurt or going *just* limp enough to let them restrain me while still looking like I was fighting back.   Xavier didn't like the idea of throwing matches, but Charlotte supported it full-heartedly.   They'd actually broken up over the subject, though considering they were back together again by dinnertime, I didn't hold it against them.

Either way, the fun was ending.   Lopez's deadline loomed, and if I wanted any leeway in case the combat two or three instructors proved problematic, time was officially up. Tomorrow morning, just after breakfast, I was taking a transport pod to housing A to issue a formal challenge to one Senior Cadet Long.

Then the game would be up. If I lost, my time at the Dragon's Right Eye would be over. If I won, I'd rocket up the rankings, and everyone would know I was more powerful than I was letting on.

I couldn't wait.

"Ready." Nick directed my attention to the next seed he'd isolated from the pile. "On three."

I again leaned in and channeled a small cloud of qi at the seed on Nick's cue, taking care to add just a *little* bit more than last time.

It popped like a balloon.

"Damnit," Nick cursed. "Too much, Cal. Way too much."

"That was barely more than the last one."

"Obviously not. You overloaded it."

"Maybe I need one of those stylus things," I tried. "It could just be an issue of foreign qi entering—"

"Cal, we've been over this. I modified it to match your spiritual signature. Your qi isn't foreign to it."

"Right, right, the seed's technically my cousin and all that."

"What? No. What are you talking about? Cal, if that's all you've taken away from my explanation—"

"I'm kidding, I'm kidding," I interrupted. "Maybe we're too slow? The dead seed you showed me earlier popped like that."

"You told me you lasted several minutes between your old qi being drained and your new qi flooding in. The scale is smaller, but these seeds are dormant. If anything, they should last *longer*."

"You're saying this seed is heartier than I am?"

"Alright. You know what?" Nick slammed both palms into the tabletop and pushed himself to his feet. "I'll do it myself."

"That's your plan? Find the infinite sea? Nick, you've been trying for months."

"And I'm closer to it than you are to basic control," he growled at me as he stepped past.

"I'm telling you, it's harder than you think."

He stopped at the door. "Go practice for your fight tomorrow. We both know that's where you'd rather be." With that he vanished, out into the hallway and whichever window he planned to meditate at.

I stayed on my stool and quietly sighed. Teenagers, right? No matter what I said, I couldn't seem to get it into his head that this all frustrated me more than anyone. *I* was the one who couldn't do any magic.

Shaking my head, I pushed myself to my feet and waded through the forest of potted plants for the door. By the time I made it out into the hallway, Nick was nowhere to be seen.

I shoved aside that problem for later. He was right about one thing, if for the wrong reasons. There *was* somewhere I'd rather be, if only for tonight, if only for Nick's benefit. Wherever he'd stormed off to, I couldn't look after him if the sect kicked me out.

I arrived early at the sparring ring, skipping dinner entirely. I wasn't hungry.

I ran through my forms while I waited, both the entirety of the Dragon's Fang and the handful of steps I'd borrowed from Cedric. They flowed together neatly, the product of months of practice with a handful of AI analysis tossed in. The bots weren't great at telling you when or where a particular step would prove useful—too many unknowns —but they knew better than anyone which motions combined best.

By the time Xavier arrived, I'd already broken a sweat.

"No Charlotte?" I halted my practice as he climbed into the ring.

"Charlotte's not speaking with me," Xavier explained. "She... doesn't think you should challenge Long."

"I knew that. *You* said I could win."

"It's not just that." Xavier exhaled. "Right now Long considers you an annoyance, a weakling that doesn't belong here. He'll take personal offense if you challenge him. He'll probably try to maim or kill you in the ring, and that's if you lose. Should you win, Long will drop at least a few hundred ranks and suffer a major embarrassment. He and anyone aligned with him will be your enemy for life."

I sighed. We'd been over this before. Threads, I hadn't stopped thinking about it since I first decided to challenge Long. Lucy'd warned me before I even set foot on Fyrion that I should avoid making enemies, especially powerful enemies.

The problem was, I'd already failed. Weak as he thought me, I disrespected Long merely by existing. Once it came out how powerful I really was, I'd morph from an intruder to a threat to his entire worldview. Beating him in the ring, showing that I wasn't only strong but stronger than he was for all the world to see, was my best shot at asserting my right to be here.

Putting Long in his place was just a side perk.

"He's already my enemy," I summarized. "And I won't abandon you guys. I won't abandon Nick."

Xavier shrugged. "Charlotte's words, not mine. If Long is weaker, he deserves to lose. If Long is stronger, he'll win. His opinions on the matter are of no consequence."

I spent a moment staring across the sparring ring at Xavier, trying to parse the sheer dissonance between the two perspectives. "It astounds me that you and Charlotte are a couple."

"Right now, we aren't," Xavier replied like it meant nothing. I supposed after the fiftieth break-up, they stopped hitting so hard. He raised his practice sword. "Ready?"

I charged him.

He met my advance, lunging forward with aggression of his own. I slipped into Cedric-three—we hadn't bothered coming up with creative names for the borrowed forms—and caught the weak of his blade against my lowered crossguard. The move knocked my sword out of position, but it raised my elbow just in time for it to collide with Xavier's face.

He stumbled back.

I got my sword back up first.

"Touché," Xavier stepped back.

I grinned at him. "Again."

Xavier burst into motion, exploding across the arena almost faster than I could raise my weapon. He went into The Dragon's Raised Ire, an overhand strike that brought his superior reach to bear.

I tried to counter with Cedric-six—a weak deflect designed to leave my blade at his throat—but as I committed to the move Xavier's feet shifted, his sword pulled back, and his left hand shot forth.

He grabbed me by the throat. I tapped his wrist to signal my concession.

"Again."

Back and forth and back and forth we sparred, the hours drifting by as we came at each other again and again. Xavier got the better of me more times than not, a worrying prospect but for my own smattering of victories. Thankfully—no doubt intentionally—Xavier called a halt with his back on the floor and my boot on his chest.

"We'll stop here. Don't want you to wake up sore tomorrow."

I held out a hand and helped him up. "What do you think?"

"You beat me one in three fights," Xavier reasoned, "and Long is a stronger fighter than I. He's over a thousand ranks higher, but that's in part because he's been copper for years as opposed to weeks."

I grimaced. "That puts my odds at... below one in

three? Call that one in ten?"

"No, no." Xavier shook his head. "They're better. Much better. I've been sparring with you for almost a year now. I know what you're capable of. I've seen all the steps you learned from Lucy's recordings. I've practiced against them. Senior Cadet Long thinks you're beneath him. He'll underestimate you, and he won't expect forms that aren't a part of the Dragon's Fang."

"Good," I muttered. "That's good."

"It is good, isn't it?" Xavier grinned. He stepped up and placed a hand on my shoulder, looking me dead in the eye as he told me, "You can win this, Cal. I know it."

I returned a weak smile of my own.

"Now, get some rest." He clapped me on the back. "Tomorrow there'll be glorious victory."

"Thanks, Xave. Really. I wouldn't even be remotely close without your help."

"The only greater honor than making it through one's crucibles is to see one's friends safely through their own."

I blinked at him. "Did you just come up with that?"

"Come up with...?" Xavier squinted. "It's a simple statement."

"Right. Of course it is. Nevermind."

"Goodnight, Caliban," Xavier bid me as I gathered my things. "Dream of triumph. You'll find it come morning."

As we went our separate ways, he back to housing B and I up to the third floor, my mind pondered Xavier's words. It struck me as odd—odd that he'd pull such a poetic platitude out of nowhere, odd that even after defeating me he still thought I'd beat Long, and odder yet that for all his idiosyncrasies and blatant overconfidence, by the time I made it into bed, I'd arrived at a startling conclusion.

I believed him.

33

I slept like the dead. I dreamt, as I did most nights, of the infinite sea, drifting along in pleasant nothingness. The all-important duel the following morning didn't matter. Nothing mattered.

So it was with a full eight hours I plodded my way downstairs, waved to the custodian as he vacuumed the second-floor hallway, and headed to the gym. There, I did a light twenty-mile run and a few stretches to get my blood flowing without tiring myself out, and went to breakfast.

I smiled to Wilma on my way over, who seemed marginally less grumpy now that management had given her Arthur's dayshift. Kidnapping or otherwise, you can't just no-call no-show without scheduling consequences. Arthur seemed happy enough on the nightshift anyway.

Charlotte and Xavier beat me to the cafeteria, making the trek over to housing D under the cover of strategizing while we ate. They revealed their true nefarious purpose soon enough.

"Cal, you have to *eat*." Charlotte shoved a plate of hash browns across the table at me.

"I told you, I'm not hungry."

"Even the mightiest of the ancient soulships needs to

refuel," Xavier said.

"It's a good thing I'm not a ship," I countered.

Xavier shook his head. "How can you hope to find glorious victory if you deny your body the strength it needs?"

"*My body* is not hungry," I repeated.

Charlotte took a different tact, picking up my fork and skewering a bite of the fried potato. She pointed it at me threateningly. "You can either take this and eat it like a grown adult or I'll feed it to you like a petulant infant."

I stared into her eyes.

She stared back, unflinching in her resolve.

"Fine," I grumbled and snatched the loaded utensil away from her.

It didn't escape my notice that the pair of them watched me like particularly judgmental hawks as I slogged my way through bite after bite of hash browns. The breakfast was hot and crispy and wonderfully salty, yet no amount of deliciousness could materialize appetite where there was none.

It came as no surprise that they'd shown up for breakfast together. Whether or not they'd been speaking with each other last night, they lived together, and like clockwork they always managed to resolve their disputes by morning.

I similarly didn't bat an eye at Nick's absence. Sure, I hadn't seen him since he'd stormed out yesterday, but the kid slept through breakfast more days than not. I wasn't worried. Not yet, at least.

"Try not to use the same trick more than once," Xavier said as we bussed our trays. "Surprise is your biggest advantage, and Long will be quick to adapt."

I nodded along to his advice, only half-listening to the tips I'd heard a dozen times before while my mind scrambled through a much more important element of my strategy: finding some good zingers.

Jokes aside, there was only upside to getting Long riled up. He would almost certainly try to hurt me anyway, so I didn't have to worry about the repercussions of disrespecting him, so any way to throw him off his game would favor me.

Besides, making an ass of myself was my greatest talent.

I even had the advantage that while his qi would make him quicker to anger, mine kept me calm. Way, *way* too calm, but still calm. I figured with Long actively trying to kill me, *motivation* would be the least of my worries.

The three of us sat in tense silence as the transport pod whisked us to Long's residence.

For all its hallowed name, prime location, and position as the sect's most fiercely sought-after accommodations, housing A looked remarkably like housing D. The same sparsely occupied seating filled the lobby; the same hanging plants dangled their leaves above; the same circular reception desk greeted new visitors.

I noticed three differences. The first was the crowding. Unlike my own abode, cadets filled housing A to the brim, doubling or even tripling up in every dorm on every floor for maximum access to that sweet, sweet qi.

Which brings me to my second observation. The air was thick with it. Easily triple the qi pervaded the environment here than at housing D, a quantifiable advantage for those that would win their way here.

The final, and perhaps starkest difference was the looks we got as we crossed the lobby. I was used to glares of superiority. I was used to morbid curiosity, disdain, and even predatory hunger, the disquieting leer given a meal to be devoured, a weakling to be exploited.

I wasn't used to dismissal.

It… bothered me, more than perhaps it should've, as cadet after cadet looked up at us, lingered for under a second, then returned to whatever they'd been doing. There was no interest in the strange offworlder, no disgust at the upstart mortal, only the quiet glance of momentary diversion followed by the immediate decision that *we weren't worth their attention*.

It felt like I'd discovered an entirely new form of cultivator egotism. Neat.

"What do you want, mortal?" a voice snarled behind me.

I spun to find Long and his lackey Charleston sneering at us. Where Davis, the only combat instructor who didn't hate me, was, I couldn't guess.

I saluted as sarcastically as I could manage. Have you ever tried to *salute* sarcastically? It's not easy. Good thing practice makes perfect.

"I would like to test out of combat one, Senior Cadet Long, sir."

Long raised a perfectly shaped eyebrow—did he pluck them? I bet he plucked them—at Charlotte and Xavier behind me. "And your… reinforcements are supposed to intimidate me?"

I stayed at attention. "No, sir."

"Too bad. You failed." Long stepped in, bringing his face just shy of licking range as he glared into my eyes. "You don't belong here, *mortal*. You're not talented enough, not dedicated enough, not *good enough*, and by the end of the week, the esteemed Elder Lopez's timer will run out, and the entire sect will see you for what you are."

He spat at the floor beneath my feet.

"Request denied." Long turned his back to me.

I let out a long, overdramatic sigh that, in hindsight, was probably too much. "I'd hoped I wouldn't have to do this," I muttered just loud enough for the eavesdroppers to hear. I raised my voice again as I addressed the asshole in front of me.

"Senior Cadet Bao Long, I, Caliban Rex, hereby challenge you to a duel."

An overpowering silence filled the air. Nobody spoke. Nobody breathed. Nobody blinked. A chill ran down my back as I felt every eye in the room on me, every ear eagerly awaiting Long's reply.

He let out a laugh, a single, deep and throaty outburst that tried and failed to pierce the tension in the room. "The jokester's finally said something funny." He spun to face me. "You formed your core, what, a week ago?"

I blinked, somewhat surprised he'd been following my progress in the official sect records. I hadn't even seen the man since I'd stopped attending his class.

"Your attempts at humor have been duly noted," Long sneered. As he moved to again turn his back to me, I raised my voice once more.

"I've challenged you to an official duel, Long." I spoke loud enough for the whole crowd to hear, purposefully foregoing the honorifics. "By sect law you're bound to either accept or forfeit your place at the Dragon's Right Eye."

Long stopped short as he realized his attempt to blow me off had failed. I wish I could've seen his face, but he'd kept it turned.

He rounded on me. "I will offer you one final chance to recant and apologize for this grave insult," he growled. "I am Bao Long, chief enforcer of sect security, instructor of our most precious young, and the one-hundred-eighty-ninth strongest cultivator on all of Fyrion. You, mortal, are an upstart weakling who's only just begun to understand what a cultivator even *is*. So before you open that foul mouth of yours, I'd urge you to remember your place here, and know that with these next words you speak, you court death."

I raised an eyebrow at him. "No, no, you've got it all

wrong. Death and I had a fling last year, but it went kind of sideways, and now things are awkward between us." I flashed a mocking grin. "We dueling, or what?"

His left eye twitched—actually *twitched*, at the glibness with which I'd ignored his threat. He replied under his breath, low enough that even I mere inches away barely heard him. "You'll pay for this." Then he pulled back, seeming to collect himself as he answered differently for the audience. "I graciously accept this opportunity to educate. Come." He beckoned. "To the ring."

The silence popped like a balloon as Long turned on his heel and strode towards the gymnasium. The crowd flowed like a tide after him, a din of excited chatter and rampant speculation and blatant offense blaring through the air around them.

Charlotte, Xavier, and I followed. The housing A residents kept their distance, the space around us an island in the river of cultivators, but that didn't stop me from overhearing snippets of their conversations.

"—practically committing suicide. He can't be that—"

"—either an idiot or he has something up his sleeve. Maybe the rumors are true about—"

"—care how many tricks he's hiding. No way a tin beats a copper. It's impossible."

"—put five hundred credits the outworlder doesn't survive the fight."

I leaned in to whisper in Charlotte's ear. "There're rumors about me?"

"Of course there are. Don't worry about them. They've mostly been working in your favor."

I furrowed my brow. "Mostly?"

"Focus, Cal," Xavier interrupted.

"Right, right. I'm focused." I ran qi through my heart to slow its pounding, fighting off the mounting nerves. The attention was almost worse than the looming duel. I'd been preparing for this fight for months now; I was ready for it. I *hadn't* been ready for so many of the sect's top cultivators excitedly chattering about watching me die.

Too bad I was going to disappoint them. I hoped.

Much like the rest of it, the housing A gymnasium was the mirror image of housing D's but for a few minor details. The track, the dueling rings, the glass roof were all the same, yet the exercise equipment that lined the walls seemed newer, more advanced. That didn't come as a surprise. Threads, it even made sense. Coppers needed more intense workouts than tins.

The chatter slowly died down as I caught up to Long and the mortal official who'd spotted our approach. The official made no attempt to raise his voice for the audience, though I imagined plenty of sense meridians caught the exchange nonetheless.

"Registered duel between Bao Long and Caliban Rex." He looked to Long. "Weapons?"

"Free choice," Long said. The decision was technically an insult as he gave up his right to force me onto a weapon I may've been less comfortable with, but it was one we'd expected. Against an opponent so much weaker than he, Long couldn't afford to look like he needed such advantages.

I simply nodded and picked up a training sword from the ringside rack. Long followed suit.

The official tapped a few more times at his holopad. "Very well. You may step into the ring."

Long effortlessly jumped onto the shoulder-height platform as if it were nothing. I handed Xavier my sunglasses and Shiver and took the stairs.

We crossed to opposite sides of the ring. I took a breath. Long glared at me.

I started cycling.

The crowd erupted into a cacophony of whispers. I saw

fingers pointing and wide eyes staring as my skin went deathly pale and my eyes turned black as the night sky. The world dulled around me as my qi-enhanced mind made sense of the mess of information. In hushed tones our onlookers spoke of secret techniques and black Ways, of a heart that didn't beat and lungs that didn't draw breath. The words *demonic* and *necromantic* came up more than once.

What I didn't see was Nick. A pang of worry arose at the bottom of my stomach.

Through practiced discipline I blocked it out, reasoned against my own uncaring thoughts that right now, only Long mattered.

I caught the slight twitch of tension in his forehead as the visible effects of my cultivation made themselves clear. That was it. He otherwise masked his surprise expertly. If doubt had reared its ugly head in the dark corners of his mind, it stayed confined to there alone.

I raised my sword. The Dragon Prepares.

Long mirrored the motion. He knew as well as I did I'd never beat him at his own game.

The crowd fell silent. The starting gong rang.

Long charged in.

I kept Cedric's moves in reserve for the first exchange, relying on my first and foremost surprise to overcome his superior technique. My heightened senses spotted the tension in his calves as he approached. My hyper-analytical mind recognized the form before he even entered it.

The Breaking Swipe, step forty-four of The Dragon's Fang. It was an appropriate choice, a basic forehand swing whose only counter forced my blade to meet his. Against a weaker opponent, he'd break right through.

I stepped into The Fifth Guard anyway.

Long's sword crashed into mine with all the force of a

copper-tier cultivator backed by self-righteous fury.

And my defense held.

His weapon bounced back from the collision, putting it just out of position enough for my fist to shoot past his guard and collide right between his shocked eyes. Red dripped down his nose.

Long backstepped.

We'd trained that exact counter a thousand times. He should've been ready for it. He should've known exactly what I'd go for and found a way to either exploit it or a flaw in my execution.

But Long hadn't fathomed that my scrawny, "tin" self could've repelled his strike.

And now I'd drawn first blood.

I flashed him a shit-eating grin. "You fell for *The Fifth Guard*? Really? And they let you *teach?*" My jibe came out in the inhumanly calm tone my brain and lung meridians inflicted upon me, simultaneously robbing it of its comedic timing and creating the illusion I found this whole duel beneath me.

A blood vessel bulged on Long's face.

I stayed on the defensive, leaning into my spirit's natural tendency towards stillness as Long resumed his attack.

In an impressive display of stubborn arrogance I couldn't help but admire, he fell into The Breaking Swipe a second time, daring me to repeat my same defense.

I wasn't *that* stupid.

I tensed my muscles in just the right places to imply I intended to use The Fifth Guard again, but instead slipped into my true counter for Long's assault: Cedric-seven.

I brought my wooden sword up and at an angle just shy of parallel to his swing. The maneuver deflected his strike ever so slightly upward, just enough to send it sailing over my head as I ducked beneath it.

I leaned into the strike, slipping under Long's guard to retaliate with a blow of my own, but the senior cadet hadn't gotten this far without honing his instincts. Sensing the danger, he leapt back the moment his attack missed. I scored a grazing hit against his left ribs, not enough to end the duel, but a hit nonetheless.

I dashed past him before he could bring his sword to bear on my exposed back, crossing to the other side of the ring before I spun again to face him.

"Where did you learn that?" Long snarled at me.

"Not from you, obviously," I answered glibly. "That move's actually *good*."

Again he charged, abandoning The Breaking Swipe for The Fang That Bites. I met it with Cedric-two, again forcing Long onto the back foot, again failing to land a lethal blow as he reacted just in time to mitigate the damage.

The fight began in earnest.

Back and forth and back and forth we struck, our exchanges growing longer and more intense with every pass. It didn't take long for the obvious pattern to emerge. Whenever I pulled out another of Cedric's forms for the first time or used one against an attack I hadn't yet faced, I gained the upper hand, either forcing Long back or landing a superficial hit. Whenever I repeated myself, Long found an opening.

I realized quickly I was on a clock. I only had so many steps in my bag of tricks.

My greatest advantage, however, wasn't physical. It was emotional. I took every opportunity to demean the egotistical man, mocking his skills, his appearance, the very fact that he seemed unable to beat the lowest ranked cultivator in the entire sect. More so than at his defenses or stamina, I chipped away at his pride.

He charged me again.

I met his advance with Cedric-three, the same sword-tip down maneuver I'd first used against Xavier. Long recognized my second use of the form, and ducked beneath my counterattack. I transitioned into The Plunging Fang, but had to abort the attack to jump over Long's leg-sweep. I landed unevenly, and he struck out with his offhand.

His fist collided with my chest and knocked me off balance. I danced back as best I could, but Long came unrelenting. Cedric-two, The Third Guard, The Seventh Guard, Cedric-four, The Dragon's Scales, parry after parry I evaded Long's furious assault, his blade inching closer with every exchange.

"For someone named Long, you seem to keep coming up short," I taunted even as the tip of his sword passed barely beneath my chin.

Long didn't reply. He didn't have to. The sweat dripping down his brow, the increasingly red hue of his face, and the wild fury of his attacks offered reply enough.

I was running out of tricks.

Long was running out of patience.

His hands trembled with rage. His eyes stared wide and bloodshot.

His sword slammed into mine with unprecedented force, a torrent of qi shooting through his muscle meridian almost certainly more than it could handle. He'd probably damaged the meridian, actively harming his cultivation for the blow.

But it worked.

My weapon wrenched from my grip, tumbling to the padded floor on the other side of the ring.

I didn't concede. I didn't panic. The adrenaline pumping through my veins failed to pierce the icy calculations of my mind. I recognized the disarmament for what it was and took the only action available to me.

I stepped closer.

The willingness and lack of hesitation to remain in range earned me but a handful of milliseconds' worth of surprise —just enough to wrap my fingers around his left wrist.

I yanked with all my copper might, pulling Long off balance and sending him stumbling forward even as I used the inertia to launch myself past him.

By the time he spun around, I'd already reclaimed my sword.

"Wow, you are bright red." I smirked at him. "You must be *so* embarrassed. I know I would be if I'd torn one of my meridians to disarm an opponent only to just *let* them get their sword back."

A wave of chatter ran through the crowd.

"I'll kill you!" Long roared in defiance.

I smiled and fell back into The Dragon Prepares.

I'd shown my full hand. I'd run through each and every one of Cedric's forms and wrung every bit of unpredictability I could out of them. By all rights, Long was the superior fighter.

But I'd already won.

His blows came wild and uncontrolled, his technique falling by the wayside in his desperation to finish the job. Better yet, they fell weak upon my guard, as his injured muscle meridian flagged.

One by one I countered his flurry of blows, struggling to find opportunity to riposte as Long's fury drove him ever deeper on the aggressive. I kept my face calm and my smirk steady, feeding Long's rage, his embarrassment, his need to put this upstart mortal in his place.

For nearly a minute the exchange dragged on, Long's crazed onslaught failing to penetrate my guard, yet leaving me without an opening to earn a decisive blow. I was holding. Against one of the best fighters on all of Fyrion, I was holding. I was holding beautifully. It was only a matter of time until—

Something invisible slammed into my stomach.

I doubled over, falling to my knees.

Panic reared its ugly head at the back of my mind, eroding my focus as my analytical mind spiraled down the obvious path.

Long stood over me.

I desperately tried to raise my sword, to roll back, to duck, to dodge, to do *anything* to avoid the killing blow I knew was coming, but I couldn't move. At each wrist and each ankle, bands of golden qi held me in place. I tried to raise my head to look my murderer in the eye, but it too refused to budge.

This was it. I was finished. All the training, all the meditating, the friends I'd made and the questions I'd left unanswered, it was all over.

And of course it all came down to a fucking qi attack.

I didn't mind it. My death didn't matter. Nothing mattered.

"You'll pay for your insolence," Long snarled his final words to me.

I shut my eyes.

I heard a flurry of footsteps, the telltale swish of a sword swinging through the air, and a great gong.

The official's voice droned, "For use of a qi attack in an unscheduled duel, Senior Cadet Bao Long is disqualified. Cadet Caliban Rex is the victor."

"Stop! Unhand me!"

I blinked my eyes open. Long's sword lingered above my scalp, wrapped in tendrils of shadow, a field of shimmering translucent force, and even encased in ice as three different cultivators from the crowd moved to restrain him. The golden bands fell away from my limbs as a dozen more leapt into the ring to hold Long down.

I knelt there, staring wide-eyed as he railed against his

captors, struggling desperately and futilely to escape and act on his grisly intent.

Charlotte was the first to my side. "Pretend you're injured," she whispered sharply into my ear.

I blinked. "What? Why?"

"Just do it," she repeated. "Xave, help him up."

I pantomimed a broken ankle as Xavier's arm snaked its way under mine and pulled me to my feet. I let Charlotte do the talking.

"Out of the way, out of the way. We'll take him to the infirmary."

"This isn't over!" Long spat as we passed. "I'll kill you for this! Nobody disrespects Bao Long and lives!"

I ignored him.

Looks of shock and fear and curiosity washed over me as we descended into the crowd. A few of the bold coppers reached out to pat me on the back or congratulate me on the victory, but most kept their distance, frozen in place by both the intensity of the morning's events and their own unwillingness to impede the injured victor.

Far and away the most common reaction, the emotion that projected itself across the gymnasium to reach my gaze and pride alike, was one I hadn't quite experienced in all my time on Fyrion.

Respect.

Even beneath the dullness of the world, the meaninglessness of our insignificance, the veil cast over my emotions by the qi coursing through me, my heart swelled at those looks. I was still an outworlder. I was still a stranger, an enigma, something not quite to be trusted. But for the first time in my life, in the eyes of those that looked upon me, I'd finally become something else.

I was a cultivator.

We continued our charade all the way onto the transport platform and aboard the pod bound for housing D. Only once the doors had shut tight behind us did I finally cease my cycling, and did Charlotte speak.

"We needed an excuse to get you out of there. If you'd given everyone who wanted to a chance to congratulate you and introduce themselves, you would've been stuck there for hours. There'd be at least twenty people lined up to challenge you before you could even take a breath."

Grateful as I was for her maneuvering, I only half-listened to her explanation as my emotions finally caught up with me.

I'd done it.

I'd fucking *done it.*

I had to call Lucy.

She picked up immediately. "Cal?"

"I won! I fucking won!"

"Language," she chided, but didn't press the issue. "Congratulations, Cal. I'm proud of you."

"You need to get down here. We need to celebrate!"

"Docking request is already sent. I should be there in a few hours. How did it go? Is your rank updated?"

My brow shot up. "Good question. Let me just…" I didn't have to go looking for it. A notification popped to the front of my holopad informing me that I'd climbed from sect rank five thousand and eight all the way to three thousand eight-twenty-six. I relayed the info to the others.

"That's housing C!" Xavier clapped me on the back hard enough to nearly throw me from my chair. "Congratulations! I may disagree with the indirectness of your methods, but cannot help but admire the warrior's spirit you showed on this day!"

"Thanks, Xave," I told him, brushing past his endearingly strange compliments. "Thanks to all of you. I couldn't have gotten close without your help."

"You're not out of the woods, Cal," Charlotte warned. "Things are about to get a lot more difficult for you. You have a target on your back, and surprise won't be in your favor for long. Your only advantage is that you're still only in housing C. Pretty much all of the people lower-ranked than you are still tin, but that won't stop people higher up from taking a shot at the guy who humiliated Bao Long."

"I'm not moving to housing C," I said simply. "I told you. I'm not abandoning Nick."

"That'll raise questions."

"And I'll answer them as they come," I countered. "Let me just have today, please. I *won*. I get to stay with the sect. I can worry about everything else tomorrow. Tonight, we party."

The pod doors slid open as we arrived at housing D. I led the way, pride in my step and victory in my heart. Word had apparently yet to spread all the way out here, so we made it unimpeded across the lobby and onto the grand stairs. "We can hide out in my room until Lucy lands," I told the others. "I have a bottle of champagne stashed up there for *just* this occasion. Our celebration starts—"

I froze mid-sentence as we reached the top of the steps. My heart stopped. My breath hitched. Joy turned to ash in my throat as my eyes trailed down the third-floor hallway to a sight that haunts my darkest dreams to this very day.

There stood Nick, his eyes black as the endless abyss, his hands twitching with unsettling arrhythmia, and at his feet, the pale and qi-drained corpse of the housing D custodian.

34

Cold sweat ran down my neck. Shadows crept in along my periphery, blotting out the others, the hallway, the window. I saw only Nick, deep in the throes of void-induced psychosis, standing over Brady's pallid corpse.

No. Wait. That wasn't right.

The housing D custodian, the faceless mortal whose name I'd never bothered to learn, lay dead. Did his life matter so little I had to substitute another?

I'm not in deep space anymore.

The words came unbidden to my mind, a desperate denial, a futile prayer that maybe, just maybe, all was not as it seemed. I blinked.

Nick was still there. His eyes were still black. His hand still twitched.

This couldn't be happening. He was just a kid. He'd already suffered through so much. He wasn't even qi-deprived. Threads, he was getting extra focus hours!

I'm not in deep space anymore.

I clung to that mantra as if it could save me. As if it could save Nick.

In the face of cruel reality, my protests, my pleas, my frenzied rationalizations didn't matter. Nothing mattered.

That's when I gave in.

Amidst the horror, the panic, the quiet wrenching of my heart and the black ichor wrung free that was despair, a hauntingly familiar sound echoed through the hall.

Cedric laughed.

I took an instinctive step back. The boot of my vac suit clanged against the maintenance tunnel's metal floor. My muscles locked up. My thoughts scrambled. I tried to run, to turn, to at least avert my eyes from the nightmare before me.

I failed. As that vicious cackling seized control of me, I could but look down roofie's dark hallway, the emergency lights dull and flickering from the core's failure, and gaze into the abyss of insurmountable power and inevitable defeat.

I'd been here before. I'd dreamt this dream a thousand times. I'd seen its grisly end. Its terrors never changed.

But I had.

I'd grown. I'd learned. I'd overcome the hurdles in my Way and come out stronger for it.

I'm not in deep space anymore.

Qi flooded from my copper core into my heart, my blood, my brain. The laughter fell silent. RF-31 dissipated around me. I stared not at unstoppable Cedric and my fallen brother, but at poor, young Nick, the lonely kid I'd taken under my wing.

And I knew what I had to do.

Charlotte and Xavier kept defensive positions as I advanced down the third-floor hallway. Even a stage above, they knew the dangers of approaching a VIP. I carried no such risks.

If he could've drained *my* qi, he wouldn't have hungered so.

Shiver was already in my hand before Nick's vine lashed out at me. I severed it with a sharp, decisive swing. That trick may've worked on me once, but against the speed and strength of my copper body, it made for little more than an annoyance.

It didn't even slow me down.

I stopped just shy of the custodian's body and stared deep into Nick's eyes. I scoured them, searching their black abyss for a spark, a single star in the endless night, some small part of him that yet remained, that rejected the hunger, that might still flail against infinity rather than succumb to the madness that it wrought.

Only emptiness stared back.

I plunged Shiver into his chest. It was easy. The blade slipped between his ribs and pierced his racing heart.

Nick collapsed.

I followed him to the floor.

He reached out a balled fist towards me, craning his neck to meet my gaze.

As I took his hand, it opened to press two tiny lumps into my palm. He looked up at me with a smile on his face and triumph in his voice as he breathed his last.

"I found it, Cal. I found it."

Nicolas Vesper, sixteen years old, the youngest cultivator to reach tin in Fyrion's history, and one of startlingly few that I called friend, died with my sword through his heart and his hand clasped in mine.

Xavier and Charlotte raced to my side, the former stopping to confirm the custodian's death as the latter wrapped an arm around my shoulders.

"You did the right thing," she told me.

"I did this to him," the words came cold and quiet, an admission more to myself and to the Threads than to Charlotte.

"You couldn't have known—"

"The signs were there," I interrupted. "The depression, the appetite, the staring off into space, I saw them. I *recognized* them. And I did nothing. I wasn't in deep space anymore. How does someone planetside, someone getting *focus room hours*, contract VIP?" I looked up at her, gazed at her with my qi-enhanced eyes, black as the night sky, only a few specks of starlight different from Nick's, from Cedric's. "How, Charlotte?"

She didn't answer.

Xavier placed a broad hand on my back as he knelt next to me. "You did everything you could have. You were his friend. You looked out for him. You r*isked your life* to avoid abandoning him. You can't blame yourself for this, Cal."

Oh but I could. I could blame Cedric for making me like this. I could blame Nick's parents for their mistreatment. I could blame this entire cursed sect for creating such a hostile environment for those that needed help the most.

Above all I could blame myself. I'd alerted him to the vast well of power in the emptiness. I'd driven him to try injecting seeds with dark qi. My own inability to complete his experiments had sent him to find it for himself.

But that didn't matter. Nothing mattered.

Together the three of us stayed there, kneeling in silent vigil until the paramedics forced us away. We watched them gather up the two bodies, cover them in a blanket as they readied to wheel them away. Xavier took it upon himself to clean Nick's blood from my sword. I didn't thank him. I should have.

Through it all I clung to the qi running through my mind, chilling my heart and slowing my breath, like my life depended on it. In certain ways it did.

The world moved in a blur around me as I gave the medics my statement, heard the others corroborate my story, and watched the two shrouded forms disappear into the elevator. Only when but a bloodstain in the lush carpet remained as evidence of the day's tragedy did I return to my room.

Charlotte and Xavier tried to follow, tried to offer their sympathy and support.

I locked the door behind me.

Lucy had sent me a message. She whispered comfort and condolences in her gentlest of tones, assured me she would land as soon as she could. Apparently there was some sort of delay in obtaining a berth.

I paid it no mind.

I sat on my bed and finally opened my fist to stare down at the two lumps Nick had handed me, the obvious source of the grin on his face, of the victory in his dying words.

A pair of apple seeds greeted me, one alive with light and fire and a complex weave of qi I couldn't begin to untangle, the other quiet and dark, its center wrapped in shadow and familiar stillness.

He'd done it. Of course he'd done it. He'd always been a prodigy.

For some time I sat there, gazing down at Nick's achievement, his one and only bid to leave his mark on this uncaring galaxy, until it proved too much for even my qi-hardened heart.

I slipped the seeds into my pocket. I lay back. I expanded my spiritual sense.

And I drifted off into infinity's uncaring solace.

35

There's a hideous temptation the nothingness offers to those in pain.

Escape is the wrong word. There is no escape. There's only a deadening, a sense that for now, if only for now, you've hidden it away, locked in a closet as it hammers at the door, rabid to break free.

The tooth may be numbed, but the dentist's drill still buzzes, still presses, still vibrates your jaw around it.

Obscure it as you may, it remains. It screams for your attention, and you cannot, you *will* not, ever forget its presence.

But only a madman rejects the novocaine.

So, I drifted. I hid away from my trials beneath the depths of the infinite sea, a black and icy stillness that enforced the smallness of my own grief.

They say time heals all wounds. That's a lie. Time erodes. Time abrades. Entropy must increase, and there is no healing to be found in a world that little bit colder.

Time *contextualizes* all wounds. It offers distance and perspective. It hurts us in so many more and different ways that how could we ever believe that first injury had affected us so much? Time demands our pain be no less finite than we are. It offers solace only in our own mortality, in the heartbreak of insignificance, in the fearful yet inescapable axiom that *this too shall pass.*

Pretty words fare little better, but any port in a storm.

I lied when I said there was no escape. There's exactly one escape, one so horrible it warrants no further mention here nor anywhere else less its insipid romance spread.

There's a hideous temptation the nothingness offers to those in pain.

* * *

It was the incessant beep of an urgent message that finally brought me to shore.

The last vestiges of sunset peeking through my window gave some hint at the hours that'd passed. A glance at my holopad offered the truth of the circadian time.

Just past three AM. The first of the ungodly hours.

Upon the holographic screen flashed the name of the sole individual I'd permitted to send me such disruptive missives. With a tap, Lucy's voice filled the room.

"Cal, there's something wrong. They're refusing my requests to dock. The harbormaster has stopped answering my messages entirely. You need to get somewhere safe. Arthur's been trying to contact you. Answer him."

The line went dead.

Adrenaline took over. I flipped through my notifications to find a series of hastily scrawled messages from my mortal friend.

[Arthur - 0304:14] Can't talk. They're in the lobby.

[Arthur - 0305:53] There's an enforcer squad here for you. Armed to the teeth. Still setting up.

[Arthur - 0307:04] I'd bet you have fifteen minutes before they break down your door.

I tapped out a reply.

[Caliban - 0311:09] I did nothing wrong. I'll talk to them.

He responded in under a minute.

[Arthur - 0311:46] Bao Long is with them.

"Shit," I audibly cursed. Long couldn't have asked for a better opportunity to take me out while I "resisted arrest."

[Caliban - 0312:08] What do I do?

[Arthur - 0312:25] Call Mindy.

I obeyed.

"Caliban!" The fixer's voice came labored and breathless as her mic picked up the telltale whirr of a treadmill. I didn't question why she'd be going for a run at three AM. "It's my understanding you need a walk-of-shame package pronto, yes?"

I blinked. "A what?"

"You aren't the first cultivator I've had to smuggle out of a bedroom. I've got it down to an art."

"What do I need to do?"

"There's a food delivery cart outside your door. I set it up hours ago when Arthur warned me you might need a quick exit. Your pal Charlotte had your dinner brought up after you locked yourself in your room. The enforcers don't want it in the way, so they've already got a member of the waitstaff on their way up to inconspicuously clear it. Before that happens, you're going to hide inside."

I scurried around my dorm room as she explained, frantically stripping off my sect uniform and throwing on a set of Cedric's old clothes, complete with a brown leather jacket I rather didn't want to leave behind.

A pang shook my heart as I transferred Nick's seeds from one set of pockets to the other, but I shoved it aside. I had more pressing matters to worry about.

"When I say go, a device in the cart will project a holo of your closed door to fool the surveillance cameras. You'll have twelve seconds. I hope you have a good veil. There'll be a lot more eyes than this trick normally gets, and if any of them get even a whiff of your qi, you're done for."

I smiled as I strapped Shiver to my back. "That won't be a problem."

"All set?"

I stopped just in front of my door, quickly patting myself down to confirm I had everything I'd need. I crouched to keep below the camera's line of sight. "All set."

"And... go."

The door both opened and not as the hologram masked the change. To the naked eye the illusion crumbled, noticeably two-dimensional and slightly transparent. I crawled through it.

Outside I found myself face to face with a fitted white tablecloth, beneath which four simple metal legs held the table up. A secondary surface of thin stainless steel a few inches from the ground made for my hiding spot, obscured entirely by the cloth. I wormed my way in.

The line in my ear went dead. I'd have to find a way to thank Mindy later. I couldn't afford the noise of a call, and the cramped space limited access to my holopad.

So I waited.

I ran qi through my senses to better hear the world around me, through my heart and lungs to muffle even the quietest sounds my body made, and through my muscles to keep me perfectly still.

I may've lacked a single qi technique to call my own, I may've struggled to stay focused and compassionate under the influence of the uncaring cold, but this? I was made for this.

Silence and stillness became me. My hunters would sense nothing for all that I *was* nothing. If a well of power so vast and deep as to drive men mad could go so unnoticed, what chance did they have of finding little old me?

Cowardly or underhanded as some may've thought it, I couldn't deny I had a penchant for shadows.

My mind raced. If they'd sent enforcers after me, someone clearly thought me responsible for Nick's death. I supposed they were right, though probably not in the way they thought.

My money was on Elder Lopez. She'd used Long to screw with me before, and I didn't doubt she'd do it again. My only uncertainty was if she intended him to kill me or had some other scheme going on.

The speculation came to an end as I heard the footsteps tap against the carpet as they climbed the stairs, the unlabored breaths of someone well accustomed to such activity, the racing heart of uncertain nerves. I wondered what Long and his lackeys had told this person about me. I doubted anything good.

The table lurched into motion as its wheels overcame the carpet's resistance. I felt the familiar bumps as we passed into an elevator already waiting for us.

I dared not open my spiritual sense as we reached the ground floor for fear one of Long's men could feel my attention. The cart stopped. The mortal conversed with one of the enforcers, a woman whose voice I didn't recognize. My nerves mounted.

I knew they were looking. I knew they were listening.

They heard nothing.

My heart beat so infrequently as to be unrecognizable as such. My breath came slow and soft, gentle enough to spark little turbulence in the air around me.

"Alright, you're clear. Get that thing out of here."

I held back a sigh of relief as the table pushed forward once more.

I gave up my attempts at tracking my position not long after, as multiple seemingly conflicting turns brought us in a circuitous route to *somewhere*. The path itself didn't matter. I could guess the destination well enough.

The clashing aromas of sweet and savory and stale

leftovers hanging beneath the overpowering scent of lavender dish soap made it clear. The cart came to a halt.

I waited.

The mortal cleared the various plates from the table top, tossing the uneaten meals into the composter where they'd go to feed the gardens.

Still I waited.

Nearly five minutes passed as I crouched motionless beneath the table while the worker who'd brought me here washed dishes. I cursed to myself as I realized they gave no sign of stopping. I only had so long before the enforcers stormed my room to find me absent. I dared not burn any more of my head start.

I spent another thirty seconds tracking the mortal's movements, listening for every footstep, every turn of the faucet and swish of brush against pot. Right as they leaned in to scrub a new dish, I made my move.

I slipped out from under the tablecloth to find the other side of the dish bus I'd returned countless trays to over the past year. I'd only seen the space in glimpses through gaps in the track, but I recognized it well enough. Staying low, I slipped out the only exit.

The kitchen itself was smaller than I'd expected—a limitation, I imagined, of valuable ground-floor square footage. Here, surrounded only by mortals, I stretched my spiritual sense to its fullest.

A skeleton crew worked the stoves at this ungodly hour, but a handful of dull blobs that represented a mortal's uncultivated qi. A year ago I might've found them blinding and headache-inducing, but I'd spent longer staring at brighter.

Maneuvering through the area proved trivial, a simple task of keeping below the rows of stainless steel tables and avoiding line of sight with the night shift as I tracked their positions in my mind. A number of times I had to pause and wait or otherwise backtrack, but in a scarce few minutes I escaped the kitchen free and clear.

I abandoned stealth entirely as I slipped into the hallway. With clear sight lines and nowhere to hide, I couldn't prevent the infrequent passerby from noting my presence. At least in these halls I was a strange presence rather than an obvious intruder.

The sect's own ego proved my saving grace. Housing D, as with all the outer housing blocks, had been designed to allow the various mortal staff to keep out of sight as they came and went, hiding away those most cultivators thought beneath them. It meant as I walked with confidence and purpose down the cramped back passage, I only came across the odd bleary-eyed employee on their way to an early shift.

They saw me. They saw my civilian clothes. They saw the sword on my back. And they decided not to risk bothering me. I was certain once the enforcers realized I was gone they'd be able to track which way I went, but for now I had a head start, and I intended to make the most of it.

"Lucy," I spoke into my holopad as I strode away from housing D. "Where are you?"

"Cal! Are you okay? What's going on?"

"I made it out of housing D, but I can't run forever. How soon can you get planetside?"

"They won't give me a berth," she replied. "I could shoot my way in, but that would take—"

"Don't," I interrupted. "I have a better idea." I tapped at my holopad. "I'm sending you the place. We'll meet you outside. How soon can you land?"

"I'll beat you there."

"Perfect. See you soon."

"And, Cal..." For a brief moment the urgency, the professionalism, the calm confidence of someone who *knows what they're doing*, all slipped away to reveal the deep, earnest worry beneath. "Please be careful."

"I will. I promise."

I hung up, and immediately tapped away to make my second call.

"Cal?" Charlotte greeted me. She didn't sound like someone I'd just woken up. "What happened? Are you out?"

Thank the threads, Arthur had told her. "You're up to date? Good. Please tell me Xavier's with you."

"I knew you would escape!" Xavier's voice boomed over the comm line.

"Where are you?" Charlotte asked.

"I thought I might buy some flowers." I kept my answer cryptic as a mortal passed by. "You should join me."

"Got it," Charlotte affirmed. "Meet you there."

She hung up.

I quickened my step as my mind settled on a plan.

These back passages would only get me so far, especially once my pursuers realized I'd taken them. The transport network was a no go—all it would take was one camera and they could lock down my pod with me inside it.

I guessed I had maybe twenty minutes before the enforcers realized which way I'd gone and took a pod of their own to cut me off. That was nowhere near enough time to get where I needed to go, which meant I had to either hide or find some other way of getting to Lucy.

Thank ever-loving fuck for Arthur and a little tidbit he'd dropped months ago when we'd first gone out for drinks.

Some days he walked to work.

That placed Arthur's apartment within walking distance of housing D, and I happened to know of another remarkable asset within walking distance of Arthur's.

Gordon Street was dark.

With neither the clubs nor bars of Droe Lane, the

revelers and prostitutes and alcoholics abandoned the quiet avenue for more exciting pastures. The storefronts had all locked up, the lights gone out, the word "closed" displayed prominently in every window.

That meant nobody to see me break in.

For the second time in my stay on Fyrion I kicked down the front door to In Full Bloom.

I winced at the crash that echoed out, but as the reverberations died down, no lights came on. No windows slid open. The locals had long learned better than to investigate weird noises coming from Victor's place.

I left the lights off as I stepped inside, content to navigate the near-perfect darkness by touch and by ear rather than risk announcing my presence. It took under five minutes for two figures to make their approach. To my spiritual sense, they shone like suns.

"Cal!" Charlotte whispered sharply into the dark shop. "Are you in here?"

"Threads, it's good to see you two. C'mon. Let's get underground." I stepped to the back room, where I dared to turn on a light to lead the others in. I shoved the sink back into the wall to reveal the ladder down into the transport maintenance walkways. Only once we were cleanly down with the way closed behind us did I turn to face my friends.

Charlotte darted in for a hug, practically snatching me up. "I thought you were done for. When Arthur told me they'd let *Long* on the arrest team…"

I pulled away. "Arthur's a treasure. Mindy too."

Xavier stepped up to clap me on the back, an awkward motion on the narrow catwalk. "Already your legend grows."

I smiled uncomfortably at the strange praise before my eyes turned to suitcases they each carried. A flush of warmth flooded even my qi-cooled heart. They meant to come with me. They'd give up their focus rooms, their mentorships, the ranking they'd fought so hard to achieve, just to stay with *me*.

Two thoughts robbed me of those fuzzies. With me gone, they'd be the next targets for the investigation into Nick's death. *When* it got out how much they'd helped me, how much they'd hidden from the sect for me, I doubted it would end well for them. The second though I voiced the moment it struck.

"Are those vac safe?"

Xavier's brow shot up. *"That's* your plan?"

"Of course," Charlotte said. "Lucy's a *skiff*. Half a skiff's job is to ferry people to and from the mothership. She'd be equipped for a ground landing."

I nodded. "Airlock and everything." I gestured again to their suitcases. "Are those vac safe?"

"No, but they can be," Charlotte answered. "All it takes is a quick and dirty qi field."

"That'll do." I turned. "C'mon. Let's move."

I ran the navigation software locally on a city map I'd downloaded months ago just in case they could track my localnet activity. We moved in relative silence along the maze of catwalks, neither stopping nor stumbling as the floor shook with each passing transport pod.

I took the time to send messages to both Arthur and Mindy.

[Caliban - 0351:51] Thank you. I know you took a huge risk in helping me, and it means a lot. I'd be dead or somebody's science experiment without you two. Seriously. Thank you.

[Arthur - 0352:43] Just returning the favor :) Stay safe out there.

Mindy didn't reply.

With any luck, the sect's investigators wouldn't even consider the mortal staff as possibilities. Assuming I managed to escape, they'd have no way of tracing Arthur's messages back to him unless they checked *his* holopad. I hoped they wouldn't.

Mindy I wasn't worried about. With all the secrets she knew, none of the elders would move against her. Having a dedicated walk-of-shame package made for a lot of blackmail material. Maybe her friendship with Arthur might extend him some of the same protections.

We'd been walking for nearly an hour before Charlotte finally spoke up. "Something's bothering me about all this. Who in their right mind would let Long onto the arresting team? It hasn't even been a full day since he tried to kill you in the ring."

I shrugged. "Maybe it was an oversight? Either that or he pulled some strings for a chance to come after me."

"Or someone powerful wants you dead," Xavier said plainly.

I gulped.

Charlotte glared at him.

"What?" he asked. "It makes sense. Why else would someone give Long a chance to finish the job?"

To be honest, I was more surprised that *Xavier* of all people had come up with something so underhanded than at the idea one of the elders may've been trying to kill me. "All the more reason to get off world as soon as possible."

I was fairly certain we'd long escaped the enforcers' search radius by the time we climbed over the railing to drop down onto the track itself. Already at five in the morning, traffic had begun to pick up, leaving us a short window to leap up onto the platform.

A familiar staging area greeted us, one thus far vacant of workers, with benches and cubbies and, more importantly, vac suits lining the walls.

Who said working as a vac-welder didn't have its perks?

I made straight for my usual gear as Charlotte and Xavier scurried around in search for suits that would fit them. A message popped up from Lucy confirming she'd landed some hundred yards from the airlock. If I craned my neck, I could see her through the window.

We were close. We were gonna make it.

I transferred Shiver to the outside of my suit and guided Charlotte and Xavier to do the same with their rapier and great axe respectively. The weapons would survive just fine.

A knot of trepidation formed in my stomach as I helped Xavier squeeze into the largest vac suit he could find. Lucy was right there. The airlock awaited us.

It almost felt—and these are among the most cursed words anyone as ever uttered—*too easy*.

Still, with our helmets under our arms we crossed the wide staging area, maneuvered past the collection of torches and scrap metal and maganchors, and approached our exit. Via my holopad I entered the access code I'd used a hundred times at the start of my shift.

The airlock's interior door slid open.

My stomach sank.

Xavier gripped his axe.

Charlotte cursed.

Out strode Elder Maria Lopez, her uniform decked out in full battle regalia, her hand around a gnarled wooden staff, and her bronze core ablaze with power. "Cadet Rex," she greeted us with a thin and taunting smile. "Took you long enough."

36

Maria couldn't keep the smile from her face. She had him. She *had* him. She almost wished she'd taken a picture of the looks on the would-be fugitives' faces as she'd emerged from her hiding place. It would've made a wonderful decoration for her new office.

That is, Honchel's and Velereau's faces. Rex simply stared at her with that inhumanly blank expression behind those sunglasses of his.

"You didn't think I would let you escape, did you Mister Rex? Or should I call you Andrew?"

That, at least, managed to get a rise out of him, as his brow shot up.

"My name is Caliban."

"Is it now?" Maria asked, bringing up a pair of documents on her holopad. "Because this crew manifest lists one Brady Rex and one Andrew Rex working as vac-welders on refueling station RF-31, and this salvage report confirms Brady's remains but notes Andrew's are mysteriously absent."

Rex paused.

Maria beamed. There was nothing better than looking a man in the eyes as you told him all his secrets.

"In fact, Andrew seems to be the *only* survivor of RF-31. If the unidentified viscera we found hadn't been clearly a bronze-tier cultivator, you might've stayed hidden. It was sloppy not to change your last name, but shared surnames aren't unheard of."

"I wasn't hiding," the man snarled. "My name is *Caliban*."

"A monstrous name for a newly made monster, then? The John Doe had clearly undergone void-induced psychosis. Was he a failed experiment, or part of the process?"

"What are you talking abou—"

"I know about your qi vampirism," Maria cut off his weak attempts at lying. "I know you've been giving away all your focus room hours to fatten up your lackeys, and I know they've been feeding you that qi under whatever enchantment is hiding your core. What I don't know is who created you. They must be powerful to have a soulship under their sway, but whoever they are, their little experiment ends *here*."

The three cadets stared at her agape, clearly in awe of her brilliant deduction.

"I've had my suspicions ever since you asked me for a way to bind your spirit to your body. At first I thought it was necromancy, especially after your little display during the void horde attack, but then I realized: all that conflicting, stolen qi is probably driving your spirit in a dozen different directions. Of course you needed to reign it in. The security footage of your two friends joining you to open your spine meridian confirmed my theory. I just had to prove it."

Threads this felt good.

"That idiot Long made for the perfect poisoned pawn, just hateful enough to bait you, just powerful enough to push you to reveal your true colors. I was disappointed when he survived that duel of yours, but you embarrassed the fool enough that he would've forced your hand sooner or later. It was sheer luck you killed the Vesper boy before that happened. Then it was just a matter of using Long to smoke you out, send you running somewhere I could catch you alone. After all this work, I can't very well allow anyone else to claim the glory."

She drummed her fingers against her harrowwood staff. "You see, you're my ticket off this desolate rock. Maria Lopez, savior of Fyrion. It has a nice ring to it, don't you think?"

* * *

This lady was off her rocker. Qi vampirism? Seriously?

I was pretty sure the fumes from all that synthetic wood in her office had gotten to her.

I suppose I shouldn't have been too surprised she'd found out about roofie, even if the rest of her absolutely unhinged supervillain monologue treated jumping to conclusions like a competitive sport.

At least it gave me time to think.

From the sound of it, she planned to attack once she'd said her piece. My immediate impulse was to surrender. Even three on one, taking on a bronze cultivator felt like a marginally slower way to die than just opening the airlock and letting the vacuum take me. On top of that, Lopez was absolutely kitted in enchanted gear and natural treasures. I counted no fewer than five items on her person that screamed into my spiritual sense.

I wondered if she could still be the savior of Fyrion if she let me live. I didn't have to wonder long.

"Senior Cadet Honchel, Senior Cadet Velereau, if you aid me in putting down this dangerous experiment, I can see your punishments for aiding him reduced. There's no reason for the Dragon's Right Eye to lose any more of its young prospects."

"Not a chance!"

"Xavier," I whispered at him sharply. "She's *bronze.*"

He spoke through gritted teeth without diverting his gaze from Lopez herself. "We can beat her."

"Stop thinking we can beat everybody!" I snapped back.

Before Xavier could reply, I heard a familiar *shing* to my left.

Charlotte had drawn her rapier.

"It seems your hold on their minds is as strong as I feared." Lopez smirked. "You won't find *me* so easily ensorcelled."

Huh, apparently I had mind control powers. Why hadn't anyone told me?

Elder Lopez raised her staff.

Xavier reached for his axe.

I let my vac helmet fall to the floor as I wrapped my fingers around Shiver's hilt.

Lopez swung first. I could feel the qi as it gathered into a blinding mass at her staff's tip just moments before a burst of golden light shot directly at me.

Charlotte darted in front of me and *parried it.*

Before you ask, no, I don't know the physics of how a rapier parries a fucking laser beam. I'd seen Charlotte pull out the technique a few times, but she always got a bit cagey whenever I pressed her for details. Until proven otherwise, I'd chosen to believe with the proper timing she could parry anything and everything.

Except, apparently, Lopez's second attack.

The blast came mere milliseconds after the first, slamming into Charlotte's forearm well before she could bring her saber about for another parry. Her vac-suit—thank the gods for solar radiation-resistant polymer weaves—managed to bear the brunt of the bronze-tier attack's heat, but the force behind it still sent her rapier flying.

That was our cue.

Xavier, in typical Xavier fashion, charged directly in. A battle cry echoed through the staging area.

Lopez fired upon him.

Xavier's own defensive technique flared up, the front of his chest transmuting into shining silver—a suitable element for a man born and raised on a silver mine. Both of Lopez's bolts refracted off Xavier's silverskin, bouncing off at odd angles into the wall.

She didn't even bother to raise her weapon against Xavier's as the axe blade took on its own silver sheen. Without so much as a gesture, a transparent sphere of light blinked into being around the smug elder. Xavier's axe failed to so much as leave a scratch.

That didn't stop me from trying. Masked by Xavier's advance, I ran in unassaulted. For lack of qi attacks or defenses of my own, I ran my meridians at full capacity and forced the rest of my not inconsiderable reserves running through Shiver.

The blade grew cold. Moisture in the air crystalized upon its edge as it seemed to gain a weight to it, an immense inertia against anything that would infringe upon its stillness. The qi flowed remarkably easily, a benefit of its spiritual significance. Both Vihaan's and the void beast's blood had stained the steel from which it'd been forged.

That *meant* something.

Not that you'd know that from the way my overhand strike bounced right off Lopez's shield.

I do mean *bounced*. My blade didn't scrape or skid off the brilliant bubble as Xavier's had; it seemed to push its way just a tiny bit in before exponentially increasing resistance threw it back out. In hindsight, I'd realize the strange behavior *probably* had something to do with the absence of detectible qi in my weapon making it harder for the shield to recognize something was trying to pierce it.

In the moment, I managed a "huh, that's weir—" before another burst of light slammed into my chest.

With neither silverskin nor a well-timed parry to fend off the attack, the beam's full force tossed me aside like a particularly surprised rag doll. I heard a crack. The icy chill of spine-meridian-suppressed pain welled up just beside my sternum, but my breath didn't suffer for it.

At least the broken rib hadn't punctured a lung.

I landed hard against a shelf full of welding torches, sending the heavy tools crashing down beside me. Shiver skidded across the floor, some dozen feet away.

For an embarrassingly long moment I sat there, stunned, as I watched Xavier continue to hammer away at Lopez's shield. By the time she managed to sneak a beam past his silverskin's limited coverage, Charlotte had reclaimed her rapier and reentered the fray.

The latter darted in just in time to parry the follow-up beam aimed at Xavier's head.

I forced myself to my feet and ran after Shiver. A shot to my ankle sent me tumbling before I could make it halfway.

Even as I hit the deck I thanked the gods Lopez had been arrogant enough to let us put vac-suits on before making her move. Threads, if the wisps of smoke coming off my suit were any indicator, that laser would've melted my foot clean off. The supremacist cultivator probably couldn't imagine mortal-made gear could make such a difference.

Her loss. Well, probably still our loss, but I wasn't going to complain about keeping my flesh attached to my bones for a few minutes longer.

I lost my view of the fight as I caught myself on my palms and scurried on hands and knees over to Shiver. By the time I made it to my feet, Charlotte was on the ground —thankfully still in possession of her weapon this time—

while Xavier faced the brunt of Lopez's focus alone.

I charged in.

Lopez clenched her eyes shut.

From a ring around her finger, a brilliant flash filled the room. Xavier stumbled back, blinded.

I blinked away the dark spots in my vision and kept approaching. For a half-second I thought the graying effect of my sense meridian had protected me from the flash, before I landed on the much more obvious truth.

I was wearing sunglasses.

Surprise washed over Lopez's face as she opened her eyes to find me bearing down, her spiritual sense blind to my presence. She didn't seem to find her powerfully enchanted ring being foiled by a pair of dark aviators as amusing as I did.

I lunged.

With an icy torrent running through my bones and muscles and weapon alike, Shiver's tip slammed into Lopez's shield like a torpedo into a dreadnought's hull. Nearly an inch it pushed through the golden bubble, forced its way past that seemingly impregnable bronze technique, before the higher tier won out.

Shiver flew from my grip as the shield ejected it.

Lopez didn't even bother firing another light beam at me. With a swing of her staff I could barely even *see*, she swept my legs out from under me and sent me to the floor.

I rolled to the side, building distance as the gnarled wood slammed into the ground beside me. It left a dent in the sheet-metal flooring.

But then Xavier's axe met her shield again.

Charlotte darted back into the fight.

This time, I didn't hesitate to take advantage of the opening and sprint across the room to reclaim my sword.

We fell into a cycle.

One by one Elder Lopez would land a hit or manage to

disarm one of us, forcing the other two to cover for them as they returned to the fight just in time for someone else to lose their footing. By the skin of our teeth we pressed her, always on the offensive, aways just barely enough of a distraction to keep her from delivering a finishing blow.

I took the worst of it. With no way of my own to deflect her light beam, I depended entirely on Charlotte, Xavier, and the weave of my vac-suit for protection. Time and time again I hit the floor, taking bruises and sprains and the infrequent fracture as her technique overwhelmed even my copper qi-enhanced bones.

Lopez herself showed no sign of flagging. She didn't look desperate or worried or even frustrated as we hammered away at her.

Of us all, I'd come the closest to penetrating her defenses, but even on the odd instances I made it into melee range without tanking a laser to the stomach, Shiver never pierced further than an inch into her barrier.

It was a war of attrition, and we were getting nowhere.

I heard my wrist break before I felt it. I smelled the acrid fumes of my vac suit partially melting. I saw Shiver fly off into the wall when my grip failed.

I leapt back to dodge the base of Lopez's staff. I landed on my ass, failing to catch myself as I clutched my broken wrist in my left hand. I cursed.

If my attacks hadn't been working before, they stood little chance one-handed.

A brief, dark thought crept through my mind as I realized what absolutely *would* shatter the bronze's defenses. Lucy was just outside.

I entertained the idea no further. Lopez had come to prevent our escape. There was no way she'd let us build enough distance from her to survive artillery designed for taking out entire ships.

It was up to us.

I lurched forward to bring myself to my feet. I looked to Shiver. Lopez stood between me and it.

I darted to the side, putting Xavier and his superior defenses between me and our opponent before shutting my eyes and doing something I'd deeply wanted to avoid.

I opened my spiritual senses.

The light and sound and *heat* of a dozen qi techniques crashed against my brain like a tidal wave, overwhelming and unceasing. Lopez's shield shone above it all, a blinding star screaming its presence against all of existence.

I didn't look at it too long.

What did catch my attention was the cloud of qi that hung in the air, saturating the space around the combatants with its brilliance as technique after technique dissipated its energy into the environment. Better yet, I watched as three vortices drank it up, two small drains and one massive whirlpool that sucked up the ambient energy nearly as fast as it gathered.

The sheer amount of qi, far denser than any of us could've managed, that Lopez expended was matched only by that she then consumed.

I had an idea.

"Conserve your qi!" I shouted to the others as I stretched my senses outwards, past the blinding shield and deafening cores and the maelstrom of ambient qi, past the airlock and outer doors, and into the emptiness beyond.

The infinite sea stood ready.

For all my effort, all my practice, all my fruitless attempts at forcing my qi into *anything*, be it a seed or a technique, it only ever left my body as a shapeless cloud.

It was time to see how big a cloud I could make.

Qi raced from my core in a torrent, billowing limply out into the air around me. It wasn't an attack. It wasn't a technique. It *certainly* wasn't magic.

But it was a lot.

When my reserves ran dry of what they could expend without depleting my core, I refilled them from the infinite sea, channeling a river of shadow, of ice, of quiet stillness into the staging area.

It didn't suppress anyone's abilities. It didn't chill the air or drain the oxygen from the room. Threads, most of it washed back out to rejoin the infinite sea.

But some lingered. Some joined that bright miasma from which the others drank. And as I dumped more and more dark energy into the air, the stillness slowly took over. Something about it tickled at the back of my mind, plucked at the strings of interest as I watched it hang there dense enough to force the other away. I ignored it. I had bigger things to worry about.

By the time I snatched Shiver from where it'd fallen, my own umbral cloud had fully driven away that of the ambient light. My qi sat still, hanging increasingly dense in the air, readily making way for the light qi that would float through it, yet refusing to be displaced for long.

First Charlotte's, then Xavier's, then even Elder Lopez's influx of qi dried up as mine claimed the air around them.

I hoped that would be enough.

The cacophony muted beneath my dark cloud, I kept my spiritual sense open as I ran back into the fray. I kept my broken wrist behind my back as I wielded Shiver in my left hand, an eventuality I wished I'd had the time to train for. I mirrored the forms as best I could, but the movements came awkward and inefficient.

Lopez fired on me.

Xavier sidestepped into it, tanking the blow on a silver-covered shoulder.

I slipped past him and jammed Shiver into Lopez's shield once more.

It pierced no further, but with my mind's eye open, I could *see* the qi she'd expended deflecting my attack. I could watch it drift up and away, unable to linger in the already-saturated air.

A beam of light slammed into my chest. It knocked me back, bruising my pelvis where it collided with the ground.

But I could still fight. Already I'd denied Lopez some of her precious qi. Threads knew how long it would take, how many close calls we'd have to survive to outlast her reserves, but they would, in time, deplete.

Only the void was endless.

* * *

Maria masked her disappointment.

She hadn't exactly expected a fight for the history books against three coppers, but she'd expected more than… *this*.

It was this planet, this weak, desolate, *shithole* that produced such pathetic cultivators. Threads, she wanted to get out of there. She *needed* to get out of there. Of course, she couldn't let her victory seem too easy. If *any* of the elders could've dispatched Rex with an idle thought, it'd undermine her success.

Curiously enough, Rex proved the least troublesome of his little posse.

She could deal with the Veleraeu girl easily enough. The fencer *depended* on her speed to counter attacks, and nothing moved faster than light. It was some annoyance having to fire two Divine Piercing Lights every time she wanted to penetrate the girl's guard, but it wasn't *difficult*.

The Honchel boy, in contrast, countered her quite effectively. He'd improved in leaps and bounds since she'd first written him off as lacking potential, and his silverskin technique, though flawed, deflected her Divine Piercing Lights quite effectively. He even moved so fast it seemed like he knew where she was going to strike before she did, an unheard of level of celerity for a copper. Were he a stage higher, she might've struggled to survive his relentless assault.

As it was, he failed to so much as scratch her Blinding Bulwark.

Rex himself seemed curiously helpless. His sword—unenchanted as far as Maria could tell—somehow made it far further into her Blinding Bulwark than anything his tier should've been capable of, yet she repelled him all the same. The odd Divine Piercing Light his way kept him at bay well enough.

Whichever mind technique he'd used to influence Honchel and Velereau, Maria had it well in hand. Her Silver Diadem of the Untainted Mind guarded her thoughts from outside intrusion, and the Fallen Petals of the Helix Bloom she'd tied to her wrist prevented emotional manipulation. Together with the pouch full of bark shavings from a Keeper's Oak to stop him from stealing away her qi, she'd amassed three bronze-level artifacts and natural treasures to perfectly counter Rex's skillset.

They'd cost her nearly all the wealth she'd gathered over decades of hunts on Ilirian, but any price was worth paying if it secured her a position off Fyrion.

Now it was just a matter of finishing the job.

A beautiful *crack* reached Maria's ear as her technique shattered Rex's wrist. She swept her harrowwood staff at him to press her advantage, but he clumsily dodged back, falling to the floor in the process. She swiped down to end him, but he was already rolling out of melee range.

A second drain at her qi pulled Maria's attention away as the Velereau girl returned to her pointless assault. She'd just about sent the girl clambering after her sword *again* when Rex's voice called out.

"Conserve your qi!"

Maria scowled as the silver edge faded from Honchel's axe blade. Velereau too, she noted, had withdrawn the flow of qi that'd been solidifying her otherwise flimsy rapier. She batted the former away with the tip of her staff, holding further Divine Piercing Lights in reserve for whatever Rex had planned. Moments later, she felt it.

The ambient qi had all but vanished. Rex's vampirism must've been more powerful than she'd expected as he stole away every scrap of qi her techniques emanated. Of course, he couldn't touch the qi directly under her control, but every technique she threw, every attack her Blinding Bulwark blocked, sent dissipate into the air. Maria, like all cultivators, had long learned to reclaim and recycle that loss.

But now Caliban Rex had taken it for himself.

This wouldn't stand. Maria worried little about the personal loss—these pitiful coppers would break long before she ran out of qi—but however Rex intended to *use* all that power gave her pause.

Just in case, she eased up the Divine Piercing Lights to better reinforce her defenses. It was better safe than sorry. Besides, her victory had been assured from the start. It was better, she reasoned, to avoid undue risk.

Maria could afford to take her time.

* * *

I had to keep myself from cheering as Lopez slowed her barrage to shore up her defenses. It was exactly the wrong thing to do.

She didn't cease her bursts of light entirely, and I worried each one Charlotte or Xavier deflected cost them more qi than it cost her, but that couldn't stop the faintest glimmer of hope from rearing its head as I watched her shield shine brighter than ever before.

For the first time in the painful encounter, all three of us managed to close in on the powerful elder, raining our admittedly ineffective blows down onto her shield in tandem.

But Lopez didn't need her qi attacks to prove a lethal

threat. Her staff passed seamlessly through the barrier that caused us such trouble, knocking aside blades and forcing retreats even when it failed to make direct contact.

When it succeeded, bones broke.

An overhand swipe snapped Xavier's collarbone. In practically the same motion a backwards jab fractured Charlotte's shin. They kept fighting. One handed, one legged, one *eyed*, they kept fighting.

Twice Lopez brought me to the floor. Twice Charlotte and Xavier, with their qi and with their blood, bought me the chance to get back up again.

Through it all Lopez barely moved. Either by some limitation of her shield technique or the simple knowledge *she didn't have to*, she remained nearly stationary, standing fully upright in open rejection of any combat stance I'd ever seen.

The final time Lopez knocked me away, I wouldn't be getting up so easily. Again her strike landed directly against my chest. Again I heard a crack. Again I flew into the back wall. My sunglasses snapped and fell to the floor.

This time, my lung didn't dodge the jagged break. I heard the hiss of air. I felt the bubbles in my blood. I fought to inhale, but the breaths came ragged and labored.

I glanced down and saw Cedric's bone piercing my chest. His blood coated the walls of the narrow gangway.

I looked across the room, past Xavier with his left arm hanging limp, past Charlotte keeping weight off her right foot, past Lopez's brilliant bubble shield, to what lay beyond. To the airlock. To salvation. To Lucy.

My gaze fell again, to where the bone fragments had peppered my vac suit with more holes than I could've counted. But there were no punctures. My suit was singed, burned to near melting a dozen places, but whole.

Then it hit me.

For all my life I'd waged war against the cold. I'd

patched holes and mended tears and suited up time and time again to maintain that flimsy wall that kept it out. I'd trapped the life within its shell, disallowed the warmth and light and precious air from breaking free.

But that light was no longer mine to keep.

Ever since that horrible day, ever since I'd died for those four minutes and twenty-three seconds, I'd surrendered all claim to the warmth in which I lived.

I belonged to the cold now.

No more was I a creature of the light constrained to the walled garden of life amidst the infinite night. I was of the dark, entombed by the faults of my biology, by the contradictions inherent to my existence, to that very bubble of warmth on which my body depended.

How that bubble burned.

I found it fitting, in hindsight, that my Way began with a punctured vac suit. How better to mark my spirit's inversion than the literal tattering of that which had, for so long, kept me separate from the cold?

Today, my vac suit did the opposite. It shielded from the oppressive heat and light wielded against me. It formed a bubble of its own, a tiny island of calm and cool amidst the torrent of energy and life.

I found it poetic.

I found it beautiful.

I found it *inspiring*.

The sigil came to me unbidden, a hollow shape of gentle curves and twisting edges. I held it in my mind like a mother cradling an infant, and it held me back like a child grown an aging parent. I found no need to memorize or optimize or rehearse ad nauseam. I *knew* it. In a way, I'd always known it.

I forced myself to my feet. I took a breath, long and deep and agonizing against the pressure of my collapsed lung. And, at long fucking last, I used my first ever technique.

Qi cascaded down my body like a waterfall, forming a thin and narrow shell, a second skin like those I'd worn for so many hours out in the cold. The more power I fed it the denser it grew, never thicker, never bulkier. Like a vac suit it moved with me, preferring stillness—always stillness— but more than willing to wade through this sea of light in which I swam.

I raised my sword. I took a step, back to the fray, back to my friends, back to Lopez.

And I smiled.

* * *

Maria diverted the bulk of her attention away from his two thralls the moment she first fathomed what Rex was doing.

It was insidious in its simplicity, brilliant in its underhandedness, and the perfect explanation for the powerful enchantment that so hid his qi.

By clearing the air of ambient qi, he'd not only robbed her of the chance to reclaim her spent power, but opened the door for his true technique. She'd have noticed it carving its path through all the dissipate, so he'd removed it all.

Even now she couldn't truly feel the tendrils of his qi worming their way into her body, but she knew they were there. She felt the resistance where they impeded her own qi, recognized the way that—with remarkable precision— they targeted each and every empty space within her meridians, rushing into the tiny gaps left by her own expenditures like oxygen sucked into a vacuum.

How she wished she could've sensed it. It must've been a remarkably complex technique.

For the time being, it did little more than slightly resist her cycling, little more than an annoyance, but Maria had seen what'd happened to Nicolas Vesper. She'd seen the way Rex had taken hold of Xavier Honchel and Charlotte

Velereau. She had no intention of letting the same happen to her.

It was time to end this.

She slammed the head of her staff into Rex's chest, rejoicing at the sound of shattering ribs as he flew back. She raised a hand for a Divine Piercing Light to finish the job, but Velereau darted in to parry the technique. The girl took a strike to the shoulder for her efforts.

In a halfhearted hope that ending him would break his control over the senior cadets, Maria conserved her qi for a few moments as she fought to maneuver Honchel and Velereau away from between her and Rex. By the time she did, he was on his feet.

And he was *smiling*.

Unsurprisingly, she could see no technique in action around him, but he appeared… darker, somehow. As if he stood in a shadow that fell upon him and only him, leaving his surroundings as illuminated as ever.

Maria knew what to do with shadows.

Technically speaking, The Light Which Banishes the Darkness was an iron technique, one that would strain her bronze core significantly with each use. She was loath to spend it here. Maria had kept the trump card secret for a reason, and not even she held enough sway to delete *these* security logs. The details of Rex's downfall would spread throughout the Dueling Stars.

But cards unplayed did little good.

The entire staging area fell into darkness as Maria absorbed every bit, every mote, every photon of light in the room. It raced into the sigil at her fingertips, gathering into a single point that shone like a star in the night. In and in and in she pulled, weakening her defenses, ceasing her cycling, fighting through the increasing resistance within her meridians to put anything and everything into her final technique.

Maria fired.

The Light Which Banishes the Darkness blasted through the room, a sustained beam of blindingly bright prismatic light over twice the width of her Divine Piercing Light, with enough power behind it to punch a hole clean through several inches of solid steel.

Against Caliban Rex, it washed harmlessly to the sides. The shadow across his form seemed to flicker and waver, but it parted her technique around him as if the light itself sought to ignore his presence.

Maria pushed harder. She wouldn't let this *copper* overcome her. She couldn't. Whatever he'd done, no technique could survive her onslaught. Not for long. She fed it more.

She fed it her ambition. She fed it her pride. She fed it her disgust at being trapped on such a miserable world. Most of all she fed it her need, that same, essential need that drove all cultivators to defy the heavens, to reach for immortality, to become *more*.

She knew she was damaging her core. She knew she was exposing herself to Rex's own invading technique. That didn't matter. This weakling, this monster, this *mortal* would not withstand her. Would not outlast her.

With every hard-earned scrap of qi, every hour of painstaking meditation, every agonizingly perfected technique, every bit of asskissing and information trading and political maneuvering to earn the resources she deserved, Elder Maria Lopez, one of six bronze core cultivators on all of Fyrion, flailed against infinity.

And infinity flailed back.

Even as her greatest attack failed to pierce his shield, that faint resistance she knew to be Rex's technique advanced through her now empty meridians, encroaching further and further through the vacuum she'd left it. Still she channeled. Still it came. Until, at last, it reached her core.

Her qi didn't drain away. Her thoughts didn't cease or lock up or fall beneath the influence of Rex's control.

His qi touched upon her core and for but a paltry moment, Maria *saw*.

She saw the black miasma that hung in the air around her. She saw the technique filled with more qi than she'd ever imagined clinging to Rex's body.

Above all, she saw the well of power from which he drew.

Maria glimpsed infinity, and her world changed.

This wasn't qi vampirism. This was so, *so* much more. This was eternity. This was inevitability. Maria Lopez looked upon the unending, and for the first time in her life, she knew what it was to be small.

Then it was gone. The miasma, the technique, the infinite sea all vanished as her body ejected the foreign qi from her core.

She fell to her knees.

She knew it was still there, that wellspring, that *power* beyond the finite minds of humanity, but scramble as she might, she failed to catch so much as a glimpse.

But that wasn't true. There was but one, a single window into those cold depths. She found it as she gazed up, past the sword that had made its way to her throat, and into a pair of eyes as black and full of stars as a summer night's sky.

Infinity lingered within them.

And Maria couldn't look away.

* * *

I rushed forward as Lopez collapsed to her knees, a look of reverent awe on her face. She offered no resistance as I pressed Shiver to her throat, ready to end her life at the first sign of trickery.

None came.

473

She looked up at me, stared into my eyes with an expression of unfettered surrender, not only of the body, but of the spirit. Something had broken within Elder Lopez, something profound of which I couldn't begin to guess the meaning.

She didn't speak. She didn't have to. Her captivated eyes, her slack jaw, her staff left carelessly to fall to the ground offered answer enough.

For some time I stood over her, continuing to channel vast swaths of qi through my as of yet unnamed technique. Around us Charlotte and Xavier checked over their various injuries, confirmed they could make it to Lucy's open airlock, and gathered up their belongings.

I spent that time coming to a decision.

By all logic I ought to have ended Lopez's life then and there. She'd already proven herself my enemy. She'd taken my focus room hours, schemed and manipulated both me and others to hamper my progress, and now she'd outright tried to kill me for her own gain.

Little good would come from letting her live. I knew that. Much as I searched for any basis on which to offer mercy, any reason to spare her the very fate I'd hours ago delivered unto Nick, I came up empty.

The non-zero chance that Lopez would offer me more trouble if I let her live won out. It wasn't like I was committing some foul act by cutting her throat.

Her life didn't matter. Nothing mattered.

"Cal!" Xavier's voice pulled me from my thoughts as he tossed my vac helmet to me. I had to withdraw my sword from Lopez's neck to catch it with my good hand. "Let's go."

He and Charlotte had already limped their way to the airlock. They were waiting for me.

I spared Lopez one final, pitiful glance, slipped my helmet on, and moved to join them.

Together we stumbled our way across Fyrion's ragged gray landscape, past rocky crags and exposed silver veins judged too small to be worth mining, until a wondrous matte white greeted us.

For the second time in just over a year, I collapsed into Lucy's airlock with a punctured lung and a damaged vac suit. For the second time I carried the grief of recent loss and the wounds of narrow survival against seemingly insurmountable odds.

But this time I had friends at my side.

This time, it felt like coming home.

37

Maria only made it to her feet as she felt the whirr of thrusters quake the floor beneath her. Her hands shook as she moved to the window, pressed her face up to the glass to watch the soulship shrink into nothingness in the starry sky.

She kept her eyes fixed upon that spot, as if even too far away to make out, she could still watch Caliban Rex fade into the distance.

Maria didn't resent her defeat. How could she? She'd set herself against a force far beyond her comprehension. Her defeat had been an inevitability. His mercy hadn't.

The thought of it sent chills down her spine. She'd gazed into the abyss, experienced the revelation of infinity in a way few if any had the privilege, and at the end, even after all she'd done, He'd seen fit to let her live.

This changed everything. For all her life Maria had lived a world of little things. She'd become so embroiled in petty squabbles and sect politics and her own advancement, she'd failed to grasp the larger truth.

None of that mattered.

The cadets had seen that. It all made so much sense now. Honchel and Velereau weren't thralls under His control, but disciples, the lucky few who'd understood His significance, who'd proven themselves worthy of His teachings.

Maria, in her selfishness, had failed to earn such an honor.

But she would. She understood it now. She'd *seen* His vastness.

Maria knew His power still lingered, still waited for her just outside that window. It'd always been there. It'd always been *everywhere*. She didn't go looking for it. The human mind had never been meant to perceive such greatness. Even the tiny glimpse she'd been given had driven her to near madness.

She touched dearly upon the places within her His qi had traveled. Along her body, through her meridians, into her very core it'd come. To think she'd been so dismissive, so arrogant, so afraid. She saw it now as the blessing it was, the chance for redemption she'd so desperately needed.

She'd have to rebuild her foundation from the ground up. Her Way had begun with errant steps. That would need correcting. The light she'd spent so many years contemplating, cultivating, *understanding*, felt hollow now, a futile gasp against the reality of the infinite dark.

No, she'd walk a path more suited to one of His followers.

Plans began to circle in her mind. She'd have to leave Fyrion, of course. Its people were too small-minded to grasp her message. The Right Eye would do for now. After that, who knew?

It'd mean abandoning her position at the sect, but she didn't need *them*, not when she knew what true power looked like.

A gentle hand upon her shoulder tore her from her revelations. She turned to find the morning vac-welding shift lined against the wall as far away from her they could manage. Apparently one of them had called her assistant.

"Elder Lopez, ma'am, are you okay?   You look like you've seen a ghost."

"No, not a ghost," Maria replied, turning back to gaze out the window. "It's worse. It's so much worse." Despite the words, a smile crept across her face.

"I've seen a god."

* * *

Martha Vesper clenched the fingers of her good hand until the nails drew blood.

She sat perfectly still in her front-row seat, resisting the urge to fidget with the funeral veil that shrouded her face. Threads, the thing itched.

"—a dedicated cadet, perhaps the most promising youth the Dragon's Right Eye has ever seen. Nicolas reached tin younger than any in Fyrion's history, a testament to his talent, his drive, and his will to defy the heavens."

Martha chewed her lip as Elder Smith droned on. As his assigned mentor, Smith had been responsible for Nick's wellbeing and advancement within the cadet program. If this speech was any indicator, her brother hadn't even met the man.

It was bullshit. It was all bullshit. She wanted to jump up there, to shove that snide elder aside and inform the crowd that her brother had wanted none of this. He hadn't wanted fame or glory or cultivation.   He *hadn't* been dedicated. He'd had no will to defy the heavens.

And his name was *Nick*.

But Martha knew she couldn't disrespect Elder Smith like that. She couldn't disrespect her parents like that, even as they all disrespected Nick with this farce of a lie they kept telling that he was just as ambitious as their parents had always wanted.

The coffin sat empty. They all knew it. The sect had

hardly tried to hide the fact they'd taken Nick's body for themselves. Her father had taken the handful of credits recompense with a smile on his face.

Even in death they wouldn't let Nick be.

He lay in a lab somewhere, someplace dark and quiet where a team of scientists could take him apart piece by piece in their greedy attempts to figure out what exactly Caliban had done to him. It wasn't difficult to guess what they wanted. The ability to inflict void-induced psychosis would make for a powerful—if indiscriminate—weapon.

Martha cared less about the what and more about the why.

Over and over she'd run it through in her head, how the Cal she knew could've done something so terrible. He'd seemed so... *nice.* He'd befriended the mortals. He'd saved that kid from the void beasts. He'd looked after Nick.

Obviously not.

At the time she'd never doubted the speed of his advancement. It was fast, sure, maybe even prodigious, but *possible.* The first recordings of his duel with Senior Cadet Long had dismissed that notion. She'd had Long for combat one, studied under him for her very first swings of a blade. That a fresh recruit could beat him after a single year of training was impossible.

Caliban was no ordinary recruit. The way his skin had gone pale, his breath near stopped, his eyes gone black as the night sky... it gave her chills. It was clear he'd been lying from day one. The extent or breadth of his lies she couldn't guess. He certainly hadn't come to Fyrion for simple training.

But why else? Why Fyrion? Why *Nick?*

And why oh why were they sitting around an empty coffin spouting lies instead of tracking down her brother's killer?

Martha glanced down to her half-formed right hand. It'd be another year at the minimum before she recovered full use of the limb. At least she'd finally rid herself of that cursed sling.

If her injuries, if her parents, if *Nick* had taught her anything, it was that if she wanted something, she had to seize it herself.

She had a long way to go, a mountain of recovery, of cultivating, of training between her and her vengeance. She'd have to advance at unprecedented speeds if she hoped to catch up to Caliban's breakneck pace.

But Martha was no stranger to pushing herself. She better than anyone understood the sacrifices it took, the pain one had to endure to temper oneself and survive the crucible.

If no one else would, Martha herself would track down the man who'd killed her brother.

This, to the gods, to the threads, and to herself, she so swore.

* * *

Three days gone from Fyrion's gray wastes, just enough time to begin to recover from our injuries, we gathered in the garden to say goodbye. Already we'd spoken, already we'd gone over our options and made our plans.

We hadn't yet decided whether or not we'd look for sect positions on a different planet, but to get them we'd need to be impressive; we'd need to show potential.

We'd need to reach bronze. Either way, that was our goal. None of us wanted to let the week's events stop us on our Ways. But getting to bronze meant crafting a focus, and crafting a focus meant natural treasures, and obtaining natural treasures, with our limited funds, meant one thing and one thing only.

Ilirian.

Already Lucy and Charlotte had begun to work out how

we'd sneak onto the system's sole habitable world.

But that was for tomorrow. Today was for goodbyes.

My right hand in a brace, my chest bandaged where Lucy had cut through to mend my ribs and patch my lung, I knelt in the unsowed loam.

Xavier and Charlotte stood at my back, the former with his arm in a sling to help his collarbone heal, the latter leaning on him to keep weight off her right shin. I'm sure we made a sorry sight, beat to shit and in the mismatched garments that made the best approximation of funeral blacks we could manage.

I could feel Lucy there with us, a warm and comforting presence I'd come to lean on heavily. She didn't call attention to herself, didn't intrude upon our grief, but she was there, ready to offer support to those who needed it.

I reminded myself to thank her for that later.

After a moment's breath, I let my hand fall to the cool earth, and I began.

"Nick... suffered. I think it would be dishonest to say otherwise. He was lonely. He was depressed. He lived his life under the yoke of potential from which he never quite broke free. Those of us who've experienced the kind of cruelty Nick has like to say that it gets better. Just hang on. Just a few more years. Soon you'll be old enough to leave them all behind, to escape their harsh words and crushing expectations and live the life you've always wanted.

"We say that as if it makes it all suck less, as if the promise of a brighter future somehow softens the gloomy present, but the cold truth of the matter is, however better it may get, some of us don't make it through.

"Nick didn't. He lived and died in the same shit situation in which he was born. Sometimes that's just how it is. Shit all the way down."

I swallowed down a knot in my throat. "Nick suffered, and I refuse to romanticize that fact. Maybe a more poetic mind, someone who's never *been* where Nick has, would look for beauty in all he achieved, would ascribe his momentous rise to tin, his botany research, that he found the infinite sea through sheer force of will, to his suffering. He overcame adversity, reforged himself in the fires of his hardship, and came out stronger.

"That's bullshit. Pain never helps. Nick accomplished everything he did in spite of his suffering. And I respect him all the more for it."

With my uninjured hand, I dug out a half inch of soil. From my pocket I pulled two seeds, one brimming with light, the other with shadow. They were all we had of him. I closed my fist around them and held them to my lips before lowering them into the earth. Only as I tossed on the first layer of topsoil did I speak the final words of my eulogy.

"I'm so sorry."

As Charlotte and Xavier each knelt in turn to add their own fistful of dirt to the planting and say their own goodbyes, I sat back, I shut my eyes, and for the first time since I'd first seen him standing over that mortal's body, I cut off the flow of numbing qi to my brain.

And I wept.

Epilogue

Chairwoman Alabastra Verenzia Ren cycled the sweet qi from the air, through the tiny black speck of immeasurable mass at her center, and back out into the environment around her. At the peak of the black hole stage, she had little use for such trifles, at least not until she made the inevitable journey across the frayed veil to join the others at Ascension's End.

But the super mass at the center of the galaxy would have to wait. The rest of the galaxy still needed tending.

So for now, she meditated, searched for peace among the ongoing maelstrom of ideas, complaints, and problems all begging for her attention.

She'd long learned to tune out her immediate surroundings. The hundred-thousand seat arena in which she sat offered plenty of those.

Technically, these free meditations of hers were open to the public, but as cultivators flocked for the opportunity to be near someone at the true edge of possibility in this plane of reality, the queue had outgrown the average lifespan. Positions mere years from the front bought and sold for millions of credits. Any closer, and the numbers grew staggering.

In truth, it made for quite a stable investment. Its value

could only go up, after all, at least until Alabastra finally resigned from her position as chairwoman of the board and left Illustrious Sky Holdings behind. Much as the inequity of the system may have irked her, Alabastra had to admit, she *did* appreciate a good investment opportunity. She herself owned six spots in the queue.

Of course, nobody who owned a position actually waited in the line. They had mortals for that.

Since a high-level cultivator could meditate for days or even weeks before the need to drink or relieve themselves forced them from their seat, turnover within the amphitheater itself stayed relatively low.

Sometimes, when she was feeling generous, Alabastra even offered advice to those who'd made the pilgrimage. She could hardly help but hear every uneven breath, see every misaligned bone, feel every imperfection in the cycling of the hundred thousand souls around her. A simple exertion of her will sent a list of corrections to offenders' holopads.

On this particular meditation, she pondered how best to resolve the ongoing border dispute with The Glenn Conglomerate, if Emperor Jen would accept her offer to expand trading operations on Vareek-4, and, as with every meditation lately, what to do about her errant son.

She'd come no closer to finding a solution to any of the day's three dilemmas when she heard, somewhere else on Yabilon, her assistant, Telbraun, say her name. Within moments, her attention was three thousand miles away, on the words the portly old man uttered next.

"The Kai'Deiron are speaking."

Alabastra blinked. He'd said "are." That implied... "More than one?" she whispered on the winds to him and him alone.

"All of them, madam chairwoman."

Without hesitation she ripped a hole into the Threads

and vanished from the arena's center. Her visitors knew to wait for her return.

She stepped from Faith to The Depths to The Bulwark to Winter, a familiar journey along the Threads that bound the universe together to an unassuming black marble building.

The pale blue light of the neutron star they called their home shined down from the mirrors above onto the streets of Yabilon. While Alabastra might've preferred to build their corporate headquarters around a black hole like the other great powers, she couldn't deny the advantages of natural light and free heat.

Telbraun was waiting for her at the door. "Madam chairwoman." He nodded respectfully.

"Any word on my son?" Alabastra didn't stop walking.

Telbraun fell into line behind her. "No, madam chairwoman. The Kai'Deiron have had little to say on the matter since his disappearance."

Alabastra didn't react. She'd expected as much. Oracles were famously erratic, and the Kai'Deiron in particular had always been fickle in their attentions. One of them had once told her her son had a weight to him, a significance to the tangle of fate that would see his actions influencing the galaxy for generations to come.

They hadn't spoken on him since.

She continued her interrogation as they seamlessly passed through two dozen security checkpoints. "Then what do they want? When was the last time they've all spoken at once?"

"Never, madam chairwoman. The most we've ever seen is three at once, each sharing a part of a larger message. This is... different."

"How so?"

Telbraun stopped at the final set of doors, massive round obsidian things carved with the great mess of a tangle they called fate. "See for yourself." He pulled the door open for her.

Alabastra stepped inside.

Each of the nineteen Kai'Deiron lay naked, afloat in their own pool of body temperature saline. Their eyes were bound, their noses plugged, their ears blocked, their senses diminished as far as science could take them to better hone their gift.

True sight came perhaps once every billion years, and the recipients of such power never lasted long. Assassination was easier than war, after all.

Most of the great powers instead relied upon their own version of the Kai'Deiron, those with but a tiny echo of the gift enhanced as best they could manage. It wasn't an exact science, but Illustrious Sky Holdings had found the most success through non-maiming sensory deprivation combined with a particular cocktail of hallucinogens they'd come upon through decades of trial and error.

They were finicky. They were fickle. But they were the best Alabastra had.

Today, as she strode into their chamber, each and every one of the nineteen oracles spoke in hauntingly perfect unison, a message of three words they repeated through cracked lips and dried out throats.

"The stargazer comes."

"The stargazer comes."

"The stargazer comes."

Alabastra froze as a chill ran down back. "Telbraun, run a scan of the archives."

"I already have, madam chairwoman. There are no relevant mentions of a stargazer in any of the languages we have on file."

"Something new, then..." Alabastra let her voice trail off. She looked back to the Kai'Deiron. "I'll meditate on this. Let me know if they say anything else."

"Of course, madam chairwoman."

She opened another hole to the Threads, but paused before stepping through it. "In the meantime, keep looking for that ship. Wherever Cedric went, that soulship of his has to be close by." Alabastra turned to deliver one final meaningful look into Telbraun's eyes to reinforce the severity of her message.

"Find out what happened to my son."